I0592309

Wormhole Alleyoop
Copyright © 2022 by Simple son

Book
ISBN: 9798218007751

First Editon

Simple son novel

ACT I

Mom and Stepdad
September/14th /2023

Faint jazz music running in the background of the restaurant.

Ivory adjusted her cleavage inside her corset. She was freakishly beautiful sitting across the round table. Her big bright eyes darting across and a soft smile with high cheekbones.

"you hear me, Fritz?" She uttered toward her husband. He had a well-trimmed beard and blue eyes glimmering under the candle light on the table. He wore a black Versace button-up baseball style shirt with gold symbol designs running down his shoulders like a king of France. A black wifebeater underneath. His arms lifted from his lap and he grabbed his fork and pulled the plate closer.

Fritz's large fingers were squeezing his fork, He had a wedding band on it shining with a gold luster. There goes her obsession; Lindsey, the red head waitress glared down the far row of customers and walked back to the table while bending her fingers in an awkward way.

Ivory grabbed her pearly white plate of pink shrimp, alfredo sauce smelled like buttery garlic. She pulled the handkerchief off her fork and stirred the noodles into the milky pepper sauce.

"Phillip is probably is keeping secrets, he came to Lucy's house with a busted lip," Ivory uttered in conversation.

Fritz's eyes bulged.

"in Crown Heights?" Fritz responded with a grimace "with Shandy I bet! that little whore has been nothing but trouble ever since she—."

Ivory reached forward,

"stop!" she uttered "you know Shandy aint have no father growing up, because—because of me!"

Fritz took a deep exhale.

"so that means we should let them have a brother—sister relationship after all these fucking years?' Fritz shouted a whisper through his teeth.

"they—."

"no!" Fritz muttered under his breathe, "you're opening up a can of worms that we won't be able to close. What if they find out we lied about Merlo being Phillip's real—."

"don't—not in public."

Fritz formed a knuckle and pulled it back to torso.

"—over some fucking money Ivory! We did that, you forgot?" he slammed his knuckle against the table and the surface shook.

Fritz had eyeballs that were glossy, his nose red and his teeth showing. His gums were bright pink.

Ivory smiled awkwardly, beaming yellow restaurant lights shinning off her eyeballs. She pushed his fist off the table.

"Lucy met the girl! not me! I wouldn't go looking for some shit that's going to put us on blast!"

"why would Lucy screw us."

"They just happen to have the same appointment at the cardiologist on the same day."

Ivory's eyes were wide and her nose twitched.

Fritz hunched forward.

"Lucy is going to get it the worst if shit backfires! she is Phillip's guardian! what the fuck was Lucy thinking—wait, what was a young girl like Shandy doing at the cardiologist?"

"Shandy has a best friend, Abdul from north Philly, he used to be a boxer or something, he has heart disease now. Lucy happened to walk in the cardiologist and she saw Shandy Jenkins written on the damn sign-in sheet."

Ivory took a bite of her noodles; the alfredo stained her lips as she slurped it.

"Merlo must of did that from heaven!" she uttered while chewing.

Years prior ....

I

Merlo's Family
October/6th/ 2020

Suddenly, the houses front door swept open, and Orlando walked through the frame with his bald head shining. He had a navy-blue security windbreaker on his chest, a black belt and some black boots that trembled the house. He was an ugly troll of a man, overweight, had a gut, the size of a full laundry bag and a hunched posture.

Sometimes his gut would get caught in his belt buckle and he had to stand up while working to avoid the pain.

Orlando smiled when he saw his mother. His arm stretched and his armpits were moist.

"there you go Ma." He spoke in an anxious voice.

Although Mother Megan was an older sixty-eight-year-old woman, she had perfect hearing. When it came to her son Orlando, she seemed deaf. Deaf! As in hello?

Are you there Ms. Jenkins? Old age is something that every human had to deal with and while she was vegan, her only unhealthy eating was the words she swallowed for her son. She lowered her armpit and climbed from the ladder with a funky look on her face. Funky like when you listen to a mean beat and the rapper says a hard punchline, but Megan had a punchline of her own, the joke of a child she had to deliver the day he was born. She dropped the duster on the oak coffee table, next to the remote control and her Granddaughters pink charger rolled up like a snake. She turned her back, stared into the fireplace while casting a long shadow across the wall. She tucked her silver chain into her turtleneck in a fast-paced motion and adjusted her silky black hair.

"You ain't come here for no reason," she spoke in a shrill voice. "What is it, are you here to remind me of the mistake I made."

"Mistakes?" He uttered back, "Mother I missed you."

Orlando tried to hug her from the back, but she moved to avoid the kiss and her neck stretched like an ostrich. Her hand slapped the fireplaces mantle, and each of her fingernails were black with white stripes. She tapped them against the mantle for eight seconds.

Megan turned her face and kept her elbow stiff. "Why did you miss your brothers gathering in September?" she screamed in a soft voice. Megan placed Merlo's golden urn closer to the wall so it could not slip again. She reached for the fireplace knife leaning on the side with the bricks next to a metal golf club bag. She squeezed the knife hard and poked a charred piece of firewood. She turned over her shoulder and stared with a threatening look.

Orlando walked closer to the mantle and shut his eyes. He had eyes that looked like two dimples. He tongued a prayer, but his lips didn't move. He looked like someone who was sleep talking and speaking gibberish. He reached toward the clean mantle with each of his fingernails dirty. Megan slapped his hands away and made a wrenching face.

Orlando turned his back, he walked toward his father Remson Jenkins, who was also known as Grand Pooba. He was dark skinned like a Choctaw Indian, he had wavy whirlpool waves that slipped off his hairline. He had big ears like Dr. Sebi. He had a protruding goatee with a shaved mustache and a muscular neck full of veins. Orlando slapped his father's shoulder, and he bounced in a spry motion. Father was athletic even in old age. The floor tiles bent as Orlando walked past the living room. He noticed his niece at the corner of his eye. Shandy Jenkin's was Merlo's twenty-three-year-old daughter. She had a puffy brown ponytail, a slender build and long brown nails on her finger that she filed herself. She tapped her cellphone screen while playing SZA in Apple music. The family called her Shandy bear because of her bear slippers, which spread from the house into the streets and now everyone in Crown Heights calls her Shandy bear.

Orlando walked to the back of the house with a Chanel paper bag dangling in his four fingers. There were two rooms with off-white doors and gold knobs. He stuck his bald head through and caught a glimpse of the most beautiful woman in the world! Cyn! He lifted his Chanel bag and smiled with his butter yellow teeth.

"Cyn, this is for you baby." He uttered while handing her the dangling bag. "I just wanted to show you a different side of me."

Cyn scrunched her face with a Latina attitude. She had pale brown soft skin, ringy black hair that curled naturally without water or gel. She had wet eyes, a thin nose, pink lips and an exotic Tiger tattoo on her sideburn. She was inside the backroom, wearing some yellow booty shorts and a grey sweater with Merlo's face on it. She was feeding the baby Junior with a bottle of formula while watching FaceTime with her girlfriend.

Cyn held the bottle into juniors' mouth while rocking him side to side.

Orlando's gust of wind stunk as he walked past, he leaned over and placed the paper Chanel bag into the baby crib, his fingers wrapped around it, and it teetered slightly.

"You don't see what I got you? Cyn, you don't hear me talking to you?" He shouted softly. "I'm trying to show you a different side of me."

"Nigga, how about you show me the side of ya bald head and walk the fuck out, don't you see me feeding junior, Move!"

"I'm about to get some money tonight with the biggest dealer in the city. Remember back in the days when my brother used to take you out of town and shit, I can take you out."

As Orlando spoke, Cyn scrunched her face. She put the bottle down and it rained milk in a sluggish movement, she put the baby on her shoulder and tapped Junior's back for a loud burp.

The baby's face was reminiscing of Merlo and anyone who represented Merlo in the slightest way, was someone she loved unconditionally. Merlo was her forever love. The house was Merlo, from the bedroom's color, carpet, satin cream sheets, satin cream curtains, basketball trophies and pictures of him all around the hallways with flower frames and incense burning. Which is why Orlando left the house in the first place, and why it wasn't wise to come back home even if it was a pending recession.

Orlando walked closer to Cyn and he reached for her purple waistband and it retracted like a rubber band, slapping against her booty cheek.

Cyn froze, she pulled away while holding the baby away from her stomach.

"No" she sucked her teeth loudly. "Orlando! Merlo is my man! Shandy is your niece you forgot? which means we family so act like it nigga." She had a Latina accent when she spoke.

Orlando's face flexed, he stepped toward Cyn, and they were the same height.

"Bitch! My brother is protein powder! he dead! get over it! y'all still on his fucking dick. Get over it!"

Cyn turned the other cheek, walked out of the room while breathing hard. She sat in between Shandy and Grand Pooba on the couch.

Orlando reached into the baby crib and pulled out the Chanel bag. He walked with a mean mug, through the hallway and back to the living room. There was a hateful silence. Megan, Shandy and Grand Pooba stared at Orlando without any blinking. The silence was so loud that when their brown-blackface pug scurried inside the living room, it just froze with its ears high and its tongue curling back into its mouth.

Megan was so angry that she was shaking, her nostrils were snarling, and she held a fireplace knife that looked like a poker tool. She held it with the sharp end down, squeezing and rolling it around her palm.

Orlando walked toward the front door, he pulled the silver knob and slammed the hinges after he was out. To the porch, he walked into the garage that smelled like cement. He pushed boxes out of the way and his body slammed on his old twin sized bed. There was a black milk crate with an old airsoft BB gun. He pulled it out, and grazed it across his head like a cellphone. The gun's steel was cold against his face and while humans are known for being warm blooded, he felt the coldness in his body. The coldness to do something crazy and not even feel it.

First, he fantasized about Cyn and how she used to strip at a spot near Citi Filed. Although she played hard to get, one summer night, before his little brother got with her, Cyn and Orlando were touching and flirting in the private room. The whole scene was dark with some old Master P music playing in the background. That southern shit that the stripper hoes like. Orlando rubbed a stack of fifties down her bra, then down to her stomach and legs. It felt good to rub that musty money on her panties and see her eyes brighten like Christmas lights. The money was falling like leaves in the autumn down to her little pink toes. From the backdoor, to the parking lot and into his blue minivan. She threw her legs up and let him taste her kitty for ten bands. When he tried to reach for his underwear, she reached for hers as well and put her foot into her black dress. She was giggling with her ass pointed at the window, pulling her dress upward. She opened the passenger door, back peddled out, holding her palm over her balloon shaped cheeks while laughing to her stripper friends who stood in the parking lot.

Orlando still remembers the chocolate strawberry-lime taste of her pussy, and sometimes at night he would jerk himself while imagining going in-between her legs. He shivered while lying in his bed, squeezing the head of his penis. Fucking tiny penis, fat, bald, short, ugly ass nigga that can't get no pussy even if he paid a bitch.

Orlando's perfect clean-as-a-whistle brother had

Cyn wrapped around his finger and chose to marry another woman. Goddamn! A dead man's decisions surely seemed foolish in hindsight. Especially because Cyn was the most beautiful woman on the planet.

Orlando snapped back into reality and his frog shaped eyes fell at his shot down dick. He glimpsed around for some lotion, and his eyes flickered at the Chanel bag with the perfume inside. He opened his lousy pants pocket, then snatched a half a Percocet that he stole from work. He had it on a balled-up security log sheet. He pulled it out, opened his mouth and his tongue snapped on it like a piece of candy. He felt an electric body chill, his mouth salivating, and his neck stiffening like arthritis.

In the center of the Livingroom Megan grabbed her pocketbook from the dining table near the basket of apples. She stood up and put on a fur jacket that had a hood that looked like fox fur.

"I have to go and get my sons deaths benefits before you know who gets his white hands on it."

Shandy bear stood up, she folded her arms while walking with ghetto body twist.

"Nah Grandma, what if you go over to the house and catch Covid?" Shandy blurted.

Mother Megan smirked,

"Lucy is a devote Christian, but she never told the pastor about her wrongdoing with Merlo's death and Ivory, don't get me started with that Jailbird!" Mother Megan's eyes popped out of her face and her nose was stiff. She went silent, then she stared at Shandy's bright eyes that looked like a twinkling star was swimming inside her pupil. She was brown, petite, and a little sassy, but her eyes were the eyes of a good child, even as an adult, she still had the same innocent eyes. Those same innocent eyes were only five on the day she realized her schoolteacher was marrying her father. Mother Megan broke focus, she stared at the rotten apples in the trash bin and thought about Ivory's rottenness. She deserved to be in the trash along with the other bad apples.

Mother Megan had a vein at each temple.

"Ivory was a homewrecking schoolteacher turned convict and Fritz is the white man who had something to do with the death of my son. Covid is the last thing I am worried about when it comes to the modern-day Adams family."

2

Vegan Carrot cake
October/19th/2020

Mother Megan came to see us during the pandemic. I remember Mother Megan as much as I remember the smell of Big momma Lucy's cooking that day. The house smelled like paprika, grilled onions, seafood, pepper, and curry. Big momma Lucy twisted the knob on the stove. The hot smoke made her nose sweaty, so she removed the steel top from the pot, and she stirred while an inch of sweat dripped down her cheek.

Fritz tapped me on the shoulder,

"Phillip! get the tablecloth while I organize the dishes." He wrapped the spoons and forks in napkins like how they do in Red Lobster. My stepdad was a white man who looked like Tom Brady but with blond hair, blue eyes and he had these thick fingers that looked Italian pork sausages. Speaking of Italian, we had A large loaf of Italian bread, seasonings, and white wine were in the middle of the table. Fritz loved to drink beer or whiskey, but he wanted to impress Mother Megan, so he popped his wine that he had gotten while on his trip to France. He was traveling all over the world because he coaches professionally.

Big momma Lucy diced a bowl of tomatoes and olives; she leaned up and gave Fritz eye contact from the kitchen.

"I hope Megan doesn't bring that damn vegan carrot cake," she said, "that stuff tastes like cardboard."

Mother Megan was a tiny woman; she had wrinkles all over her neck and face. Her pants were always slightly baggy; she wore turtlenecks with orthopedic shoes. She was a tough cookie; she always said things that offended people and that day was no different.

Mother Megan walked into the doorframe. She looked like me but with darker skin. She had a wide-eyed smile, her hands rubbing together and wobbling as she took steps. A tall, lanky man by her side who was much younger than her, he was brown skinned, with a low cut, and a part on the left side of his head. He had black buttoned shirt with straight- legged jeans and Jordan's. He squeezed a plastic bag in his palm, there were aluminum pans stacked to the top and veins were protruding out of his wrist.

Mother Megan slightly turned and put her hands on his bulky bicep.

"I hope y'all didn't mind my company," she said with a high-pitch voice as if she were singing a song.

"This is Jeffery, he's going to be joining us. I hope y'all have extra because he sure can eat." She rubbed his brown arm, smiled so hard that her lips receded over her gums. She stepped inside the house, hung up her jacket on the coat rack, and then reached for Big momma Lucy's emerald necklace.

"Lucile, you look adorable," she said, "you always have the rarest gemstones." She smiled with bright teeth.

In my opinion, it seemed like she was throwing shade the minute she walked in; she disrespected Ivory on many occasions, so the compliments she gave to us were full of shit.

Mother Megan spread her arm and gave Big momma Lucy a half hug as if she didn't want anyone touching her. She then pointed to Jeffery's bag with a wide smile from cheek to cheek.

"Jeffery, I made the best dessert for tonight," she uttered with her long teeth showing. "This is the best vegan carrot cake you will ever taste." She pointed to the foil pan.

Big momma Lucy glimpsed at Fritz, she snatched the foil pan, placed it on the counter, opened it up halfway, and the cake was the same shit as last time. Cardboard! Big momma Lucy forced an agonizing smile to the point that her cheeks looked like a celebrity with a ruined facelift.

"Yum," she uttered sarcastically, "Can't wait to eat cardboard. "While Big momma Lucy worked in the kitchen, Fritz pulled the chair for Mother Megan and stood there as if he wanted her to sit. She glimpsed at him while folding her arms, then her teeth snapped, her forehead crumpled, and her eyes rolled. "Shouldn't we wash our hands first," she grunted, "nasty ass white man, that's how y'all spread the virus, doing stuff like that." She rolled her eyes, dropped her bag in Jeffery's hand and walked to the bathroom. The house was breathing in silence and the only thing we could hear was Big momma Lucy's spoon carving around the pot of slushy chickpeas.

Mother Megan flushed the toilet about five times; we listened to it while making comprehensive eye contact.

"That vegan poo be stink," Big momma Lucy

whispered while laughing, then twisting the knob on the stove.

Mother Megan's lip untwisted as she stepped out of the bathroom.

"The tiles in there are gorgeous," she said with an agonizing smile, "you have a beautiful home."

"Thank you," Big momma Lucy replied.

Mother Megan stepped over to me with a devilish smile. She spread her arms out and hugged me, then pulled out of the hug and touched my chin with her underhand.

"Phillip, you're so tall," she shouted, "what's your height now?"

"Five foot nine," I responded with a look of shyness.

She turned around and slapped Jeffery with the back of her knuckles. "Jeffery, you hear that! You were about five foot nine when you were fifteen too right," she uttered, "you'll probably be as tall as Jeffery when you get older; I don't think you'll reach my son Merlo's height because he was taller than the both of y'all in his freshmen year."

Big momma Lucy dropped the spoon on the ground, she turned around, and her lips started to pulsate. She wiped her hands on her apron and took a deep breath.

Mother Megan had a Ziplock bag full of photos in her palm. She held them like playing cards and her gold rings on her fingers made her look like a kingpin holding cash. She distanced her neck, squinted her eyes and slapped the photos down on the table when she was done. The pictures were all glossy, half-bent and some with specs of paint. They were all pictures of My Father. He kind of looked like Michael during his rookie season before the bald head. Merlo had many photos, some were of him as a lanky tall youth on his bikes, holding basketballs and even wearing a football jersey. I reached to the back of the bag where he was a grown man.

Vegas, Atlantic City, Miami, Virginia, Ohio. He stood in front of cream-colored Benz's and red Cadillacs.

Mother Megan turned her cheek.

"My son was all over the world," she smiled, "now Phillip, Lemme see a child photo of you, I want to see how you looked when you were younger because Lucy never brought you around."

I stumbled out of the chair and ran towards Big momma Lucy's dresser drawer. There was a huge mirror, makeup, perfume bottles, and an unused checkbook at the edge. I picked up the wooden picture frame of myself in kindergarten. I snatched it and brought it back to the kitchen table with my wiry frame. Hella Skinny!

Mother Megan's eyes swelled, she put on her glasses and everyone's faces weren't as blurry. Her eyes ping-ponged from the photos of my dad and then back to me.

"He doesn't look like you very much," she said. "Merlo is so handsome, I mean, you're handsome too, but my son used to get all the little girls in his class."

Big momma Lucy's face tightened, while she stepped out of the kitchen, she blinked at Fritz and twisted her lip to the side.

Fritz's neck turned towards the photo; he glimpsed at both pictures with a slack neck.

"Are you kidding," he scoffed. "Phillip looks just like Merlo, you know Merlo is just a more dark-skinned version.

Mother Megan leaned back into her seat, both arms crossed and her legs kicking forward,

"White men always think they know things about black men's melanin," her lip twisted, "you ain't got it, so how the heck would you know, I wasn't no Biology major or nothing, but dark skin is more dominate, so the likeliness of a light skinned baby is kind of low, but Phillip is light so who knows how that happened."

Big momma Lucy rolled up her sleeves, "His mother is light," she snapped, "Ivory has always been light since she was a baby girl; that's how that happened."

Mother Megan shrugged her shoulders, took a sip of wine, and leaned further back into her seat. She had a tasteless smile; she gave me back my photo and didn't look toward the side I was on.

Big momma Lucy walked out of the kitchen holding plates like flying saucers. Her palms upwards with the dishes tilted from her hands to her wrist. The sauce on curry chickpea moistened the taco bread. There was lettuce, tomatoes, and white rice on the side of the plate. She rested it in front of me first, then on Fritz, and Mother Megan.

Mother Megan hunched forward; she picked up the wine glass and swirled it around. "Phillip, you were a fat little white baby," she said. "Jeffery, weren't you the same way as a baby boy." She touched his biceps again.

Big momma paused, she squinted at Jeffery and her wrist stiffened. She retracted her plates back towards her chest.

"Enough is enough," she snapped with the plate on

her breast, "who is this Jeffery man? Why did you bring him to my house? We don't know him."

Mother Megan tilted her head.

"Jeffery was a correctional officer in Obbit Thorn," she yelled. Then immediately swallowed a spoon full of rice and chewed it with her long teeth. Her gums were purple; there was rice and eggplant stuck in her teeth as she smiled.

Fritz sucked his teeth softly, his mouth wrenched, and his face reddened at the cheek. He leaned forward with both of his palms shaking the dinner table.

"Hell no," Fritz yelled, "my girl would never do anything with this clown." He inched backward out of his seat and curled his fingers into two bulged fists.

Big momma Lucy put the extra plate down right beside me, she took her apron off and threw it on the ground like a server who was quitting a waffle job.

"What are you trying to do here?" Big momma Lucy snapped, "Is this about money again? Ivory wasn't no hoe like I told you, she was pregnant by Merlo before she went to Obbit Thorn, so why are you bringing Jeffery here to scare us, do the math! you don't even know your grandson's birthday."

All eyes turned to Jeffery, Mother Megan pulled him by the arm, and her eyes narrowed into his half-twitching face.

Mother Megan snapped her neck.

"Jeffery, what do you remember about Ivory?" she asked. The color drained from his face; he had a whimpering noise coming from the back of his throat. He took a deep swallow, his fingers loosened from his palms and slapped across the table.

"I can't do this," he responded awkwardly, "I don't even know who Ivory is— I'm just a lost prevention security guard at Macy's, she paid me to come to scare you all with fake secrets."

Mother Megan grunted; she pushed Jeffery's arm to the other side of the table and put her sharp elbows inches away from the knives. The table wobbled, and the plates and spoons made a trembling noise. She picked up a fork and pointed the sharp end at Big momma Lucy.

"It's been twelve years," she shouted calmly, "your family took all of my son's money and left me with nothing; you owe me something; I want a big house, I want emeralds, the vacations to Europe, he was my son so everything should be mine, what about Shandy! She will never have her father!"

Mother Megan's grandchild, Shandy Jenkins is Merlo's biological daughter. She is my only sibling, a sister, six years older than me and never comes around.

Big momma Lucy said that Shandy is even less mature than I am which says a lot. Her Mother, Cyn was a half- Mexican, half-black stripper at a titty-bar not too far from the stadium.

Big momma Lucy slammed her foot on the floor and the table rocked side to side.

"Cyn was a stripper! Ivory was a schoolteacher— Cyn had the baby and didn't get a ring. Ivory got a ring twice! But y'all adore Cyn and treat my daughter like gum under ya shoe. Aint no competition, you call my daughter a hoe dammit but Cyn stripping while living at your house, I bet the daughter ends up stripping too, y'all need Jesus."

At first, when Big momma Lucy found out about Shandy, she gave the broken family a bunch of cash to help. Even though Big momma Lucy extended a hand to the family, we've never been invited to their house in Crown Heights, and I haven't even met my sister Shandy.

Mother Megan snatched every dollar of Big momma Lucy's money and still wanted more cash, even if it meant disproving that I was Merlo's real son.

In the morning, when I went to put the wooden

frame back, Big momma Lucy was in her bed asleep hugging her body purple pillow. I walked to the dresser and noticed the checkbook was on its second page and jagged at the edge.

3

Megan's close call
October/19th/2020

Fritz squeezed the doorknob and held it open wide enough for Megan to walk out. She had her purse at her rib, her right arm in her leather jacket, shoving the left arm in while rushing out.

"I'll take the garbage out," Fritz shouted loudly, he snatched the hefty bag full of garbage from dinner and a bottle of wine and started stepping down behind her.

Mother Megan could feel Fritz at her backside, so she made snarling remarks into the second floor. And each step looked more dangerous with him behind her.

Fritz was holding that bulky black trash bag and there were veins in his wrist and forearm. Suddenly he wasn't a bozo that she could slick talk at dinner. He was a large mountain of a man. He was a strong man, so strong he could toss her down a whole flight with a wrist thrust. In his left-hand Fritz held a bottle of empty wine with the bottom up as if he wanted to whack someone with it. Megan had never seen anyone dispose of empty wine like that, so she walked faster. Poking her lips out, grazing the handrail and stepping out of the shadow he cast from the top of the stairs. She saw his large dark shadow extending after each step, so she squeezed her purse and felt the plastic crinkle of her photos in the ziplock, but also the hard imprint of her deuce-deuce handgun. She walked from the last brown staircase, turned over her shoulder and the wind hit her from behind. Not the wind of the wine glass, but the wind of Fritz climbing back upstairs with speed.

.

4

Seven sisters

January/14th/2020

The pandemic was an eventful time for our family, and I think my grandmother could see the destruction of her house before we did it.

On the fourteenth day of January 2020, was a frigid cold evening, so we kept away from the fogged windows. The radiator steam shot out and left sweat beads across the walls. Big momma Lucy walked over to the crinkled curtains with her hips wobbling. Her brown eyes protruded, she stared out the window at her new tenant and her neck snapped back.

She stared from the large, landscaped view of the sidewalk as the woman walked toward the house as if she owned the damn thing. Ms. Moss had a slow strut, with a wide hip bounce and an animated body gesture. She had long green and blue hair that looked like it was done by a curling iron.

She had a white bubble jacket, black leggings and

aqua Jordan's. She had a bone structure like Naomi Campbell, very curvy and had a pale tint in her skin that looked like she was cold from the neck. She lifted a large box at her breast, walked slowly from a Range Rover truck and held it into the door frame. A large man walked out, he kissed her on the mouth and walked into the range rover to grab a stereo set.

Each of Ms. Moss's daughters lifted boxes after her, giggling and talking loudly. Deon, her son was carrying a TV with his arms around it as if he were hugging it. He was a lanky dark-skinned boy, with a square shaped head. He was practically a celebrity because I heard of him playing basketball through the High school outlet, and even more about him sliding in the streets with the R.S.I gang.

I didn't tell Big momma Lucy that he was a gang member because she would have beat Fritz with her cooking spoon.

Big momma Lucy unloosed the flaps in her ruffled blouse, she fanned herself and then her eyes landed on Fritz. She folded her arms, while hugging her own breast, then she took a deep breath and her skin crept from brown to pale. She was always wearing her emotions, and you could always tell when she was upset because she wore a nasty smile.

"Fritz,'" Big momma Lucy shouted with her nostrils wide, "I thought there was only one tenant lady renting that little room, who are all those extra people?"

Fritz took a deep swallow, he backed away from the window, picked up a Bud light beer and lifted it to his upper lip. Big momma Lucy extended her arm, snatched the beer and the fuzz splashed onto the floor.

"Fritz, you know her," she shouted, "who is the lady? One of your little whores or something." She dropped the beer can on the coffee table and wiped her hands across her slacks. She placed her rump on the couch armrest and crossed her arms.

"That mother looks like a junkie," Big momma Lucy shouted, her nose peeking through the curtain and snapping her head left and right.

Fritz rolled his blue eyes, he took a deep breath and wiped his face with the collar of his blue polo shirt.

"The room was supposed to be for Charlesha, but I guess she brought her eight kids."

"I don't know them kids, I don't want them tearing my doggone house up."

"Come 'on Luce, they are just kids."

"We don't do donations Fritz, so get them people off my property before I have to sue that junkie bitch for eviction."

While Big momma Lucy and Fritz argued, their voices stretched into my room. I peaked my fuzzy head out to hear them. I opened the door, stopped at the dining table and neither of them said anything to me. My building interior is brown like the color of hummus and off white. Then there's dark brown flower designs under the lining of the ceiling. There are staircases that spin from each floor into the next, brown arm rail, steps with brown carpet and gold steel at the edge. Deon was sitting on the last three steps with his square back turned. The hallway lobby was full of cotton bleeding mattresses, TV stands with missing drawers, clothes and boxes of canned food stacked over the mailbox. I walked down the steps which made a bending sound and Deon turned around with his eyebrows scrunched. He was coddling his smallest sister in his arms, holding her by the pits and letting her walk on his knees. She was wearing a pink onesie, socks and her little fingers holding a tablet. As I walked closer to them, I could see that the tablet had a cracked screen that resembled a daddy long leg spider.

"Wassup," I uttered while reaching out my brown hand. "Y'all need any help?"

He tucked his bottom lip, rocked his sister, and turned the other cheek. Then, I saw Ms. Moss walk inside with a large factory box of Ramen noodles with the orange chicken flavor sign on it. She dropped one on the floor, she breathed heavily and flared her nose as she picked it up. She didn't say anything to me, but when she went into her apartment, she was screaming at her daughters.

She seemed like one of those mothers who liked her son more than she liked her daughters because Deon did bare minimum work, while they had the responsibility.

Fritz sat right besides Big momma Lucy and took his Bud Light beer from the coffee table,

"Lucy, the lease is already signed," he uttered "I didn't know, I didn't know, please, why would I lie! She has all those children, but what can we legally say? Tell her not to be a mother?"

He took a sip, and his golden mustache was moist after he held his beer away from his mouth.

Aunt Yata came to visit during the pandemic.

Yata had her hair in African braids, gold bangles around each wrist dragging on both sides. Yata was my mother's only other sibling. While She looked like my mother Ivory, she has a coffee skin color that made people ask if she was from Nigeria. They used to say she looked like India Arie, but she didn't have a soothing voice and I know first-hand that her voice wasn't soothing because she yelled at me on every occasion.

Aunt Yata turned her back, her hips jiggled. She was wearing a long dress with vibrant colors. She carved a wooden spoon into a whistling batch of macaroni shells. The pot had fumes coming out that looked like a witch's spell.

There was Some juicy baked turkey wings in the oven oozing on the colorful peppers. The aroma made me go into the kitchen and salivate. Yata was dancing next to Big momma Lucy. She always trying to show out, be the best version of herself to prove that men were the problem and not her. She opened the oven, placed the aluminum pan of baked macaroni in the oven above the turkey wings. The heat was so intense that her face turned a shade browner. Her temples moistened, and she used her hands as a fan. Big momma Lucy stood inches away from the counter with a handful of cashews and berries. She felt so hot, that She placed the snacks onto the counter and walked towards the window seal to lift it. When she arrived at the rug, she saw a red light bouncing through the curtain. She opened it and Her eyes twitched, her heartbeat was in her ear, and she felt even hotter than she already was. Dopeboy Q's flashy black Range Rover was double-parked outside. The hazard lights blinking like a UFO.

Big momma Lucy slapped the window glass. "Oh Lord have mercy," she shouted. She put her hand on her chest and rolled her eyes.

Yata dropped her spoon. She ran towards the window with her eyebrows on her brown forehead. "What's wrong, mama," she replied, "you good?"

Big momma Lucy backed away from the window curtains with her fingers curled around her breast. "That old drug dealer boy Q, beat that lady downstairs until her front teeth came out."

"Her teeth?"

"Yup, the lady's teeth came bouncing out her mouth sounding like a bunch of dice in a crap game."

"What! Why did he beat her?"

"Because Rhonda, the second eldest daughter, stole from him."

"Which girl is the eldest?"

"Dutchess," She uttered, "Dutchess, Rhonda, Livonia, Mary, Ginger, Onyx, and Draya! In that order! Seven girls and one boy."

"Why did you let them people rent the

apartment?" "Fritz did that foolishness," Big momma Lucy sung her words. Her brown skin crept pale, she backed away from the lamp near the table, while fanning herself.

"I can't wait to get them out of my doggone house."

"Evict them momma!"

"Fritz is Lucifer in the flesh!" Big momma Lucy's eyes strained, she looked over her shoulder at his room door and rolled her eyes at the gold knob. Fritz's room door had the cross in the middle of it, just like all the others in the house but Big momma Lucy thought he needed Jesus the most. On winter nights, his side of the house was always the coldest, there was always bad spirits and the feeling of fainting once she walked to close to his door and it was probably because of his pet spider or the fact that he was a fucking manic!

The cardiologist told Big momma Lucy to keep active because of her lagging blood, and its inability to get to her heart. Any time she felt stress, whether from Fritz or Ms. Moss, she would walk circles in the living room and take a deep breath.

While Big momma and Yata gossiped, a hissing cockroach flew into the apartment window. Its brown wings stood on the wall upside down with its antennas moving. Yata clinched, her hands retracted towards her chest, she stood up and screamed while running in fear. Her body knocked over a vase of flowers and the soil spewed onto the surge protector with plugs. Big momma Lucy lifted the broom above her shoulders and swung it like a lacrosse stick. The broom landed on one of Fritz's championship trophies. Dozens of ribbons and pictures tumbling down to the floor. The cockroach flew from the wall, spun around like drone and back out of the window.

Yata was inside Big momma Lucy's bed with the burgundy comforter above her head. "I'm not eating none of that," She screamed. "I swear to god if I see another water bug I'm going to stay in a hotel."

She had her arms covering her legs while sitting on her rump in the mattress like a scared child. It was hard to believe that she was a thirty-eight-year-old woman.

Big momma Lucy stood barefoot in the kitchen. She was picking turkey wings from the pan and placing the peppers with the potato. She thought about Fritz and how he is always luring cockroaches into the house so he can feed his pet spider. She sucked her teeth loudly, she turned towards me and asked me to bring her some plastic forks and spoons. She wrapped up the extra food in aluminum foil.

I stood under her watching her arms jiggle as she packed it up.

"Phillip, Give the food to Dutchess and her sisters on the first floor," she said, "ring the bell and put the food on the mat."

I walked downstairs; coming out of apartment one was a hefty brown man. He was out-of-shape, wearing a black durag with the strings hanging. He had wolfed out facial hair with bald spots and some fake jewelry that barely shined. He had on a leather jacket with a black eight ball on it. He wore some Beef-and-Broc Timbs. He walked with a limp as if he was shot in the past. The center of his face brightened brown; he had a single headphone in his ear while shouting. "It feels better than before," he chuckled. Then he opened the lobby door while shouting some old school gangsta lingo.

I knew that Dopeboy Q sold drugs, but it didn't make sense why he always stopped by to see Ms. Moss. I could not imagine him doing anything sexual with her, especially in that tiny room, plus she has her baby crib in there.

I knocked on the door; the welcome mat was all sticky and dirty, as if someone vomited on it and didn't clean it. I held the plates; the food was making my palm hot, so I switched hands.

The front door opened. Rhonda's flat brown button nose poked out of the darkness, she halfway opened the door with the chain under her chin and flared her nostrils. The skin around her eyes tightened like a person who needs glasses. She shut the door and reopened it with the chain off. She had the door into her chest, with her eyes stiff towards me.

"What do you want," she asked with thin lips, her eyes bobbled towards my wrist. "what's that."

"I have some leftover food for your sisters," I responded while handing the plates over to her. Rhonda's neck snapped back, she sucked her teeth and balled her fist.

"Are you trying to play us?" she responded, "you're beating around the bush, you're just in our business because you heard what the coward did."

My face froze,

"What coward," I responded, "what are you talking about Rhonda?"

"The coward just left—yea, I stole from him, —you better hope I don't steal from you and your white-ass daddy next. Me and my sisters will get our food—we don't need any damn donations bitch."

She exposed her teeth as she talked, and her

eyebrows got higher and higher with every word she said. Rhonda's words were so loud that the hallway walls were vibrating like tremors in California. She had veins in the side of her head, and her chest was bouncing out her shirt.

"Y'all think y'all better than everybody," she screamed, "y'all ain't nothing, don't matter if your grandmother is the landlord, y'all just like every other family! You ain't perfect!

She was right.

Dutchess, the eldest sister with pale skin, copper colored hair and slender build. Some people said she looked like Dua Lipa the singer but with hair that looked like curly fries. She stood in the middle of the hallway with her towel and a comb full of hair dye. She walked toward the bathroom and stepped on a spaghetti noodle that looked like an earthworm. Her facial expression changed from content to curious as she lifted her foot. She noticed the spaghetti and the angled spine of a little child sitting with her legs folded. Mary Ann, her badass little sister was blowing through a cheap whistle with chips of dirt on her elbow. Every time Dutchess took a step, the troubled sister blew the whistle louder. Fucking kids are hella annoying! Dutchess slapped the light switch, stared at her sister and she could smell a strong stench of vanilla coming from the floor tiles. Mary Ann smiled with her lips stretched. From her collarbone to her lap, she was full of what looked like tree droppings from a sparrow's nest. Her two fingers were holding a ripped Black and Mild and there were tobacco guts everywhere.

"Look Dutchess I found a Peter Pan flute" she laughed while holding the lip piece above her nappy head. Her laughter was if she was having a chest spasm, she was slapping her hand against the solid wall and kicking her legs. As she slapped the wall, the paint chipped and the cracks behind the wall looked powdery green.

Dutchess's lip twisted, staring with her brown eyes shaking and then kneeled. The tobacco for the Black and mild smelled like vanilla chocolate.

"Mary, what are you doing with this? Ughh."

She let go of her sister's arm and brushed all the tobacco with the tip of her fingernails, sweeping it to the corner with the side of her hand. While she cleaned, she slipped on another spaghetti noodle and her towel almost fell off.

Dutchess's light brown eyes strained, she lifted a

single finger and aimed.

"I'm sick of you touching everything," she shouted "If there was ever a forensic scene, you would have your fingerprints on everything wouldn't you. Where did you even get this crap?"

"Godfather." Mary Ann blurted with a playful smile. She looked like Rudy Huxtable if Rudy Huxtable had an evil twin. Her brown skin looked like spiced rum. But even though she was the one standing under light, Dutchess straightened as if she was thunderstruck.

"What?" she shouted, pinning her towel against her breast. "Where did you get this?"

"Godfather." Mary Ann blurted louder.

Dutchess's heart pinged with adrenaline. She felt as if her little sister was spilling the beans. Spilling the beams on a certain someone who needed to be banned from their family for good. It wasn't no game to Dutchess, she dropped to her knees and squeezed both of Mary's shoulders.

"What!" Dutchess shouted with moist eyeballs. "Did Edward do something strange to you?"

Mary Ann stared with a senseless look, then giggled with her nose wide.

"Not Edwardo Dorko," she uttered while snapping

her head playfully. "Deon's Godfather movie case, the Cigarette- whistle was inside the case." She pointed like a crossing guard.

Deon, the eldest of eight, loved gangsta movies and left them all over the house in a messy manner. Whenever he was home, He'd stare at the TV and smoke weed as if he were a grown man with real life stress.

Mary Ann's feet thumped to the shelf, she tippy-toed, and you could see the whiteness of her soles. She snagged the dirty DVD case which had spaghetti stains on each side, and She used her little thumb to press the rainbow DVD back inside.

As Dutchess stood there, she felt her heartbeat pumping, she stood up and her head was swollen with bad memories. She was a tall girl for her age, five-foot-eight but she wasn't big enough to deal with what she was hiding. She walked to the bathroom, shut the door, and stared into the mirror. She bent over the sink, while running her fingers through her copper brown hair. She bit her lip so hard that it turned red.

The apartment was narrow, just as a railroad apartment but had a vast space for the Livingroom. It was a large space full of bed sheets and pillows on the floor. There were two large wood closets near the open kitchen, one off white and the other, wood brown.

Deon's bed was a crooked black pullout in Livingroom, an iron and iron board near his bed with a flannel shirt hanging off it. Mary Ann loved her brother so much that she slept on a blow-up mattress next to him and tolerated all his shoot-em-up gangsta movies.

There was a tenant who rented a room on the front side of the apartment. Fat short Shaq, the man with the sumo-built body, short neck and arms that looked like he was bound for a mobility scooter eventually.

Dutchess didn't like dropping his packages, she wished that he would drop dead instead. Not because he did anything to her, but because he knew her deepest-darkest-filthiest-Secret.

5

The secret

November/20th/2020

Dutchess was lined-up in the center of the pink carpet with tough fibers, under the ceiling heater with orange bulbs and the sink that dripped water when the faucet was shut. All the girls at Pink Blossom wore different bright colored sheer dresses, with pin-ups and smelling like and Iranian madame's perfume. They stood, shoulders tucked, skin showing and smiling through their face mask at every old man who walked inside. Elmhurst was a predominately Spanish speaking community, and Dutchess stood confidently because she knew a little bit of the language. She was wearing purple- eye shadows, her copper-curly hair in a ponytail, gelled back with a mask on her mouth, but she was so tall that you could still notice her beauty.

It was three minutes after twelve and the police car flashed red and blue through Roosevelt Avenue. An unknown officer opened the door, walked down the steps and the boss of the establishment rushed up bumping him by accident. A small stack of fifties dropped to the ground and the boss smiled while bending over to pick it up with an awkward smile.

"Sorry Mr. policeman." he uttered. He lifted eyes and saw the officer's utility belt. The officer tapped his own Glock, his eyes bounced into the establishment and then back to the boss. On the ground he stayed with his head down.

The officer held his utility belt, ducked his head to peak in at the fine girls.

The boss stood up, gasping while smiling; he plopped all the money into his hand.

The officer cracked a smile that looked like dry clay. "Just checking on you Mr. Brut Han." The officer smiled while turning away.

Behind the officer was Dutchess's quirky Godfather Edward Aberdeen. He walked around the handrail, stumbled through the beaded curtains, and smiled at the ladies. In the Pink Blossom spa, there wasn't a door, there were those pink and purple beads that clicked and rattled. Dutchess always heard when a customer walked in, and her ears would rise.

Her eyes would wander, and she'd always hide at the end of the line of Asian bombshells. The front desk had a gold Chinese cat toy with a moving paw, posters on the wall of white people getting foot rubs, a neon entrance with padded pink walls that feel like a sofa.

Edward stood there in his brown electrician uniform, his hands on his hips smiling as his eyes twitched down the row of girls.

Edward looked back, then his eyes darted toward the girls. His hair was oily and black, and he had wrinkles on his forehead but still looked like a man who could get a woman in his age group if he wanted. He made eye contact with Dutchess, then he twisted his neck and rubbed the back of his head. He introduced himself to the girls while still side eyeing Dutchess. He crossed his arms, leaned back, and kept smiling. He had eyes that looked like he took a line of coke, drunk a Red Bull and then ran five miles straight.

Brut Han, the Boss of Pink Blossom was boldly peeking out the beaded curtains, speaking fast with his arms folded and tapping his foot against the floor. He cursed in his language as cars drove past. He turned his cheek, moving his red neck back and forth and lowering the curtains to block the beam from the window. He moved away from the beads, then flailed his wrist towards Windy and Sue, and stopped at Edward who had his eyes on Dutchess.

Edward talked with a thick accent, repeating her name as he walked down the line of girls, you could hear the scuff of his boots knock to the sound of his Hispanic words "Sasha, hermosa" he uttered. He walked past Sue, Windy, and Lia and stopped at Dutchess's dainty little body frame. He locked his fingers around her thin wrist and spun her around as if he were listening to his favorite Salsa song. Dutchess felt that same feeling you get from riding rollercoasters as she spun. She looked down to the floor, watching her feet as she walked to her massage room with him. The design on the room curtain was red lotus buds but she wasn't thinking about nature or tranquility. She was thinking about pushing his ass to the floor and hauling for the beaded entrance at the front of the shop. The room was dim, with a scented candle on top of a white cloth with lilies. There was a black towel folded on a massage bed and a cold breeze coming from the ceiling that made the candle sway. The window was covered in newspaper and black spray paint.

Through the spray paint you could see high heels on the street. Another set of feet from a man with large mountain boots. Edward hunched, he was talking like a Hispanic poet, while kicking off his battered construction boots and sitting on the massage bed. He grabbed the towel and wiped the sweat off his face. He gave her eye contact as if he knew who she really was. As he unbuttoned his shirt, he had the sniffles, so he sucked air through his nose and his face looked pale.

He wiped his nose again then lifted his shirt above his chin and his pit's smelled funky. When he got the shirt off, Dutchess turned her cheek and reached for a mask. He rolled his eyes and put the strings over his ears. His black beard was covered but his daunting eyes looked the same. He had a chest full of hair covering his sternum, which she had already seen at a waterpark when she was eleven but when he dropped his silver belt, along with his underwear, she wished she had never seen that.

As Dutchess rubbed the oil in both palms, she peeked at him from the side of her eye and blinked back to her moist fingertips. The only thing she thought about was whether to take her N95 mask off so he could see her whole face. Her body was a foot away, on a white stool with lotus buds. She pressed her palms into his spine, rubbing his brittle back bones and dropped low to the groove in his lower back. She rubbed in rotation, while preventing her breast from touching his back.

Dutchess's eyes stared toward the curtain, she

envisioned someone walking through her room to prevent the happy ending but there wasn't anyone coming, Suddenly, she stopped, and the oil leaked from her palm like a drip of water from a closed faucet. She stood there, still, and soundless. She lifted her light blue mask off her face and placed it on the side of the massage bed. She waited for Edward to say that he had a Goddaughter that looked like her so she could scream that she was her; but he didn't. Edward turned the other cheek, he laid on his muffled chin and groaned in Spanish while stroking himself. Dutchess could see the long dark shadow against the hallow wall and even though his shadow appeared long his penis wasn't. After three minutes, He reached for the purple basket of condoms near the body oil and used his sharp tooth to bite the wrapper. He sat upward on the massage bed, with his mask half-way off breathing hard. Dutchess was inches away from his hairy legs, so his arms stretched toward her, and he pulled her blue dress at the shoulder. Dutchess turned her neck toward the lotus curtain. She could feel the acid in the back of throat, pushing up to her tongue and the moistness of her seltzer-water-saliva that let her know she was preparing to vomit.

Fat short Shaq wore a green T-shirt with a jean jacket, leather shorts and a green checkerboard Louis Vuitton bandana on his head. He liked to dress with vintage shit and stuff that wasn't out yet. His sneakers had tags and his clothes always looked like they had never been washed.

There was never a greyish washed look in his fabric. The fat boy walked toward the Pink Blossom, and you could hear his Volvo car keys slap against his thigh with each step down the stairs. There was a giant brown rat that ran into a hole when it seen Fat short Shaq coming. He was a mountain of a man; his body was so large that he could eclipse sunlight to anyone smaller than him. He pushed the beads, walked inside and he smelt the stench of perfume intensify until he turned his cheek and saw five girls lined up about five feet away.

Windy, was in a yellow sheer outfit, she had ink black hair with a single blonde streak coming down her eye. She had the perfect bone structure with a round booty that looked like two bowling balls. She had a slim face, perky breast and thick knees that always looked lustful in Chinese dresses.

Brut Han sped from his bedroom-office; red curtains swayed as he handed Fat short Shaq an N95 mask with the metallic nose strip.

"You need mask." he shouted while wining in crooked English.

Fat short Shaq's friend walked inside behind him, and Brut Han handed over another N95 mask while jittering.

He knew them fools were dirty.

The establishment was so lowkey, out in Elmhurst Queens but once them Brooklyn niggas heard of it, they'd drive out looking for a good old time which they always got.

Each room was dark, orange candle lights looked like a ceremony for Catholics in the hall, but it was nothing godly about that place.

Fat short Shaq's best friend walked in the Pink Blossom, and he pointed directly at Dutchess at the tail end of the line

"ain't that the girl from Brevoort." He shouted. But Fat short Shaq nudged him in the rib with his sharp elbow.

Fat short Shaq shook his head left and right and leaned on the padded wall with a headphone string bouncing on his gut. He walked backwards and peeked out the service window.

Brut Han glimpsed at Dutchess, then he glimpsed Fat short Shaq and flicked his fingers to come.

"All my girls very clean." he uttered, he put his wrist around Dutchess's hip. "What's wrong?"

Dutchess pushed off, she walked to her room with the white curtain, and held her face with her palm. She twisted the faucet and let water run while hunching in between the stool and mattress. Such a short area, but she was skinny enough to fit. Her knees were on the cold floor, she panicked as her arm reached for the power outlet in the wall. First, she removed her cellphone cord, then she removed the outlet face, and it was a bundle of cash stuck inside next to blue wires. She didn't think about Edward or Fat short Shaq. She only thought about the extra money she hid from Brut Han. She reached forward, pulling out hundred-dollar bills with blue faces on them.

Fat short Shaq chose Windy, and his homeboy chose Sue. From the back room, there was lot of skin clapping and gasping which all sounded like it came from Fat short Shaq. He sounded like he was having a heart attack. After his happy ending, he peaked his head through Dutchess's curtain and his eyes bulged twice their normal size.

She was fully dressed in jeans and a white bubble jacket half-way on her right arm. She was still on the floor, with her bills scattered, looking like a complete wreck.

Dutchess looked upward, she froze up with the money in her hand and the silence was loud.

Fat short Shaq took a deep breath.

"I'm not here for that, or to expose you." he uttered.

She swallowed her saliva and at that point it was as thick as peanut butter. She turned her neck and stuffed her white Old Navy hoodie pocket with a wad of cash. She loosened her hair, took the rubber band off her ponytail, and tried to tie the cash with it.

Fat short Shaq walked through curtain and his face was dark, but the movement of his mouth was visible.

"Do what you do." he uttered. That's when Fat short Shaq leaned closer and reached forward. He plucked a hundred-dollar bill from her rubber band. "Big Fellas don't close their mouths unless they get fed." He uttered down to her. "It's a pandemic, you understand right mama." He tapped her on the back.

Dutchess looked at his hairy brown legs and nodded.

Fat short Shaq turned his back, he walked with

bulldog feet and with each step, his car keys slapped his thigh. Every step he took, Dutchess felt the vibration in her gut. The curtain swayed vertically but Dutchess stayed on the cold floor swaying horizontally. She shivered into tears that dragged down her cheek and wiggled at the bottom of her jaw.

Months after, on a red leaf rainy day of October 2021.

Fat short Shaq was gunned down in front of a bodega. Coincidentally, Edward Aberdeen was killed five months later with shots to the body, head, and pelvis area. The murders were strange even for Brooklyn homicides.

I never suspected that Dutchess killed them or got them killed because that meant that she told someone her deepest- darkest-filthiest secret. It rules out Me, her boyfriend, and her big brother Deon because it's something that Dutchess would have never mentioned to a boy.

6

Piece of the Pie
March/7th/2022

Detectives smoke weed? Imagine being high as shit and someone trying to explain their story on why they are not the killer. I'd probably laugh through my nose and say bitch you the killer. While I play Sherlock homes for a second, I have to keep in mind that Dutchess being the actual killer would sober me up faster than hearing your boss telling you your fired or your dog died, or you have an illness that's a life-or-death situation. Dutchess was my world.

Anyways, finding a killer isn't always easy because no one is going to be dead honest about murders except for people like Lance. He raps, and the lyrics are always about the kids he shot at and stabbed.

I was hanging with my no-good gang banging homeboy.

Lance was my friend, but to keep it a hundred, he was a menace to the progression of the black folk.

There wasn't a logical way for our race to progress when he out there stabbing niggas, shooting and beating up people over colors. Lance was at my house, he sat with his legs wide open, a PlayStation game controller in hands with his spine bent closer to the TV. He sat on my grandmother's favorite brown suede couch and his friend T.T. sat right next to him with her kneecap touching his leg. She was licking a vanilla backwood. When she first came upstairs, I heard some fools blasting Gin and Juice from a grand Cherokee. They stopped at the light and screamed Foxy brown from their rolled down car windows. T.T. did look like Foxy but younger and slightly taller.

Lance tossed his game controller to the other side of the suede couch and grimaced because he got shot in Grand Theft Auto again.

Suddenly, we heard pounding knocks at the door which was odd because Big momma Lucy was in the hospital and Fritz was in Berlin for Olympic elimination. The knocking at my front door persisted and I could see two sets of feet underneath as if we were getting spied on.

I signaled Lance and T.T. to move out of the door's view in case it was the police officers. I was paranoid when I blew it down. Everything sounded like a setup or something, which is why I'm how I am to this day. I picked the baggie up off the floor, sprayed some freshener, but when I looked through the peephole, it wasn't anyone important. Sophia, the tenant with the air bag boobs and facelift chin. She and her boyfriend Jay stood there with their arms folded while rambling with Caribbean accents.

They were the tenants on the second floor, and since they paid rent, they thought they could just come up and complain at any time.

I opened the door with a careless half-grin, my eyes were crooked, and my shoulders were loose like when you get a massage. I didn't give a damn about shit.

Sophia was wearing an orange blouse with palm trees, white pants, and shoes with a buckle on the side. Jay, her boyfriend, was next to her with his paternal potbelly. He looked like Uncle Phil from Fresh Prince. Old Jamaican school chef that can throw down in the kitchen, but don't know how throw down his foot when his woman yells at him.

The hinges creaked, the light from the hall shined on my smacked face. Sophia's index fingertips pointed at the center of my eyes and her long nails looked like the back of a hammer.

"See, I knew he was getting high," she yelled. "I'm

going to call the policemen right now."

"Wait, Sophia, I'm not high. Wait ..." I responded.

Her eyes popped out of her skull, and her bottom lip was pulsating. She waved her hand across her nose, left and right while dialing into her android phone.

"What di ass is dis? Your grandmother just had a heart attack," she screamed, "she is hospitalized, and she will probably have another one when she finds you smoking herb and carjacking." The tone of her voice amplified loudly

She turned her back, walked toward the roof door and took a step up to the emergency handle. There were a bunch of old boxes that Fritz had there for painting. Sophia bent over, her arms tightened as she dragged the boxes from the roof entrance and pushed the roof door open wide. The bright light beamed into the hallway, through the roof door frame you could see the slanted windshield and the groovy black passenger side of the car. There was a luxurious sports car on my grandmother's roof, like something from a video game that we were playing.

Sophia's face shook.

"What di ass is this? Are you Batman and dis your Bat- mobile? where is your stepfather?" She yelled with her chest bouncing, "Where is Fritz?" she slapped the roof door in the center, making a loud thud, "Tell me where he is —right now!"

I took a deep breath.

"Fritz—Fritz went to Berlin," I responded in a casual tone. Lance and T.T. bussed out laughing in the background, but I wasn't lying or telling jokes. Fritz went to Berlin twice a year for basketball coaching, but there's something about being high and explaining shit; everything sort of sounds like a punchline.

Sophia lips went thin to the pinkest of her gums, and she stomped toward the doormat.

"Fritz isn't home, Lucy isn't home, no one is ever home!" she shouted while stomping her feet. "You need a mother to whip you! No! They need to lock your black behind up in juvie with the rest of the thugs."

Jay pulled his woman by the waist, while tugging her away from the roof door and when he placed her to the side, the roof door closed and light from the sun cracked away.

"Your granny usually runs a tight ship," he uttered, "we aren't paying rent this month."

"Because of the smell?" I yelled back. "Weed is legal."

Jay's eyes narrowed toward the roof door.

"Are you insane?" he said with a nasty mouth

twist. Sophia followed behind him, flicking pictures with her phone camera. "I bet you this car is stolen property," she uttered. "He and his little criminal friends are bunched up inside like a chicken coop, smoking crack and carrying on."

"Shut up, stinking ass breath!" I responded with my face twisted sideways.

Jay crossed his arms while shaking his head left and right. "We are not paying rent because this house is unsafe, this place isn't a parking lot young man."

"I know it isn't."

"So why is there a car on top of the roof like Grand Theft Auto," he snapped, "are you off your crazy pills?"

After Sophia and Jay were back in their apartment, I shut the roof door and the gold lock clicked. Back inside, Lance had his arm around T. T's neck.

T.T turned around towards the door.

"Who was that bitch?" she uttered. "And why is she trying to act like she is ya mother."

"I don't know," I replied. I shrugged my shoulders, "She a hater."

"What does ya mother look like?"

Lance's eyes beamed towards the pale wall and then he removed his arm from T.T.'s neck.

"Roll the weed hoe, why you are worrying about

my boy's mom, you came here for Milf pussy or to fuck with a real nigga?"

"Stop it, Lance." she uttered while rolling her eyes. "Ugh"

I sat across from Lance and T.T. Tahiry Thaud was her government name. Up close She had lips that always look glossy as if she used her whole cap of Blistex. Even though she smoked all that weed, she still had the pinkest set of heart-shaped lips.

She had a petite upper body and a meaty lower body. She could put on sweatpants that aren't ironed, but once she slides them on her figure it makes it look like it was ironed. That's how thick she was. She wore a pink hoodie with white sweatpants and some UGG boots with white fur on the top.

Whenever Sophia complained about me being too careless, a part of me knew she was right because Lance and T.T were in my crib like it was a hotel.

I didn't care about them being all Boo'd up in my house, but I wasn't getting no action which is why I thought about Dutchess. Deon's younger sister, only by a couple of months so she is sixteen just like me. Everyone in Brevoort thought she was my girl, which was good for me because I didn't want anybody else busting a move on her. Since her family got evicted from the first floor, I was having a lot of guilt and even more sleepless nights.

Christmas Day of 2021. The snow on the steps had salt pellets in them. The road was greyish, slushy, and Dutchess walked with her eyes to the footprinted ground. She strutted slowly while struggling with the last bag, her chin down and each of her sisters jumping over piles of snow.

Ms. Moss was near the trunk, she looked like Naomi Campbell, but the drugs sucked the muscle out of her cheeks, so her bones were more defined. She was a good-looking older woman with a huge apple-bottom ass that moved like a waterbed. But on that day, her brown chest was bouncing, and she kept yelling.

"Nobody's gonna help me," she screamed in a high-pitched voice, "y'all motherfuckers don't see me standing here with these big ass bags, my gawd." She grabbed Dutchess by the arm and pushed her into the midsized taxicab. The driver was a big Armenian guy with a balding crown on top of his head. He wore a button-up shirt, bubble vest, and a thin gold chain on his chest hairs. When he saw Ms. Moss's ass in the rearview mirror. He got out of his seat like someone being released from an electric chair. He lifted the bags with one hand and squeezed them into the trunk. He smiled with his stained teeth, leaned on the car, and started swinging his gold watch.

While all of that was going on, I leaned on the kitchen wall and cracked my knuckles. There was music being played so loud that the walls wobbled. The music was coming from Big momma Lucy's computer sitting on the marble table next to the ketchup and pineapple juice.

Big momma Lucy snapped her fingers and took slow steps as she rocked her body to music.

"Come on, Phillip," she uttered. "Why are you looking so stiff, dance with me baby boy." She had an apron on with a cinnamon stain. She leaned over the stovetop. Her famous sweet potato pie was cooling off.

Big momma Lucy slowed down but still moved her hips.

"What's wrong, Phillip," she uttered. "You're not being yourself tonight."

I took a deep breath,

"Deon and his sisters going in the shelters because of us?" I uttered.

She gasped, turned away and put the nutmeg inside the cabinet. She turned back around with both hands on her hip and her neck leaning towards me.

"Who told you they are going to the shelter." Her forehead creased like sneakers from the thrift shop. She put her hands an inch higher above her waist and walked closer to me.

"Boy, stop taking guilt for things that have nothing to do with you," she snapped. "Charlesha is on crack, she chose to smoke that junk, you didn't put crack to her lips, did you?"

"No."

"Okay, well, hand me those mitt's so I can get this pie out the oven, or are you too guilty to take a piece of the pie?"

She opened the fridge and the light shined onto her round face. She reached into the top layer, grabbed the vanilla Almond milk, and placed it on the table. There was a shiny plate and a tall glass that looked like it was cleaned in a dishwasher.

"There you go baby." she uttered. Her back leaned over, she sat on her hemorrhoid pillow in slow motion and her eyes ping ponged.

"Listen Phillip," she spoke with a downturned mouth, "I know you have feelings for Dutchess, but Charlesha spent almost two years on the first floor with those kids and didn't pay rent, I did what I had to do."

My eyes strained downward; I saw a cheesy shell

of macaroni on the table that we didn't wipe. I picked it up with my napkin. "At least their mother is around," I responded. My hands pressed down on the plastic tablecloth. I got up and dumped the napkin in the trash bin. The macaroni shell was cheesy and so was Big momma Lucy's excuse for not helping the girls.

Big momma Lucy's eyes turned glassy, her hand retracted to her lap, her cheeks swelled twice their size and she turned away while taking a deep breath. "Eat up, Phillip," she said. "Come on back to the table and eat boy, I tried telling you in the kindest way I could, if you want me to be the public enemy then so be it, but my pie got the flava-flav baby."

She pressed the computer screen while laughing, "You heard me boy," she danced with her hips moving side-to-side. Her music amplified in the background, she held her wooden spoon at her chin like a microphone and hit all the high notes. She looked like a real singer in a concert in front of a live audience. She had charisma, presence, and charm. Big momma Lucy couldn't sing, she could sang. Her voice was so soothing, and she could dance while doing it, it was a side of her that was absent throughout the pandemic.

After eating, I dumped the pie crumbs into the garbage, I walked toward Fritz's bedroom and pushed the door open. He had the sunny room in front of our apartment, so he always kept his lights off. He was inside, leaning over his tank, feeding his pet Tarantula, Kenny.

Fritz didn't even move. He held the brown cricket on a tweezer and dropped it inside the tank. The cricket quickly twitched towards the glass, but the tarantula's legs were faster, and its fangs opened like a Venus flytrap.

Big momma Lucy hated the spider, she called it white people shit and hardly ever went near his room door unless she was pissed off.

I leaned on the door frame with my head to the side. "Fritz, can you help?" I asked while staring at the back of his head. "Dutchess and her sisters, can we bring them back to live in the basement?"

Fritz put the tweezers down, wiped his hands with a blue rag, and sat down in his Coney Island themed beach chair that had sand, Ferris wheels, a picture of Nathans hotdogs and the boardwalk.

Fritz shook his eyes,

"I tried to help," he responded, "but that lady is sick, your gram is even infuriated with me ... sometimes you have to let people suffer, you saw that cricket get ate right, well it's a cricket and you shouldn't feel guilt for it because it's purpose is to get eaten by Kenny." He hunched his shoulders and popped the top of a Bud light can.

He burped loudly, and when I stared him down, he asked me if wanted one.

Fritz didn't have any beef with Fat short Shaq or Ms. Moss, but Sophia from the second floor was a wildcard because she yelled at everyone in the building. However, when it came to Fritz she would smile and wave hello. He once put a broken dented refrigerator into their apartment, and she still spoke to him kindly. She had the door to her chest smiling and laughing while talking and he walked inside and pushed it out of the frame. I've never seen her smile like that, not even with her own boyfriend. My aunt said it was because Fritz was a white man, and that Sophia's country acknowledges the British as kings and queens, therefore they come to America with a high sense of respect for white men like Fritz.

But since we are brainstorming of motives and what not, I kind of know someone who fit the bill as the killer. Me! First, I'm smart, slick, always in the mix of things and I'd do anything for Dutchess. But I been pussy since I came out of pussy. The type of nigga that would hold a gun and drop it while aiming it. I was always that scared kid who hid behind his grandma or called his stepfather if someone beat me up in the yard. That would be an enjoyable book twist, but I didn't bust no lead because I didn't want to get booked at central bookings. Lance, on the other hand, was a goon. I've seen him get questioned by white officers and he'd tell them to suck his dick. They stopped and frisked him during the pandemic because he was in the park while the sky was dark. The officers shoved him toward the gate, snapped cuffs on his wrist and while most young boys would have been shaking, he was telling the police officers that he is indeed packing; but not packing a gat, packing a big black limp dick to fuck their wives. Reckless!

Me, Lance and T.T were on the rooftop with our bodies leaning on the side of the car. The wind pushed through our shirts and pants, and I could feel my skin chime. A few feet forward was the ocean blue sky and an aerial view of the projects and the streets. The projects looked like a maze.

Everyone planned how to get out the hood, but the question I asked was how did they get in.

I caught a glimpse of the sparking concrete from

the height of the sky, I saw Sophia's feet dragging her luggage and it made a thumping sound at each step. It had a missing wheel, so it shifted side to side until her boyfriend helped her. His pits were wet at both sides and his sweat made his hairline curly.

T.T lifted her ass off the car, she spun around and glanced at the license plate.

"Why does your license plate say Georgia." she uttered. "Are you from Atlanta?"

Lance held the spiff to his lips, sucking in the smoke with his eyes low.

"You the feds?" He uttered with a deep smoke-filled voice.

"No."

"Then stop being weird and smoke this."

Supercharger Revolt GTSS was written on the back of the black vehicle. Its exhaust pipes looked like a double chrome shotgun, and the glossy paint was shiny like one of the models at the car show. Lance pressed the car key, he opened the door, and it dinged repeatedly. The car seats smelled like leather and chronic so whoever owned it was a habitual smoker. Confession time! I didn't own it!

T.T.'s ass sunk in the leather seats, she crossed her brown legs and her eyeballs bounced across the dash like a pinball. Lance walked around to the driver's side, he pulled the handle and sat down next to her with his legs open wide. When he turned his cheek, he noticed that the glove department was wide open, and she had the registration papers in her hand.

"What the fuck are you doing?' He screamed. "Who is Lia Stennod?" she uttered. "And David Stennod?"

Lance's eyes turned red, he reached over and snatched the papers. He shoved it back into the glove department while biting the spliff with lips.

"Yo! you blowing mines.' He shouted.

T.T was smiling with an angry glow in the center of her face.

"Damn, this car is sexy though," she said, "how did you park it up here?" She slapped his arm while hunching over, "Y'all didn't even tell me."

Lance hitched his chest; he scratched the red lighter to spark up another joint. His eyes dragged downward, puffed it, and blew sour smoke into her face.

"This ain't no normal V," he responded. "This is the Vroom Deady!"

"Vroom Deady," she repeated, "Mmm, I like that."
"Bitch, roll more weed den."

"Don't call me no bitch—just because you have a

car don't mean you can talk however you want."

Later that evening, it was time to go because of Lance's Mother, who had concerns about him being outside late again.

T.T. sucked her teeth, she leaned over the couch, flicked through their rollup papers, napkins, and Fronto. She dumped the red rice and skinny chicken bones in a plastic bag, put on her sweater, and walked to the front door. T.T kept her chin down with a slow-building smile, she zipped her hoodie and it stopped at her breast. She noticed me watching her, so she turned sideways and straightened her neck. When her face perked up, her eyes rolled at Lance as if she had an attitude. She hiked up her leg on my grandmother's piano seat and slipped her socks into her UGG boots.

Lance stood near the door, staring into the wall mirror while tying his bandana like Pac.

"I wish I had what you had," he uttered, "your stepdad is always in Berlin, you don't have to worry about bitch ass parents all up in your shit—your lucky son." He turned around and tied his bandana more aggressively. I could tell he got a headache with how tight he tied it.

They walked towards the staircase; stomping and

their height dropped as they took delayed steps. I tried to stop Lance and ask him if he had my orange lighter, but he reassured me that he didn't take it.

"Nah—why would I take your lighter," he said, "it was on the couch, go look, bitch." Once I shut the apartment door, I walked over to Big momma Lucy's furniture set, I stuck my hands into each couch cushion. Big momma Lucy has plastic over her seats, so my forearm was slightly red as I dug. I reached the bottom, and my fingers were covered in dust. I stuck my hands into the suede one closest to the TV, my curling fingers pulled up a half-wrinkled paper, it was Fritz's dusty Covid-19 vaccine card. Fritzen Clayed written on the top.

I leaned my head on the couch and stared into the ceiling, but I saw how trashed my apartment was when I got up. Red rice pebbles all over the floor, ripped Fronto leaf and guts on the suede couch seat.

The ceramic ashtray was downward, it left black ash smudges all over the living-room carpet looking like a charcoal blemish.

7

Barbara Has Roaches
March/7th/2022

Fritz always lied to us, Last spring he told Big momma Lucy that he cleaned the gutter. But he didn't and the rainwater ruined her daises, flooded the basement, moss grew along the ledge, and we even saw a wasp nest. That same day, Big momma Lucy stirred her egg batter aggressively while cussing him out.

She knew stuff about him that made her angry, but she never explained in distinctive detail.

She lifted her eggbeater and pointed it at me while the yolk dripped in slow motion.

"Your stepfather is a doggone fibber," she uttered.

While I reminisced about Big momma Lucy, I leaned back into the suede couch near the piano and bookshelf. I stretched my arms and my chin dropped to the side, between my thumb and my index was Fritz's wrinkled vaccine card. I lifted it, squinted into the words, and something became alarmingly clear. Why would he leave this behind? Didn't he need it to fly out to Berlin?

I opened my phone to write to him.

"Pop?" I didn't send the text, my eyeballs stung as I read the earlier messages and I took a deep breath. There was a text where he said he'd find Dutchess and her sisters to give them a place to stay. That was in February; he still hasn't done anything to the middle of March. He was the perfect stereotypical super because they always fake-fix things just to shut you up. He liked to gas the tenants, like yes it will be done on Saturday and when Saturday comes no one knocks on the door, except the Grim reaper when he comes to collect your lungs from the Carbon monoxide that no one smelled.

Suddenly, I heard the doorbell rung, a set of footsteps darkened the bottom of the crack, so I got up and twisted the gold knob. Through the side of the open door, T.T. was standing there with her belly button exposed. She had her pink sweater with a knot in the back. And belly ring exposing her chocolate waist. In her hands, she held a black plastic bag at her thigh with a brown corked bottle poking out.

Her eyes shook left and right as she stood at the

door. "So, are you going to invite me inside? can I stay here for a little while longer, or no?" she asked, "I don't want to go home yet."

She seemed innocent but at the same time direct because of her wide eye contact. She talked like a businessperson who was impatient. She was one of those girls who didn't say much, but she knew how to position herself to get what she wanted. The only thing was, Lance is a gangsta, so why would she try to go behind his back. In my hood, most gangsta's were paranoid, always thinking someone betrayed them and skeptical of their friends. I wasn't down to play those games with her.

My face flushed, "Iight T.T.," I responded, "you can stay for a little, want me to call Lance or you good?"

"Nah," she uttered, she put her fingers on the knob and shut it fast. She walked inside with her belly out. Her body posture loosened, she kicked off her Ugg boots and took slow steps. She stopped at the couch, swiped the cushion seat while giving me darting contact and she sat down. She always did that every time she squatted for a seat, and I think it's because she wore light-colored pants and didn't want to sit on something dirty by accident. She reached into the bag;

her nails squeezed the cork of the bottle, and she opened it with her ring of keys. It was the 375 ml (about 12.68 oz) bottle of Casamigos Tequila resting in her lap and two plastic cups by her thigh.

T.T. smiled with her white teeth showing.

"You ready to get lit," she shouted with an amped voice.

She swung her hand over her head and rocked her shoulders.

She mixed the Tequila with Tropicana pineapple juice like a chemist. The plain drink looked like rubbing alcohol, but it became tangy when she poured the juice. She poured my cup like a bartender, then leaned into my face while handing it over. She crossed her legs and smiled with her shoulders hunched.

"That's enough?" she muttered while giggling. "I bet you a lightweight."

"Nah, I can handle that—I drink henny."

"Nigga please—you know damn well you can't handle no henny—you green."

"Green? nah I'm brown—just like the hen."

It was the first time I drank anything, and I didn't feel it right away. The back of my throat tasted like citrus and gasoline. It burned my whole respiratory system, and I felt a rush through my skin that made me feel relaxed.

T.T. took a sip, she crawled closer to me while squeezing the couch and the cloth in my clothes and snapped her fingers.

"Aye," she uttered, "I'm gonna make you feel good, don't worry," she spoke. She leaned in closer to me, her words sounded louder, and I could feel her nostrils breathing on me. I stared at her neck and down to her shirt, where her chocolate skin looked as mouthwatering as a bag of Hersheys.

T.T. slapped my kneecap. "You're tall, so the drink takes longer to hit, but it's gone hit."

She turned her cheek, relaxed her posture, and spread her wrist to my lap.

I thought about where things might go, and I couldn't help but consider spanking her out, but then I glimpsed my cellphone at the corner of the cushion.

My cellphone was ringing like a slot machine.

Lance sent a text that lit up the screen. "Yo, what's cracking, appreciate you, my nigga, we bro's fa life," He wrote.

T.T.'s neck straightened, she moved closer to me and placed one hand on my shoulder.

"Nobody is here?" she asked in a high-pitched tone. She bit the rim of her cup while looking at me in a seductive way. "It's getting late, and I don't want to disrespect ya house?"

"My stepdad is in Berlin," I muttered back in a shouting tone. "You can make noise,"

"I can make noise?" She bent over and let out a fake moan. She looked over at me and laughed while holding her claw-like hands over her stomach.

"Can I ask you something? In the Vroom Deady car, the registration said Lia Stennod and David Stennod, are those your parents?"

"Damn T.T! Lance was right, you are acting like the feds." I uttered back with a chuckle.

"I'm not the feds, that car has me curious that's all, like why is it on top of a roof, how did it get there? You know cars are like two-thousand pounds and I don't see a freight elevator in this building nigga."

T.T rolled her eyes in a ghetto way, leaned off me, folded her legs, and poured some more Casamigos until it dripped on the sides of the glass. The alcohol was clear like water, but it smelled strong enough to blow the house up.

"I hate my father," T.T. uttered with a husky voice, she randomly blurted, shook her head at me with her brown eyes and hunched. "He lives out in Harlem, I will never go back out there, I don't ever want to see him again." She scooted closer to me, her soft thigh rubbed against my leg. Her arm pressed down with her boobs, she perked upwards and her other hand around my kneecap. She bit the rim and took a deep breath that looked like she was gulping the liquor, "I would rather live in the streets than stay with him again." She leaned over like she was about to hurl. She put the drink on the coffee table with a twisted mouth. She reached back and cupped her hand to my kneecap.

"Can I take a shower here?" She removed her hand from my knee, "If that's okay with you." Her face ticked awkwardly. "I'm not a bum-bitch or anything, I just don't want to go to the shelter smelling like that Cassa."

"Which shelter are you in?"

"Ralph Avenue family shelter," she responded with a look of shame. "Why you so quiet." she touched my arm, "don't judge me of nothing, shit happens."

My heartbeat skipped a beat, and I felt clouds opening in my mind. Dutchess's face showed up in my head and I remembered that's the same shelter that Ms. Moss stayed in with her daughters.

I put the drink on the coffee table and wiped my bottom lip. My eyes ping-ponged because my brain was moving fast. "You know a girl named Dutchess Moss,"

I asked, I leaned up. T.T.'s eyes dotted, and she turned around with a smile that turned into a confused face.

"Yea, I know her," she responded, she retracted her brown hand away from me and put it in her lap. She straightened her shoulders, stared with a single eyebrow.

"Dutchess is like sixteen, she a kid, wait how old are you?"

"I'm sixteen and a half," I uttered back.

T.T.'s eyes widened, her face froze, she looked around and blinked her eyes into soberness.

Her circular eyes blinked hard one last time and then protruded.

"Wait, how old is Lance?" she said, "please don't tell me he's a kid too. Why are men always fucking lying to me, do I have a sign on my forehead that says I'm a dumb-ass-bitch."

She reached forward, took my drink, and reeled it towards her kneecap. "You are a damn kid," she uttered with a hateful face, "you ain't supposed to be drinking." She turned the bottle around where it says you must be Twenty- one years old. I stared back at her because she wasn't Twenty-one either and we both were tipsy enough that the words on the bottle didn't even exist.

She snatched her cellphone, stomped towards the

bathroom, and slammed the door so hard that a gust of wind made the portraits on the wall wobble like a haunted house. She cursed Lance out on the speakerphone for an hour and a half. I heard the roll of toilet tissue rolling and rolling and her voice cracking dramatically.

"Short dick bitch," she shouted, "half midget, full fuck boy." She had her cellphone in her hand, spewing fragmented words while sitting on the toilet seat with her knees knocking.

"I hate boys," she screamed. "Y'all all are creeps, just like my father, I swear to god."

She turned over and flushed the toilet. Her half-spewed vomit spun in circles.

She crept out of the bathroom with the side of her hand against her eyes. Her hair looked like strings, her skinny neck was bloated and veiny as she screamed. She stomped her feet to the area rug and balled onto the couch.

She was holding her legs to her chest. She glared at her time, slapped herself on the forehead and screamed, "I missed curfew." She shouted. "Can I stay for the night?" she asked while tightening her arms around her knees, "I'll be gone by the morning. I just need a fucking shower."

It might seem kind of bizarre that T.T. was all up in my crib asking for showers, but I'm used to it. Every time someone comes over, they don't want to leave my spot to the point that my grandmother has to step in and tell them to go.

I handed T.T. a white towel and wash cloth from Big momma Lucy's room.

She walked into the bathroom and pushed open the door with her hip. The hot shower water came pouring down, and I heard her cursing at herself loudly.

I was inside the Livingroom walking around like dickhead, first because I ratted out Lance and couldn't think of whether to tell him. I bumped my leg on the Coffee table with the Casamigos bottle and the glass shattered beautifully.

T.T. dropped the soap,

"Phillip," she yelled from the bathroom, her voice echoed through the tub, tattering rain. "Is everything okay," she uttered with the showerhead scattering over her face.

"Yea, I dropped something, my bad, fuck."

A half-hour after, the showerhead squeaked, and she stepped out of the bathroom fully dressed in her tight pink shorts and a long shirt that I gave her.

She walked into the living room heavy-footed. Her

eyes froze as she watched me with the mop in my hand.

"Be careful," I uttered. "I dropped the Casamigos bottle."

Her face flushed, "It's okay because the party is over anyway." she said with her eyes low. She stepped towards me, took the mop from my hands, and started swaying the shards out. She had her head down, baby hair still wet and her shoulders tight as if she were cold.

"You wanted to know about Dutchess, right," she uttered without staring. "She was in the shelter for a month, but they placed her with a foster parent. Her Godfather in Nassau County until she turns eighteen."

A month ago, Ms. Moss and her boyfriend Q, parked the Range Rover in front of my house, blasting Drill music that throttled the car hood. The bass of the music was so hard that it made the side mirrors tremble like a jackhammer on concrete.

Fritz's room door extended, and he crept out his room fully dressed in a grey tracksuit, some blue Air Max shoes, and a Yankee fitted. He pulled his jacket from the coat hanger, put his arms through and then zipped up. He bent down to tie his shoe with aggression as if he were tying up Ms. Moss.

My eyes beamed,

"Why is she doing that?" I asked. I walked to the window and put my palms on the cold glass.

Fritz squeezed his keys, and turned his cheek.

"Because she got kicked out, why else, the lady is a complete psycho."

Fritz ran downstairs, he approached the Range Rover at the curb and people's faces in the car became clear. Ms. Moss loosened her seatbelt, pulled the handle, and hit Fritz on his knees with the passenger side door.

"I need a place to stay," she shouted particles of spit "I ain't staying at that fucking shelter no more, how y'all gone put me out in the damn streets with seven girls, are you fucking dumb, bozo?"

Fritz's eyes bounced from across the street and back toward her face.

"Charlesha, are you nuts." He shouted softly. "They are taking my daughters away from me," she

yelled dramatically. "They took Dutchess, she is living with her godfather now and they are coming for Livonia next, I shouldn't have to beg so hard, you hear me, dickhead." She threw the paper from child services into his face.

"I will fix it," Fritz uttered. "You remember Barbara? She rents her rooms across the street, in

Apartment 1H."

Charlesha removed her hands from her cleavage, "Barbara has roaches," she snapped back in rage. "I don't want to live in the projects no more, just talk to that old bitch upstairs, she would let me come back if she knew.

8

Some Kind of Drug
March/8th/2022

The sun crept through the cotton clouds and shined in the southern part of the sky.

T.T. was still at my house, she had her perky buns hitched up while her face was in the armrest. I was Amused that she slept with her face down because of limited circulation but she looked comfortable. The TV was running infomercials for knives. From the open window, I heard a loud scraping noise, along with car horns honking. I walked over towards the window, pulled aside the curtains, and stared at Brevoort projects. Through my high window, I glared at the silver curb, I saw an old Trinidadian lady standing on the corner with bakery bread hanging off her cart. At the same time, clanking bike handles hit the concrete; children ran towards the street with their eyebrows arched above their foreheads, pushing through without an excuse me.

Ms. Moss was there, at the center of the madness with her shoulders squared. Her legs buckled, her breast dangling out of her green shirt, and when she was ready, she started swinging her fist through the air like propellers. She landed on the staircase and lifted herself off the ground with a weird eye twitch.

Mr. Allen walked out of his chop-shop gate, rubbing his oily hands on a rag, and shaking his head in disappointment.

"Charlesha, what you got yourself into now," he muttered.

Ms. Moss had ashy lips that looked like she peck-kissed baby powder, broken skin around her mouth area, and snot on her nostrils.

"Bitch, I would fucking stab your guts out," she screamed from her guts while squeezing her fist, "Don't play with my children because I'm ready to go."

The ACS workers were two women wearing black suits, slacks, flats, and white-collar shirts half-buttoned at the top. They kept their clipboards over their heads.

"We'll have you arrested for assault," Shelly Wallace spoke with direct eyes. "This time, we are serious, Charlesha."

The suited women went into the project building

with clipboards over their heads. Drips of water was dripping from the lobby. There was water damage on the ceiling that looked like brown mold. The ladies walked side by side, they stepped towards the elevator and entered the raggedy orange and brown project building to pick up the girls, Onyx and Draya. The youngest two girls who hadn't been to school in weeks.

When the women stepped out of the broken door frame, the two little sisters both dressed in matching yellow and black outfits, had their fingers locked together while their mother was being held back by the security guard.

The woman in the driver seat started the engine, it cranked heavily, she turned the wheel and it hauled off. The ladies watched Ms. Moss shrink from the mirrors. Shrink as small as they've ever seen her. It was a joy to see her that small, that far from her children, who had the potential to be big.

Ms. Moss had feverish bright eyes, protruding without blinking and her chest bouncing rapidly.

"Y'all all up in my business," she screamed, "that's y'all problem, mind ya damn business." She roared at people snapping their phones at her. There was a trash bag near the curb for sanitation. She kicked it as if it were a soccer ball.

Half-eaten pieces of chicken, burnt rice, and crumbled tissues spewed out. She walked to the other bag and kicked it into a parked car, then she kicked every bag until she got to the end of the block. The leaky sour scent of the trash lingered through the streets. Pampers, orange peels, noodle wrappers, and fish heads were in the middle of the pavement like roadkill. Before she reached our trash, I sprinted downstairs, but I noticed that our garbage bags were already blowing in the wind when I got there. Each trash bin had its lid removed.

Although Ms. Moss just had her episode of kicking trash, this old street dude named Alcoholic Mike was the main culprit for plastic tampering. He wore overalls, a bucket hat with magnolia, and sneakers with holes in the front. He liked to pop the trash bags open with his fingertips and dig until he reached the bottom.

Ms. Moss strutted from the block with her shoulders slouched, she walked by trash that she kicked. Her thighs bounced, and her lips making an ugly twist and then loosened when she stopped in front of Jazz-Mack. An old hustler from Brevoort who still served outside his mother's house. He had dreads with a cap over, a red hoodie and his pants sagged while leaning on a burgundy Charger.

She exchanged money for a bag of powder, and then sped into Brevoort projects rambling emotionally. She saw the other neighborhood drug dealer coming from the parking lot, and her eyeballs became as bright as an elevator button. She lifted her hand and scrambled towards him.

"Miles, can I trade you this for yours, baby? You got the best shit," she scratched her nose while she stood there.

Miles's neck snapped back,

"Nah, why would I want another nigga's dope," He uttered back. "I only take bread."

"Only cash Miles?" she walked over while blinking fast, she yanked her boob out of her green blouse. "You sure about that, remember how good I sucked that dick last time." She leaned towards him, grabbed his dick like she was throwing an underhand pitch.

"Nah." He uttered. "Dead that," his forearms pushed her off.

I didn't know exactly what she was buying, but she barely took care of herself while she lived downstairs, so I knew she was on some kind of drug.

9

Tenant beef
March/8th/2022

Ms. Moss, I'd hate to say it, but her potential for violence puts her on the list as a main suspect too. Fat short Shaq and her rented the same apartment, and there were many wicked stares between them. Low eyed stares, snarling, and stomping.

Fat short Shaq would always complain, so they'd have to separate until he comes out to use the bathroom or kitchen again.

Murder? Maybe.

As far as Dutchess's Godfather, Edward, Ms. Moss had a good relationship with him. Whenever she needed to get in contact with Dutchess's biological father, she'd call him, and he played a middleman role. Which is why Ms. Moss would have splattered his guts on the street pavement if she knew Dutchess's deepest-darkest-filthiest secret.

After Ms. Moss destroyed everyone's trash, the

seagulls flocked down and pecked the trail of fishbones, rice, and bread.

10

Obbit Thorn Born
March/8th/2022

I've watched Dateline and seen Detectives get murder cases wrong. Dead wrong, actually because they let their suspicion lead them astray. Surely the black guy must be driving dirty, packing gats, and committing felonies because he is uhm, well he's black and that's supposedly our nature. Wrong! Sometimes you must cut off your suspicion and just gather the facts. The killer is sometimes right under your nose or, in a dirty police officer's case, in the next cubical office. They can't see it because their tied up with your own racism. Where we are from, I feel like police officers are policing stereotypes, so a detective just might investigate a crime in the same way. Nigga, guilty closed case.

In Dutchess's case, she and her mother, Ms. Moss, fit the glove more than anyone else did because they knew both victims, Edward and Fat short Shaq and had a constant streak of violence in her.

I tied my last garbage can. I twisted the flap, and boom, I smelled utterly rotten just like that. I sat down on the stone stoop, pulled out my cellphone and texted T.T.

"I got your dub," I wrote, "are you awake?"

She didn't reply, I knew that she was probably sleeping because of the way her body was aligned on the suede couch. She slept like a boxer that got knocked out on a ten count.

She had her chin down, as if she was swimming and drowned. T.T. was comfortable in her own way.

I've heard that Ralph Avenue family shelter doesn't even have soft beds, that they give you a bordered dorm room and you have to sleep on half ripped mattresses that they provide. When you wake up, you'll have thick dust all over your sheets that make your skin itch.

T.T. was happy in my crib.

The spring leaves always made a crisp sound when they rubbed together. I enjoyed listening to that more than gunshots because when niggas get shot, there's nothing but frantic anxiety. The day they hit Fat Short Shaq on the corner, people scattered like mice. I've heard different stories about how he died, but the most consistent was a random shooting. Random! But so intentional.

Fat Short Shaq was walking out of the Patchen avenue Deli, and someone stepped toward him with an orange flag wrapped around a gun handle. The killer didn't even say anything, he flared up with a flashing muzzle. The glass from the Deli shattered and fell like crystal rain. Shell casing bounced across the concrete sounding like pennies, and the gun powder smoke looked like cloud of powder. Shaq was on the ground pulsating with his eyes frozen, horrified. He stayed out of street politics which is why the shooting stunned him.

As I was thinking about Shaq, I noticed something that made me twitch forward. From the corner of my eye, Alcoholic Mike limped through the block with a potbelly, skinny arms that didn't match his body and a bald head with grey hair on the side. He had a button-up flannel shirt opened, and his chest hair was curly and grey. He had a frail set of rotten teeth that showed every time he yawned and sniffled. He had a brown paper bag in his hands and each of his fingernails were brown like roach wings.

"Do you have change," he uttered to Barbara while interrupting her chess match.

Barbara's head snapped back.

"Spare change," she sucked her teeth and rolled her eyes. "You want the change so you can buy more bourbon," she snapped, "get the hell outta here Michael."

I stood motionless, my legs straightened, and then I darted towards him. I could feel the tension building as I approached him.

"Mike, wait," I yelled, "did you pop my trash cans this morning?" My fingers pointed to my house. "Why do you keep digging through our can." He had a hitch in his chest, and a snot bubble stretched from his nostril. One eye opened wide while the other sealed.

"The lid was on top, the can was closed," he screamed.

Mike walked away while rubbing his palm against his nose.

I crossed the street and yielded as I saw a speeding navy- blue car speed across the road with student driver written in the window. I stared at my Brownstone home to the roof, and I could see The Vroom Deady's exterior at the edge. The car looked dark and demented even from the ground view. It looked like it didn't belong so high. How did Something so dark get so high? Something so heavy ascend and take place at the top of the whole neighborhood without being detected and removed. It was like a sky throne, my roof was, and the Vroom Deady was a bastard king that rose above our heads.

I looked both ways to ensure I didn't bring any unwarranted attention to it. Some little girls were playing Double-Dutch on the sidewalk, some niggas smoking in front of Brevoort, and a couple walking up the block arguing. A fat kid was walking past my gate latch. He had an almond- shaped head, small arms, and legs, and he wore church shoes with blue jeans. The kid's name was Dennis and I remember him from school, but I tried not to give him the satisfaction of being remembered. He stood there chomping on some candy. His eyelids were flinching. He kept scratching his elbow and blinking like a person walking in a blizzard. When I came close to the gate, I pulled it and stared at him in the center of his face.

Dennis took a deep swallow.

"Sup Killip," he whispered while holding my gate latch, "I want to see the Vroom-Vroom." He opened the gate and walked inside with entitlement. He froze once I stared him down. He had an awkward smile, and you could see his red and blue braces "You look tight," he uttered, "did I do something wrong?"

My eyebrows flattened as I moved closer to him. "What car?" I muttered, "and who sent you?"

"Lance told me, "He replied, "and he told me about your mother. I ain't going to cause no trouble. I know y'all dangerous. I just wanted to see the Vroom Deady."

I stared at him up and down, "Why would Lance tell you anything?"

"Lance is my cou—cousin."

"He never mentioned you."

"Lance told me not to tell—because I could get targeted."

"Targeted?"

"—you know my cousin stabbed those gang members on the train—they might come back."

I stared at his church shoes, then lifted my eyes towards his blue jeans, up to his fat throat and eyes. I held the gate open wide. "What did Lance say?" I asked calmly. "He told you about my mom, right?" I shut the gate and stared at him, "What did he say?"

"She shot your daddy," he responded, "and you and your family were able to afford this big building cuz your daddy died and then your mother married a white man to replace him."

The center of my face was twitchy as if I felt an allergic reaction. Whenever someone walked past our brownstone, they'd investigate the garden first, each green slender stem of the daisies, thorns, vines, and buttercup sprawling through the gate, then lift their head to examine the reddish-brown brick structure to the top. They'd tell their stupid horror stories, but the allure of our home came at a harsh price. A price that Big momma Lucy couldn't have much pride in.

It's true! She killed Merlo while seven months pregnant with me and the was imprisoned for murder in the third degree and delivered me at Obbit Thorn medical center while handcuffed to a bed with bars.

II

Galaxy Motel
March/8th/2022

Ivory wasn't a killer like those women on documentaries who snap. She was a perfectly well-rounded woman who passed her mental evaluations for a career as a teacher for first grade students.

Big momma Lucy said that Ivory was a good child. She loved to go to Botanic gardens or Prospect Park in the afternoon. Ivory loved watering daisies and feeding snails that she found along the moist concrete. She used to let them slither on her fingers and let them slither off onto a garden. She was a peaceful woman, much more peaceful than anyone else in the family.

One afternoon, during the pandemic we were bored so Big momma Lucy held Ivory's old purple volleyball in her lap.

"Phillip." she uttered, while her tea bubbled on the stove. "You know how your mother got the name

Bumblebee?' One summer afternoon the Bee's followed us to volleyball practice, they stung Me and Yata, but Ivory was so calm that she never caused them to be riled.

Big momma Lucy tossed the volleyball, she turned around and pulled a jar of honey from the cabinet.

My face wrenched.

"If she was so calm, why did she do what she did?" I replied.

Big momma Lucy pulled the tea bag out of the kettle, she dipped it inside and the steam lifted above her face.

"One day I'll tell you the whole story." Big momma Lucy grimaced while staring at the sink, dropping a spoon on the counter, "Oh lord, It's too much for me baby." She held the spoon and didn't move.

I stood inches away from Dennis, the heel of his church shoes was clicking, he was all hyper and ready to push the roof door open.

My face tightened,

"Hold up," I uttered, "Don't tell nobody bout this car kid."

I pushed through, letting him see a glimpse of the

car, then yanked him back away from the windy roof door. He kept touching my forearm, jumping up and down and voicing his excitement with eyes like fireworks.

"The Vroom Deady is awesome," he said. "Wait, can I use the bathroom fast, I have to go, and Nana always tells me to go before I leave so I don't have accidents."

What the kid did not realize was that he was a walking accident, that's why I didn't let him get any closer to the car because he'd be the one to try to touch it and fall off the edge of the sky; holler through Bed-Stuy as he smashed to the concrete.

His legs kept grinding against each other. He was holding his crotch and his cheeks were puffy pink. I didn't want him to pee on the floor, so I opened the apartment door. It cracked partially. My eyes exploded out of the sockets because T.T., who was in the center of my Livingroom had the ceiling light shining on her chocolate backside. She was standing up, stretching both arms over her head as if she was playing Twister. She was wearing her pink spandex shorts. They were tight around her pelvis like a chick in a Pilates class. I pulled the door closed, pushed Dennis out and squared my shoulders.

"Hold on, Dennis," I said with my chest bouncing, "give me a second."

I reopened the door, slipped inside, and walked towards the couch.

T.T. stood up with her arm straight, her other arm over her rib and both knee's knocking together.

"wassup."

"Hey, T.T.," I uttered, "here's your dub. Can you go to the back room, it'll be quick?"

Her half-shut eyes strained, she scratched her prickly weave while yawning and twisted her lip to the side. "Phillip, you were just mad cool and now you pushing me to the back," she shouted, "I can't stand you." She turned around towards the mirror, put her earring inside her ear and sat back down while avoiding eye contact.

My eyes bounced,

"I ain't mean it that way," I responded, "Lance's cousin is about to come through, and I don't want him to see you here."

"His cousin?" she uttered, "I don't care what his cousin thinks."

"Lance would kill me, he is—he might think we—." She sucked her teeth, took a deep breath, and stood up.

Her bare feet slapped against the floor as she

walked to my bedroom. She has one of those asses that switch hard when she walks so it looked like she had an even worse attitude. She shut the door, lunged forward, and laid on my mattress with her back leaning on my pillows.

I grabbed the gold knob to get Dennis, my apartment door made a sweeping noise as it opened but when I investigated the hallway; he was invisible; I looked down, and I saw a yellow puddle dripping from the flooring down to the second floor. The kid pissed in our halls like a dog.

I poured some Pine-Sol, lifted the mop, and cleaned the puddle of pineapple juice piss. It stunk. People were always pissing in Brevoort projects, but this was a private house, and I didn't expect anyone to ever do that wild shit over here.

Big momma Lucy would have whooped him if she caught him.

After all that, I went back inside, I kicked off my sneakers and the laces looked like squiggly tapeworms. I sat down across from T.T.'s clothes; her pink hoodie, white pants, and bra were folded neatly. She wasn't messy, even after all those Casa drinks she had. I walked towards the back room, but suddenly the house phone rattled with red flashes. There was a red strobe light on the side, and it vibrated until it reached the edge of the coffee table. Super Galaxy Motel was glowing on the caller ID, my first thought was Dutchess, so I rushed towards it and picked up.

"Hello! This is a Rosette, calling from Super Galaxy motel," the voice of an older Hispanic woman greeted "We couldn't find your wedding band, Mr. Clayed."

"What," I responded, "what wedding band?" "Your ring, you lost it in room two hundred seven,

right?" she asked, "Is this Fritzen?"

My face flushed,

"Excuse me, Miss. Is Super Galaxy Motel in Berlin?"

"Sir, we are in Brighton Beach, Brooklyn," she uttered, "This not Fritzen Clayed?"

As I held the phone with confusion, the top lock on the door clacked, the front door pushed outward, and Fritz's leg planted on the inside of the house. His hand was wrapped around the aluminum luggage handle. He was wearing his Burberry jacket with a plaid collar shirt inside. He had some grey pattern pants and brown Stacy Adams shoes with no laces.

Fritz's eyes narrowed, his hand cupped his nose and his face shrunk like he smelled something sour.

"Jesus-hell Phillip, will you open darn a window," he uttered while waving. "It smells like pot and alcohol in this fucking living room."

His fingers were at his nose, and I watched each one. There wasn't any gold luster. There wasn't any sign of commitment for his wife. Just a man with some luggage, a fly outfit and hatred for his stepson.

Fritz slammed his luggage,

"Phillip, it smells like shit in here, were you smoking while I was in Berlin?" He stood at the center of the Livingroom, inches away from the coat rack. Big momma Lucy's favorite coat that looked like peacock was next to his shoulder. It twirled as grabbed it. He took off his Burberry jacket and put the loop on the hook. He walked closer to me, and his face crumpled. He stretched his arm across the coffee table, lifted a pack of cigarette papers and tossed them into my lap.

His face turned into stone,

"Smoking in your grandmother's house," he shouted softly.

His blue eyes dotted side-to-side like a snake moving in slow motion, and he grilled the fan spiraling out the window. The wind from the blades was blowing on the reverse side and pointing outside into the streets rather than the house. He turned the fan back to the normal side, with his nostrils flared and his lips tight around his teeth. While his face pointed downward to the white power cord, he saw a silver ashtray lid was flipped on the carpet with black charred stained that looked like a whole can of black pepper fell.

Fritz's face tightened,

"Phillip," he shouted, "What have you been doing in this damn house? I won't snitch to Lucy or anything, but this looks like something, you have a fucking new smoking habit, goddamnit."

Whenever I was guilty about shit, I was quiet and red in the face. I always gave it away because I wasn't the best liar. I squared my shoulders, lifted my jaw, and used my body to block him from seeing T.T.'s clothes folded along the armrest.

"What's that," he uttered, "That behind you." He tilted his chin up and took a long stride as he stood in front of me.

My cheeks turned puffy,

"Nothing," I responded, "I just had my friends over, they smoke but we didn't do it in the house."

"What!" He shouted, "are you nuts? His palms spread and he slapped me so hard that my eyes shook. He knocked my brain to the back of my head and I could feel skin tingles on my cheek.

"What did I say about those little weed-head fuckers around here." He screamed with his jaw stretched.

"Move let me see what's behind you." He grabbed the top of my shoulders and pulled me out of the way. There was T.T.'s white pants lined against the suede couch.

He took a deep breath.

"That's not Charlesha's daughter, right?" he uttered. "Don't let her spend a night because the girl would want to move in, and we will be going through the same situation as Charlesha's daughter, everyone wants to move in, and nobody wants to pay the fucking rent."

Fritz walked towards the coat rack, he pulled his other jacket out of his luggage and hung the loop along with the other. From the mirror's reflection, he saw that I had new Jordan's lined up in the corner next to the wood seat piano.

"Where did you get those new Jays?" he uttered. His eyes glimpsed toward me.

We had a large dining table with an extra fridge near the pantry. Inside the small kitchen there were a bunch of cooking pots on the stove that looked untidy.

Fritz's face went pale, his eyelids tightened around

his eyeballs and his neck turned stiff as if he had been shot with an ice gun.

"What are all of them pots doing on the stove?" His Adam's apple went up and down, "Were you cooking crack with your grandmother's pots?" He stood there waiting for an answer. One thing that always pissed me off about him, besides his mean streak, was when he acted like I was bound to be a criminal because Ivory was one. Fritz always jumped to conclusions. It's like he always thought I'd get into selling dope like them niggas on the corner. It was as if he pushed me to be a dope dealer instead of keeping me away from it.

I lunged off the couch and planted the house phone into his well ironed grey shirt.

"I'm not your real son," I shouted, "you should be worried about finding your stupid ring at the Super Galaxy."

After I told him off, I walked away but through the reflection of the kitchen oven I saw his face shivering.

He stumbled into the couch seat, then he stood up with his neck growing veins. He balled up his fist and held them at the bottom of his chin with his eyes closed. He laughed with anger, he stood up and punched the wall so hard that the picture frames of

Berlin wobbled.

Fritz's eyes shuttered,

"You think you're so smart, don't you?" he uttered with a smile. Then his blue eyes opened and closed. "Your real father, Merlo thought he was smart until Ivory blasted him. Yea! You want to end up in a body bag then fucking keep it up."

Fritz took a long stride towards me and grabbed me by my skinny arm until my body swung around.

"You hear me kid! You want to be in a body bag! You want the truth, you little piece of shit?" he yelled, "You want the truth so bad don't you," his fingers squeezed harder, and his teeth were showing. "I didn't mean to assume that you were hustling drugs out of Lucy's house, but your dad was a drug dealer. So that's why I worry about you, how do you think Charlesha got into that junk? Because of him! He was a hustler— Merlo! Yea your father, sold crack from Brighton Beach to the boardwalk—."

My eyes beamed into nothingness.

"What no he didn't!" I turned around and glared into the darkness while hearing the shifts of my heartbeat.

Fritz stepped into the light, he stepped backward, landed on the edge of the couch seat, and cracked his knuckles.

"You think your mother was so bad," he whispered aggressively, "you walk around calling her Ivory instead of Ma. What the fuck is wrong with you! I would love to see you around your real pops, that drug dealing piece of shit."

Fritz's face was red, his neck shivered, and he bit his bottom lip in an angry way.

I usually laugh or shrug it off whenever I felt awkward, but at that moment I couldn't laugh or shrug. My head aligned with my body, my balance was gone, and I leaned against the solid wall. I tried to smile, but my cheekbone turned swollen. My eyes shivered, my shoulders curled, and I crumpled down to the hard floor.

It made sense that my father was hustling because in pictures he had a lot of expensive cars, out-of-town trips, sparkling gold, diamond studded jewelry, and European clothes.

I lifted myself, stomped towards my room, shut the door, and leaned on it.

Behind the wooden door, T.T. was lying on my bed, with her hair spread across the sheets. When she saw me come inside, she put her cellphone aside and scooted closer toward me.

"What happened," she uttered, "I heard a bunch of yelling, you look tight." She lifted herself from the mattress and stayed right at the edge.

I squeezed my knuckles and held them down on each side as if I wanted to punch something.

"It's my stepdad," I responded. "I hate him."

T.T.'s face went blank, she got up, she spread her arms as if she wanted to give me a big hug, then dropped one arm for a friendlier one. She stared at me with a look of care blended with confusion and fear. She removed the pillows off the mattress and sat slowly while pulling me to sit.

"Tell me what happened." She uttered softly.

As we were behind closed doors, I explained everything to her and didn't even notice that my cellphone was missing.

The cellphone was flashing while laid across the Livingroom floor. The cased gadget was lying right next to Fritz's shoe. My friend Lance texted me multiple messages and a bell sound alerted Fritz.

"Yo Phillip, you heard from T.T." the text read, "Yo Phillip, why you ain't reply nigga, you good?"

Fritz reached for my cellphone, his eyes had a muscle twitch and sweat tears as he invaded my security system. His fingers clicked the phone screen with aggression. He held the phone to his gut. He typed while wobbling, a single inch of sweat dripped from his mottled nose and his eyes didn't blink.

"Yo—homeboy. You have a connect for dope?" He wrote, then he removed the messages and dropped the phone on the couch. He slapped his forehead, bit his bottom lip, and walked into his bedroom. He thrashed all his drawers, and the knobs came tumbling off. He opened his luggage case and tossed his clothes all over his room. His underwear dropped across the floor like confetti and sock balls went bouncing.

He lifted his desert eagle from his luggage and held it against his cheek.

"Fuck!" he screamed with veins in his neck "I need to get back in the fucking game or else I'm going to fucking shoot someone's head off.

12

Thong Chandeliers
March/8th/2022

Fritz's room was on the Sunnyside of the apartment, which is far from mine, but I could hear a loud carpet thud all the way from my room.

T.T. was a few inches away from me, sitting on my bed with her tight shorts squeezing her thighs. She was lighting the spliff with her hands forming a barrier. She dropped her eyes into a much fresher Fronto leaf bag then glared at me. She kept staring at me, waiting for me to start talking about the drama between my stepdad and me. She stretched her brown arm and squeezed my kneecap.

"Start from the beginning," she said. "Tell me everything that happened." she blew the spiff and the smoke pushed toward the window to the point it looked like fog.

"You might need to roll some more weed for this."

I responded.

"Nigga you aint gotta ask twice." she smirked.

T.T. squeezed her packaged dub and a nugget came out the size of a Brussell sprout, so she shielded her fingers away from the door. She had a bangle wrapped around her wrist that dropped to its lowest point; when she crushed the weed down, she kept looking over her shoulder and bouncing her eyes back to me.

"It's okay," I muttered, "Fritz don't be coming in here, but here is what happened. Dutchess's family was evicted by my grandmother."

T.T.'s eyes popped out of her head as if she were getting helium pumped into her face.

"Your grandmother is the landlord," she replied with a loud pitch, "damn bro, she must be making bank off this like them white people do... keep going, tell me what happened."

A year ago, I stood at the dining table smelling the buttermilk pancakes, grits, and scrambled eggs with pepper specks. Big momma Lucy was sitting down across from me, she had buttered toast on a napkin, but she didn't even take a bite. She rubbed her knees and her chest bounced like she had just ran in a marathon.

"I worry about your stepfather sometimes," Big momma Lucy uttered. "Fritz told me to let him make more decisions about the house, and he then put that lady with eight children into a doggone room, is he insane!"

Big momma Lucy twisted her lip, her weight leaned over to the side of the table I was on; she folded her arms over her chest and grilled me. Fat Short Shaq's real name was Shaqkris, he was about five foot nine and stocky, dark-skinned with a tapped-up afro. Some people would say he looked like Zion Williamson. He did whenever he got a fade or grew his afro out at the top. He was Big momma Lucy's longest tenant because he stayed there with his parents until they moved four years back. Big momma Lucy loved Fat short Shaq, so she let him keep his large room and only charged him six hundred dollars for rent. Six-hundred dollars was considered cheap rent in Brooklyn, but it wasn't worth the price since he had to deal with that ratchet bitch Charlesha. One morning Fat Short Shaq came upstairs with the muscles in his jaw flexing. He took a deep breath and shook his head.

"Charlesha handwashes her lil panties and lines them up all over the shower rod which makes it hard to shower." He shouted softly. "I don't want to see her panties all the damn time, I have a *shorty already dam!*"

Big momma Lucy stood in front of Fat short Shaq

shaking her head. She adjusted her silk pajamas, then held the door open for him so he could come inside. She walked towards Fritz's room, put her ear to the door, then knocked on it with her index curled.

"Fritz, we need to chat," she hollered, she folded her arms and stomped. "Right now." She twisted the knob, went inside his room, and flicked his lights. His head bobbled upwards from his flat pillow, his face was flustered, and his eyes had cloudy red veins. She had her brown hands on her hips, shaking her head while leaning to the side.

"Fritz!" she screamed. "I told you that your plan was not going to work, the lady downstairs is a dang freak! She has her panties all up in the bathroom while Shaqkris is there."

The morning sparrows were chirping from outside the window, but my family was chirping even louder. Big momma Lucy, Fritz, and Fat short Shaq argued while walking downstairs. I shoved my foot into my Jays and rushed behind them. First there was Ms. Moss's voice yelling fast, like she was speaking Spanish, but she was talking a lot of gangsta lingo,

"Nigga are you dumb?" She hollered, "Nigga are you dumb?" While slapping the wall.

From the staircase on the second floor, I heard their

voices get loud, and I could make out some of the daughter's voices screaming. The walls shook, the door slammed like those paranormal ghost movies, and I heard their voices get louder. I walked inside the apartment door frame and saw them in clumped between the hallway and the kitchen. The eight children surrounding Big momma Lucy as if they were against their own mother. Ms. Moss was standing in the bathroom, her arms flailing dramatically, and twisting her head to the side.

"You have a problem with a bitch's underwear?" her neck rocked from left to right, "they are just panties, man the fuck up fat ass nigga!" She pulled a set of yellow ones down from the shower, winded her overhand, and threw them into Fat Short Shaq's face. It unraveled against his nose, and his head jerked backward in a delayed motion. Fat short Shaq could have pushed through everyone like a tight end on a football field, but he held threw the panties off his face and rinsed his mouth over the kitchen sink. While he was bent over, Ms. Moss ran towards him while swinging her hands. "Look at that Fat fuck! He is talking about how I'm a crackhead! He got more crack than all Bed-Stuy combined, pull Ya pants up stinking ass bitch."

Hours after the chaos, Big momma Lucy glimpsed at Dutchess standing in the Livingroom. She was hunched in between the burned-marked iron board and a laundry bag full of clothes. Her legs extended into a bookshelf, each of her fingers wrapped in her coily hair and she hunched down with a deflated body.

"Lemme talk to you," Big momma Lucy uttered, she reached out her hand and touched Dutchess's shoulder "You are the eldest girl? right? Well, I have a washer and dryer in the basement, you can use it anytime. With her left hand, she reached over and touched my shoulder. "This is my son, Phillip, he has the key to the basement. Y'all can wash clothes down there if you need to, no more handwashing in the sink, please." Big momma Lucy lifted her off the floor and grabbed my hand to make us touch each other's hands.

Dutchess had that copper-colored hair gelled down into a ponytail with a red scrungie. Her skin was light brown like those Spanish girls who might have had a black parent or a mixture from overseas. She extended her arm forward, and her pink fingernails were bitten down to the white part. When my hands touched her, I felt shelves of moistness in the crevasses of her palm. She retracted her hand and rubbed them on her Levi jeans.

"I'm sorry," she said, "because of all of this." Her eyes bounced back and forth, her chin dropped down, and she used her shirt sleeve to wipe her eyes' edges "On Sundays, I'll do it," she uttered while staring at Fat short Shaq. Then she bobbled her head at Big momma Lucy. "Every Sunday at three."

While Big momma Lucy and I exited the apartment door frame, I noticed that Fritz stayed behind. He had his hands around Ms. Moss's shoulder while mumbling fast.

Fritz was the perfect super because he thought he could fix things that were damaged. Sure, you can fix an apartment, but you can't fix a Person.

13

Tumbling Tissues
March/8th/2022

T.T.'s neck snapped back as if she was catching an attitude. She was quiet, rocking her legs and looking downward.

"Wait I have to say this," She uttered, "your stepdad is the super for this building? So why was he all up in the tenant's apartment like that."

"What you mean," I replied. "Fritz was trying to calm her down."

"Nah. That's not his job, he should stay out of shit, he seems shady as fuck—I wouldn't want the super in my apartment unless he is fixing pipes—sounds like he is getting his pipes fixed instead—Continue the story."

"Nah, Fritz was just trying to help!"

Big momma Lucy's church was a packed house during Sunday service. The gospel rang through the roof; the air was dense as the drummer banged out every verse. The choir would sing, and he'd go bang right in rhythm. There were rows of enthused women clapping and bouncing on their toes as the preacher spoke. He was so sweaty like he had come out of a sauna.

Big momma Lucy told me that I looked happy, and she was right, but it wasn't because of the atmosphere of the church; it was because I was imagining being with Dutchess from downstairs. It was a couple of hours till three, and I texted all my friends and told them.

"Ima chill with Dutchess from downstairs," I texted. "Nigga, you finally gon lose your virginity, lame," Lance wrote back.

As I waited at the basement door, I could feel my stomach bubbling with hot lava. The lock to first floor apartment went click, and Dutchess ruffed her way out of the screeching door. She stepped out of the apartment with a pink laundry bag. She had a black T-shirt with spangled words that read pretty girl. The shirt exposed her belly button and her panties stuck out her jeans slightly. She had on the same blue jeans from last Saturday and blue slides that separated her big toe from her others. Her pink laundry bag had gaping holes on the side and an assortment of ragged fabric poking out of the edges.

"Do you need help," I asked.

"No," She responded with her nose down.

She dragged the bag towards the door, her arms tensed up, and there was a vein in her temple as if she were using force. I put the key into the gold lock, twisted it with my wrist, and the chilly air from the basement brushed against my skin. There was a bulb hanging in the dark basement, I flicked the light, and it illuminated the center. The couch in the basement was royal blue with puffy white pillows and a TV remote on top. There was a kitchen with a fridge, washer, and dryer. I stood there for a second, sat down awkwardly and the couch tilted upwards on the opposite side.

Dutchess leaned over, segregated her laundry clothes, and kept her face to the side while kneeling. She never looked in my direction, not for a second to see the other side of the basement. She put the underwear into the machine, and it was so full that the door could barely shut.

Next load, she dug into the bag and lifted a pair of blue denim jeans. They were larger than her legs, so they were either Ms. Moss's or Ronda's. She pulled the pocket's inside out and her wrist froze. The light from the ceiling bounced on her skin, but she did not move.

Her cheeks went pale, she dropped to her knees in slow motion, and her shoulders slumped into a slack, lifeless way. She stared into her other hand and sucked her nose to hold back the tears.

I stood up and walked towards her. "Dutchess are you good," I asked.

"Leave me alone." she muttered while scrunching her face. She extended her arm, twisted her body, and hunched again.

She was breathing hard like she had asthma, her eyes trembled with moistness, and I could see her face bones tighten. She slouched, then stretched her arm forward, In the center of her palm was a twirled plastic baggie with powdery dust remnants.

"I hate her" Dutchess shouted, she dropped the baggie on the ground and stepped on it with her big toe. The whole basement was silent, and I could see Dutchess stretching her fingers and placing them across her face.

"She was supposed to have quit, but she didn't—She is going to die and leave us to take care of ourselves."

Her head snapped downwards, and her back bounced as she cried. I ran into the bathroom, grabbed the box of tissues, and handed it to her. The clothes in the machine stopped, but her tissue balls kept tumbling.

The machines with the underwear stopped, Dutchess's arms extended, she hugged the pile into a basket and put the colored clothes inside. She bent over, her low belted jeans exposed the top of her ass crack. Her posture became rigid, her jaw clenched, and she side-eyed me with her lips twisted. She poured the detergent into the machine, and she saw that my eyes were beaming from the metal machine.

"I can feel you staring," she said with an empty voice, the light shining on the side of her cheek as she turned towards me. "Everything makes sense on why you are acting nice to me—You can stop that because it's weird, just fuck me and get it over with."

My face crumpled, "What you mean?"

She dropped the detergent bottle on the machine, blue detergent dripping off her nails at the end of each fingertip. Her fingers pressed the button on top of her jeans. When she reached the bottom button, unfastened, and I saw that she had a patchy birthmark on her thigh. She kicked her jeans off like a snake shedding its skin. She dumped them into the machine and her panties were cream-colored and wedged between her legs. She had her arms folded, shirt slightly above her belly button. She glanced at the cheap blue couch in the corner, raised a single eyebrow, and then looked back at me.

"That's all you want, right," she said with her finger pointing, "You want me to suck your dick?"

My right hand extended and waved side to side. "Dutchess, nah," I uttered, "I'm not a thirsty-ass-nigga." "All boys want that —all y'all the same, so don't try to act like you different—you just want to use me for whatever—so be direct because I don't like getting attached."

"It's not even like that—."

"Just don't stare at me then," she shouted while trembling, "ughh and stop being so nice, don't feel sorry for me, I fucking my hate my life too."

She turned around, with her hair bouncing on her back, she put one arm on the machine, pressed the button, and the water splashed against the glass. I still remember the dark area of where the laundry machine was, and how the light crept against her back, legs, and hips. The machine made that snapping noise, spun counterclockwise, and the zipper made a ticking noise as it hit the inside of the machine. There was a silver knife on top of the machine, Dutchess picked it up and I could see the veins in her back moving. She used the blades tip to stab a pack of tide over and over until it bled scented white-blue dust.

14

Stay
March/8th/2022

The pack of weed had me smacked like Snoop. The more I smoked, the bigger my eyes got and the better I got at telling the story. Across from me was T.T. biting her bottom lip and rolling another one to match the two blunts rolled near her thigh.

"Wait," she interrupted with her neck snapping in a ghetto way. "Dutchess's mom is on drugs, right? Is the super on drugs too? Because he makes some interesting decisions."

My face flushed, "Nah Fritz ain't on drugs," I responded, "Not that I know of."

"I'm telling you there's something sus about him ... and the tenant lady."

"I don't know, maybe Fritz was just being a good guy."

"You are so naive, Phillip," her eyes shuttered as

she scratched the lighter, "You don't see what's going on here?

"what?"

"Whatever, go on, continue the story because this is getting spicy."

A month passed, after Fat short Shaq's funeral Dutchess seemed a bit happier which boosted her case as a suspect. She walked into the basement, pulled the metal chain down and it lit the ceiling. It illuminated the center of the living room area and there was a small set of black jagged nails in the middle of the floor. Fritz was always down there doing work and sometimes he left equipment out in the open.

Dutchess's arm stretched toward the second bulb.

"Oh, I didn't know that this light worked," she uttered while clicking the string. "It looks better here, I'm just saying."

The basement had three rooms, two in the back and one in the front, that were cluttered with old fitness machines, dingy clothes and antiques. Dutchess walked toward every room, sticking her head inside and touching whatever looked interesting. A box of old Vinyl, some old knob-less cabinets, large silverware that looked like it should go into an antique shop and dolls. Big momma Lucy used to collect all that stuff years ago in hopes of selling it to a collection shop.

Dutchess spread her arms across the door frame

"Y'all can rent this basement." Dutchess uttered with bright eyes.

"Big momma Lucy said that basement apartments are illegal."

"They are?" She walked towards the window and pulled the curtain from the side. The view from the window was a glassy view of plants and flowers coming from the dirt. If someone lived down there, it would have been like opening your window to a science project.

Inside the last room to the right, it was a wooden door, full of boys' clothes and piles of old dusty furniture preventing the door from budging open.

Dutchess pushed the caved door and opened slightly. She stretched into the room, took a large stride, and stood in the center. From outside the room to me was only a foot. She slouched, then touched some clothes with both fingers stretching them wide open. The clothes were a bunch of polo shirts for someone around my age. She turned around towards the wooden door and saw what caved the room shut. It was a red Rover bike covered in dust as if someone threw protein powder on it. Its pedals were pressed against the door and Dutchess's finger prints were all over it.

"This your old bike or something," Dutchess uttered while giggling.

"No," I responded. "I've never seen that bike before."

She then turned towards me, took a stride out of the room and her bare foot slapped the tiles. She pushed me backward onto the couch and got on her knees.

"Is the door locked," she uttered while looking into my eyes.

"Yea."

"Let me show you this new trick"

"New trick?"

While squeezing my balls, she sucked the head and Dutchess started slurping, gagging, and spitting all over my dick. Her hair was so long that it covered my whole pelvis. I mean not to say that my penis is short, but her hair is so goddam long. She turned around, and she had black pepper dots in her skin, spine and down her cheeks. She spread her ass and her butthole had a diamond plug glistening. She pressed her brown pussy against my dick, so I grabbed her hips, put it inside and the head slipped in slowly.

She shook like the holy ghost, while backing her

body until it was all the way inside.

"Choke me," she screamed, while reaching backward and making me put my fingers around her neck.

Her face dropped down, and each curly strand was inches away from touching the carpet. She threw her ass back on my dick until it looked like a line of yogurt milk was on my shaft.

The tint of the window curtains went from bright to dark and as the machines rumbled, her ass was clapping in the same rhythm. The echo of the body slaps sounded like a seal clapping its hands. She was skinny, but her body had a jiggle to it like a larger girl.

Dutchess slapped the couch cushion and it bounced with no sound.

"Woo!" she yelled "that was better than last time."

She walked to the machine naked with an avatar-built body. She opened the little glass door and squeezed the underclothes into the metal dryer.

I directed my attention to my cellphone screen, and I saw an Instagram post about Fat short Shaq, so I leaned upward and lifted my chin towards her.

"Crazy what happened to Fat short Shaq." I uttered with the phone light shining in my face.

"Hmm." Dutchess responded with her back turned.

Her shoulders slacked and her eyes bounced around in a nervous way. "Why you say crazy, niggas get shot all the time, there's nothing crazy about it."

"I meant like it's just crazy."

"It's not crazy, stop saying that word." She turned around with her hair bouncing. She hunched down across the blue carpet,

"I mean, don't be so judgmental to people's mental health."

She dropped her foot into her panties and lifted them up to her hair stubbed vagina.

"Judgmental?" I replied, "What you mean?"

Redflag. But of course, my dumbass didn't notice.

Dutchess's inner thighs clenched, she rolled over with legs shut and crawled towards me. She reached for my cellphone and lowered it.

"Phillip," she said, "I don't want to leave here—I want to do this every day—I can't move with my Godfather—I just can." She crawled even closer to the point where her nose was touching mine. "Can we stay here, just me, you, and my sisters?"

"What do you mean," I replied while wiping my hands off with a tissue.

She lowered her chin, took a deep breath and her eyes had a look of terror. She had her face down on the carpet, and her body was full of static. "My mother is going to get evicted," she uttered, "Can me and my sisters stay her." she smacked the carpet. "Please, get Lucy to take us! Please try! do I have to beg because I would do it, deadass."

She put her palms together as if she was praying.

We looked at each other and then bussed out laughing.

She grabbed my left hand, and I could feel her pulse bouncing an offbeat rhythm. She led my hand to her body so I could feel her and then linked her fingers around mine on some spiritual shit.

"Foster care," she whispered. "Lucy won't have to worry about us I promise, all she has to do is attend orientation, get certified, claim us and I can pay Lucy too."

Dutchess walked over toward her Levi jean pocket. She had a white sock rolled into a ball. She peeled it open and there was a wad of cash flicking like a booklet. It was Hundreds of dollars folded on top of one another.

My face went pale, I dropped my phone and scratched my elbow.

"Where did you get all that."

"it's nothing, you know I work overnights in a restaurant." She glared at me with her eyes bouncing. She stuffed the money back inside her pocket and walked over in a seductive way. Her body weight pressed on top of me, the warmness of her fat pussy felt good on my dick. I nodded my head while rubbing my fingers on her Jell-O soft ass. She moved closer to my face, her doe eyes swollen with moistness and conviction.

"Please," she said, "please let me stay." She grabbed my hand and pressed it against her titties. I could feel her heart throb like a drum solo. "I can't live with my Godfather."

"Who's your Godfather.?"

"He is—somebody that I just can't live with."

15

Eviction for Christmas
March/8th/2022

T.T. made a stink face as if she smelled something rotten and shook her head afterwards.

"—You were really into Dutchess huh?" she asked with her neck snapping back. She held her spliff with her index and thumb and flicked her finger at the ashes while letting it fall into a plastic up. The room was silent for a minute, then T.T. slapped her thigh and turned her neck in a ghetto way.

"Yea you don't even have to answer," she replied, "you really was on her, she had you hooked like the little boy you are—her and her little tricks—you know she was too fast for you right?"

While T.T was talking all that shit, I noticed her clench at the window as if she were cold.

I opened my closet and lifted a comforter from the top row, spread it out, and put it around her shoulders. It was the same brown puffy one that Big momma Lucy told me to give Dutchess.

T.T.'s face froze as if she were confused about something. She stared around my room from the carpet to the ceiling, the closet, the mattress and back at me. She felt like she was the luckiest girl on the planet, and it was all because I put a comforter on her bony lil shoulders. She blinked uncontrollably and kept blushing with a smile that did not hide.

T.T. shook her head,

"That Dutchess girl is getting on my last nerve," she said with a stink face, "the whole damn family is suspect if you ask me."

"What do you mean?"

"Dutchess doesn't even like you that much, she just didn't want to go to the shelter with her sisters, so that's why she tried to stay in the basement and hump you good—but whatever, continue the story."

"No way."

"Yes way! And wait, how come Dutchess wanted her sisters to stay and not her brother, sounds like they were beefing."

"What do you mean?"

T.T handed me the spliff and it burned like volcano smoke.

"Go ahead and finish the story." She pulled the

comforter around her arms.

A couple of weeks before Christmas, it was colder the usual. The doors screeched louder, and the lights looked dimmer. When I walked down the steps to see Dutchess, it led to a steamy kiss. She sucked my spit; my tongue, everything. That is how I learned how to kiss, make it as sloppy as possible and do not hold back. We blindly kissed into the dark frame of the basement, tripping and slipping. Her ass slammed against the cushion, and we tore each other's clothes off in perfect blindness.

Dutchess moaned into my ear.

"Am I all yours". She uttered while yanking at my belt out of the loop.

My face tightened,

"Big momma Lucy ain't going for it." I uttered.

Dutchess gasped heavily, her wrist loosened, her fingers unwound, and her eyes swung back and forth.

"So, what will I do? I'm going to end up killing him, I know it! wait but will my sisters do?" she shouted. "Maybe I can ask Lucy?" She hunched her way off me and held the couch pillow to her brown nipples. "Would that work?"

"It was my grandma's decision —She just didn't want to put up with your mom anymore."

"Did you tell her I have money." Dutchess scooted toward her sock rolled into a ball. "Your grandma is so nice to us, why do people act nice then do stuff like this," her cheek turned, and her face went red in the center. "You just don't want me here," she shouted, "you just used me, you're so confusing, you should have just taken what you wanted and left me alone because I can handle that—I'm used to that."

She grabbed her shirt, dropped it over her head, put on her panties on, then grabbed her laundry bag while stuffing the clothes inside. When she reached the door, she pushed it with all her might. It slammed against the brown wall. The door was propped open, and a beam of hallway light shone onto me as I leaned on the couch. I laid there with my skinny bird chest, long feet hanging, and a confused eye bounce.

T.T. cleared her throat. Her face flushed, she squeezed the blunt and took her last hit of the roach.

"Dang y'all got mad drama in this big ass house," she snuffed the fire out and placed the roach on the window ledge. The AC had a bunch of older blunt ash on it, she wiped it off with a swipe. She turned around and sat down on my bed with one leg straight and the other one bent.

"So, what did your stepfather say to you?" Her

eyes beamed towards the stiff off-white closed door. "Why were you so mad when you walked in?"

My eyes dropped to the mattress. "My biological Dad, Merlo was the one who sold Ms. Moss the drugs in the first place. He got their mother hooked on that—, so my family is responsible—for everything."

"Wait—Dutchess don't know? —that's drama!" T.T.'s face busted into a painful laugh, "Sounds like you and, what's her face can never ever be." T.T. giggled, "Womp, Womp, Womp—I hope you find her so you can tell her the truth— you might as well get over her now because she is going to ghost you for life—your grandmother was better off letting them stay."

16

Dutchess
March/8th/2022

T.T. sprayed a bottle of air Freshener. She stood up like she had a broken hip walking around with that big ole meaty booty. She has those Hershey bar-brown legs, curvy calves with prickly little hair stubs from shaving. She reached up and sprayed at every corner of the room. The mist dropped into the carpet, and it smelled fresh.

T.T.'s heavy body rocked against the springy mattress with her head back like she was posing to be drawn.

"Look at me, nigga, I look good right?" she uttered "don't even need to reply because I can tell by the way you were all in my ass with those little beady eyes." she pointed to her nail, yellow and square at the tip of my nose. She turned the other cheek, glared around my spacious room, and her face landed back to my peach-fuzz face. She sat on my bed with one leg stretched while the other was folded.

"No offense," she uttered, "but you need to stop talking so highly about that Dutchess girl. Her face trembled, and her eyes were enlarged. "Why?"

"She is way too fast for you—she could run circles around you—she is probably doing the same thing she did with you to another boy in Nassau County or even a man."

"Nah, I doubt she is—we took each other virginity."

"Virginity" oh please, the girl puts plugs in her ass, and she was fifteen, she is a nasty bitch."

"You would know." I uttered while staring into my cellphone, dodging eye contact.

T.T. rolled her eyes. She sucked her teeth and looked away from me with her knuckles on her chin. Then she removed them and flicked her hair in the direction that I was sitting in.

"I don't even care about Dutchess." she responded. "Tell me more about your stepfather though, because he is shady— hold on let me roll another one because you going to need it with his crazy ass."

17

She Fair Skinned
March/8th/2022

Fritz did raise me my whole life, dinners, graduations, basketball games, birthdays, Christmas, he never missed anything, but Big momma Lucy had suspicions about him since last year's Easter. It is some dark shit that could break up my family but let me explain exactly what happened.

After the service, Big momma Lucy and I arrived home. There were creases in her blue dress and a white blouse with ruffles. She loved to dance and most of the time paid the price. Wrinkled clothes! Her dress swayed from side to side as she walked up the concrete staircase of the stoop, she held the gate open and pulled the keys out of her purse. She saw Barbara cross the street and waved.

"Hey girl," she said. "I'm making some smoked ham later, come by and get you some." She said with a wide smile on her brown face. When we reached our apartment on the third floor, an unusual draft brushed against her ankles. Big momma Lucy's fingers froze, her face flushed, she lifted an eyebrow and her neck turned slowly towards the roof entrance. She retracted her hand with the key and held it to her rib. Her eyes glimpsed by the exit sign; the roof door had an outline of ultraviolet leaking through the edges. Big momma Lucy's eyes strained, her ears stiffened, and her right hand grabbed me without looking. I took the keys from her hand and held it.

"Maybe it's Fritz," I said.

"No, Fritz shouldn't 'be up there." she snapped back. Her face was haunted, her eyebrows lowered, she kicked off her high heel and held it like a war hammer. She pushed the brown door open; it screeched like a car with busted rotors. The rooftop shined bright silver because of the sunlight beams as she turned around. In plain sight was the chard chimney, near the hinges of the wobbly door, a small pale child was sitting in the corner with less wind. She was on her rump, her knees bent into her chest and her arms tied around her legs. Big momma Lucy dropped her high heels, she walked across the simmering rooftop. She kneeled, put her hand on the little girl's shoulder blade.

"Baby, it's dangerous," she said, "what are you

doing up here?"

The pale child lifted her face. Her eyes were quivering and moist. She had redness in her forehead and freckles that looked like melting cinnamon. The little girl was Ms. Moss's third eldest daughter Livonia. She had her shoulders slumped, agonized sadness in the middle of her face, she was wearing a yellow T-shirt that said had pretty girl written in glitter, some white shorts with stains and scuffed payless sneakers. She had wavy-coiled blonde hair with a jagged part down the middle.

Big momma Lucy extended her hand to help her up, "Baby is that allergies?" she asked.

"Yea," Livonia replied, sounding like she choked with tears. Her face was agonized, looked like she was in pain. "My momma told me to leave the house because I keep sneezing around the babies."

Big momma Lucy's face tightened, her eyes ping-ponged to me and then back to the little girl. She clutched her stomach in slightly and took a deep breath. She grabbed Livonia's small fingers and led her back inside.

One thing about Big momma Lucy is that her family is from the south, so she understood the hospitality of all people, even the ones who trespass and solicit. If there was a home invasion and niggas ran up in your cribs with guns blazing, she'd treat them to dinner and ask why they chose to rob people.

Livonia sat on the couch, her skinny little legs dangled as she leaned on the couch pillow, and I noticed how fair her skin was. Her clothes were stained, she stunk like outside and she had a constant sneeze that pushed her head back into the cushion pillows.

I stood near Big momma Lucy with my arm nudging her to get her attention.

"Boy, what it is." she hollered.

"What if she has Covid?"

"Boy, that ain't no Covid that's allergies, your stepfather got em too, don't be a fool now."

After a while, Livonia stopped sneezing so loudly and was able to hear cartoons on the TV, it was Marvel, my favorite stuff to watch, and she did not even budge. She just stared as if she had never watched TV before. Big momma Lucy stood above her and smiled.

"It's time to fix that bun, baby," she said. "I can't let you leave the house with all that bug food in your head."

She sat the grease on the chestnut stool for her

thousand dollar living room set. She combed through her hair in silence, and her coils stretched out down to her back.

"Oh my god, honey," Big momma Lucy said. "Your hair is so beautiful, it's blonde, just like."

Big momma Lucy went silent.

There were a bunch of photographs of Fritz smiling while holding big bright orange basketballs. One photo he was holding two basketballs like he was Wilt Chamberlain and there was smaller picture of him smiling with the commissioner of the GBA in Berlin. He's an old white man, with gray hair, a hunch back and thick-framed glasses. Fritz had his arm around the team smiling with his dimple-chined smile. The team was about to splash him with ice-cold water in the background. They won their championship the first year with Fritz; which was great. Underneath the photograph's was other gleaming gold trophies and medals with German words on them and Livonia was holding her head still while staring at him.

Big momma Lucy smiled while raking the comb through Livonia's head, "The super ain't just a boring old super, he is a championship coach," she uttered, she looked at Fritz's freckled face while greasing the little girl's ponytail. Her eyebrows squished at her blonde scalp. She swallowed her foamy spit and held a piece of Livonia's hair.

"He doesn't look like he's one of us," she laughed awkwardly, "but he is a part of my family." When Big momma Lucy said the word family, her voice was high-pitched, as if she was telling a lie because she was. She hated Fritz, but needed him around.

Livonia's shoulders went limp, her bottom lip swelled twice its size. "My sister Rhonda treats me like I'm not a part of my family," she said with her shoulders slouched, "Rhonda is always saying I'm white."

Big momma Lucy's eyelids dropped, she walked from behind the little girls back and stood in front of her. She leaned in and rubbed her shoulder.

"Honey you ain't white, you're just fair skinned, that's all, chocolate comes in all colors, right?"

Big momma Lucy walked to the bathroom with her dress swaying side to side, she opened the medicine cabinet and her hands extended to a dark blue bottle of Vicks. Fritz was using it last because he has severe allergies too. The eye- rubbing, swollen-face, shotgun sneezes, yea, we delt with that all the time in the spring. Big momma Lucy stood at the medicine cabinet with the bottle in her hand, looking at it while spinning it around. She had a look of concern on her face as if she couldn't believe that she was thinking what she thought. She prayed to Jesus that it was nothing because if it were something, she'd be ready to go to jail for what she might do to Fritz.

She came back from the bathroom; her hands extended the Vicks towards Livonia.

"Rub it on your chest and throat, darling," she said. "It will help you breathe and clear up your sinuses."

Livonia stood up, then she honey-dipped her two small fingers into the bottle and spread the Vicks on her throat while rubbing it in a circular motion.

Big momma Lucy smirked, she turned to the girl facing her eye-to-eye and caught Livonia's chin dimple. Then she turned her chin toward Fritz's photograph on the living room wall underneath the piano. He had the same chin dimple that looked like a BB gun pellet hit him in the jaw.

"You have a dimple in your chin," Big momma Lucy said, "where did you get that."

Livonia had an embarrassed glow on the center of her face and shrugged her shoulders with her chin falling into her neck.

18

Olivia
March/8th/2022

Big momma Lucy held her brown hands over the faucet and the water gushed out, splashy as it went through her fingers and down the drain while swirling. She froze, looked into the mirror, and stared at herself as if she were angry.

"It can't be," She uttered with confusion, they are black kids, there's no way that Fritz had them black children, but Livonia is mixed! that's his kid fa sure."

She twisted the faucet, shook off her knuckles, and wiped her hand on the paper towel. "I need him around! Without him everything crumbles. Lord have mercy." She shut her eyes and shook her knuckles.

Big momma Lucy liked to buy those expensive towels that don't rip easily; she hated unreliable stuff, which is why she had a problem with her fake ass super, Fritz. She rubbed her hand a green towel.

She opened the bathroom door; Livonia was in the

middle of the living room with her back turned. Next to her, I was leaning on the armrest telling her about Deadpool and why he is different from the Avengers.

Big momma Lucy walked from the bathroom, through the kitchen, and to the living room with her wrist bent.

"Baby girl," she said softly, "are you ready to go home?"

Livonia's body sagged into the seat, her shoulders slouched, and she had a look of confused nervousness.

"Okay," she replied, "Can I come over more?"

"sure darling."

Big momma Lucy slapped her hand on my shoulder.

"Let me know if Fritz comes," she said, "we have to talk about something."

At that moment, I knew that Big momma Lucy was ready to kick some ass; whenever she spoke calmly, that meant shit is gonna get real for yo ass and you better dip.

Livonia's footsteps were soft as she walked down the staircase, she arrived at the second floor, and her chin shifted up at the cream and brown paint design.

"How did they paint it, and what year was it built?" she asked.

"In eighteen-ninety something," Big momma Lucy replied. "The design was done by a French artist who lived in Harlem, they built these Brownstones like it was nothing back then."

"What about this, Ms. Lucy," she uttered while pointing at the off-white part of the ceiling.

"The Brownstone was old — A man by the name Buckeye Bill sold it to me and it still had rats and roaches but me and Fritz renovated it to make it look modern." With her hands on Livonia's shoulder, she whispered to the side, "This place is worth one million dollars, and design plays a big part in its value, my daughter Yata went to college for design maybe you can too since you like to talk about Buildings and what not."

Big momma Lucy and Livonia stepped to the first floor, the hallway tiles were sticky, so when you walked on them, they made a syrupy noise underneath your shoes. Slow walking water bugs crept from the creases of the door frame and scurried across the door lining.

Big momma Lucy stood on the doormat with her heart jabbing through her dress. Yea, she was the damn property owner of the building, but she was always afraid to have encounters with Ms. Moss because of the rent situation. She felt a shortness of breath and anxiety fire brewing in her stomach; she lifted her index finger, pressed the bell, and stepped backward. Clacking footsteps inched closer from the other side of the door, the lock clacked and Ms. Moss pulled it open with a forearm full of gold bangles. Her head poked out, her nostrils flared and her lips so thin that she could have caused her lip ring to rip. She was wearing a wifebeater with her nipples drooping out of the side and her areola looked like smushed chocolate on a sizzling summer day.

"Ole bitch from upstairs," she scoffed. Then she smiled with swollen eyes, and at the ends of her fingertips was a plastic cup with brown liquor jiggling. "I knew this day would come."

Big momma Lucy's neck snapped back, she put her fingers across her chest, and her eyeballs widened. "Excuse me!" she snapped. "Who in the heck are you talking to, don't start with me Charlesha, because I didn't come down here for that." Her neck snapped side to side, and her raspy voice echoed.

Ms. Moss laughed, she took a sip of her drink and rubbed her weave with the other hand. She smiled with her missing front tooth, looking like a grown-uptoddler. "What's done in the dark comes to light," she said in a loud voice. She took another sip, standing to the side with her hand on her hip, drinking her liquor and giggling into the cup's rim. In the background of the apartment was complete darkness. One by one footsteps crept behind and her smaller daughters walked closer to see.

Big momma Lucy glanced, took a step back and she reached for Livonia, who was at her thigh.

"I'm not even going to get into it with you around your daughters because you're not worth the jail time. Livonia told me that she has hay fever. Do you give her allergy medicine?"

Ms. Moss's eyebrows tightened, and her lip thinned as she moved the cup away from her mouth. "Medicine?" Her lip twisted to the side, "For allergies? I don't give a damn about that. That shit ain't killed nobody, so why you making a big deal out of nothing bitch." Her arm extended to Livonia's head, she grabbed her by the bun and pulled her into the dark door frame.

"Olivia! Get cho dumbass in here," she barked with anger as if she was mad at her daughter for existing.

Big momma Lucy's hand reached, "Livonia is her name, not Olivia." The door slammed loudly and the breeze from the slam gave her goosebumps.

19

Damn to the Devil

March/8th/2022

The basement door swung wide. A gust of wind pushed through.

Fritz's dusty steel toe boot stepped out and he had a swollen face as if he were sleeping down there.

"Hey Luce," Fritz uttered, "I was just fixing the leakage in the basement." He reached for Big momma Lucy, but she jerked away from him, and he stood confused.

"Stay away from me," she snapped, "stay the hell away from me." She angrily sung, she lifted the sides of her dress and ran up the staircase with a hunched back. They bickered and argued about Ms. Moss all the way to the top floor and the shouting was so loud that I could hear it through the walls. Big momma Lucy slammed the door, connected the silver chain across, and placed her weight on the handle.

"Phillip, go to your room," she swung her arm towards the back of the house, "Me and your stepdad are about to tear this place up, and only God can judge me for what I'm gone do to his old no-good-scheming white ass."

I stood there, my face blanked, and I scratched my head while standing up. I pulled my videogame cord out of the TV and walked to my room with the cords dragging against the tiles.

Big momma Lucy slapped the center of door,

"Fritz, get the hell away from my house," she shouted with her voice stretching as if she was singing a song. "We didn't do no background checks on Charlesha," she hollered, "I know why you brought them, that crazy heffa here, it's because you the father of them damn kids."

Fritz extended his hand to the knob, "No, Lucy, please, that's not true." He leaned forward, but Big momma Lucy pushed back until it slammed shut again.

She leaned her body weight on the door with both feet spread open.

"You think I'm stupid? Livonia is your twin," she shouted, "you been cheating on my daughter, dammit, and then you brought that filthy whore here to live for free! Are you nuts?"

Fritz's face crumpled, his pink fingers dug into his pockets, and he stuck his key in the door, but the silver chain jammed his entry.

"Luce come on," he shoved his lips through, and she slammed it on his face. "I would never do something like that," he uttered back with a high-pitched voice "I'm married to your daughter. I love Ivory! you're not thinking straight right now."

"Is Livonia your child—Devil, Yes, or no?"

Fritz's face reddened. Whenever he got hostile, his nose slightly ran, his cheeks shook, and his hair gets all sweaty and messy. "No," he shouted, "I've never touched Charlesha in my life, I swear to God that those aren't my children."

Big momma Lucy kept him on the other side of the door like a priest yearning for confessions. He was sitting on the hallway floor with his legs wide open, a screw in his fingers and his toolbox near his thigh. He rolled the screw around his finger while telling Big momma Lucy a story. A story that brought her to knees. The same story puts Ivory in jail and her Merlo full of bullet holes.

After a half hour of talking, she took the silver chain off, opened the door wide, and spoke with a choked voice.

"You remember how you got close to this family," she muttered. "You told me the truth about that god-awful night that we lost Ivory and Brian! You were honest with me to help me find peace. I still feel guilty about it you know?"

She wiped off her dress, which was dirty from sitting on the dusty floor. She stood in front of the entrance with her long finger pointed at his mottled face.

"If she aint your Baby's Mother and they aint your children, right! you should have no issue with me evicting the whole family," Big momma Lucy uttered.

"No, we should evict them," he said with a fast twitch, he walked into the house with a stiff face and his blue eyes didn't even shake.

ACT II

Mom and Stepdad

September/15th/2023

11:00

Ivory took a bite of her noodles

"Merlo must be haunting us from heaven." She uttered.

Fritz's eyes bulged and his body straightened as if he felt a stinging feeling. He stared downward while chewing his pork ribs. He glimpsed at Lindsey; the red head waitress who walked with a tight ass. She was smoking hot like a barbeque on the fourth of July. She was all awkward looking as if she had never been with a man in her life. Small thin pale fingers with damaged cuticles. Her fingers rested on her apron, bending her thumb in nervousness. Her skin around her nails were slightly chewed. She turned around, took a step, her ginger hair strands shook and her back jiggled in her pants. She was animated at retrieving the wine cart at the bar. The cart squeaked, she grabbed it and jogged back slowly.

Ivory's eyes froze.

"what do you think about her?" Ivory aimed her fork while chewing, flicked her index finger toward the kitchen door.

Fritz shook his head.

"what the fuck is your deal!" Fritz screamed. Ivory's eyes were darting across the table.

"what do you mean, that waitress is fucking beautiful. She has that ginger look, you know? she has big brown lips, she has green eyes and she has fat ass."

"—you're my fucking wife!"

"—so, you telling me you wouldn't fuck her?"

"no!"

Ivory smiled in a suspicious way, she lifted an eyebrow and sat back in her seat. Her shoulder blades flattened.

During Ivory's stint in prison, she became very suspicious of Fritz. She heard a lot of shit about him and another woman. She was going to get the truth out about Charlesha one way or another.

Fritz leaned back into his seat, staring his wife dead in the eye. His lips went thin around his teeth, he wiped his nose with his index finger.

"first Alejeh and now her?" he shouted softly "we

going to keep doing this? I thought last time was a one-time thing."

"well it's your birthday, so everything is on the table tonight." Ivory smiled, the skin around her cheekbones looked shiny.

Lindsey pulled the finest wine bottles from the bar, she grabbed the cork from the bartender's hands and placed it on the wine cart. Giving a soft smile, a finger wave and then she rolled her wooden cart with a hair thrusting innocent eye sparkle. She looked very innocent. Probably a Taylor Swift fan who was against war, crime and bad doings. She stopped at the circular table with two bottles of wine. Lindsey stretched her hand to grab the bottle of red wine with a black label. Portiere was a French classic. She placed the tall wine bottle right next to the white candle with the dancing flame and poured until the empty glass was bloody red. While she poured, she noticed Ivory's eyes darting from the side. Ivory was beautiful, she had almond shaped eyes like an east Asian supermodel, cheekbones and a smile like Beyoncé Knowles. Ivory removed her hand from the table cloth, she lifted a fork of Shrimp alfredo. The steam from the food was smelling like garlic at her nose. She bit into it and shut her eyes.

"mmm," she moaned.

Lindsey bent down. She angled her body under the cart and lifted a bottle of white wine for Ivory. Olenoteja's wine; which was two thousand Euros a bottle in Italy.

Ivory smiled, impressed that the restaurant remembered that she only drink whites, so she slapped her palms together for a silent clap with her shoulders hunched.

"Olenoteja's," she shouted "is it my birthday? or his? Her eyes squinted in happiness "lord have mercy I'm about to get faded."

Lindsey's eyes exploded, startled by Ivory's body movement while holding the most expensive bottle.

She reached forward, creating a safety net with her fingers.

"sorry, "Lindsey uttered. "the bottle."

"it's the wine for me, girl." Ivory replied, smiling with a underbite and the bottle top glistening under the dim light. Then she locked eyes with Lindsey and poured the wine without looking. She gave her a hand gesture to come close.

"Lindsey, right?" Ivory uttered, slamming the bottle on the table. She bit the rim of her glass and drunk a whole inch down. Then her fingers curled around the menu. She lifted the menu to cover her face so her words were dark.

"I saw you looking at my Husband, but it's okay, I need a favor," she uttered.

The waitress hesitantly fell to her lips with her ear open wide. A single strand of ginger brown hair slipped in slow motion. She was a natural beauty.

"it's my husband's birthday babe." Ivory uttered in a low tone "let's make it rememberable, you know any ginger desserts that we can take home?"

Fritz's eyes bulged.

Lindsey's eyes shuttered, and there was an awkward silence. She blinked fast while twirling her shirt sleeve, then bobbling her head at Ivory.

Lindsey glimpsed over at the corner of the restaurant near the white drapes and Alejeh was at work. She was still like a wax figure. Her thick black hair dangling, she was holding a customer's debit card twenty feet away with her beady little eyes protruding. Hating!

A single line of sweat inched down from Lindsey's forehead, she glimpsed at the clock which read eleven thirty.

"I get off at twelve." Lindsey uttered, "I guess I can help him find some."

"okay Doll." Ivory dropped the menu, covering her nose, bottling her maniacal laugh with a sip of white wine.

Ivory grabbed her sparkly fork, twisted her noodles and the alfredo sauce dripped onto the table cloth. She lifted her knife and stabbed a pretty pink piece of shrimp at the tip. She chewed with her mouth shut and her eyes closed.

"mmm," she muttered while wrapping her big platform boots around Fritz's ankle.

"daddy this is some good ass alfredo." she glimpsed into his blue eyes. She raised her fork over the table and led the noodles into his pink lips.

Fritz smiled, he wiped his hands on his handkerchief and took a sip of the bloody red wine. He wiped his palm on his pants, feeling a huge bulge that was down there. He looked towards Lindsey with a giddy flinch, turned his face towards the window with white curtains and mean mugged.

"we have to go." Fritz uttered to himself, awkwardly jittering. He blinked towards the drape-less wide aquarium-like window. There were Manhattan pedestrians walking in silence.

Ivory hunched, she smacked her teeth into the shrimp, drinking white wine and even took a few puffs from her vape pen. Ivory loved to go out. Every moment in public with Ivory was a nervous moment for Fritz because she was so carefree about her life.

They say ignorance is bliss and rather than tell her the truth about his drug dealing, snitching, cheating and murder, Fritz let her be that happy woman. Their marriage would hit the rocks and there would be an unfixable shipwreck if she knew what he did to people. His past was as dark as the darkest whiskey behind the bar.

Ivory's brown hair was shaking, blue streak of weave running through it, wearing a nude brown corset, a pink skirt and knee-high bedazzled boots, squeezing them around her husband's foot. Freakishly gorgeous. He would gaze back, stare at her chest plate. Although she had medium sized boobs, she had these gigantic nipple rings poking out of her top. Ivory wasn't so innocent herself, when they were in Vegas she told Fritz to have another fucking drink because tomorrow isn't promised. Yea she used the word fucking in almost all her sentences. She told Fritz to bet it all at the gambling table while squeezing his fat dick, getting him hard and giving him the adrenaline to bet it all at the poker table. Tongue kissing, fingerfucking, cupping her ass in public while she shouted his name. Fritz; but mainly daddy. Ivory was wearing nothing under her dress, she whispered in his ear that she wants to make love on the balcony so she could scream his name into the boundless Nevada sky. Scream his name until the gods wake up like moody neighbors and strike them down for sinning in Sin City.

If the average person judged Ivory by her appearance, they'll probably think she's a smoking hot shorty whose down for a good time and most niggas would want to wife her but no man; I repeat no man would guess that she had completed sixteen-years in prison for murder. She was too soft, too sweet, too beautiful but just like Fritz, looks were horribly deceiving. The two was a nightmare couple and another Murder was bound to happen.

Years prior ....

I

Berlin, Germany
March/ 7th/2022

Rosa, the Hispanic cleaning lady lunged towards Fritz, flailing her wrist and her muffled face scrunched through the facemask.

"Estupido," she snapped, "Irse!" She waved towards the elevator, signaling him to leave the motel. One by one the doors on the side opened and people stuck their foreheads out to see what was happening.

Fritz's ghostly white skin turned fever red. He stood there with his shoulders squared looking like he was a hunchback.

Rosa snatched the half-empty bag of drugs, got on her knees, and lifted the dusty pills while cursing in Spanish.

Meanwhile, the bald security guard, Orlando Jenkins stepped from the staircase while holding the rail, to the second floor. His eyes narrowed down to

Rosa who was on her knees picking up the pills. He planted his first foot forward, poking out his bottom lip and walking closer with his hand squeezing his belt buckle. He stopped near her cart and his bald head shined like a bowling ball from out the rack. He had a wide skull and an Adams apple that looked like he swallowed half of a peach seed.

"Hey, mama," he uttered with a wide voice, a single eyebrow lifted. "You okay back here." His fat throat stretched. Rosa mumbled in Spanish while pointing at Fritz.

"Him," she shouted.

Fritz slammed the door, he let go of the knob and the light from the television shined onto Dawn. She wore a lace front wig with those baby curls around her edges, full nude curvy body, and Brown legs the same color of caramel. Her forearm was over her knee with a clear cup of Hennessy in her hands.

"You took a long time," she said with a docile smile, bending the plastic cup with her grasp, "I thought you got lost at the gas station."

Fritz rested his back on the door with his chin up high and both hands squeezed into a fist.

Fritz's fist squeezed tighter.

"I think the cleaning lady found some Fentanyl in

one of the rooms," he muttered with gazing eyes.

"I need to get that shit."

Dawn's eyes bulged, her face ticked, and she lowered her cup of Hennessy down near her foot.

"Oh, my fuckin lord, please don't," she uttered desperately, "aren't you done with that hustling shit, did you come here for me or for that?"

As she nagged, she heard a raspy voice coming from the motel window. A homeless girl was outside offering dick sucks for drugs. Dawn got up and slammed the window so hard that a beer bottle dropped from the ledge to the concrete.

Fritz shifted his chin upwards, and blinked slowly, his eyes were bright blue and scattered back and forth as if he were reading something at super speed.

"The street price for that stuff is worth a couple of grand," he uttered to himself with those racing eyes, "I could make some fucking bank, I can gun down that cleaning lady, but my steel is in the rental."

"Hell no!" Dawn screamed. She lifted her bra, spread it open, put her arms through it, and snapped the back without turning around into the mirror. She picked up her skirt, navy blue, and silver, see-through at the hips. She squeezed her multicolor fingernails into it, walked closer to him, and dangled it like a fresh piece of meat.

"Are you done with the streets or not," she said, "because I can just go, you told me you aint never going back, that I would never have to help you hustle ever again, I don't have time for that shit again."

Fritz shut his eyes like he was exhausted, he put his fist over his jaw and pushed his bodyweight off the door. He grabbed Dawn by the upper arm, squeezed her with a smothering tight grasp like a blood pressure machine when the doctor holds the pump. His grasp was so aggressive that her petite arm turned red on the insides.

"Dawn, sit the fuck down," he screamed with darting eyes. His nose had a muscle twitch, and his ears were red on both sides.

"I'm sick of you saying that, I already told you before, you aren't going anywhere you fucking disloyal whore. You already know too much about me. Do you think I'll just let you up and leave me? ... it's too fucking late for that."

He stood over her, he had a snarling nose and eyeballs that shook with every word. He walked back to the silver knob and twisted it. Through the cracked door, he let a single eyeball through. He saw the security guard talking with two officers who looked like newcomers.

Fritz removed his palms from the knob, he shut the door and locked it with a silver latch. He hated the police and he'd never expose himself to them, especially over some sketchy pills. He took a deep breath, sat next to Dawn, and put his palm over her kneecap.

"Stop trying to leave me," he shouted, "you know how complicated things are at home, I need some fucking money."

Dawn flinched, she stared downward with her beautiful, slanted eyes and directed them towards the window. She looked good whenever she was pissed. She had wide cheekbones, a round hairline with baby curls and a perfect set of plump lips. She was so beautiful that she'd get offers from modeling agencies but always turned them down because she knew Fritz wouldn't stand for it. Even her best friend Savannah would tell her to start a modeling page so she could help her brand it, but she was already branded by Fritz, and he was a selfish man with his real estate.

Dawn yanked her brown leg away from him so he couldn't touch her with his pale fingers.

"Money!" she responded. "But y'all own property, right? "The building in Bed-Stuy, right? Isn't it a lot of money in renting apartments."

Fritz rolled his eyes,

"Yea, there's money in it, but I haven't gotten a dime,"

"Ask Lucy."

"Fucking silence, yourself." He responded while nudging his shoulder to the other side of the off-white wall, "You wouldn't understand this shit, you don't know anyone with property so shut the fuck up Dawn."

The TV was shining on their faces. One side was light, and the other side was dark. Live news coverage was playing on channel eleven. A reporter had a crisp voice full of terror and confusion.

"Fifty-nine-year-old man Edward Aberdeen killed in queens," he uttered, "witnesses say that the getaway car disappeared." The hopeless news reporters always had a story, but Dawn didn't want to hear drama. She just wanted an enjoyable time with her man and by that point felt like it was never going to happen. They spent ten years fooling around and she knew that once Fritz set his mind on getting bread, he'd do anything, even use her if necessary.

Dawn's eyes whitened, she sucked her teeth, then she pressed the button on the remote. Wheel of Fortune popped up on the screen, making that clicking noise in the background. She had her Fendi purse near her thigh with a golden emblem. She pulled a zip lock bag from it and reeled out a deep brown fronto leaf that looked like a bat's wing.

That's how we roll our weed in the city, papers and fronto so it burns slower, and we can preserve more weed.

Dawn's eyes blinked at a fast pace.

"Fritz, did you get the papers?" she asked. She put her palm on his knee.

"Yea, I got you the papers, why do you need papers if you already had fronto?"

Dawn rolled her eyes.

"You been in the Stuy long enough you know that's how we do it."

She eagerly reached for the flat stack of papers. She noticed the gleaming wedding band wrapped around his chubby pale finger but didn't ask why he was still wearing it. She rolled her eyes and rocked her leg impatiently. Her chest was steaming hot like a pot of crab legs, she flicked her hair and turned her neck the other way. She pressed the lighter with the side of her thumb, put the blunt to her lips, and sucked the fire with her face turned to the side. She coughed with her hand at the center of her chest, she put it to her lips again and it made a faint crackling noise, and the smoke went straight to her brain. Straight to her brain exactly how Fritz words went. "You're my girl Dawn." He said at Metaford hotel in Virginia Beach. After a couple of hits, she leaned over for an ashtray, but there wasn't one on the TV stand like before. She sucked her teeth so loud that it echoed onto the ceiling. One of the ashes dropped on her thigh and she flinched so hard that she kicked her cup of Henny.

"Dammit Fritz!" she screamed, "This motel is cheap! you must really think I'm a cracked-out whore." Her eyes beamed. "Because why are we here! y'all own the whole brownstone in Bed-Stuy, I wish you took me over there instead of here that way I wouldn't have burned my fucking leg."

Fritz snatched the remote control, the gummy button turned red like laser. He tried to switch his attention, but Dawn's eyes kept beaming brown.

"Hello," she uttered, "you hear me? I don't want to be at this fucking cracked-out motel." She slammed her palm against the stiff mattress.

Fritz's face flushed pale.

"It's my stepson," he leaned away while talking. "My stepson is doing remote learning, he is home all the time because of the pandemic."

"Phillip? I told you that I would make a good stepmom to that boy," she snapped back, "you should stop worrying, unless you got something else you are hiding from me at that house."

Fritz took a deep breath, grunted, and wiped his palms on his pants.

"Fucking Dawn its complicated..."

"I know about the boy's mother," she responded, "if I had a husband and I was—" Dawn stopped mid-sentence. Her heart fluttered fast because he was across from her with his fingers curled into a fist that looked like he was ready to knock her head in again. He stared at her with his blond eyebrows straining and his teeth showing. "Forget it," she muttered, "I won't talk about your wife because I know how you get, always ready to violate me because I'm telling you the truth and shit."

Fritz leaned backward, put his palms over his eyes, and his chest inflated. His dark blond hair looked sweaty, and his skin mottled like sunburn. He turned around and Dawn stared at his bald spot on the back of his head.

"Sorry," he said, "I've just been a little uneasy. Lately, you don't know what it's like living there, you don't know the life I used to live and how much I changed."

Dawn rolled her eyes, she got on her knees and crawled over the mattress like a cat. She looked so exotic, her hair dangled across her shoulder and the well-cut strands slid against the mattress like sex spikes. She swayed her long fingers across his crotch, put the blunt down into a plastic cup and continued to crawl over him. The light from the TV showed her full body figure. She was curvy, exotic, leg tats down to her calf. She stretched her legs over his lap like a motorcycle rider and in-between her legs were warm like a pot of home cooking. She loosened her bra straps, a cherry tattoo right above her cleavage and stretch marks on her breast leading to her nipple. She had a focused gaze on his disgusting finger—the one she hated because the wedding band shined even in the dark. She tilted her head sideways and bit his bottom lip like a piece of chewing gum. She kissed him, put her tongue into his mouth and he tasted her snake eye piercing.

"Take it off," she muttered into his mouth while kissing.

Fritz's hands reached for his shirt, he pulled it upwards towards his ribs, but she wrapped her fingers around his wrist and tightened her thighs around his bony pelvis.

"No, I wasn't talking about the shirt," she said. "You know what I meant." She breathed into his mouth while kissing him.

He had an embarrassing glow in the center of his face, without breaking eye contact, he spread his fingers, swiveled the wedding band off, and placed it at the edge of the mattress.

While she sat on top of him, he could feel her cat getting all wet. The kissing led to him whipping out his growing penis, and it easily sliding inside.

Her eyes rolled back to her head like she was having an orgasm, but it was attitude, something she couldn't control when it came to Ivory. She stared at that putrid ring gleaming with a yellow luster on the white sheets and kept thinking about Ivory.

She slammed her ass down on his dick as she rode him. Her brown eyes bounced from his blond bearded chin back to the flashy ring while the bed spring shook and she could feel the sting. Not from sex, but the sting from him wearing that ring and worshipping his wife after all they've been through.

"Oh, yea daddy," she moaned dramatically while her nails spread across his chin. She moaned extra hard as if he grew a couple more inches, but she was putting on a show. A show more dramatic than anything running on the TV.

Minutes after Fritz came, it shot up like a volcano all into her fat pussy and the heated liquid made her clench. Her eyes bounced toward the shut curtains, while fanning herself and breathing hard. She sat there for minutes, holding him, and pressing her head underneath his chin. He yawned and shut his blue eyes. His eyes always shut as if he were winking, then opened and shut until he knocked out. He pushed her off, rolled over on the white pillow and squeezed it at his chest like a little boy with a stuffed animal. That's what he was; a little boy trapped in a massive man's body and his wife was the stuffed animal; full of cotton and stitching. He could have had a real woman, but he wanted that play-time-make-believe relationship. He could never be with Ivory for real.

Dawn turned her cheek and checked her cellphone, which was messages from her best friend Savannah.

"Girl where you at," she texted.

Dawn looked around the room, ears lifted, hearing treacherous footsteps from behind the weak white walls. she abruptly stared towards the end of the mattress and saw that ring. She shook her head and tried to text but couldn't think of any words to say. She dropped her cellphone, reached forward, and snatched the ring. She slid it into her blue Jimmy Choo heel.

"Got him," she whispered. The TV screen flashed against her exotic frame. While unbaling her blue camouflaged thong, she felt a tear drop inching from her face, not because she was crying, but because she stared for so long at the ring without blinking. She tried to wipe her face but when her thumb met her nose bone, she smelt the bleachy scent of semen on her fingers. She looked down and felt the semen leaking down her legs. She was familiar with it because Fritz liked it raw.

Dawn walked towards the TV stand, she opened his royal blue wallet, and the Velcro made a ripping noise. She hunched, lifted her cellphone, and snapped a photo of Fritz's address. She was ready to see what Fritz was hiding at his house.

2

The Cold Blue eyes
March/7th/2022

Fritz was a large man with flabby chest and a stomach that looked like he threw down a lot of brew in his spare time which made him appear more intimidating as he stood over her.

He yanked the sheets back, lifting his wrist high enough to see his underarm hair and dropping his own clothing onto the floor. The room was quiet, you could just hear him breathing hard and cars swishing the road from the outside window.

"Where the fuck is it," Fritz yelled with his lip twisted.

"Let me help,"

Dawn walked toward the mattress with her arms reaching. He suddenly turned around and threw a nasty backhand punch that grazed her but still made her stumble to the rug with her naked body. Her fall shook the whole room and gave her an earth flipping headache. Not because of physical force, but because of the extent he would go for Ivory—his wife. The woman he chose to be with forever, while he only indulged with her for a moment.

Fritz's face shivered, his pale fingers grew red as he tightened them, and he shouted particles of spit over her body. "Dawn! stop fucking horsing around with me," he screamed with his bare chest jiggling.

"You scared that I'll tell Ya wife what we be doing huh?" She shouted back, she lifted herself off the ground and slapped him with both of her palms back-to-back, "I can't take it anymore." She pushed her palm into his chest. "Fritz, I been ready to be your girl and you fucked with my head since we met at beach, how could you lie to me about leaving your fucking wife." Dawn's eyes bounced side to side, her chest wobbled, and she gave him one last palm push.

Fritz walked to the end of the mattress, his face twisted as if something stunk, he bent down to see if his ring had fallen but it wasn't there. He was inches away from her blue Jimmy Choo high heel but didn't look inside the toe part. His face trembled, he reached and clawed under the bed but saw darkness, old crumbs, and carpet lint. He lifted from the crease of the bed. His fingers curled against her clothing, and he started throwing it toward the carpet in short order; her bra, then her thong and her dress.

Dawn's face shook,

"Please Babe can you just stop." she shouted with her fingers pressing into her eyes.

Fritz didn't care that she was crying, he was angry, so he wanted her to feel his white madness.

"Fucking worthless hooker," he shouted with his finger aimed.

"The only reason why I let you live every day is so I could fuck you the following day, but I'll send us both to hell along with my urges to rip your sweet little asshole." His hands trembled as he tore her fashionova blouse, then lifted the Hennessy bottle under the light. A small piece of her blouse sleeve was shoved inside. The cloth hung out of the bottle hole as if he created plenty of Molotov cocktails in his day.

Dawn's face made an ugly twist,

"Fritz, wait what are you doing?" she shouted.

He lifted his red lighter, scratched it, and sparked an orange flame. He brought it closer to the cloth and the flame danced.

"Dawn, I'll burn this whole motel with me and you inside! along with all of the other bitches and hoes, give me the fucking ring! you lousy smut."

Dawn's face lit up from the flame, her voice went high-pitched, she retracted her hands to her breast and trembled naked.

"I swear to god, I don't have it," she shouted with her mouth stuck in an ugly twist. Her bottom lip trembled, she grabbed her breast tighter and curled her knees away from him. "You can check all of my pockets, I don't have it Fritz, please don't start, we were having a good time."

Fritz trembled in anger,

"I saw you about to leave—why were you in a rush to get out of here?" He yelled.

"Because I have work."

"Only work you'll ever have is between your legs, you lousy streetwalker." He held the bottle inches away from his rib. When he shouted, the liquor inside the bottle jiggled against the glass.

Dawn panicked, she clutched at her stomach while scooting backwards slightly squeezing the sheets. Fritz's eyes beamed down to her vagina. His blue eyes were so cold that it made her skin grow goosebumps and her nipples hard. He put his knee between her legs and grabbed her by the waist. Dawn's eyes beamed, "stop! why would I put a wedding band in my coochie. You need to be logical. Fritz lowered the bottle, pulled her by the ankle until she reached the edge. At that point, she didn't feel like a two-hundred-pound woman; she felt like an open door the way yanked her with ease. He had strength like one of those Greek gods in Homer, but he wasn't a God, he was a man with insecurities and a potential for violence.

Dawn's right foot was at his flaccid dick and her other foot was at the ceiling. She dropped her left heel and kicked near his balls sack, but he tightened his legs around his penis and her heel only grazed his inner thigh.

He grabbed her tightly and yanked her like a ragdoll.

"Bitch!" He screamed. His hands were so massive that he held both of her wrists with one grasp.

Her face shivered with terror, her naked body was under the light, and he was so close that he could see her vagina had some razor bumps.

"Okay," she shouted, "I'll show you that there's nothing in there, you're scaring the shit outta me." She blinked hard under the light, she spread herself while looking away and shook involuntarily. It was the most jacked up situation that she'd ever been in, other than the time when he asked her to hold some cocaine for her. Not only did he unzip her jeans, but he also shoved them up there with his bare hands. The girl's bathroom was known to be bugged with cameras, so he was scatterbrained, sweating at both temples, on his knees with his eyes bouncing at the ceiling. While most men prayed to a God for good fortune, Fritz prayed to God that there wasn't any camera staring him down because he would have to gun it out with T.S.A or the police. While they were crammed in the airport bathroom, Dawn felt like she found true love because there wasn't any other reason for being so stupid. Shoot-outs with T.S.A.?

How foolish!

Dawn peeled her lips open, dug her hand inside wrist deep and her vagina bulged open looking like a snake throat. Pussy was like a snake, the way it grabs you and lock you in its clutches, but Dawn swore that hers wasn't working because no matter what, he'd go back to his wife. Her nails were moist and sticky from her natural fluids. She was always so wet whenever Fritz raised his voice, even when she was afraid that he might do something impulsive like snatch every dollar out of an Arabic man's taxi or beat up a mechanic for messing up his Alternator and charging him for it. She always liked guys who she couldn't control but Fritz was just a different breed. He had a temper like a nuclear weapon and was ready to blow everything up over his ring—over his wife. She never met a white man like him, she was almost certain that white men were all soft, but she found out first-hand how cold a person could be. Sometimes she would stare into his eyes and wonder if blue eyes meant that he had a heart of ice.

When she finished inserting her wrist into her vagina, she folded her legs and scooted to the other side of the mattress. She turned over and cried into the pillow with her back bouncing uncontrollably.

Fritz turned around, he planted his foot, winded up his arm and threw the bottle of Hennessy against the wall. When it shattered, the sharp glass shards made a crashing noise and the liquor splattered back into Dawn's face and backside. There was glass in her hair and the liquor was warm and thick.

That's the type of man Fritz was, I knew he had a temper because he's my stepdad, but once he entered the house's front door and see Big momma Lucy, he'd turn into the good-spirited handy man.

3

Fritz's Outburst
March/8th/2022

Fritz walked towards the coat rack, he pulled his other jacket out of his luggage and hung the loop along with the other. From the mirror's reflection, he saw that I had new Jordan one's lined up in the corner next to the piano.

Fritz face wrenched,

"Where did you get those new Jays?" he uttered. His eyes glimpsed toward me and he had that pinging in his pupil. Everything stops when he stares with that cold hypnotic gaze and things that weren't weapons seem to become one. Like that edge of the chair. I think Fritz is so loony that he might push my head into the edge of a wooden chair and run my skull across it while screaming in my ear that I'm not his real son anyways.

We had a large dining table with an extra fridge near the pantry. There was plastic over the table so he could have killed me, but he didn't. Inside the small kitchen there were a bunch of cooking pots on the stove that looked untidy so he walked towards it.

Fritz's face went pale,

"What are all of them pots doing on the stove?" His face twitched, finger pointed, and Adam's apple went up and down. "Were you cooking crack with your grandmother's pots?" He stood there waiting for an answer and his eyes twitched.

One thing that always pissed me off about him, besides his mean streak, was when he acted like I was bound to be a criminal because Ivory was one. Fritz always jumped to conclusions. It's like he always thought I'd get into selling dope like them niggas on the corner. It was as if he pushed me to be a dope dealer instead of keeping me away from it.

I lunged off the couch and planted the house phone into his sternum.

"I'm not your real son," I shouted, "you should be worried about finding your stupid ring at the Super Galaxy, you wasn't in Berlin your lair!"

After I told him off, I walked away with ground shaking stomps. *Domp! Domp! Domp!*

Fritz stumbled into the couch seat, then he stood up with his neck growing veins. He balled up his fist and held them at the bottom of his chin with his eyes closed. Spit bouncing from his bottom lip, he laughed with anger, he stood up and punched the wall so hard that the picture frames wobbled like a haunted house.

"You think you're so smart, don't you?" he uttered with a smile. Then his blue eyes opening and closing. "Your real father, Merlo thought he was smart until Ivory body bagged his ass. Yea! You want to end up in a body bag then keep it up."

Everything in the house felt as if it were spinning.

Fritz took a long stride towards me and grabbed me by my arm until my body swung around.

"You want the truth, you little piece of shit?" he yelled, "You want the truth so bad don't you, you little nimwad," his fingers squeezed harder, and his teeth were showing, "I didn't mean to assume that you were hustling drugs out of Lucy's house, but your dad was a drug dealer. So that's why I worry about you, how do you think Charlesha got into that junk? Because of him! He was a hustler—Merlo! Yea your father, sold crack from Brighton Beach to the boardwalk."

My eyes beamed into nothingness. All I could think of was Dutchess; My girlfriend.

"What no he didn't!" I turned around and glared into the darkness while hearing the shifts of my heartbeat and my words jumbling beneath my feet.

Fritz stepped into the light, he stepped backward, landed on the edge of the couch seat, and cracked his knuckles.

"You think your mother was so bad," he whispered aggressively, "you walk around calling her Ivory instead of Ma. What the fuck is wrong with you! I would love to see you around your real pops, a real goon! that drug dealing piece of shit woulda dealt with you."

Fritz's face was red, his neck shivered, and he bit his bottom lip in an angry way.

I usually laugh or shrug it off whenever I felt awkward, but at that moment I couldn't laugh or shrug. My head aligned with my body, my balance in my equilibrium was gone, and I leaned against the solid wall. I tried to smile, but my cheeks felt swollen. My eyes shivered, my shoulders curled, and I crumpled down to the hardwood floor.

It made sense that my father was hustling because in pictures he had a lot of expensive cars, out-of-town trips, sparkling gold Diamond studded jewelry, and European clothes. I lifted myself, stomped towards my room, shut the door, and leaned on it.

Behind the wooden door, T.T. was lying on my bed, with her long needle black hair spread across the sheets. When she saw me come inside, she put her cellphone aside and scooted closer toward me.

"What happened," she uttered, "I heard a bunch of yelling, you look tight." She lifted herself from the mattress and stayed right at the edge.

I squeezed my knuckles and held them down on each side as if I wanted to punch something.

"It's my stepdad," I responded. "I hate him."

T.T.'s face went blank, she got up, she spread her arms as if she wanted to give me a big hug, then dropped one arm for a friendlier one. She stared at me with a look of care blended with confusion and fear. She removed the pillows off the mattress and sat slowly while pulling me to sit.

"Tell me what happened." She uttered softly.

Fritz. My stepdad married my mother while she was in prison. Word on the streets is that they knew each other before she got locked up. Fritz was in infatuated with her and my Grandma allowed him to stick around for some reasons that I still don't understand.

T.T.'s eyes brightened, she pulled me by the arm and took me to my mattress.

"why would your grandmother let a strange man around y'all, that doesn't make sense! Have you ever seen him do something out of the ordinary?

It was a Monday evening in the year 2019. I was in the kitchen eating a chop cheese from Patchen avenue deli. My best friend from apartment One downstairs, Fat short Shaq was on the opposite side of the kitchen talking to me about how to play craps with three dice. Suddenly, the front door busted open. Fritz stumbled inside the house while carrying and he had a suitcase full of clothes. Shaq was a dark-skinned man, I saw his whites in his eyeballs. Fat short Shaq had a zig-zag fade was like Zion Williamson, a white t shirt and some green camo shorts. He stood up.

"yo, super? You need help."

Fritz rushed to his bedroom, a pack of cigarettes fell from his pocket along of coins and keys. He extended his arm, standing in the middle of his room while the front door was still open. He flicked through the news. He smashed the remote-control buttons, going channel after channel until the light glistened over his eyeballs. Then we could hear the broadcast reporters talking about a 29-year-old man in Brownsville who was found dead. The man supposedly hung himself in a mechanic shop with dangling chains. Fritz gasped for breath, shivering and not blinking. He was obsessed with that case; he had footage, newspapers and even some paperwork on the man.

Fat short Shaq had mouth full of bread and cheese, he turned towards me while grabbing an Arizona sweet tea. He gave me an eye bobble.

"yo! Check ya pops kid!" he uttered, he lifted his green dice and dropped it at the center of the table and it was a four-five-six. "Ya pops looking like he guilty of something."

"My pops is not even like that." I uttered with a smile.

My eyes dropped to the aluminum foil and I couldn't eat another bite of the chop cheese.

"Nah, Fritz is just a basketball coach." I uttered back, "he aint never do nothing bad before. He is a square."

The cellphone was flashing while it laid across the Livingroom floor. The cased gadget was next to Fritz's shoe. My friend Lance texted me multiple messages and a bell sound alerted Fritz.

"Yo Phillip, you seen T.T." the text read, "Yo Phillip, why you aint reply crippy, you good?"

Fritz reached for my cellphone, his eyes had a muscle twitch and sweat tears as he invaded my security system. His fingers clicked the phone screen with aggression. He held the phone to his gut. He typed while wobbling, a single inch of sweat dripped from his mottled nose and his eyes didn't blink.

"Yo—homeboy. You have a connect for dope?" He wrote, then he removed the messages and dropped the phone on the couch. He slapped his forehead, bit his bottom lip, and walked into his bedroom. He thrashed all his drawers, and the knobs came tumbling off like the toys for Hannukah. He opened his luggage case and tossed his clothes all over his room. His underwear dropped across the floor like confetti and sock balls went bouncing. He lifted his desert eagle from his luggage and held it against his cheek.

"Fuck!" he screamed with veins in his neck "I need to get back in the fucking game or else I'm going to fucking shoot someone's head off."

4

Brownstone

March/8th/2022

My eyes bounced through my cellphone gallery. My contorted neck was over the screen while I stared at pictures of Big momma Lucy before the heart attacks. She loved to pose sideways while smiling with her teeth covered, it was a soft smile, but it was so calm and soothing. She had shiny pearls on her neck and gold earrings that looked like they were from Egypt. She would always ask if she looked fab, and I would nod my head.

"Yea, you look, good mama." I replied.

I missed her, so I pressed the call button on her number, and after the fifth ring, Yata's voice barreled through the phone line.

"Hello," she said in a snappy tone. "Don't worry about mother. You can stop calling here with your concerns and just let her recover from Covid."

The call went silent. I took a gulp of my own spit

and held back the tears.

Suddenly, as I held the phone to my ear, I heard Fritz's creaking footsteps from outside my wooden white door, he walked slowly, but the wood from the floor still made that bending sound. Like that quiet creepy noise from ghost movies—that was him slowly creeping around here and grazing his ear against my door.

I lifted myself and moved closer to the window, my head turned away and I stared out into the city view "Okay, Aunt Yata," I replied, "but can I speak to Big momma?"

"She's not right," Yata snapped back in an agitated voice "I might have to get her to another specialist, just give us some time," she uttered, "if Lucy dies then make sure y'all get those papers for her will. You remember where she keeps it, Phillip?"

I took a deep breath, raised my chin over my shoulder towards the door and I could see Fritz's sneaky shadow from under the cracks. Stalking me!

Some days he was normal, and other days he was downright weird. Every tenant in the building knew he listened to the house as a doctor listened to your pulse with a stethoscope.

Big momma Lucy's bedroom had colorful fabric dangling down out of closets and drawers. She had a Persian carpet that brushes once you walk across it. She had a wood ceiling fan above, a purple love seat, and a big mirror with a table full of perfume and brushes. On the right side of her room, directly underneath her portrait of Jesus Christ walking on water, was her most valuable thing. The file cabinet that she never spoke of. It was made of black steel, had a vault on the front with a red light blinking on the top. Only Big momma Lucy and Ivory knew the combination for it.

Fritz entered her room, he squeezed the vault and it didn't budge. The top of his teeth clamped down on his bottom ones, and the veins in his wrist were pumping like he finished taking a dose of roids. His gelled-down comb over hairstyle was all prickly like a porcupine. He kept pushing the steel as if he were about to get into a fight and was warming up before the first punch came. He was ambitious at times, but I've never thought he was dumb enough to get in Big momma Lucy's file cabinet.

Fritz was banging and hammering in the room as a plumber fidgeting with pipes, and then the walls shook with tremors of dust particles.

In the same hour of my worrisome thoughts, Ivory called me from Obbit. My face shivered, I put the phone to my cheek, and Once I picked up, it sounded like she was having a panic attack similar to mines.

"My mother is in critical condition," she blurted. "Fritz might be the wrong person with this information. This Berlin shit; and his attitudes lately have been the center of my headaches. I want you to open the file cabinet with your Aunt Yata."

Ivory sucked her tears back, and at that moment it sounded like my mother had feelings. I've never heard her sound sad about anything, not even my father's death.

Ivory's voice cleared,

"Phillip, your grandmother's file cabinet," she uttered, "the code is two-nine-nine-seven-nine-two."

At that moment, she didn't sound so hard and coldhearted. Her voice sounded as if she wanted to bond with me. Like her whole life was a mistake and she wishes she knew me like Big momma Lucy knew me.

Fritz's foot tattered across the hallway, bending the wood with his heavy body. He entered Big momma Lucy's room, kneeled, and dialed the combination in. The file drawer turned green, and the vault popped open with a slow screech.

5

Dawn's Dagger
March/8th/2022

I stood at Big momma Lucy's door frame with my fingers reaching toward the cable wire, then tugging to get his attention. It was as if I were a child again and I was tugging him like those times I wanted to get snacks.

Fritz was hunched down, realigning at the cabinet on one knee like a proposal, but he wasn't taking anyone's hand—he was taking Big momma Lucy's paperwork and money. My Grandmother was recovering from her heart attack—and he was stealing from her.

My face flushed pale,

"What are you doing?" I asked.

Fritz's blue eyes gleamed, his breath plummeted, and he kept digging with his chin down.

"I'll explain later, Phillip," he replied, his eyes bounced at my brown skinned face and back to the cabinet, "this is grown-up stuff that I have to handle for your gram."

I let go of the cable wire and folded my arm. "Okay, but who told you to do it," I replied. "And why do you have your shoes on Big momma's carpet?"

Suddenly, the doorbell electrified the tension-filled house, and I had a feeling that the bell saved us both.

Fritz froze, his nose bounced toward the door, and he stared like a guilty dog. The sweat on his temples poured out and the veins in his eyes looked like red beetroot.

"I'll get that," he muttered while straightening his wrinkled shirt.

I raised my palm to block him from standing up.

"Nah, I got it," I responded.

I walked out of Big momma Lucy's room into the spacious living room, I buzzed the door, waited for the person to walk up, and to my surprise, it was a curvy brown woman. Her skin was moist like droplets of fresh flowers; she had thin drawn eyebrows, high cheekbones, and a wide head shape with a single strand tucked behind her Diamond-stud on her ear lobe. The hallway smelled like coconut and honeysuckles. She wore black leather pants and red high heels that made her look as tall as a Macy's mannequin. She had red lipstick around her lips without a smudge. Long brown curly hair that tickled her shoulders. She stared at me without saying a word, her face clinched, she blinked three times in a row, and her lips parted.

"Phillip?" she said. She squeezed her purse handle, looked downward at her Jimmy Cho heels.

She took a deep swallow,

"I'm Dawn," she said. "I'm here to tell y'all about me and your stepdad, Fritz."

"What about him?"

"Is Lucy home." Her eyes shook, she leaned closer towards the door and peeked into the house.

"No, She's at the Presbyterian."

Dawn dug into her purse, and at that moment I noticed that her wrist was red as if someone squeezed her by both arms. She extended her right arm, holding a piece of gold and unraveled her fingers. The gold wedding band was gleaming in the center of her palm. I lifted it and held it in the light. Ivory's name was engraved on it along with the year Fritz, and she got married in script.

Dawn's face squeezed as if she were nervous. She placed her red nails across her left arm and hunched over like she was about to be sick.

"I know all about your mother, Ivory," she said,

"he aint no good. He has done a whole lot of sneaky things to your family—I mean we—I'm so sorry, Phillip."

"How did you get this ring?"

"I took it while we were in the motel—the Super Galaxy—that cracked out hell hole."

My skin buzzed, my face lowered, my eyes were still, and the color drained from my cheeks. I turned my neck to the back of the house, and at an angle, I saw Fritz forcing stacks of folders into a black Dunlop racquet bag with white words. He used that bag as a conversation starter to get to know white folks in Bed-Stuy, but at that very moment he was taking a backhanded swing at our whole family. He was as good as Venus and Serena—metaphorically of course backhanding us like we were green furry balls from the field.

Each of Dawn's eyes looked like glass as she stood there. She squeezed her Christian Dior leather purse handle with both hands.

"He's a sociopath—somebody that would do anything to get what he wants—He always gets it," she uttered with a vengeful voice "He won't get what he wants this time." She stared towards her stomach. Her eyes bounced from her stomach to me, and she spread her fingers through her blouse. "It's my turn to get what I want—it's my choice and we are going to be safe this time." Her fingers spread and rubbed her stomach like it was a crystal ball.

My face went pale and there was no noise except air creeping in from the roof door.

Her brown eyes darted, and she took a step forward with body shivers.

"We met ten years ago. It was the fourth of July, and you were wearing a blue Germany jersey, blue jeans and Jordan's. You had rainbow cotton candy and a soccer ball. You were so cute back then with your little fat cheeks. I was by the beach with my best friend Savannah. She is my family—she cared for me before I lost myself to him—I regret letting my friend see me become this unhappy person. —I'm leaving that Elf looking son of a bitch and Ivory should too—If he shows his true colors on you or your grandmother best lawyer up, okay?"

I nodded. I understood what she meant by leaving, just didn't know what she meant by lawyer up because Fritz was our family. The fuck was I supposed to do? Sue him for stealing? who is going to help me tie my tie on my way to court.

Dawn sucked air into her nostril, she gave me a

half hug and walked down the steps. Her red high heels clicked on the steps, and it sounded like she was walking on daggers.

That was the day that Dawn warned my whole family that he was a monster. See the thing about the mistress is that they know things that the family would never know—could never know. They serve the real monster deep down inside of a man. Even though mistresses are typically condemned, they are the keeper of secrets that we aren't privy to. Information that my mother and grandmother should have known before we accepted him into our family. My mother wouldn't have married him if she knew what he was doing.

6

Karma

March/12th/2022

The morning after, I heard Bulky garbage cans topple down from outside. I reached over to my curtain, and I saw Fritz being pushed out of a moving car with his T-shirt stretched into strings. His pale skin was rash red, and his head was swollen in the front and side. He buckled down on one knee, walking on his kneecaps and reaching with his lanky forearm. He had a faint movement as he crawled over black pavement. He lifted and then collapsed at the curb like a drunk person who couldn't stand anymore. He lifted once more, grabbed onto a garbage can chain to keep himself up and wobbled into the yard gate. A big stout man walked over, grabbed his neck like an owner who wanted to discipline a mutt and tossed him into the stairs. He stood over Fritz and punched him repeatedly in the spine. The loud assault sounded like skin drums. With each punch landing, his flabby back wobbled, his neck snapped back, and blood splattered in a drippy burgundy line.

"I'm not done yet," the man shouted while slamming his knuckles into Fritz's head.

He was a Latino gang member, a bunch of tattoos on his neck, skull, and fingers. He was about six feet, half balding wavy hair and a thick beard that looked like it had been braided and taken out. He wore a blood-stained wifebeater, baggy black slack pants with a leather belt in the loop. He looked like a crooked narc, but he aint have any weapons on him and he wasn't law abiding.

I ran down the steps, skipping two and three at a time, to the lobby and then outside. The man loosened his fingers; his knuckles looked like a skin rash straight across.

"Ayo Pablo," he yelled something in Spanish, "pop the trunk and get that."

"Iight Osane." he uttered.

They looked dangerous, like on some mob shit, but they were all Hispanic. Slick, disciplined motherfuckers with nice clothes.

Fritz reached toward the door and Osane stepped on his fingers so hard that you could hear bones snap. Fritz's hand went limp, and he screamed with his mouth wide like a dentist visit. Osane squeezed his neck while punching him in the head with blunt force. His knuckles slammed over several times before he stopped. Fritz spat out a string of blood that landed like maple syrup on pancakes. Real thick and nasty.

Lil Tony retrieved a scratched up black Glock from out of his trunk. It was next to a spare tire and a box of Chardonnay. He grabbed it by the handle, sped with his head low and handed it over to Osane. The gun looked heavy as if it had one in the head already. One in the head meant that the ratchet wouldn't jam once you squeeze the trigger. Osane stood with his chin up, he rubbed the Glock-thirty against his black slacks then brashly shoved it into Fritz's temple.

"You was the biggest drug dealer in Brooklyn, and now you are stealing from Merlo's son! Fritz you bitch ass nigga! you hear me." He shouted with the cold gun hole imprinting a ring on Fritz's pink skin.

Osane wasn't related to Dawn, he wasn't doing it for her, or clout or women's empowerment. Fritz had so much beef that something else caught up to him— something so treacherous that related to my real father's death and although Osane caused a crowd to watch, he didn't hold back. It was a public beatdown for all to see. It's strange how life works, how everything you've done can come back around.

*

At the Liberty Jet airport, Dawn wore her blue uniform with her collarbone showing in a V-shape. She had white choker around her neck, two hoop earrings and her hair dangling down her backside with brown tips. She was sitting at the concession chair, picking at a plate of onion rings and daydreaming of children's names. She dipped the onion ring into tartar sauce and bit slowly. She had her phone at her cheek listening to her best friend chatter.

Melvin, the custodian pushed the rolling trash bin while walking from the T.S.A private room. He had a low cut, with a part that looked like it was from some fancy clippers. He had big brown biceps and tattoos on his fist. He swept trash into his metal dustpan while glimpsing at her.

"Hey Dawn." He uttered while holding his broom to his stomach.

She glimpsed over her shoulder, rolled her eyes, and looked away into the large window with the wide blue sky. There were no planes with turbulence, but her body shook. Her onion rings felt like they were causing a gassy feeling in stomach. She pushed the paper plate and kept her shoulders slack.

"Girl, Melvin just said hi to me" She whispered into the phone, "Ughh, I hate that he looks so good."

"Girl, y'all need to talk." Savannah responded. while her child was making rattling noises in the background of the phone. "Give him a chance, girl."

"No, Fritz would kill me and Melvin."

"Uh, Unn, girl You aint never going back to Fritz—Remember when he hit you with an umbrella in Sunset Park and the damn traffic cop tried to break it up and he beat both y'all asses—if you ever get back with him, I'll fight you myself." Savannah made suckling noises in the background of the phone, then kissed her son Dayton with a wet smooch.

Dawn's shoulders dropped,

"You don't know Fritz like how I know him." She uttered back and then sipped her white and blue straw with cherry coke inside.

"No, all dumb bitches say that."

"Maybe I should give Fritz another chance—he is the father of my child."

"Bitch, He's married." Savannah snapped.

"Don't throw that in my face, Savannah—I only told you that because I thought you would understand the situation."

"Understand Ivory?" she snapped. "Do you even know what kind of bitch Ivory is—she is a jail bird—she is doing time for murder—bitch you want to be her next victim?"

Dawn was a thick two-hundred-pound woman, but when she was a child, she got bullied for having barbwire braces. She still feels the effects of being a bony preteen who got pushed around by kids younger than her because she let Savannah tell her what to do and she is only five Feet tall. Dawn was bigger than most men too, but she would cave in if there were aggressive enough.

She never wanted to be involved in people's marriage's so whenever Savannah mentioned Ivory, she was willing to listen.

Dawn opened a cup of fruit and picked up a grape with a stem attached,

"You right, I've been so reckless," she uttered "I love you girl because you always tell me the truth about myself."

Planes looked like missiles sometimes when they landed, and while Dawn daydreamed, she thought about Melvin's missile. He was a war head, for sure, dangerous for any woman. Thirty-two-year-old young man who worked hard and never had drama at his job.

She took her girlfriend's advice and asked Melvin for a ride home.

*

At Twelve, Melvin walked out of the silver turnstile with a brown book bag on his back. The bag had a Gatorade bottle in the net pocket. They stood side by side and there was a major height difference. He was candy bar brown skinned, tattoos that looked wild and exotic and had 360 waves that spun with square line-up, a part and a coily beard that covered his throat. He was the most handsome man she'd seen in a long while.

"What's the bag for." Dawn asked while smiling.

"I'm getting my G.E.D." He uttered back. "Mostly be studying in-between my cleans."

"Oh, that's good." Her eyes lit up as she stared at his arms but then she was taken back because she knew there was no chance.

Things were awkward at first with Melvin because he was such a gentleman. He kept his face on her brown eyes and didn't glimpse at her breast like most men in the Liberty blue airport. Even the supervisor Roger had a thing for checking her out, which was against policy rules, but he still did it. Dawn's heels clicked against the marble floor until she reached terminal five, and while she walked, people in the airport watched to see who she was. A white couple from Turkey asked her for directions, and she pointed them toward the terminal with the white and gold train called the Zipline. It could get you to the city in less than ten minutes. Dawn and Melvin arrived at the last terminal and then the exit. They were outside next to the men who landed the large planes, walking near the steps with the glass doors that open from the top down. They looked like a power couple coming out of the airport together, but she made sure to keep her distance just in case someone saw her and him driving away. At first, she was nervous walking side-by-side with him, but once they reached the parking lot, they got word from the loudspeaker that Plane M-45 had some smoke coming from its right wing. She wasn't nervous after that. Work always made her snap back into her desk duties. Miles away, where the plane was, there was heavy grey smoke dispersing into the boundless sky.

"I hope Julie off lined up the plane." Dawn uttered. "Julie is so damn slow."

Melvin looked over and smiled,

"You are clocked out Dawn" he uttered "the whole airport is about to go up in flames, you know black women get things done."

They walked to his parked car in the airport lot. He

had a silver Hyundai with rusty paint on the door lining. A large dent in the passenger door that looked like a ram spearheaded it. It had a missing hubcap on the back wheel, the rest were silver, and the wheels looked partially flat while parked. She opened the door, sat in the polyester seat, and it had a stale dip.

Dawn thought about Fritz's rentals, which were always clean and stable. She sat in the seat with her hands crossed. Her eyes paced side-to-side. She wanted to ask Melvin why he didn't use his employee discount on rentals but did not want to offend him on their first date.

Melvin looked over,

"You smoke? he asked. As he turned the engine on, the lights in her head lit up too. Dawn smiled "yup, I smoke just like that burning M-45 plane, probably not the most suitable joke for work though, but that's what I like to do." She stretched the seatbelt across her chest, and it clicked. Once she heard the click sound, her face became woozy because she remembered that she couldn't smoke.

Melvin backed out of the spot, his forearm had some fine hair and tattoos that looked like they were gang related.

"We can go get some bud tonight, if your down."

Melvin uttered.

Dawn folded her legs,

"—I kind of have a man—its compli—it's complicated."

Her iPhone was on her lap face up. She had a selfie of her and Savannah in the background hugging in front of a large baby shark birthday cake. While the car was moving, her phone buzzed like barber clippers over and over. The screen was bright, and the name Kate popped up with sporadic messages. Dawn's chest trembled, she unfolded her legs and put the password into the phone,

"Someone tried to murder my brother again," Kate wrote. "He is at Brooklyn hospital, if you are involved or did something to make this happen then don't come here! contact the police."

7

The real Ms. Clayed

March/13th/2022

Melvin's car squeaked at the wheel when he met a traffic light. Then he imploded with speed, swerving around a red Pontiac that was in head of him and leaving it in dust clouds. His car had a busted taillight, but it still signaled correctly enough not to get tickets. It made a clicking noise and then he sped once more. Dawn had a face full of moist saltwater, she stuffed a tissue into her nose and shook because the thought of her losing her child's father made her sick. Not sick like a cold either, sick More so like quitting heroin and your body getting the chills. Electric chills, that's what her love for Fritz was and it wasn't illness that she could survive. She thought about him possibly dying and couldn't leave him. She thought about Ivory being behind bars for at least five more years. She thought to herself maybe she's lucky that Ivory wasn't seeable.

She'd never run into her or anything, so maybe their love could work if he survived.

Dawn's screen lit up, her best friend texted her saying that she hopes she is having a good time with Melly-Mel and Dawn closed the screen.

*

Melvin was a great driver. He arrived on the circular driveway of Brooklyn hospital and turned over to give Dawn a half hug. He didn't ask her any questions or force himself into her business, but his eye contact was different. He just held the steering wheel with his left, bit his nail and looked through the windshield.

Dawn pushed the car door, and it sounded like a briefcase opening. She dropped her tissue on the concrete and her eyes bounced as she walked into the revolving doors at the hospital. Her heels clicked over the carpet. She stopped at the front desk with her chest bouncing uncontrollably. She put her palms on the desk, picking up the pen attached with a string.

The lady at the front desk pointed towards a mask for her to wear. Dawn put it on. She signed the logbook as Dawn Clayed instead of Dawn Spaige, which was her way of assuring that she got to see Fritz. She fidgeted while panicking, fanning herself and stumbling over her fragmented muffled words. She pulled her white choker off her neck and her body bounced.

"I work at the airport, Liberty blue, I'm Fritzen Clayed's wife and I heard that my husband was stabbed and shot or something in Brevoort."

The lady at the desk offered her a cup of water from the machine with the aqua blue jug that looked like a plastic turban. She poured it into a paper cup, pressing the blue tab until the water overflowed onto her wrist.

The lady at the front desk stretched out her index to point towards the half empty waiting room.

"Wait this way." she uttered.

"I need to see my husband now" Dawn whispered softly while squeezing the cup.

"Wait, which one of you are Mr. Clayed's wife." The lady at the desk replied. She pulled in the sign-in sheet and read it with a look of confusion.

"What?"

"He has his family in the waiting room already." The lady said while rolling her eyes.

Dawn's chest bounced. She thought about Ivory first, which was terrifying, so she backed out into the lobby between the glass. She leaned over a potted plant and felt herself about to vomit into the stiff soil.

She opened her phone to text Fritz, while peeling her uniform sleeves and walking through the automatic door.

Her eyebrows scrunched, she took a deep swallow and kept her chin down in an embarrassed way. She turned to the lady at the front desk and gave her a fake smile, she walked over beyond the white wall, to the vending machine and peeped her head out. There were a dozen metal chairs lined up against the white wall, and in the corner directly under the TV was Kate Clayed who is Fritz's sister. There was Me; his stepson, who brought him with the ambulance. But at the corner next to the window, was a beautiful woman with orange hair down to her shoulders. She looked like Rubi Rose, she had brown skin, tattoo's all over her neck and a piercing in her nose. She wore a blue Dolce and Gabbana track suit with white Yeezy's. There was a blue baby carriage at her kneecap with a toy car that lit red. It was Savannah, and her son Dayton in the waiting room. Waiting for what?

Once Savannah saw Dawn, her jaw dropped, and her fingers covered the bottom of her mouth. Her eyes bulged like it was filled with helium and her neck was involuntarily shaky. She placed Dayton into his rocker seat. He was light skinned with sand brown hair. Hazel eyes and short legs just as any baby. But he wasn't just any baby. Savannah stood up to block the baby with her behind and tears came rolling from her large emotion-filled cheeks.

"Dawn, girl I love you. I should have told you about Dayton's real father— it wasn't Ishmel. I lied to you and to him. I'm sorry." She glimpsed toward the security wearing an Allied uniform and her eyes bobbled like she was reading the room. "Girl, you remember when I was homeless and you let me stay at your apartment on Throop—he gave me money for my mother's Kemo, then one thing led to another, but I see that now he was only trying to come between our friendship,"

"Who's he?" Dawn walked over aggressively, and she stopped at the metal seat with her hands shaking "Who the fuck is he? Who is he? huh!" She stood inches away from her friend with the cup in her hand.

Savannah held her forearm out to prevent her from being hit in her face.

"Fritz!" She responded, "Me and Fritz was fucking while you were at the airport," Her eyelids squeezed. "I didn't have nobody, my mother was in Kemo—,"

Dawn threw the paper cup forward, and the water splashed into Savannah's face with a stretching effect. Dawn lunged forward, kicking, and clawing at her friend's disgusting face. Her right hand was yanking that orange weave while the left was swinging and slamming her bare knuckles into the back of her head. Over and over, her red knuckles pulverized Savannah's head and the brutal impact made a thump noise. The security guard pulled her from the back and slipped on the water in an agile way. Nurses, the front desk lady, and other hospital workers in white stood up and tried to help Savannah who was hunched-back beaten. She had rows of braids underneath her weave, and her cheeks looked puffy. Her nose ring was torn, her track suit was stretched by the hoodie and stained with blood. Her orange weave was spread across the floor in chunks that looked like tumbleweed. While fighting, the baby rocker slipped off the seat and Dayton slammed face down on the hospital floor. He had a cry that sounded like an ambulance truck from far away.

The chaos in the waiting room caused so much commotion that the police were deployed from a nearby food stand.

8

The cover-up

August/14th/2022

The sun crept through the cracks of the open door. Dawn walked into the tattoo shop, her face was clear of make-up, she had her long shaggy hair in puff ponytail and tucking her lips into her mouth. While there was silver sunlight around her, she looked like she had been in complete darkness for days. She had her hands in her pockets while stepping onto the shop's welcome mat with her black UGGs. At the store entrance, there were thousands of manga tattoo galleries with red and orange. The one that caught her eyes were the flesh peeled zombies, vampires, Japanese lotus buds and Dragons with open wings that looked like a bat's wings. There were framed skateboard bumper stickers on the walls, photos of famous rappers standing with the shop owner. He liked to smoke hookah, so he was holding his silver hookah pen in most of the photographs.

Dawn yanked out her case for her air buds, picked them out of each earlobe and placed it inside of the magnetic part. At each side of the tattoo shop, the machines were buzzing like vibrating drills and it made her ear tingle. Whistling vibrations, ink in her nose, but she walked inside staring at the walls.

There was Honcho on the left side, wearing a green apron, with a fresh fade on the side of his afro. He had an Afro like Lonzo ball, so people would call him Lonzo. He was a short man, with light green eyes and a protruding jaw. He was leaning into a brown-skinned client. Writing across his rib with ahis tongue sideways, deep focus as if he were doing surgery. At the far end, far, far, far end of the shop was the boss Enlil. He had his black pen shading a man's stomach and bopping his head to some of Future's old music.

"Stick talk that stick talk" the music blasted.

Dawn's eyes were moist red, she was sniffling, while rubbing her nose, but it seemed more emotional than a common cold. She pressed her shoulder blade against the wall, and the lights shut off. She turned around quickly and slapped the light switch right back on.

"I'm sorry," she uttered with all the attention on her. She looked a mess, she wasn't keeping herself up like she normally did, but she was still a beautiful enough face to make the fella's smile and giggle.

"Nah! you good shorty!" a man wearing a Louis Vuitton bucket hat yelled across the room. She stood side by side with her boyfriend Melvin, locked her fingers with him like a seventh-grade crush and kissed him.

Enlil, the shop owner, lifted a single brow, he had a narrow nose as he focused on his tattoo gun, rubbing off the ink with a paper towel, then drawing as if he was dissecting an animal. He had a client in the leather seat lying on his back under a yellow beam of light. Every time the drilling tattoo made that hard skin noise, that client flinched and shut his eyes.

"Dawn, I'll be right with you shorty," Enlil uttered through the loud hip-hop music while bopping his head, "have a seat love." Enlil had a beard like DJ Khaled, a widow's peak on his hairline with big ears.

Dawn sat down on the red bench next to the only person she could trust. Melvin! He was wearing a blue sweater with a Yankee jacket and some blue joggers from Sax-fifth Ave. He had his legs wide open, drinking his protein shake and licking his lips like LL Cool J.

Dawn snatched out her phone and Melvin opened

his bag strap to pull out his heavy engineering book.

"Might as well do some of this," he uttered.

Not only was Melvin still around after the Fritz break-up, but he was a big reason why she didn't break into a million subatomic pieces. There wasn't a bandage in the tattoo shop that was more capable than he was of keeping things together. For Dawn, losing a love and a best friend was something she never thought would happen. But losing a love to a best friend was the stuff that nightmares were made of. Thinking of them swapping spit, her girl bent over getting it doggy style in her apartment! What! Oh hell no. But there was more depression than rage. Not to mention her choice of outfits, some days she wore denim jeans. Dawn hated jeans! She was told by her own mother that she was dressing like an old lady on her period. That's what her earbuds were for, to tune out the noise from her mother. Yes, Dawn was always dressed down, but it didn't matter to her because her man Fritz wasn't around.

She'd often stare at Melvin and rather than cry, she'd let out a goofy laugh and they would hug and kiss with a romantic pause. Then he would squeeze her with his big biceps. He was one of those type of men where you'd be sick and look up and he's there. Pain and agony comes and you can't figure out what to do with yourself and he's there. You need to talk to someone about grief, or life lessons and he's there.

After all the work Melvin put in to completing his G.E.D, you'd think he didn't have enough time to complete a woman, but he did the impossible.

In the mattress, they locked hands, locked eyes while he gave her those hip thrusts from the front. The headrest would shake, her body would stiffen, and her eyes rolled to the back of her head like the undertaker at WrestleMania. He would move his hips as if he wanted to put a baby in her, knocking her stomach upside down and as down and out as she was about the second miscarriage, she would have been even more down to feel him bust a fat warm nut inside of her.

By August 14th, of 2022, Melvin was a student at Livingston community college, working in-between the spines of physics books twice a week, but he still had Dawn's spine as his main priority. And it was marked with Fritz's name. Most of the time he would reject doggystyle on purpose, just because he couldn't stand to see it.

The buzzing in the tattoo shop tickled Dawn's ear, she looked up at Melvin and gave him a soft smooch. His coily mustache hair pricked her lips.

"I love you," their lips stuck together with a delay. And a couple exiting the shop said "ouuu" in a coordinated harmony. Dawn dropped her chin, she smiled, kissed his bicep while sniffing his inner shirt. She stared into his textbook and saw a purple picture of a Quasar.

The tattoo shop smelled like hot Ink, metal and alcohol. Honcho leaned in, wiped the man's rib with a wrinkled paper towel. He leaned his head closer and drew some more ink lines over the man's dark colored blood.

Dawn flinched in her seat, hunched under Melvin's beard and covered her face with a look like she was in pain.

"That rib tat looks like it hurts," she uttered with her lips tight around her teeth.

"Yea, he needs a perc." Melvin responded.

"A perc just to get a tattoo? I might need A Perc thirty for all the pain I'm going to feel in my back." She smiled with a look of fear.

Melvin's lips opened in a white tooth smile,

"Nah, I'll be your perc thirty, I'll make the pain go away," He grabbed her hand and locked his brown fingers with Hers. What a hunk he was. His arms wrapped around her, it smelled like dove lotion and Tom Ford cologne. Dawn scooted closer to him and leaned her head on his shoulder while forcibly locking fingers in a sideway position.

Sketchy Taco was a rookie tattoo artist from Venezuela. He had a wildly cut highlighter green mullet-mowak, a teenage mutant ninja turtles T-shirt on and some open toe Nike slides with furry socks. He walked over to Dawn and Melvin with an offbeat head nod. He stopped at the bench with his tattoo gallery book opened wide. He had black nail polish on each fingernail and a tattoo of a fossil on his wrist.

"Hey, what kind of work y'all need." He uttered while chewing orange gun. While chewing you could see he had a Tongue ring that looked like a marble. He placed the tattoo book in Dawn's lap like a child during Storytime.

Dawn glimpsed at Melvin, she removed her head off his shoulder, sat straight and flicked through the pages with hesitation.

At the back of the shop, Enlil stopped his needle, he placed it on the side of the leather chair, stomped aggressively and grabbed Sketchy by the back of the neck with his black gloves.

"That's my client puto," he shouted. He rolled his

eyes and dragged his collar from the back.

"Dawn, be with you in a sec," Enlil shouted with a smirk, "I know you getting a cover up on your spine so take off ya hoodie and get comfortable shorty."

Enlil pushed Sketchy.

His cousin surely lived up to his name. Sketchy!

Enlil dragged Sketchy into the back of the shop, walked past the bathroom with the yellow light, and vending machine that stole everyone's money. He opened a brown office door and pushed him into a room with shipping boxes and a flat couch with no cushions. Sketchy tumbled backward against the glass desk with the ashtrays. Enlil put his forearm over Sketchy's throat.

"Sketch, it's almost dusk, what I told you about messing with my clients," he grabbed the silver piercing from his eyebrow and his skin turned red.

Enlil's lip tightened around his teeth,

"We have a shipment for Tec-nines and Draco's today, he pointed to the boxes and his eyes bobbled to the back door that was labeled emergency. "That's what I brought you here for, idiot! to move these Guns."

Enlil never sold guns straight up, he ordered parts from all over the United States and brought them together to create ghost guns. Untraceable guns without serial numbers or codes.

Sketchy swallowed his own spit, and his Adams apple shook and there were sweat beads on his pupils.

"What about Honcho?" He uttered back, "you let Honcho work, and isn't it too hot to sell ratchets."

Enlil rolled his eyes and shook his head. He dropped a single needle from one of the piercing boxes, and it sounded like a screw.

"Fool, just load up the truck so we can get the R.S.I off my ass. You know how they been after us since David's death."

"Iight Primo, I'm sorry."

David was the man who everyone feared. If David came to the shop, someone was gone die and since David is dead, and the R.S.I wants new guns, well go figure.

When it was Dawn's turn to get her cover up tat, her eyes bobbled with a hesitant stare. She pulled her arm out of her purple hoodie and walked with a strut to the black and white divider with her hands rubbing her thigh. She sat down on the leather seat, reaching for her shirt to take it off. Her eyes glimpsed at the saran wrap, and she always liked being wrapped in saran after her tats were done, but this time she just wanted to be wrapped with Melvin.

She pulled off her shirt, lifting above her chin, revealing a blue Nike training bra with black straps hugging her brown torso. She laid on her stomach like a woman waiting for a tan at the beach.

"The purple one looks cute," she uttered while removing her coily hair strands off the back. "As long as I can't see the name anymore."

Dawn's brown backside was covered in Japanese cloud tattoos. Her brown skin was under the bright beam of light. She had moles, discoloration and birth marks just as any woman. Still curvy, smooth and naturally beautiful. Her mother once told her that her skin was golden, which is why every man acted the way they acted over her.

Enlil sprayed a bottle with a nozzle that looked like a straw. He pulled out a yellow razor and shaved a patch of her spine that had the name Hannah heart Fritzen on it.

The music was blasting, people were chatting, and Dawn was just staring down at her boyfriend's pelvis. She often imagined their amazing sex life, even in public, wishing he'd take the hints and throw her against the wall while chocking her.

9

Hannah

Enlil sat in his seat, prepping with a handwipe. Dawn's curvy body was laid out, her ass upward like a fresh piece of thanksgiving ham. Mm she looked so good laying there. Enlil felt the shadow over his shoulders, he turned his head and smirked with a gap tooth.

"Is this your man?" he uttered. "He looks like Michael B. Jordan in creed, tell him to cool out, we good peoples."

Dawn's eyes broke focus, she glimpsed up at her protector, who looked all macho and serious. She loved that about Melvin, he could be tough and soft when he needed to be. Dawn reached forward and grabbed his big index finger. She'd often see images of black love on the internet but never experienced it because of her violent relationship with Fritz.

"It's okay babe," she shouted over the hip-hop music. "I've known Enlil since elementary, he's not going to stab me too hard,"

"Ayo," Enlil interrupted.

Dawn laughed with swollen cheeks,

"You know what I meant," she replied, "don't even play."

Enlil ripped a tiny plastic bag in half and placed the fresh needle on the gun. The needle bounced up and down like a sowing machine. Enlil clicked his Bluetooth, and some brand-new Travis Scott music shook the speakers. He then dapped some Vaseline on her Brown caramel skin and dipped his gun into a small cap of black ink.

"You ready," he uttered.

In actuality, Dawn wasn't ready to take Fritz's name off her body, or Hannah's, but after her second miscarriage, she had to start fresh or else she would have been in an asylum. Her first miscarriage happened seven years ago, the daughter that they would have had was named Hannah Clayed. Dawn still got flashbacks of dropping down to her knees and bleeding while she was in terminal five. No one knew that she was dealing with so much stress at home, because she was always bubbly and happy at work. She wanted to tell everyone that Fritz caused it, but she covered for him more than she covered for herself. Covered for the abuse, covered for his lies, covered for his cheating and now she was covering up his name tat. Fritz used to hurt her with his words too. He'd sometimes criticize her for being less of a woman because she couldn't cook or bare children.

"Lousy bitch," he once shouted. "Just be quiet when you are around me" and his favorite thing to say was "don't come to my funeral Dawn, because you would be the reason I died with that cooking of yours," his sense of humor was so dark and hurtful, but Dawn made excuses for it. She convinced herself that it was his way of saying he loved her.

In the bedroom, Fritz would explore her curvy body more than he explored anything else of hers. She was comfortable with it because she felt useless to him. He had a wife! He didn't need her unless it was a sex thing. So, whatever, her body had an immediate purpose, and whenever she was around him it reminded her that she had someone to serve. That's the type of woman Dawn was, and the reason why she enjoyed working so many hours at Liberty Blue. Being with him was like her job at the airport, but instead of checking passports, Fritz was a pilot of her body and flew her around and landed wherever he wanted. She enjoyed being on his undisclosed flight, but one thing that

Dawn knew for sure, is that flights get cancelled.

As Dawn daydreamed, she kept her head down and her eyes closed. Enlil was behind her, drawing more lines which changed the name Hannah into a large butterfly wing right above her waistband. Her ass was so large, wide and poked out like a thanksgiving ham on a pan. Yum, and she smelled good like Honey suckles, orchard and coco-butter.

Enlil's tattoo needle drilled into her brown caramel skin, and the noise tickled her spine which made her chin drop against the leather seat.

"I hope no one had their ass on here," Dawn blurted with her head down.

"Nah you good, Dawn," he shouted through the tattoo gun, "we keep it sanitary in my shop,"

"Good,"

"But Dawn, who is Hannah Fritzen?" Enlil pressed down on her skin with his black gloves.

"Well, Hannah, was my unborn daughter and the other name is Fritz, my ex-boyfriend."

Suddenly the lyrics in the music didn't have context, there was just a hard knocking beat and a slow fading effect. The oxygen in the shop went thin, there was a dip in the surface of the floor and Enlil's face lifted with a confused look as if he was lost.

"Wait, Coney Island Fritz?" He raised his muttering voice. The tattoo gun stopped buzzing and his arm retracted to his rib. "He a White dude with blue eyes?"

Dawn turned her chin over her shoulder,

"Yea, wait, you know him?"

Enlil eyes were still, he scooted back out of his chair, dropped his tattoo gun to the edge of the leather seat and tried to get up but knocked down all of his supplies. The saran wrap, paper towels, ink and Vaseline. He pulled Dawn by her dainty wrist. His elbow yanked the USB cord out of his laptop and the music shut off.

Whispers grew loudly and sneakers of the three people began shaking the floor.

"Dawn, you gotta get the fuck out of here," Enlil whispered while hunching.

"Why?" She replied.

"Fritz killed David's brother, and he is a rat!" He whispered through his teeth,

"Nigga what?"

Enlil peeled his gloves off his hand and threw them into the black trashcans full of plastic wraps for needles.

"R.S.I is coming, if any one of the gang members sees you here with that tat, it won't be good for you mama."

Dawn's eyebrows twitched, she turned her pupils toward Melvin and blinked in an awkward way, "Who is R.S.I?" she shouted, "Enlil you know me!" Her body jerked back into Melvin's grasp.

"Which is why I gotta get you outta here." Enlil replied, "Don't come back here Dawn,"

Through the window glass, an orange Camaro with silver rims rolled into an open parking spot that read no standing. It bumped against the sidewalk curb, rattled a little and then parked with its wheels still curved. There was grey smoke coming from the car window, looking like the same smoke that comes out of freezers when you first open them. The windows rolled down and a black man with sand brownskin was in the driver seat with a blunt at his lip. He looked like Pop Smoke, with his long braids and shades. He had tattoos all over his face leading to his neck, a ski mask rolled up into a hat and large fingers squeezing his cellphone. His name was Tripple plat, he was the new street leader of the R.S.I after the death of David.

Dawn stood by the glass lifting her purple hoodie over her head,

"It's just a cover up," she uttered "it shouldn't matter if you knew him and he's a rat or whatever, we broke-up, do your job as a tattoo artist,"

"Sis, just get out of here," he uttered "I can't do you, I just can't."

Honcho, the tattoo artist closest to the window stared at Enlil. Without the music, he heard every word of the argument. He stopped his gun. He reached down into his seat crease and lifted a shiny switch blade handle that reflected like a silver star beam. He placed it back in the seat. Paced back and forth, his eyes dotted toward the window glass, and his eyes were as if he were reading something.

Honcho's story was interesting because he is a dedicated R.S.I member. A street thug who stole from churches, then was disowned by his grandparents to live in shelters. While roaming the streets of East Flatbush, he discovered his passion for train station robberies. Months later, he came in contact with a man who he claimed was like a father to him. Guidance! Guidance was sentence to life for human trafficking and the word on the streets is that he still involved with it.

A few years back, the R.S.I leader made a lucrative street deal for guns and Honcho was appointed by Guidance to work inside the tattoo shop to ensure loyalty to the gang. He recalled the name Fritz, Fritz this! Fritz that! Fritz was one of those shoot first, ask questions later type of situations.

Honcho's black client lifted from the seat, he had an angry eye bulge and a crooked afro.

"Hey," he uttered, and his eyeballs were swollen twice its size, "I don't think my tat is done,"

Honcho's face tightened,

"It's not done, but I'm done my boy," he replied.

"What about my four-fifty and change?"

Honcho pulled off his black gloves, turned the other cheek, opened his booth drawer and lifted his Glock and slapped a magazine into it.

"What about it ya four-fifty and change, you peep steez yet or nah?" Honcho uttered, his face scrunched in an ugly way.

The client stumbled out of the mirror view and

backpaddled out the shop door with a soft whimper, his pants sagging and his shirt hanging like a wash rag.

Honcho walked to the side window, placed all his fingers against the seal, and stuck his head through. He saw Sketchy was down in the alley, moving large brown boxes into the shipping truck. It had the logo for Inky's tattoos on the boxes. A logo that Fritz could have identified to the police.

"Sketch," Honcho shouted, "clip it! It's up! We got a rat in this bitch."

Everyone in Crown heights knew Fritz, although he was a Coney Island native, he put some good people away for major drugs, Trafficking and guns.

Fritz was hiding out for so many years, no one thought that they'd hear of his name again and rightfully so.

IO

Extreme Danger
August/14th/2022

Dawn and Melvin walked out of the shop door. Arrived to his silver Hyundai car on the opposite side of the Shop. Dawn had her eyebrows scrunched cupping her hand with her purse. She felt a sense of electricity in the atmosphere, opened the door and sat fast, while pulling a stick of bubble gum.

"That bullshit got me mad," she uttered.

Melvin sat inside and twisted the key. His car sounded like a dolphin clicking and then it made a vroom.

"Why did you take me here to this piece of shit place," Melvin spoke "he was basically rubbing on your ass the whole time."

Dawn glimpsed at the shop, she turned towards Melvin and grabbed him to prevent him from putting the car in drive.

"Melvin, wait." She uttered while staring through the car window.

From five-hundred feet away, there was little to no traffic, then cars gliding through the block one by one. Through the street view, you could see a fight building through the shops glass. Rumbling walls, Honcho pushed the divider down, holding his gun and barking at particles of spit. Suddenly, he swung so hard with his left while holding his gun with his right. There was an aggressive body tug and chairs being toppled to the floor and Enlil was on his knees, her ass crack showing, tussling with his hoodie over his head and crawling to regain balance.

Tripple plat opened his Camaro door, he jumped over the curb while walking like penguin. He pulled something from behind his back pocket and wielded it across his belly.

"What's going on," he shouted with a look of anger, stepping toward Enlil and holding his weapon with a jittering eye stare.

After a second or two passed, there was just a head nod from Tripple plat and an energetic dash to the window from outside. Then there was a squalling voice and five flocking lightning flashes back-to-back.

Melvin gasped for air, he put the car in drive, he swerved out of the parking spot and drove through a red light with his car wobbling at full speed.

Melvin turned the steering wheel, almost hit a cyclist as he pulled out, but raced through Flatbush Avenue leaving behind a cloud of dust from his exhaust pipe. Flatbush was a place where crime shouldn't have been so brazen. A place where old people, young children and innocent people went to shop and they were all frozen as the shots rang.

Dawn thought about the Spanish people who jumped Fritz in front of his house, then she thought of the tattoo shop and wondered and how they bugged out over her tattoo. She wondered why she fell for him in the first place.

Melvin stepped on the gas, twisted the wheel with speed and turned towards Dawn's apartment on Throop Avenue. She lived in a one-bedroom apartment in a three-family house. It was a grey and yellow building next to a brown tree with long branches that stretched to the street poles. There was a Chinese food store, a McDonalds drive through, a Golden crust and

Applebee's across the street. She wasn't in the mood for food though, more so in the mood to vomit. How could she almost fall for a killer like Fritz? Not only was he a killer, but he was a snitch and he'd do anything it took to avoid prison. He'd even use her if he could.

Dawn got out of the car gasping for air, she opened her purse, put her key inside the lock, wiggled and gave it a hip knock. She walked into her apartment door and squeezed the faucet for water.

Melvin didn't come inside immediately, he circled the block to see if anyone in an orange car was following him and after a half an hour, his car was low on gas, so he parked it next to a champagne colored Ford focus.

The rest of the night was traumatic for the couple, so they laid in bed and talked for hours about what they saw. The mattress stunk of Popeyes fried chicken. She laid in bed naked with a red box of friend chicken near her thigh, crumbs everywhere. Dawn rolled on her chest and let Melvin rub the half-done tat with alcohol pads, but it seems as if he was angry while he doing it.

Melvin reached for her hand, squeezed her fingers and tightened them while holding them over the bedsheets. Each of his nails were oil with chicken grease,

"Dawn, we are going to pretend we didn't see that," his eyes shook, "promise me! every time we dig into your ex-boyfriend's life there's something,"

Dawn lifted herself, her nude body felt warm in his lap, she lifted his greasy finger, she held it to her mouth and sucked it seductively,

"I promise," she uttered with a whole finger chocking her words, "I love you daddy."

"No, no could have got ourselves involved in that bullshit! I'm not trying to get myself involved in that snitch niggas life! I just want to move on with you,"

"you right," she responded, letting go his finger and pulling back the sheets. He was hard. She sat across his kneecap, wrapped her arms around his shoulder and kissed him with her cherry flavored lips while jacking his hard dick. The universe slowed down every time they kissed, but this time, there wasn't any light speed.

She had her hair under his beard, face across his large chest and her long tongue running down his sternum to his rigid six pack.

As Melvin held her, he questioned if she was worth it. Not blurting the words to her but interrogating himself inside of his head. The warmness of her body felt good, but sometimes he questioned if Fritz made her cold.

After a half an hour of fucking, Melvin's face appeared drowsy. He wrapped his arm around Dawn and there was a peaceful silence in the bedroom. While he was asleep, Dawn lifted her eyelids and got on her knees to crawl backwards. Her legs jiggled out of bed and onto her blue carpet. She tip-toed into her pajama pants and buttoned her pajama shirt to her collar.

Melvin was snoring, his large chest bounced up and down at a slow pace. She stared at him as she reached into her cluttered closet. She put her arm into her light purple coat sleeve and tippy toed out the shadow black door. She walked to the front of the apartment, then sat down on the stoop. Her fat booty butt was freezing cold, so she stood up again and started to roll her weed. After minutes of smoking, the weed went straight to her head. Dawn leaned closer to the door crack, turned around to the lobby frame and saw the doorbell directory. Her name on the directory read Dawn Clayed. When she sucked the smoke, the weed went straight to her head again and she could see Fritz helping her get that couch into the apartment, He also threatened the misogynistic landlord, telling him that they were married, and he would whip his ass over her. Fritz was the only person to ever stand up for her when it came to professional settings. It always seemed like people took advantage of single black women, but not when Fritz was around. He knew how to be sociable, but serious and stern. She mindlessly started to walk in the direction of his house, saying to herself "what am I doing, girl stop" but her legs couldn't stop. Only wearing flip-flops, a coat and thin pajamas that weren't suitable for cold windy nights, she got on the bus smelling like chicken grease and cum.

II

Nuclear Love

August/15th/2022

Dawn walked through the pathway, her face and cheeks had dark spots, flesh still jittery of nerves. Brevoort projects, the big brown sign across the street. Her coat hoodie over her head, her hands in her pajama pants pocket while the wind swayed through her ankles. The ground was full of plastic cans, leaves and dumped plates of food. Her brown eyes glimpsed at the depleted projects buildings and her stomach flipped as if there was a sense of the earth shifting before a quake. Every window was bared up, every building chipped with brick and pale from rain. She saw a couple at eye level, and she paused with fear; fear of seeing Fritz with Savannah. That bitch! She walked through the projects where there were glassless entrances, graffiti on doors and low-spirited adults hanging out in large groups. On the other end, there were bright-eyed teenagers chatting loudly, shouting and ripping about each other's clothes. Hip hop music being played at full volume coming from some portable speakers next to a blue fixie bike, a brown Pitbull barking with a white bandana wrapped around its neck and a bouncing basketball dribbling.

There was a trail of bushes at every street pole. Cricket noises, she kept her eyes down, jaywalked over and there was Fritz's luxurious Brownstone house. The reddish-brown exterior looked like it was made of chimney bricks. His building was called Brownstone, just like the ones in Harlem that she had seen when she was a young child. There was a large police presence, so much navy blue, and gold badges that it looked like the president was coming. Dawn walked over to a barricade and her fingers curled around the chippy wood. A blue and white police truck was making a beeping noise as it backed out from underneath a red tree and swerved onto the long road.

There were dozens of police wearing body cams, military veterans holding weapons while standing on the sidewalk. There was a large white forensic tent, thousands of white detectives, and generals standing on the stoop coming in and out of the building. The same building that Fritz lived in, his son and Big momma Lucy.

A detective with grey eyes walked toward Dawn with his palms open like he was about to push an open door.

"Excuse me miss, you have to get back on that side of the street," he uttered, he pointed towards the curb and his gold badge was shining in her face like a Medallion. Dawn's finger unraveled, she took a deep breath and swallowed her back talk. A big soldier trailed her while hugging his AR-15.

Dawn stood a thousand feet away, on the opposite side of the street. Her feet planted side by side in the sidewalk of Brevoort projects. Time was in slow motion, her bang blowing in the wind and revealing her eyebrows. She stared upward to Fritz's window to see if his curtains would shake or light up with a dim brightness, but it didn't. His room window was the center left with the royal blue curtains that looked like silk, but there were no vibrant lights. She felt like a fiend waiting to get their fix, but she wasn't a drug addict, she was worse; a love addict. At least a fiend wanted to get high, Dawn was a black queen who was addicted to love, love don't get you high, it takes you low.

Dawn took a deep breath as if she was doing some yoga. She opened her purse strap and pulled a strip of gum out of its wrapper. She heard some squeaky wheels that sounded like an old stop-and-shop shopping cart. Directly behind her, she saw a frail black man who wore denim overalls with an off-white thermal underneath, he had shoes with zig-zag gaping holes on the front and his toes sticking out like turtle heads. He was digging into the dumpster while standing on top of a black milk crate. From the side view he looked disfigured and contorted like an oblong. He had wide eyes that looked like a fish out of water with a skinny fish bone face and a mouth that shook like he was chewing something.

"Excuse me, Sir," Dawn shouted, "you know anything about what happened here?"

The man turned over shivering, he slammed his foot against the concrete and grabbed his milk crate. He placed it back into the shopping cart, hunched and pushed his handle towards her. Cling! Cling! Cling! The wheels knocked against the concrete until he arrived at Dawn.

"Sweet pea, I am Michael Levy from Jackson Mississippi," he slurred. His lips were purple, he stared at her with a look as if he was frozen. "In Jackson, we would call that dere a murder case, I don't do no murder Ms. Lady." Mike's elongated finger pointed into the rooftop.

Dawn glimpsed up and saw a dozen soldiers on the roof surrounding something large, but it was hard to see because of the clouds of darkness. On second glimpse, she squinted her eyes and saw another white tent that was swaying in the wind.

"Murder?" Dawn uttered with her eyebrows lifted. She walked closer to Mike and could smell the strong alcohol on his tongue. Wooo! He stunk! His clothes smelled like buttery popcorn and mildew, his face was full of flesh marks and his fingers were black at the tips.

Dawn held her breathe as she spoke,

"Sir, do you know anyone named Fritz?"

Mikes smiled with his missing teeth and spoke in a raspy voice, "The master, yep, Mr. Clayed is a serious mane, when he tells me don't come around digging in his dam trash bin, I listen to him the furst time."

Dawn's eyes bobbled,

"What?"

She stared at the black gate where the trash bins used to be. The police had taken everything from the front lawn, including the bricks surrounding the garden, the hose and uprooted every flower in search of buried evidence.

"Do you know where he is?" Dawn whispered with

a desperate eye twitch, walker closer and closer.

Mike lifted a brown stained Dunkin coffee cup from his shopping cart basket and shook it. It was full of twigs with rotten leaves and Pennies.

Dawn shoved her fingers into the bottom of her coat pocket, lifted a bunch of dimes and nickels along with a wrinkled dollar bill. She dropped it into his cup.

Mike's tongue snapped against the roof of his mouth, his jaw gaped opened and thick veins popped out of his bottom lip.

"Mr. Clayed. Mmhmmm the master he is, he is helpin da policeman get his old gal back,"

"Who? Ivory?"

"Yep, Mrs. Ivory Clayed has been at Obbit Thorn maximum security penitentiary for sixteen-seventeen years, he is cooperating with them detective folks,"

Dawn's eyes became as glossy as a marble floor. Rolling tears almost sliding down her eyelids. Her brown pupils were the same color as Henny, but they mirrored the red and blue police car lights. Her lips trembled, she used her fingers to pluck her mouth and stood there rolling the paper around the chewed gum.

Mike tried to get her attention, but she stared into the hypnotizing bright lights and kept doing the same rolling finger motion.

12

Michael Levy

August/15th/2022

From Fritz's room window, to the living room or even the kitchen window, I've seen Mike in my community for as long as I can remember. Never spoke to him about anything relating to anything because he was a drunk. He knew things about my stepdad. I wish I did. I wish I talked to him a long time ago so I could know. He used to push his shopping cart, stop at a tree, and lean on it while ranting but I never gave him direct eye contact because he reminded me of Jeepers Creepers. Ugly and scary.

I was six years old, sitting with a stretched seat belt. Extending my arm while my fingers spread to the car floor.

"my Ipod!" I screamed "it fell, because you're driving fast." Fritz's face scrunched, His hand reached over, he lifted my Ipod off the floor mat, then he pulled down the sun visor, and I could see the words on the screen again. We arrived at Williamsburg, Brooklyn, and we saw dozens of people dressed in black blazer suits with white shirts. It was an orthodox Jewish community. Fritz was parked at an empty dirt-filled lot with dog poop everywhere. He unfastened his belt and got out of the seat with a fast-paced bounce. My eyes bobbled toward the windshield, the light green car freshener swung back and forth, and the door made that ding noise. He lifted me and sat me on top of the slanted car hood. He had a 98' Chevrolet back then, blue with orange stains and fading color that looked like a hippie shirt.

His attention was focused on the empty plot, he had a wide grin across his cheeks like a countryside clothesline.

"What do you see, sport?" he uttered while rubbing the top of my nappy afro

I looked around, there was a couch that bled foam, trash bags, wood pieces, a small scruffy grey cat with his head inside a jagged tuna can, and dog poop. I shrugged my shoulders, stared into Fritz's eyes.

"This is just wet dirt."

"No, little guy, this is an opportunity," he said, "one day, this will be mines, I'll build a club and make millions of dollars," He rubbed my head, smiled, and sat next to me with his hands in his Levi pocket.

An elderly white couple stopped at the curb. They weren't Jewish, or orthodox but had property in the area. They walked towards us, and the elderly man looked like as old as Joe Biden. He was wearing a yellow cardigan with brown slacks and white sketchers. His wife had a grey-haired bun and a long red dress that looked like she was the virgin Mary. The man held a leash with a bouncy, black-coated German Shepherd on its end walking in circles. The dog was so aggressive that it nearly lynched itself while jumping toward me. The man just kept eye level with Fritz. He huffed hard like a heavyset person on a treadmill, stretched out his arm for a handshake, and smiled with an elderly dimple. He smiled so hard that his hairline pushed backward, and he had green veins in his temple.

"Hey buddy, I've been trying to get this property for two years," he said, "there is no way you'll get this one, the damn nigger lady who owns it is fierce; she isn't giving it up, we have contacted her with big offers, and she shot us down every single time."

Fritz's face grimaced, he folded his arms, and his eyebrows dropped to their lowest point. "Wait, how big?"

"Big-Big," The man said, he pulled a brown cigar out of his pocket and lit it till it puffed ashy orange. "More money than any nigger bitch should have, that's for sure. Her name is Lucile, she is such a bitch that I named my mutt after her. Isn't that right babe?" He rubbed on his scruffy dog and it smiled with wide nostrils.

His wife laughed dramatically, she put her hand on his shoulder and the Botox looked like her face ripped.

Fritz turned away and smiled then placed his heavy hand over my nappy afro.

"Time to dash sport," he uttered with an awkward smile. My seat belt clicked, and we drove away from the lot. I looked at the mirror; the beastly hound barked at our car mute and kept its wolf-dog eyes on me. Maybe because I was small, it thought it could take me for lunch. It lunged forward, and its owner just stood there smoking his cigar with snowstorm eyes.

"the dog name is Lucile like grandma?"

"no, don't listen to him." Fritz uttered softly, he had an eye twitch as he drove.

When we got back to the Brevoort project, I saw

Mike standing in the middle of the traffic, he wore a bucket hat with pictures of pink shrimp knitted on it. He held a bottle of brew in a paper bag while walking with a busted kneecap. He walked in the opposite direction of incoming traffic screaming. I thought Mike was just a street bum with alcohol shingles, but he told me that he has serious anxiety and a speech disorder from his childhood. The liquor somehow helped him gain enough courage to talk.

13

Coney Island
September/15th/2004

Mike originally was from Mississippi, he traveled to Manhattan first, with a one-way ticket, some shoe polish, some leather loafers and a hefty bag full of blazers and trousers.

Back in September 2004, in the crime filled neighborhood of Coney, Mike spent weeks in Brighton Beach. A place for him was a dream come true. After getting discovered for his street art, he moved into a nice bedroom north of Brighton with Nigel. The house he stayed in was not too far from the amusement park, so he could see from the bard window, he could see the B-train roaring above with fire on its wheels, screeching until it stopped for the station. He could also see people in the shadowy ransacked neighborhood. At night you could see the big red Coney Island Ferris wheel spinning twinkles in the background.

On the corner, Mike used to see Fritz every evening wearing baggy jeans, hoodies and when he showed his face, a patchy beard with needle blond hair protruding from his head. He didn't look like a drug dealer, he looked like a skateboarder.

Mike sat next to the window, chanting the word Master because of his blond hair, his calm body language and slick mind games. Fritz used to sit on a mailbox with his scuffed converse laces dangling. While the other dope boys wore expensive jewelry, Fritz always dressed like a boy who had nothing. He carried a Jansport backpack. He had a black scull hoodie and big headphones around his neck blasting some Jadakiss. The police officers rolled through, their exhaust pipe smoking clouds, and Fritz opened a bag of potato chips and flipped a thumb up to them.

When customers pulled up looking for their guys, Fritz hopped off the mailbox and served them through the window with a charming smile.

The same Coney Island night, Mike was inside the house painting a piece about the dark side of the beach. He flicked his wrist around, drawing an abstract body shaped figure with yellow hair in each painting. It was so dark, sinister and gloomy.

"The master" Mike blurted, standing over the canvas, holding a hand full of drippy paint and throwing yellow colors that stretched with specs and splatters.

Nigel stood in the kitchen, trembling with excitement while munching on a sandwich.

"It's a masterpiece," he blurted, "every one of them are masterpieces."

Nigel stared across the livingroom, full of plastic, there were five pieces of a yellow haired character among the insidious street.

Nigel didn't understand Mike all too well because of his speech impediment. He thought that when Mike shouted "the Master" that it was short for masterpiece.

Nigel's flip phone was full of spit particles. Vein in his temple looked like it pumped oil as he yelled at his secretary.

"My client doesn't have a speaking disorder," he screamed. "I'll just give him drinks girl, he talks better when he drinks and why wouldn't he. Everyone can talk better after a few cups of wine." He stood by the fridge, sipping orange juice out of the carton. He had a half-eaten sandwich on a red plate with a buzzing gnat hovering over a mayonnaise drip. He crushed his last bag of coke, emptied it on his pinky, and snorted it. He had a fixed grin, he buckled his leather jacket and raced to the door.

"I'm going on a witch hunt," he uttered, "I'll be right back after I get that."

"Please stop sniffing that stuff," the secretary on the cell phone uttered. "But, Nigel should I write Mike or Michael Levy on the check?" Nigel licked his fingers as if he had just eaten BBQ ribs, but it was the coke remnants from the dealer across the street. He made suckling noises for each finger and licked his upper lip.

"yum, how about Masterpiece-Mike, that's his new name. Listen Karen, Michael is home. He will be in Brighton for the next few days so when you are ready to send the delivery guys, just send them here to collect the masterpieces." He glimpsed toward Mike standing with his fingers dripping. Nigel's eyesight got fuzzy because the liquor and cocaine hit at the same time.

Mike was tossing yellow paint in the corner, without a brush or ladder, every time he took a step the plastic on the ground made a cracking dent.

Nigel knew that he had something special; like Basquiat. Yes, but gothic dark and grimy.

Nigel loved to get blowjobs from those Coney

Island freaks. He liked the ones with bodies that looked like cottage cheese, fishnets, multi-colored hair weaves and G-strings with dark pubic stubs and Neptune avenue had all of the girls.

Seconds after Nigel finished with the trash bin, he slammed the door and the pot of palm leaves brushed from side to side. The apartment was so quiet that you could hear the refrigerator hum static. The ceiling vent breathed like dragon nostrils and the art on the wall looked like some old animated Jazz. All the equipment in the house sounded like music and the art pieces looked like they moved if you stared at them for long enough.

White folks like Nigel loved black Art, but he could not land any big names because of his janky reputation with mishandling Artist in Harlem.

Mike poked his pupils out of his eyelids into the window glass. He was willing to draw more details of his yellow haired character, but he wasn't in window view. He was in the handball park handing drugs to a young pregnant woman.

The whole street was dark with barely any light

source to see the stucco of brown, red and grey houses. There were five straight buildings that belonged to P-89 Suggs. He was known as a pill slinging kingpin, but nobody ever called him out on it. Women have gone missing under his influence, and the next time you would see them, they were in different states, their hair looking like knotted strings and their eyes looking like they were hypnotized.

The buildings were used for prostitution, and had not gotten maintenance in thirty years. The front doors were boarded up and the addicts outside scratched and clawed at the wood with crowbars. Once the woodblocks were off, the dark rooms would get illuminated by small torches. From far away their lighters looked like lightning bug lights. The windows were glassless, dark, but sometimes you could see the body shape of women getting fucked doggy. Long floppy breast slapping against their stomachs.

P-89 Suggs never got indicted for trapping out of his neglected property because he had corner boys pushing weight for him and they took all the risk.

It was like New Jack City, but real. Junkies in those abandoned buildings shaking back and forth, camping in the sawdust, sitting under asbestos with their jaw rotating like horses eating hay. Junkies walking the streets, hobbling around as if they were on an invisible ellipticals, laughing and rambling to themselves.

14

P-89 Suggs
March/10th/2022

The one thing about P-89 Suggs is that no one has ever seen him. Not even Nigel, or the women he took under their wing. But, alcoholic Mike claimed Fritz; the master, was indeed P-89 Suggs. He ran the whole operation by himself, but fooled others into thinking there was a big boss behind it. It was all a scheme and since Fritz dressed like a homeless skateboarder, nobody expected him to be the head guy. When you thought of P-89 Suggs, you would think of a stylish kingpin, draped in gaudy rose red ruby chains and gold grills. A fat brown cigar, dragging a white mink against the pavement as he walked around in timberland boots. But he didn't exist.

See Fritz was heartless. My friend T.T. was staying over at my house, she listened to me talk about our drama, but everything ended after Fritz stepped to her on some bullshit.

My feet shuffled up the stone stoop, I pushed the lobby door open, and I bumped into T.T. rushing down from my hallway steps.

Her eyes opened wide,

"Phillip," she uttered, "Your stepfather is inside the house tripping and I feel like I'm going to end up exposing him! I can't deal with no grown man screaming at me."

My face tightened, I stepped closer to her and moved out of the doorway.

"Wait T.T., what do you mean?"

She pulled her black head tie off her head, tucked it into her purse zipper and patted her bang down.

"He isn't right in the head," she uttered while straightening her hair. "He kept asking me do I have a connect, I was like what you mean sir." T.T. rolled her eyes and stood like she had a broken hip, "He made me feel awkward, so I left."

T.T. touched the top of my shoulder,

"I wish you were older," she said. "Thank you for letting me chill here, but I can't be up there with your stepfather, I might end up exposing him or fighting his ass." She kissed me on the cheek, her lips were so damn soft and moist. She smelled like Vickie secrets perfume as she walked by. She stepped around me and pushed the center of the door.

As I reached the top of the stairs, my eyes dotted to the apartment door and noticed that it was slightly cracked. My neck turned, and a beam of sunlight shined on top of the hallway wall. Fritz was sitting under the roof steps. He had one arm in his lap, and in the other, he had a Marlboro in between his index and middle finger.

My face went pale.

"Fritz," I uttered with my eyes beaming to the lifeless off-white wall "you started smoking cigarettes again?" I pulled out my ring of keys and tried to put them inside the lock.

Fritz stomped his foot on the dented tiles and dust shook from the flooring.

"Wait boy" He shouted. He reached into his denim pocket, pulled out a red light, and had a premeditated smile like a villain in a movie. There was a box of paint right by the roof that he kicked and made tumble. Fritz opened the roof door wide, and the hinges made a squeaking noise. The door let in a cool breeze, icy bright sunrays into the hallway that made me squint. The car on the roof! It was directly behind him. The luxurious Black glossy car with a receding windshield with a body shape like snakehead and a grove in the front, back and side doors. The headlights of the car looked like bug eyes and it had black wheels with red brake pads. As we stood in the hall, the paint mirrored his angry reflections off the car hood.

Fritz shook his head side to side, he smiled with pure rage, and his temple muscles started to pulsate like he was chewing something.

"Fucking Phillip, you outdid yourself," he shouted and then he kicked the wall leaving a nasty boot scuff. He pointed to me with the red lighter in his grasp, walking and chuckling.

"just when I was about to sell this fucking house, you go and make the shit worthless, ehh! You're going to pay for this you little shit." He put his cigarette in his mouth, his pink lips clamped tightly on it. He used his hand to create a barrier, he clicked it and took a heavy pull. His eyes strained, and his voice became deeper as he puffed.

"A car on my damn roof!" he yelled with a deep voice, "looks like a fucking hurricane accident, what the fuck is this shit." His fingers aimed. "How the fuck am

I going to sell this fucking house."

My eyes bounced back and forth. I wasn't afraid of Fritz, but whenever he raised his voice, my body would always freeze up, and I'd forget what I wanted to say back to him. He stepped closer to me, he wound his hand back as if he wanted to slap me, but his fingers loosened, and he put it in his pocket while trembling.

"you fucking remind me of Merlo," he uttered with the cigarette bouncing at his lip. "When the police grab you up for doing stupid shit like this, I'm not your dad. I'm not bailing you out even if Ivory begs me. Beat it and let me smoke my damn cancer stick in peace." His eyes broke focus with me, but he still had a look on his face like he smelled something putrid. He was the one that stunk, not just because he was smoking cigarettes, but because he was a nasty, foul poor excuse for a human being.

Fritz was going to co-operate with the police, and if that meant throwing me under the cell in exchange for Ivory then so be it. Some kind of Stepfather he was. Maybe Stepfather truly meant that he'd be willing to step on me if necessary. If so, then I understand what that meant.

15

Dawn's Regret

August/15th/2022

Dawn spent hours across the street from Fritz's house. The time was 3:15, She had her shoulders slacked, covering her nose while listening to Alcoholic Mike shout. long lanky fingers in her face, His scent smelled of pissy clothes and strong bourbon as he yapped. He babbled, slurred and threw his head back for another swig. When the wind blew, it pushed his overalls open, and you could see the imprint of his sternum. He spoke in fragmented sentences, pulled out his flask and took delayed sips.

Dawn walked off, feeling her body heat fluctuate so she unzipped the top of her coat, and her brown neck was showing. She was wearing a neckless that Fritz gave her when they flew to Italy for Easter. She back peddled into the large Brevoort residential activity park. There was a concrete chess table at the project's entrance way, so she sat there with her neck hunched.

Dawn's body vibrated, she wiped her nose, her left hand squeezed her cellphone. There were thirty-nine missed phone calls from her boyfriend Melvin. She scrolled down, her sharp blue nails clicked the screen to Fritz's phone number.

She stared at their earlier messages that she left months prior.

"Fritz?" She texted two months ago from a text free app, "I don't care about what you did with Savannah, we can make it work, I'll just handle her and her son, I'll go to the grave with you as the only one for me."

"Dawn what the fuck!" he wrote back, "have you gone insane, you idiot! Get the fuck outta New York you ditsy bitch!"

Fritz only replied once, which made his words crisper, but Dawn vomited her feelings into the message thread like how Alcoholic Mike vomits his bourbon. Even leaving Good morning text, good afternoon and goodnight. While her boyfriend of two months, Melvin was studying engineering, Dawn was defying physics.

Dawn's eyes glimpsed across the street. She examined the luxurious brick house and the gaping hole of muddy soil in the garden tracking the sidewalk. In her mind, she was thinking maybe there was something under the soil like cash or bodies.

She lifted her phone screen, squeezed it and began to type.

"Fritz, this is Dawn, I'm outside," she texted with fast thumbs.

There wasn't any movement from the high curtains.

A short black man with big lips, a nappy beard and lint-filled dreadlocks shook his head, he ate a Cheeto and chewed while sitting in front of Brevoort bench area, near a wild bush shrub.

"Somebody caught a body bag," he uttered and chewed with orange teeth, sucking his fingers and laughing. He said it loud enough for Dawn to hear as if he wanted to start a conversation with her, but she ignored it and kept typing.

Just hearing about the murder made her fingers shake, because she was almost certain that Fritz was behind it. He strangled a mechanic once in Brownsville, dragged the man onto a dangling silver chain, locked it around his neck and shut the shop's gate to make it look like suicide. Fritz knew how to kill people, and he knew how to avoid jail when he needed to, but his best attribute was laying low or twisting a situation to set himself free.

Dawn gasped for air, she opened her phone screen, back peddled toward the green bushes inside the projects and her eyes raced as if she was driving at full speed.

"Fritz why are you avoiding me!" she texted with fast thumbs "Did I do something wrong? Are you mad at me for beating Savannah's ass? I apologize for getting catty, I didn't mean to embarrass you while you were in the hospital."

She waited, but once again there was no reply, so she opened her text free app and texted him through there,

"Fritz are you fucking my best friend again? Yea! you are! You coward! What happened down here? Did you kill Lucy for her property yet? Yea I'll text whatever loose shit I want because clearly you don't care about me anymore. Did you kill your stepson Phillip? Why is everyone out here investigating? I bet you did all of this! You fucking jackass!"

Then she closed the screen. Opened her Instagram and scrolled to his Savannah's page. She was blocked.

Dawn's lip twisted,

"Fritz I'm sorry," she typed at his message thread "There is this man named Melvin who works at my job, he is only a friend I swear to God, but we did some things that I regret. If you care about me, you'll respond to my text, come down here, slap me for betraying you and tell me I can't see him no more."

The screen was in the center of her palm, still motionless, with no alerts but when it vibrated, Melvin's contact came up next to a red and green button.

Dawn pressed the red button, she went back to the text free app and started to type.

"Fritz please," she wrote again, "Melvin is at my house right now, inside my bedsheets, if you love me, you'll go to my house and threaten him, and then you'll say something like it's my fault, I shouldn't have been fucking around with anyone while you were away."

Dawn cried. She moaned in sadness, dropping her phone into her crotch and holding her head up with her eyes shut. Minutes after four, she walked to the bus stop on Fulton. She saw drug addicts, alcoholics, and homeless people. But every one of them was staring as if she had the problem.

16

Ghost of Infamy
August/15th/2022

Dawn walked with her head down, took a step on the curb and she lifted her head. Moist eyes. What a beautiful woman, she was. Too beautiful to be crying over a man. She stared into her window which was still pitch dark. She immediately thought of Melvin, so she glimpsed across the street and his Hyundai was still parked in-between a forest green Ford Mustang and a silver Nissan three-fifty-z.

"We have to get to work" she uttered to herself. She knew that there would be an hour-long argument about her disappearing. Maybe she can iron his clothes, make him some Cinnamon toast crunch and give him a nude backrub to relief the tension. She walked up her stoop, her chin up and her eyes focused on the door. She put the key inside the keyhole and wiggled the lock. She gave it a hip push with her wrist. In the lobby there was a red and brown carpet, a bunch of FedEx boxes on the floor in a tacky way and silver mailboxes for tenants with a tongue full of mail. She walked toward her black apartment door, twisted the key and she pushed. Suddenly, she felt the floor tremble as if a giant was in her home. When she placed her foot into the door there was a tall body-shaped figure standing in the kitchen resembling a shadow. "Fritz" she screamed, A second heavyset shadow turned from the bedroom side wall and spread his large fingers around her body. Dawn dropped, she wiggled in the dark and kicked backwards. The person transformed into a skinnier man, pulling her inside and shut the door so hard that it a gust of wind knocked some envelopes from the mailbox to the ground.

Dawn slipped again, her eyes bulged with terror and fear as she faced the dark body figure. She spread her hand out to the wall, and finger flicked picture frames of her mother, her grandfather and family. The frames shattered into hundreds of glass spiderwebs and the carpet slid from its natural position.

Dawn screamed horrifically with a muffled pitch. The man covered her mouth and each of his fingers were as big as Cuban cigars. He had fat purple lips and when his mouth opened, he had gold fronts, so his teeth looked like a box of bullets and his breath stunk of hemp weed. He wrapped his arm around her like a headlock and she noticed his orange wrist watch sparkling underneath her nose. A Patek Phillipe. The man's pelvis pressed against her spine in an indecent way and he pushed her in.

"you didn't see me calling you," He shouted, while squeezing her jaw, "We were looking for you, now you gonna help me find your boyfriend." He dragged her by the throat and her pajama pants slid from her waist to her ass down to her hips.

The voice wasn't Fritz or Melvin or someone she recognized. She couldn't see clearly, but she could make out the pathway the house walls and the long shadows casted against it. The man dragged her by her neck and the flashy shadow rode her face until she reached the bedroom.

He was so strong that she questioned if she was even an adult. Another body shaped man was by the bathroom door. It was Honcho wearing a black hoodie, contorting his body while spreading out a large sheet of plastic.

Tripple plat yanked her into the bedroom with his nails digging into her arm. He tossed her into the lop-sided mattress. She landed in a clumsy way on her stiff mattress with something rigid poking her spine. But her mattress wasn't as naturally that hard, so she turned her neck and Melvin's arms were spread, his body was hunched, and his feet were ice cold purple. His forehead down, his beard was awkwardly in his throat and his neck was curled at an awkward angle as if he were texting. There was beam of light shining through the curtains that ran across his bloody chest and a warm gooey feeling on Dawn's fingers that felt like red caramel. She placed her hands to her nose and could smell the foul stench of his blood running down her index. She lifted her boyfriend's face, which felt like it was fifty pounds heavier and saw the egg yolk whiteness of his eye. She jerked her hand away and his head bobbled down lifelessly. She let out an agonizing scream, jumping, scooting off the bed and standing directly on the plastic.

Tripple plat lifted his arm, sprayed his pistol in her direction and the bullets tore through her skin with rapid flashes.

Dawn's cellphone was still at the doorframe. Flashing and flashing with Fritz's phone number.

"I had plans on coming to see you one last time. you know? some red wine and medium-rare steak on a block of wood, but my mole told me you got yourself targeted by some old enemies. It has been a good one. Our time together was unforgettable."

Meanwhile, miles away At Dumbo bridge park near the windy waters, Orlando stood across from Fritz. Orlando was the fat short bald man wearing a security uniform. He was the same security guard from the Super Galaxy motel who contacted the police about those pills. Merlo's blood brother.

Fritz wiped his own eyebrows, shocked that he recruited Orlando on his side. Thinking, sweating, smelling the river waters in his nostril. Fritz took the chip out of his cellphone, tucked it in his coat and walked closer to the scattered rock sand. He flung his cellphone far off into the river dock. It flew, spun then splashed with suds.

"You surprised me, I never thought you would betray your own family over some money," Fritz uttered to Orlando.

There was an awkward silence from Orlando and then a back-peddling shoulder shrug and a half smirk. *"Fuck them R.S.I niggas,"* Orlando shouted, *"Fuck my brother, Shandy, Cyn and Megan."*

Fritz nodded his head,

"How does the Jenkins family have ties with R.S.I?

Shandy is dating Dutch, you say?"

"yea, she had a baby by Dutch."

Fritz's eyes glistened blue like the water on the outskirts, he opened his coat, and he reached into his pocket. For a minute, he thought about shooting Orlando but there was a Caucasian family about a thousand feet away watching the night boats tread suds over the river bank. The information was enough, he knew that he had Orlando wrapped around his finger. Fritz reached deeper into his Burberry coat pocket and there was a large brown paper bag. He handed it over and it was as heavy as a bag of cash. As matter of fact, it was fifty-thousand musty dollars wrapped in rubber bands.

"It's all there," Fritz uttered. "You been loyal to me, just try to stay away from them perks" The wind blew through Fritz's spikey hair, revealing his ugly stitches in his head. He leaned over to spit on the crusty sand. His spit was foamy white as if he were talking with a dry throat.

Fritz gave a business handshake to Orlando and walked off onto Fulton Ave, and there was a white limousine with a glossy body and tinted windows near the curb. He squeezed the handle and pulled the door open wide, and it made a loud chop noise as it slammed.

As he sat in his soft leather seats, he smiled and rested his palm on Ivory's brown thigh.

Ivory uncrossed her long legs, leaned closer and held her wine glass while bending her body weight over his shoulder and her dreads dangling to his crotch. She had a pink dress with sparkles, long white stiletto heels, white nails, and blonde dreads that reached her ass. She was freakishly gorgeous and Fritz couldn't stop smiling. She leaned closer for a kiss and their lips stuck together with an electric vibration, he looked at her almond shaped eyes, her flat nose, thick juicy lips. "I fucking love you" he uttered.

Ivory smiled, squeezed her wine glass and ran her tongue down his jawline.

"What did you dump into the water?" Ivory asked, she jerked away, planting her wrist down and sipping her wine.

"Nothing babe," Fritz replied with eyes that didn't even shake. He yanked the wine glass from her hand. The same hand that she had her gigantic canary diamond ring on. The ring he could afford after he gained millions within the past few months. He pulled her left thigh over his lap. His pelvis turned warm. She didn't have panties on.

Epilogue part one

September/15ʰ/2023

Then the manager from the restaurant stepped out with a large piece of chocolate cake. The closer he walked, the larger the cake appeared on a white plate with the words happy birthday written in chocolate frosting. The whole team strutted behind, singing happy birthday as a corny choir, clapping their hands and smiling as if they knew him. Alejeh was at the middle row, singing in a low tone, least animated out of the crew. She burned Lindsey with her eyes while clapping, twisting her lip, her nose was flared, her face wrenching as if she were sick. The chef was in the corner clapping, another waitress named Molly was near his shoulder and workers from the kitchen wearing black shadows was clapping in the darker end where the lights were the dimmest.

The restaurant transformed into a slow-motion

head spinning daze through Fritz's eyes. He noticed the chocolate cake slice, his wife and the scenery and he instantly felt as if we were high. Not high off a drug but high off the moment. He felt that weird tinge in her ear once more, the side of his face felt numb, a whistling of the brain, a feeling he often felt since his brutal fight at the bar.

The team dispersed, one by one walking away to the floor to attend customers when suddenly Alejeh chest crashed into Lindsey while she held plates on her wrist. One of the plates flung off her wrist and crashed against the floor in a loud thousand shard spread. Everyone in the restaurant stared with alertness.

"oops," Alejeh uttered, she walked in front of Lindsey and crossed paths until she arrived at the bar. She handed the bartender a wine cork, turned around and her rear end bounced heavily as if she was telling Lindsey to kiss her fat Latina ass.

There were crab shells on the floor, crushed in pieces in her Puma sneakers and laces. Lindsey bent down to pick them piece by piece. You could see the part running down her ginger hair.

Ivory was eyeing her husband, she wrapped her upper ankle around Fritz's calf, she pulled him closer and blinked with a fuzzy smile.

"enough about son! Him going to the past, that was like sixteen months ago, we have to focus on our own needs? Let's use the bathroom" she stretched her arm, tugging the skinny part of her glass of wine.

"we?" Fritz responded with a smirk.

Ivory reeled his right calf, wrapping both of her legs around it and bringing it to the center of her dark table.

"it's your birthday and you been talking about our son the whole time, it's time for me to swallow your kids up. I'm thirty-nine, and he's eighteen in three months, I'm done with kids!"

Fritz removed his foot,

"damn," he uttered with a giddy smile, "you can't wait till we get back to the penthouse?"

Ivory took another sip of wine, leaned back into her seat and smiled.

"remember what happened last time with Alejeh? we have to get that first nut out of the way so do how you want it? you want me under the table?" she whispered, winking down with her sexy hair bouncing at her jaw. Then she hunched, lifted the cloth higher and whispered even softer.

"we can do it under here, in the bathroom or you

can fuck me in the streets like a hoe from Coney Island. I don't give a fuck. we getting rid of the first nut either way."

Fritz leaned back in his seat, dropped his handkerchief then crossed his arms and there was a large smile across his bearded face.

"do it around all these people," he uttered with a smirk. "you wouldn't—."

"like I care about all these rich fucks." she replied. "they fucking too, that's how we all got here."

The chair clicked against the partially carpeted floor and made a long scratch noise. Ivory hunched under the table, he saw the part in the middle of her head, and then she disappeared. Her back bones were making knocking sounds from the table surface. Fritz stood up, spun around the table and grabbed her by the waist. He had a large bulge in the center of his pants.

"aright." Fritz shouted softly. "you would, you got it, you got it."

"so, what's popping daddy." She laughed, smiled with her high cheekbones and rocking her neck in a ghetto way. She stood up with her body pressed against his dick, staring into his eyes with a sunset view. Her nerves vibrating while rubbing her fingers down to his belt. The world stopped spinning and the only moment that existed was between them. Ivory turned her cheek, snatched her Telfer bag off the table. "let's go."

Fritz pulled her like his little slut dog, eyes wandering for the white and gold restroom door.

The kitchen door at the left corner busted open and the manager walked out with a giant red lobster on a silver plate. A fat chef was inside the kitchen with a silver iron cast pot on the flat black stove, chopping a pile of wild white onions and sprinkling it into a flaming pan like a ritual.

The men's bathroom cracked opened and Fritz rushed inside with his head down. The restaurant rumblings were sliced by the muffled door and the knob made a trigger noise.

Fritz twisted the lock, then lifted Ivory by the legs throwing her against the bathroom pamper change station. The cheap plastic material slammed down against the tiles and she almost fell. Gasping, hunching into silent laughter.

Fritz threw her giggly backside against the wall, one hand held her leg and the other was around her throat. She got so much thicker since jail, and a lot thicker the sixteen months she was free, but Fritz was strong.

Ivory sucked his index, using her eyes to scream fuck me and her left hand to yank his belt loop. He pulled his belt buckle, blindly forgetting and the bulge was hanging out of his waistband. The steamy sex in a bathroom dispersed into the thin air. Ivory crossed her arms, she took a deep breath and shook her head.

"why did you bring that gun!" she yelled "you promised me you didn't have another one. you remember what Judge Wade said! I'm a fucking felon remember, I can't be around that shit."

Fritz covered his face with his two palms and you could see the redness of his nose. He turned around and the Versace shirt swayed as he leaned on the wall.

"I handed it my other shit. Wade just wants to fuck us!" He shouted in a muffled pitch "it's just so much going on right now."

Ivory adjusted her cleavage, walked toward the part of the wall he was on and punched him in the chest. She loosened her fingers, then formed another fist and tried to punch him again put he caught the punch with his open hand.

"fuck Ivory," he shouted "will you calm the fuck down?"

"it's a restaurant," Ivory screamed softly. "did you think you was gonna have smoke with one of the chef's? your so fucking paranoid! It's your birthday dinner! Normal guys want to blow their girls back out, or maybe have a threesome with another bitch, but you ready to blow someone's head off."

Fritz's chest was bouncing hard, he knew his wife was right so he stood tall, walked towards the sink and twisted the faucet. The water sprayed down causing some background noise.

"I'm sorry—it's fucking Phillips fault." Fritz screamed "once they start looking deeper into my life, they will find out"

"find out about what—."

"I've done so much shit, to so many people."

Ivory took a deep swallow, she turned around, cupped her elbow with her right palm and slouched against the wall.

She eyed Fritz, slouched down to the wall until she was on her rump.

"you think they are going to find out about the drugs? Phillip? What have you done!"

"we leave America before they come for us, how about that Bumblebee? I'm serious!"

"I'm not leaving Lucy!" Ivory screamed.

"Ivory! you don't understand! if we stay, you won't

have a mother! you won't have a son, you might not have me. They will never stop until they catch us!" He screamed in a paranoid echo.

"R.S.I?" Ivory screamed, "you think that a street gang is going to fuck with us? are you on crack nigga. Nobody can fuck with us!"

Fritz removed his hands from the faucet. He put his right hand around his wedding band and twisted it around while it was still on his finger. His eyes were stuck to it. He rolled his eyes, then turned the other check and his egregious head scar was visible. The egregious scar was one hundred and fifty stitches. It was as long as a giant centipede running down his cranium. It was all nasty with blond twiggy hair protruding out, but it was slightly fading to the same color as his scalp. His Blond hair even growing over it.

Fritz's eyes twitched,

"I still feel it you know," he spoke softly "when they were singing happy birthday the right side of my face went numb."

Ivory's eyes swelled, she lifted from her knees and walked over to him with her nerves vibrating.

"is there any numbness on the left side?" she grabbed his right hand and held his golden ring finger at her stomach.

"never numbness that hand," he uttered "I will always feel this." he retracted his hand, grabbing Ivory by the stomach and bringing her closer to him. Their jaws were close as if they were about to kiss.

Ivory pushed her face through to kiss him, but Fritz moved his face away and eyeballed her.

"just fucking take your mother with us then. *Brazil? Australia?* somewhere out of this country—Somewhere far?" He uttered while tucking his heavy magnum Desert eagle into his waistband. He adjusted his shirt over the mirror with a snarling tooth.

"little Italy?" Ivory laughed. "that's as far as I want to go."

Fritz's body stiffened.

"Listen here Bumblebee, I'll never be safe, we will never be safe after what we did. Just because we moved to a penthouse in Turtle bay doesn't mean this shit is over. We are being watched. Those fucking military fucks! The cops! Those doorman douchebags stare at me every time I get out of the limousine! they got it out for us."

Fritz pressed his finger against Ivory's lip and she immediately swallowed her argument. It was then, at that moment she glared into his frozen blue eyes and slipped into her night clothes. He pressed his body against hers, grabbed her waist pulling her into his pelvis and his electric fingers crawling up her curvaceous backside. Ivory jolted forward, kissing, sucking his tongue and rubbing her pussy on his fat dick. She could feel him growing hard through his pants, she blindly back peddled into the marble sink and lifted her right leg. Fritz twisted his body, he smacked his heavy stainless-steel gun against the marble sink. He unloosed his belt, the buckle dropped to the tiles and his dick was bouncing with hardness. Ivory pulled him closer, sticking her sharp nails into his back and the first stroke was gushy and warm. While he was thrusting inside her pussy, the mirror shook, the water splashed into her asshole. Her clothes were pulled off in an aggressive way, her glittery boots made a loud thud against the bathroom tiles. She was bare assed, getting fucked like a dirty slut against the sink and loving every moment. Every thrust made her head pop back, yawning, grabbing a hand full of blond hair, screaming words that didn't make sense.

"I'm about to nnnnnnuuuutt!" she shouted softly in his bright pink earlobe.

"damn bitch, already? Why you nut so fast, you

can't handle dick bitch?" he groaned loudly while grabbing her throat. "I got more dick for you bitch,"

"it's too big." she shouted back while digging her nails into his mountain sized back. He was large sized man in stature and in his pants. Her mouth gapped open wide and she blinked blindly.

"ughh I came again." she screamed with the light-pitched voice. She moved her arm and the gun flung off the edge of the sink and landed right in-between Fritz's pant leg.

"ohh shit—." Ivory uttered, she jumped off the sink with Bambi legs, breathing hard, then she bent down to lift the gun. Her asshole was wet, drips of milky colored nut was leaking down her thighs. She felt so slutty, she bent down like a good bitch, lifting his gun.

She held the desert eagle with both hands and it was shiny. She rested it inside her Telfer bag, then turned back around, walked with a thigh jiggle, wobbled legs and open eyes.

Ivory licked her lips, got on her knees and stood under his elephant trunk sized dick. She grabbed him by the balls and slurped the head of his dick with a wet suction cup mouth. She sucked the leftover nut from his dick, her mouth salivated and she kept moaning at each suck.

Fritz groaned angrily, his head lifted to the ceiling and he used his right hand to grab her by the back of her skull.

"ughh." He groaned loudly while grabbing her whole head with one palm, squeezing her hair out of place. He twisted his mouth, wrenched his face and groaned.

She looked him in the eye while making sucking noises.

"happy birthday daddy." she uttered with the head of his dick jittering at her mean ass tongue. She sucked it, slurped it like a good little bitch. While Ivory slurped his dick, she kept thinking about her husband being so paranoid. She knew for sure that he murdered a man, hustled drugs and probably cheated on her, but she was too afraid to find out the truth. For better or for worst, maybe somethings were better left to be unknown.

"you ready for me and that ginger bitch at the same?"

"stop—." Fritz nodded, his face was scrunched as if he were pissed off. Ivory loved that face, she loved that attitude he had when it came to her mind games.

The bathroom knob clicked open, and the outside

worldly light exploded like a final gun flash. Fritz's eyes were squinted. There were wrinkles all in the fabric of his Versace shirt, down to his pant leg. He wiped it with his left hand, walked with a sped limp, yanking his wife as her boots clicked against the fancy tiles. Five feet away, there was a white family that looked like they were slightly frustrated. A kid scrolling on an iPad near the waiting area. The white woman with light brown hair tied into a ponytail wrenched her face, tugging her kid and bringing him closer to her thigh. A black gay man with a blade fade was sitting next to her, stood up to enter the restroom next, squeezing through the crowded walkway.

Fritz stood as wide as a hockey player, clearing the entryway, twisting his face into a mean mug.

"Pardon me," Fritz uttered while walking through.

Fritz walked through the chatter-filled restaurant rows, the bright ceiling lights reflecting off the tablespoons, the walls, windows and cluttered with white people kicking out of their seats. He remembered that they shut things down at twelve, and the lights shined from the door to the backside of the bar bottles. Drunk laughter from each row.

The supervisor was at the carpeted entrance, holding the door open and friends and family squabbling out. A bunch of voices speaking at once sounded like murmur. From the window view, vehicles were lined like stars on Broadway, outside in the Erie streets of Manhattan. You could count at least ten Uber sedans near the curb and they were making chopping car door sounds. One by one, people from the restaurant exiled with full bellies of wine and grub that expanded their torsos. The restaurant sounded like hollow walls and tinkering kitchen spoons.

The fine waitresses were gathered. Molly, Sarah, Letty, Gi-Gi and Rachael had changed from their uniform, now wearing their street clothes awaiting their rides. Molly had an umbrella, holding it up as if she were about to push it open and when Letty came too close, she popped the button, extending the protruding umbrella into her face. giggling while the girls recorded her for Tik-Tok. she dropped the umbrella.

"okay." she uttered "I'll do it when we get to Hunter, stupid chip challenge, but I need some water first" she shouted.

Sarah pushed the door open and the waitresses

stormed out giggling.

Ivory turned her face, twirled her fingers into Fritz's bicep. He had big shoulders, strong tanned skin and root-like veins.

Ivory turned her cheek and noticed the bar was shut down. The bartender had a rag wiping the table in circular motion, then walking over to the tables and removing each candle.

Fritz pulled a cigarette from his pack and bit it with his lips.

"where's the pale ginger" he uttered with the cigarette wobbling at his lips. "good, she's gone. she ghosted us."

"stop it" Ivory responded with a wide smile, slapping Fritz's forearm and then getting closer to him "you aint slick! she's pale so she's a ghost? ughh you're such a jerk when you want to be."

An elderly couple near the disability tables were adjusting their clothing. A green cardigan sweater for the man and a yellow sweater for the elderly woman. She had skin like she was soaking in water. Green veins, blonde silky grey hair, hunching, trembling to stand. The old fella had patchy white skin, grey hair strands coming from his sideburns leading into a scruffy patched beard. Green veins in his hands while shivering in place. "diabetes," he shouted with a southern accent, "that's why! I wish I could but these dang diabetes and I have a failing liver. I don't have much time left."

Alejeh smiled at the two, squeezing a debit card, a receipt and a blue glass pen. She handed him the receipt and the man signed it. He lifted his debit card, giving her a soft handshake.

"lovely woman you are," he uttered with an elderly smile "you made me feel like I was important!"

Alejeh covered her face to hide her blushes.

His wife shook in place, leaning her head of grey curly hair strands on his upper arm.

Alejeh smiled, she twisted her chin sideways and formed a heart with her fingers and put it to her chest.

"I have faith that you'll get your Liver transplant," she uttered.

The man smiled,

"you know there's a private company that said they found a sick twelve-year old girl who could be my donor. I might be in line to get a new liver. There's always hope. It makes me tear up inside."

Ivory glimpsed away from Alejeh. Alejeh, she was a beautiful girl, but gave them a hard time with her level of sexuality. Ivory absolutely regretted it and hated how Alejeh looked at Fritz. It was so slow, so sensual, so infatuated. Ivory knew too many things about Fritz to obsess over him, but a young twenty-five-year-old Mexican woman like Alejeh could look at Fritz and see a daddy relationship instead of his red flags.

Ivory scratched her elbow, her eyes darted at their food which was boxed in a brown bag near a bottle of Portiere red wine standing next to a note card that read Fritz in gold letters.

Ivory lifted the note card, she smiled, then turned her body in search of Lindsey.

"which one of y'all did this." she uttered with a confused grin, she turned around and her brown hair jiggled. She focused on the words, reading the card with an envious smirk.

"Fritz the greatest coach in Berlin," she stuttered "wishing you a happy birfday." love the Seabreeze restaurant.

Ivory smiled angrily,

"best coach?" she uttered with a smirk, she slapped Fritz's arm,

"see, the restaurant didn't give me credit, I am the reason he became a coach." Her eyes were glowing in envy. "but for real, these restaurants being knowing to much damn information! Hello which one of yawl been stalking us?"

Alejeh, had a sweet little face like Mila Kunis. She stood about ten feet away with her feet crossed while standing, leaning her body weight on the table edge talking to the old man about his Liver condition.

Alejeh had very large breast and wide Latina hips that looked like an hour glass. Alejeh nod her head, gave a hug to Ernest and Meredith. Suddenly, she strutted from the disability table, her cleavage bouncing, her ponytail swinging left and right like one of the super-hot suburban chicks who do morning cardio while their rich husbands work. She had a bang on her forehead covering her well-done eyebrows so she gave it a thrust and smiled. She was wearing a rose red fabric top, brown pants and some white Jordan twos. She had a make-up less face, still a Bonafide dime. She cupped her left elbow with her right hand and crossed her left foot over her right foot.

"happy birthday Fritz," she uttered, while standing with slight lean, her arms opened wide and hugged them both with an eye twisting smile. "did you like our card?" she stood there eyeing Ivory, she smelled like baby powder, vanilla perfume and drips of fresh coconut water. She grabbed Ivory's arm, pretzeled it and kissed her ear with a secret.

"it's about Lindsey," Alejeh whispered "she came in last week with these nasty cold sores on her lips, oh yea this one time I heard her talking about how she doesn't take showers every day. Somedays she skips-a-day. She is gross. when you requested her, I wanted to tell you but I didn't want to be a bitch."

Ivory's eyebrows lifted,

"cold sore?"

"uhh huh" Alejeh replied "it was all over her lips and spreading, I told my supervisor and they sent her ass home, matter fact she doesn't have a home, she lives in the supervisor's truck, I swear on my father's life. Wouldn't lie!'

Ivory reached into her Telfar bag, pushing through and squeezed her American express card that was silver and as hard as steel. She passed it to Alejeh, shaking her head and blinking downward.

"babe! she aint touching my card or my man," Ivory uttered while squeezing Fritz by the arm, "what are you doing tonight?"

"nothing," Alejeh replied with an innocent eye bobble, she was so confident that she was in Ivory's airspace. "I was just going to go home and watch Love island and eat some Torta Ahogada with Rigoberto."

"oh, yea girl, how is your dad doing?"

"he's always complaining about his neck, we have to see a specialist before thanksgiving."

Ivory took a deep swallow, her eyes bounced but she could feel Alejeh staring in desperation. Desperation that she wanted another chance to make things right for what she did last time. Ivory took a deep breath, glared at her, visualizing the sex. Alejeh's coochie juices smelled like sweet cookies, her asshole fresh as lavender, she was always wet and her fat pussy was so tight and warm. The food at the restaurant was good, but nothing on that menu tasted better than Alejeh.

Ivory's eyes bounced left and righ, she glared at her husband biting the cigarette, and he stared back. She tugged his arm and he seemed to not care, which made her decision easier.

Ivory smiled,

"okay babe," she uttered to Alejeh, "umm since Lindsey is out, do you want to leave with us?"

Alejeh's body loosened, she thrusted the hair in her bang, moving the ends from her forehead. Through the strands you could see that her eyebrows were lifted high.

"oh my god," she replied, she squeezed the top of the chair with her left hand "yea, I would love to hang out on your husband's birthday." She slammed the chair into the table.

"okay, the limo is in the front." Ivory uttered. her nose dropped, she dug into her purse and pulled out two thousand dollars in blue face hundreds.

"this is for you Doll."

Alejeh's eyes grew twice its size, she gave Ivory a hug, while rocking side to side.

"Rigoberto is going straight to the specialist this weekend! I love you!" she stared over Ivory's shoulder looking Fritz dead in his eyes

"I love you so much!' she uttered in a slick way, staring him down, looking at his zipper, "thank you both."

Fritz's cigarette wasn't lit, but he could feel fire

burning. He knew that Alejeh was the wrong girl to take home because she was too right. If he were twenty-five years old, she would be the type of spunky little bitch he would have kept around.

12:25

Lindsey hammer-punched the janitors closet door. Her fist was as red as a rash and the side of her forearm had a pulse like a heartbeat.

"hello," she screamed in a dim light, while spit particles casted the rusty door

"Earl, help me" she screamed. She used her forearm to slam against it and rust chips were falling from the ceiling. A roach spray can tipped down and landed on her shoe. She lifted it and curled her fingers around it to slam the can against the knob over and over. *Clink! Clink! Click!* it vibrated with a loud chop. The rusty lock plate was orange like crab skin and chipped, the knob was stiff and bolted with airless steel. Lindsey twisted her body around and saw a yellow mop bucket with dust, a dingy brown broom, a large blue dustpan and sticky traps for the Manhattan rats. At eye level, there was a shelf with a yellow drill. She reached for the drill, realizing that there was a dandelion spider on her forearm, so she swung her wrist upward and wiggled like she was on fire. She felt a tingling feeling down her

318

spine so she reached through her open shirt and scratched herself like the chickenpox. She squirmed, lifted her shirt from her torso and hugged herself in fear. The spider dropped like magnet landing her toe and wobbling to the floor. Her foot slammed. She stepped on it, crushing it and turning around.

Lindsey grabbed the drill and flipped the switched to turn it on, but there was no engine noise. There was no power in the drill and the screws were rotten. She held herself, leaning against the wall feeling the coldness of the freezer smoke coming from underneath the door. She yanked her shirt on tightly.

"Alejeh," she whispered to brain, "she told me to get garbage bags and then the door just locked." She instantly bit her bottom lip. Slapping the door in the center until she could hear the faint voice of the supervisor.

"Earl" she screamed with her tonsils rattling "can you open the damn door."

He triggered the lock, opening it and the sunlight stretched into the dark closet.

"what are you doing in here," Earl muttered, squeezing an apron with his fingers.

"Alejeh!" Lindsey screamed.

"Alejeh, just quit," Earl slammed her apron on the

bench and then untied his.

"no, that crazy ass bitch pushed me inside."

"well, she quit." Earl shrugged his shoulders, kicked off his shoes and hunched.

While running up the stairs, Lindsey's ass jiggled in a messy way. When she arrived at the top of the stairs, she noticed that the restaurant was dim. The computer for checking out customers was off and you could see the shuttering light bouncing into the dark atmosphere.

"*fuck!*" Lindsey screamed in anger.

1240

The white limousine was swerving through the streets of brown infrastructure of Manhattan.

Potholes caused the champagne to spill all over the white leather seats. Ivory rolled down the tinted windows and pushed her brown head out. Her blue and brown hair rattling in the wind. She held a glass of champagne; the liquid trails floated from the window and smacked the pavement. Ivory was smiling and shaking her neck to go along with the rhythm of the music. The limousine cruised through Fifth avenue. Latino rap was banging through speakers, causing the crowded streets to stare.

"Oye! Oye! Oye! Oye! Oye!" Alejeh was straddling Ivory like a cowgirl, grinding on her lap and forming an invisible lasso with her forearm. She tugged Ivory's head back in, and the window rolled up automatically. Their eyes locked, she gripped Alejeh's big fat pale ass, both cheeks the size of wedding cakes..

She humiliated Fritz. She did it right in his face and expected him to be happy about all of this. This was a way of mockery, but he deserved it.

The light from Manhattan light poles was flicking occasional brightness as the sun roof sped through city. One minute you could see those sexy brown pancake areola's, next minute you see the dark outline of her sexy figure, then next minute you see her brown areola's and then Alejeh was kissing Ivory. Ivory blindly popped that bra off, held Alejeh's bra high and then tossed it out of the sun roof into the rippling wind. Alejeh's facial structure exploded, laughing with carelessness. She then blinked at Fritz, then glared back at Ivory, cupping her big juicy tidies and sucking her own nipple. Ivory's hand wrapped around her neck while she sat, rubbing, body kissing and hot lesbian grinding.

Alejeh rocked to the music, then did a split. She stretched her legs far. Her foot was on Fritz's thigh and her toes were pretty pink. The eye-contact with Fritz was fast, but she ate him with a feisty gaze. She glared over again, mumbling the Latin rap, her long black hair shaking, her pretty yellow jaw moving. then Ivory grabbed Alejeh for a steamy kiss while still in a split.

Fritz stared angrily, he could still feel Alejeh's feet creeping on his leg so he breathed fast. Then suddenly, Ivory stretched her arm to Fritz, her fingers crawled up to his zipper and she felt the imprint of his fat dick.

Oye! Oye! Oye! Oye! Oye! Oye! Oye! The music banged harder to their heartbeats and Ivory was sucking on Alejeh's nipples. you could hear the suction sound of her lips, her sinking cheeks. Ivory's taste buds watered because her nipples tasted like honey and milk. Ivory nibbled it, swallowing that sweet nectar coming from her breast.

"Uhh," Alejeh moaned loudly, her long black hair dangling, her eyes went sideways as she shifted towards Fritz.

Fritz snarled, leaning back and spilling the champagne on the seats. He looked upward, starring at the moving sky then looked downward at his dick. Ivory's fingers curled around it, jacking it slowly as the music played. She jacked his dick and the skin was stretching up and down.

Ivory uncurled her fingers and touched Alejeh's dainty wrist. The girls started rubbing, and tidies smushed against one other. Alejeh could feel Ivory's her fat hairless pussy. She stuck her hand in Alejeh's panties and they were rubbing each other at the same time. Ivory's fingers reaching up and Alejeh's fingers reaching down for a perfect wishbone of finger fucking.

"wait uhhhh," Ivory shouted loudly while blinking. 'it's my husband's birthday," she smiled "we are having all the fun."

Alejeh moaned while rocking her pelvis.

Ivory removed her hand, still soaking with Alejeh's juices, she jacked Fritz's dick with her oily fingers. She pulled his whole dick from his pants and it flapped over the zipper, pointing upward like the Eiffel tower and flapping down again. She jacked the bottom squeezing his balls and giving Alejeh eye contact.

"you have my permission," Ivory's head nodded with a slight head bob and her hair shook.

Alejeh stumbled off Ivory's lap, kneeled over, placing an open palm on his thigh. She smiled and slowly dropped her head into his dick. She slurped the tip with her breast knocking against his legs. Her long black hair strands were swaying, so Ivory used her left hand to thrust it behind her ear. Spit leaked down from her lips to his long veiny shaft. Her pink tongue snapped against his dick head and spit was inching down like maple syrup on flapjacks. *Kuk!* Alejeh was already deep throating.

Fritz leaned back, flailing his nose and wrenching his bottom lip. He had an angry reaction, scrunching his face and licking his bottom lip. He grabbed Alejeh's head with his massive hands, slamming it into his dick and her tonsils kept stretching.

Fritz was visualizing Dawn as he got his dick sucked.

The Latin trap music shook the limo! *Oye! Oye! Oye! Oye! Oye!*

Alejeh stared at his blue eyes, obeying him as if he were her god. She moved her neck back and forth, shutting her eyes and moaning spit while whirling her tongue through her juicy lips. *Kuk! Kuk! Kuk!* You could hear her throat choking with that massive cock.

Ivory awkwardly licked her nipple ring, but Fritz didn't see her. Alejeh didn't see her either. She realized that she was playing herself. Ivory could feel the burning sensation in her gut.

Alejeh's breast were dangling, knocking against Fritz's legs and that irritated Ivory. But then Alejeh grabbed her fat brown tidies and wrapped them around his dick for a tidy fuck while sucking his dick. Ivory was stunned. She stretched her arm, pushing Alejeh off with force.

"what the fuck are you doing," Ivory blasted her with her words,

"I told you to just suck it, that's it," Ivory screamed with her neck snapping back and forth. At the same time, the limousine slowed down, rolled into an empty lane and the car music was turned down significantly lower.

There was shameful stare on Alejeh's face, her hand at the center of her chest and she backed away "sorry," she uttered in fear.

Ivory aimed her index in the direction that she was in. "no you not." She shouted.

There was a Black Chevrolet, slanted windshield and car hood behind the limousine, parked and red and blue siren lights spinning and protruding.

Ivory turned around, squeezing her nail in the top part of the leather seats and her eyes sparkling with the lights.

"the gun,' she muttered to herself, then scrambled blindly for her top.

Alejeh hunched backwards, lifted her wrinkled rose red top, and pinned it over her chest. She threw it over the top of her head, then she kicked her right foot up, wiggling her leg into her pants.

Seconds later, there was two chopping door sounds, then boot scuffing against the rigid concrete, walking louder to the side window, there was a white man stern aggression holding a flashing light aimed to the tinted glass. The walking man arrived to the driver side door. He a bent cap, a black bulletproof vest with a handcuffed holster sparkling on the backside of his belt. Captain America looking ass nigga.

Fritz's face wrenched in agony, he bobbled his eyes and dropped his champagne glass. Not realizing why he had been spilling it; he was feeling a rash of needles all through his right side of his body, a slumber numbness crawling down his cheek and a freezing right hand.

His whole right arm. It was stiff cold. It was pale, flattened in between the cake-batter leather seat. He breathed hard, wobbling his torso and he nudged Ivory.

"fucking do something! he slurred toward Ivory "I

can't feel my fucking arm."

Alejeh trembled, she reached for his lap to help him with his pants, but Ivory stiffened her forearm, nudging her back into her seat.

"Alejeh! Enough is enough! I'm his wife," she uttered with uncertainty. While aiming her index finger with white nail polish. "the fuck away." she trembled with adrenaline, "this is why we didn't want you to begin with! I wanted Lindsey because you don't know your fucking place!"

10:24

Everything made sense. As soon as the couple walked into the restaurant that evening, Ivory lifted her wrist, blocking her lips then stared directly at the manager Earl. She whispered; how they wanted someone who didn't do too much. The manager smiled, led them to their seat, and gave a head nod to the ginger girl Lindsey, the green eyed-beauty who looked like she was from Portland with her pale milk skin tone. She sleeps in her boss's trunk and attends college during the morning. Thirty-one-year-old Lindsey was seen as a complete failure, but for one night, if you want someone that doesn't do too much, then it's her. She was requested and arranged by one of the riches couples in New York City.

Alejeh shoved her socks on, slid her foot into her sneaker. She had an eye twitch, staring downward with her bottom lip tucked in her mouth like a sad child.

Ivory swung her wrist in shooing motion.

"no, you're not sorry because you always doing out of pocket shit. what happened last time during the threesome?"

Alejeh realized the first threesome. She grabbed Fritz's two fingers and sucked it like a lollipop while moaning in Spanish.

Ivory slapped Fritz in the chest, while her feet was in Alejeh's face.

"*why the fuck are you letting her suck your fingers motherfucker! I knew you was a cheater!*"

"what the fuck are you insane, this was your idea you crazy bitch." Fritz lifted from the mattress, both knuckles squeezed. They shouted at each other for fifteen minutes.

1:00

The limousine engine clicked off, and the lights from the back seat went dim like blown fuse. The darkness was silent, the only lights that poured in was from the sunroof. Cricket noises bounced off the moon back into the sunroof and a light beam shined on Alejeh's pale make-up less face.

"I'm sorry, Ivory, I thought this was a threesome, I didn't know that there were rules."

"bitch this wasn't a threesome I was a test!" Ivory screamed with her knuckles curled.

"will you stop." Fritz uttered with a slurring lip.

"you cheated on me while I was in prison Fritz, I want the truth." Ivory's voice cracked in sadness. She lifted the plastic bag of boxed food and swung it into his chest. Red sauce was all over his clothes.

"I didn't cheat Ivory! Those were rumors! You believe every rumor you hear?"

Alejeh clutched her hands together, cupping them and slacking her shoulders

"please stop."

Ivory lifted her knuckles to her jaw, squaring up as if she wanted to swing.

"this isn't the restaurant Lil girl." Ivory shouted, "we don't need no fucking help, just sit over there." Ivory stared at Alejeh, noticing that she had a beam of light on her. The beam of light shined like she was some kind of special bitch. Special bitches can get a busted lip too.

Ivory turned towards Fritz and smacked him in the jaw. His penis was still out, he locked his legs and rolled to the left side.

"you idiot! You wanted to fuck her, didn't you? I knew you was cheating on me the whole time!" Ivory swiveled his boxer briefs back on his waist, locked his belt buckle, she twisted her torso while staring at her Husband in hatred. She saw one of his pork ribs on the seat. She lifted the pork rib and threw it at his head in humiliation. Ivory grabbed her bag, dug inside and then she noticed the stainless-steel sparkle on top of her Gucci head tie.

Ivory thought about lifting it and shooting him, but it wasn't worth the jail time. Not this time.

Epilogue part two

1:05

Ivory's face wrenched, she squeezed the seat from behind the tinted glass, the reflection of the black glass showed her chest plate expanding and deflating like an unfit runner in a marathon. She straightened her shoulders, turned to Fritz handing him the handle of his heavy wrist wobbling Desert Eagle.

"take this shit!" she screamed "take it." her wrist wobbled. She kept thinking about Judge Wade ordering Fritz to give all of his weapons, and how he ignored it.

Fritz's face wrenched, he reached for his gun with his right hand and slammed it on his lap. The gun was illegally twinkling silver. A silver trigger, rubbery grip on the handle and a magazine that felt as heavy as a can of soda.

Alejeh squeezed the leather seats, her face trembled, eyes bounced back and forth as she glared at the Desert eagle.

Devious footsteps crept from behind the limousine. The dark glass had four officers flashing a bright light inside the Limousine. The door handle clicked and remained shut from the outside.

"hello?" officers shouted.

Detective Edgecomb had a cap with a fade in the back of his head, he was shaped like a hockey player, Six foot three with a bulletproof vest, a white shirt underneath, and a holster with double guns. He opened each door of the stretch Limousine until he reached the backseats.

Suddenly, Ivory's door on the right side opened and the bright light poured into the Limousine seats. Detective Latimere, was a French man, flat brown hair with a part running down his widow's peak. He was in a bullet proof vest too, holding his gun at his hip, aiming a flash light with his left.

"hello do you know why we stopped you?" Detective Latimere uttered, he had a big Adams apple that shook when he spoke, a single eyebrow raised and a full mustache that wiggled. Then the detective saw Fritz's gun on his lap, backing out to the curb.

"Detective, he has a gun!" Latimere flipped his

flashlight and screamed loudly.

Edgecomb scrambled towards the backseat with a fast leg thrust, he glimpsed inside and the surface of the cake batter seats were visible, there was a stench of sex, pork ribs, sweat, champagne, weed, food on the seat and champagne drips everywhere like a basketball team after a championship. He glimpsed down at Fritz and saw the concealed weapon on his lap gleaming like a silver death trinket. He swept open the door, squared his legs and gave his partner a wave.

Fritz slammed his head back, his lip wrenched and his nostrils flared.

"it's licensed." He shouted.

Ivory grabbed his arm,

"it's registered," she uttered "stop! don't you assholes got something else better to do?" she pulled a bottle of Poland spring water from the cooler in the car seat. Lifted it and poured some into Fritz's mouth. She had one knee on the seat, her big fat booty aimed at Detective Latimere.

Detective Spence walked toward the scene. A middle-aged cop with blue eyes and brown hair. He pulled Ivory; dragging her, until she was punching, kicking and screaming.

Edgecomb glared at Alejeh, giving a head nod to take her out too. He squeezed the handle, opened wide and light shined on her pretty brown legs. Once Alejeh was out of the Limo, Edgecomb used his foot to kick the gun off of Fritz lap. The heavy magnum gun smacked against the street pavement. Then, while aiming his gun, he bent his hairy arm down to lift it. Her gold badge grazed the floor.

Ivory wandered into the vrooming traffic, turning her jaw to the stop light and back to Detective Latimere.

"let me please call my lawyer first," Ivory uttered with the red light blinking on her forehead. Bright head lights bounced across her horrified face.

Detective Edgecomb strutted to his cruiser, wide body Chevy Impala with black windows like it was made of octopus ink. He was Holding the Desert eagle at his chest, taking chopping steps; the voice of static mutter from his radio about a homicide. Then handed it to the eldest officer Detective Faulk.

"yea." He uttered "This is Ivory and Fritz Clayed, match the gun to Rolling Street Infamy street gang."

Fritz's eyes bobbled back and forth, blinking as if he were about to pass out. Something he had been facing for the past sixteen months. He stared at his left arm which was stiff as a tree log. His pits were sweaty, his skin fiery red and pork rib sauce all over his right side of his cheek.

His breathing was as if he had peanut butter in his in lungs. He twisted his lip to the side, his mouth tightened and blood inched from his nose to his lips.

Detective Edgecomb's boots scuffed against the road, He held his gun forward, aiming it into the open car door.

"now get him out," Detective Edgecomb uttered with his cheekbones tightened.

Officer Latimere went in through the right side, yanking Fritz's arm and pulling him to the curb, but they couldn't move him.

"he's heavy." Latimere uttered. Staring at Fritz's pale eyes, his breathing intensified, blood gushing and his wide eyes rolling white.

Detective Spence placed his handcuffs back into his holster. He had an ominous presence about him.

"listen I don't always do things by the books you hear? he grabbed Fritz by the ear, he walked closer to Fritz and they were nose to nose. Even with all that blood gushing from his lips.

"I'm not going to bullshit you." Edgecomb pulled you over because your driver missed his signal, but listen here, we know about your crime family."

Suddenly, Officer Faulk shouted from the Chevy impala.

"it's clean," he walked back over to the Limousine with the gun in a plastic bag, a slight hunch and a lip twitch.

Spence grunted, backing away with a smile.

"you don't say," Detective Edgecomb smirked, he slapped Spence on the shoulder.

Fritz twisted his body, his bottom lip flopped over his chin and the blood had rushed down to his teeth,

"give me back my fucking burner pig," he slurred.

Edgecomb extended his arm, blocking his comrade from returning the Desert Eagle. He turned around and stood up, tucking his cuffs back into his leather holster.

"Fritz! you think your so fucking untouchable. We have some information about you."

Detective Edgecomb gave Ivory a finger flick to move closer, she walked a straight line until she was near the Limousine door, she touched the handle and hunched.

"Ivory Clayed right?" Edgecomb slapped his knee and was eye-to-eye with Fritz, he lifted up while smirking. "what do you know about the death of Dawn?"

Ivory's head snapped back,

"Dawn?" she screamed softly to herself. Her hair strands dangled in the wind.

Detective Edgecomb smiled with his coffee stained teeth, he dug into his cellphone files. It was a huge gadget that the police use for suspects. He flicked through the database, and turned the phone over revealing a picture of Dawn's dead body.

"Dawn Spaige?" Detective Edgecomb uttered, "she was his girlfriend from 2012 through 2022. She was shot and killed in her home eleven months ago."

Ivory's brain flashed, she stared down at her husband with her eyes drilling him and reading the horrors of his guilty emotions.

Fritz opened his mouth breathing hard and blood was gleaming from his teeth.

"he's fucking lying! That had nothing to do with

me! fucking Pig," Fritz slurred.

"whose Dawn?" Ivory uttered while squeezing the limousine door. The light from the street pole was shining on him at a gleaming right angle.

"Bumblebee please," he screamed with a smile across his face, a smile of pain and guilt. His bottom lip was hanging on his beard.

"he's fucking lying Ivory, remember what those pigs did to you, they are trying to set me up."

With the door still swept open, Alejeh walked passed Ivory, sat in the seat and crossed her legs. She bit her lip, locking her fingers while sitting.

Detective Edgecomb stared at Ivory, then Alejeh then he turned his neck toward Detective Spence.

"oh, I see what's going on" Edgecomb uttered "they have an open marriage thing going on."

"no, we don't." Ivory shouted with her hair strands shaking.

Ivory leaned in, dropped her knee on the seat and then jerked her body away. Her hand lifted along with the Telfar handbag from the backseat.

"Dawn! Who the fuck is that! That's not the bitch I heard of." She threw the door, it slammed and the seat shook. She walked to the front of the limousine demanding the wheel.

"bitch we all ready to die tonight." She uttered with her knuckles squeezed.

ACT III

Family BBQ

07/14/21

Big momma Lucy's feet were inside a blue bucket of ice-cold water. She wore a gold ankle bracelet squeezing her ankle to the point it looked like it could pop. She was never concerned with her jewelry, she barely even took a glance into the water because the spices smelt so good. She wore a yellow dress, with no straps, a long curly brown wig that reached her shoulders. She rocked side to ride, humming and singing. She held her spatula with her hand and silver tongs in the other, snapping the tongs as if they were an instrument. Dark, hefty smoke puffs elevated from the chard grill to her chin and she jerked her head away. The hamburgers, chicken, and hot dogs were oozing with juice, and the corn was Cajun orange with butter dripping into the foil. She laid the cooking utensils down and rubbed her forearm across her forehead.

Aunt Yata, was a few feet away tucking her lips inside her mouth and dancing. Her skin was just as dark as one of the charcoals. She walked towards the soca music, upped it a notch and the music from her laptop rang through the backyard. She walked back to the grill, had her sleeve rolled up, dancing over the wooden table near the white fence, she used a silver handle to scoop out clumps of potato salad, and it squashed it into my Styrofoam plate.

"That's enough for him? " She uttered

Aunt Yata brought over my potato salad. She looked at Dutchess, then she rolled her eyes at me like she knew. She knew what I was doing every Sunday, it's like all the adults knew and still let us do it.

Yata smirked,

"Finally got you a *girlfriend*," she uttered in a low tone. She swung her hip into my arm and made me wobble.

The sides of my face blushed pink.

As the music vibrated our backyard, and i held Dutchess's fingers from under the table, it was as if nothing could go wrong. She was my girlfriend and no one could take her from me, or change what we had, I didn't care if we were just sixteen years old or she had a history. She was my world! but all worlds can get crushed in a split second by a comet. That's what Ms. Moss was to us.

Ms. Moss abruptly walked in from the yards door with her hair bouncing left and right. She walked towards the tables, boobs jiggling, limping like she had a broken heel, smelling like wine and hotel soap. She had long blue crinkly weave that brushed against her behind, blue edges too as it someone died her whole head in paint. She wore a shiny white mini dress that squeezed her thighs. She looked shapely in it besides her fanny-pack gut. She wore white heels, kneecaps showing and long chocolate legs.

Dutchess's eyes dropped and her face vibrated as if she were cold.

Big momma Lucy's snapping, dancing and smiling stopped. She twisted her lip, hunched and looked away from the grill. She put her palm over her forehead while leaning away from the view.

Yata dropped the red package of Coca-Cola so Ms. Moss couldn't see. Each of the pans were dropped onto the wooden chairs in short order, the rice, the jerk chicken, potato salad and the music plug was pulled out of the laptop.

Yata stepped back, covered the potato salad with an extra layer of crinkly foil, hid the plates behind the tree. She dragged the napkins, and closed the grill behind the tree until it looked like a large stack of street junk in a yard sale.

Ms. Moss barely could keep her balance, she was sleepy-eyed, and it was as if she were staggered off of a thousand shots. Her eyes drilled, she strutted over to me, and her index finger tapped me on the top of her shoulder.

"Phillip," she muttered at the side of her mouth, "Get me a hamburger hunny." She smiled, her pearly white teeth lined up perfectly and she did a pose with her crinkly blue hair hanging. She looked just like Naomi Campbell, the model.

I glimpsed at Dutchess, the oxygen in the atmosphere turned to dust and world froze. She loosened her fingers with me and her fingers turned red. I stared at her while breathing slow and she stared back with her brown eyes. Dutchess had copper colored hair curls, and each one was hanging over her eyes. She shrugged awkwardly while turning away and tugging her earlobe. Dutchess had that pale skin too, and as pale is she was, she seemed to look more lifeless than pale. That's how her mother made her feel. Lifeless!

I stood from my seat and her eyes didn't even stare at me. She had a thing, were she rather stare downward then to stare at me and feel her mother watching us. Her mother using me to get leverage inside our building.

I walked towards Big momma Lucy's bucket with the thought of Ms. Moss. Weather she wanted cheese on her hamburger or not, and then i opened my mouth to inform her but Big momma Lucy stopped me.

The backyard was silent.

Big momma Lucy flared her face, avoiding eye contact and shaking her head left and right. Over her curly brown bang, the sun beam shined, her pits were sweaty at both ends and her Jesus chain was stuck to her oily neck. When she was ready to speak, she flailed her wrist at Ms. Moss.

"just because you dating that girl, don't mean you have to do what her momma say."

"She said she wants a hamburger, " I uttered back. Big momma Lucy skinned her teeth, she turned her torso towards Yata and widened her eye like a signal to do something.

Everyone's eyes stuck to my family.

Yata caught the hint. She took a long stride forward with her box braids swinging.

"Charlesha ain't got no teeth," Yata shouted with her head to the side. Tapped me in the middle of my chest. She yelled loud enough for everyone to hear. Yata retracted her hand and had her arms folded under her cheetah blouse.

"How she going to eat the damn burger if she can't chew it, her old ratchet crackhead ass."

My eyes wandered to Dutchess, then to her mother, then back to Yata.

"She got new teeth," I replied while pointing my finger.

Big momma Lucy made eyes as if she were electrocuted. She stepped out of the bucket, bracelet dangling half way off her ankle. Water speckles against the concrete and the ankle bracelet was left behind along with the trail of water.

Big momma Lucy had her palm over her chest, while breathing hard and flaring her nostrils.

"I wonder how she paid for new teeth before paying me my doggone rent."

She scooped out a charred burger off the closed grill and put it on the Wonder Bread bun.

The only person on her mind was Fritz. She wanted to check the whole house for evidence because she had a feeling that Fritz paid for the teeth. Money was surely going missing too and it wasn't a coincidence that he had been scrambling and leaving for weekends.

I arrived at the table with the juicy burger, and my face turned frozen. I saw that she had two gold rings on her fingers as if she were married. She had one in the middle and a skinny one on her ring. Rings that looked expensive.

I dropped the plate on the table, I turned around and walked towards Big momma Lucy. The grill was covered by tree branches, shut off, The plates, soda, jerk chicken, rice and potato salad, everything was gone. Mary Ann, the most troublesome daughter picked up Big momma Lucy's gold bracelet, opened the backyard door, she followed behind Yata and Big momma Lucy. She ran with her sneakers slapping the floor, then tugging Yata and handing it back.

As a reward for returning the ankle bracelet, She begged Yata for Coca-Cola while they walked up the tall stairs. Pulling Yata's cheetah shorts.

Doomp! Doomp! Doomp! they walked while Mary Ann tugged and pulled. "Please Ms. Yata," she yelled loudly.

Deon was helping with the foil pans. He flattened his hip, and pushed his little sister up a step so that she could stop being a menace. She walked with her shoelace aglets slapping against the staircase steel.

Mary Ann climbed the steps through the second flight, turned and placed her head over the bannister nagging Yata, and Deon kept moving her up with his forearm that he held the napkins with. They arrived at the third floor and Big momma Lucy was still at the second flight huffing and puffing.

Mary Ann stuck her head over the bannister, pumped air into her cheeks and dropped her bottom lip.

"Please Big Momma," she uttered while extending her arm "One more juice."

Yata stopped at the apartment door, she pulled Mary Ann away from the bannister, then kneeled and flicked her box braids to her ears

"It's just Soda little girl" Yata crumpled her face. "You must have an addictive personality like your mother." She whispered with a stank look. The light from the apartment shined bright on her brown lip.

"one more please." She locked her fingers as if she were doing a prayer.

"You don't give up, huh," Yata shouted. "Little girl, you remind me of myself, I was bad when I was little too."

Yata reached for one little red soda and Mary Ann

reached for the whole box. She dragged it at her hip, sped down the stairs with her barrettes dangling. She laughed with a feverish hiccup.

Yata smiled with anger, squeezed the doorframe and stood while shouting.

"Okay, take it lil girl, whatever, but If your mother can afford new teeth, then she can afford to pay some rent."

When Mary Ann reached the back yard, the twigs poked her from the fence, she wobbled with the box at her hip and kept smiling. Ginger, Onyx, and Draya all the girls wanted some soda, so they circled around her pleading and chanting,

Ms. Moss's eyes widened to the size of pool balls, she swung her wrist left and right

"Mary," she screamed with her fat neck. "Give me a soda girl, I'm thirsty."

The yard was completely silent.

Mary Ann had her back turned, bending lower, she handed her sisters a warm soda one by one while digging her short arm into the box. She pulled a warm one for herself and popped the lid.

Ms. Moss scrunched her eyebrows, she adjusted her cleavage and chewed hard,

"Mary." She yelled with chewed beef in her throat. "Give me a soda you *little rotten bitch.*"

Mary Ann's eyes protruded, she turned around with her barrettes dangling, The soda splashed from her wrist into the grass and sizzled like acid down her forearm.

"Access denied! If you can afford new teeth, then you can afford your own soda," she uttered loudly.

Livonia stood up with her hands covering her mouth and each girl followed after.

Ms. Moss stood, she lunged forward while dropping her own burger pieces onto the grass. She winded up her hand and swung but tripped into the grass. She stood up with her knees, tackled and slapped her daughter repeatedly while her dress exposed her ass cheeks.

All the girls screamed loudly.

Deon placed the pans on the table, then Big momma Lucy walked inside the apartment holding her chest as if someone shot her in the heart with a silver bullet. She was walking slow and gasping for a better quality of air. The center of her face wrenched, she breathed hard and walked shoeless like her grandparents did when they sharecropped. With each step, her lungs felt narrow, her heart skipped until it was faint. Her feet pounded and the apartment began to vibrate in her eyes. She slammed against the solid wall and realized that her own house had brought her excruciating pain. She wasn't a landlord anymore; she wasn't the lord of anything. She was weak. Way over her head and couldn't deal with the pressure of tenants nor the pressure of her own blood flow. Her eyelids opened and she was leaning on a framed photograph of Fritz hanging on the wall. It was a nightmare to feel her impending doom, as the person who caused it was staring her right in the face.

Deon grabbed Big momma Lucy by the arm to prevent her from falling.

Yata pushed through the front door, she slapped the lights and walked inside to grab Big momma Lucy's other arm and they walked her to her seat.

"Momma you good, what happened?" she shouted.

"—Water, I just need *water*." Big momma Lucy squeezed under her breast and her heartbeat was like titan stomps. Slamming against ribcage to the point that a teardrop fell from her eyes. She walked backwards and sat on her woven chair with a red hemorrhoid pillow underneath. It felt like it was full of cotton.

Deon ran to the sink, he was a tall boy, six-foot-two and barely fit through the narrow space between the table and dishwasher. He twisted the faucet and filled a tall glass full of water. He came back to the Livingroom with jiggling water dripping from his wrist.

Yata stepped in front of him with her lip twisted to the side,

"Why would you get my momma *tap water* don't you see the Poland spring by the fridge," She snatched it, turned around, and spilt the glass back into the steel sink. *"I can handle my momma, now go downstairs and be with yours."* She opened the door wide, and Deon walked down the stairs with his neck tilted down.

Big momma Lucy clapped her hands while lying in the woven chair.

"Yata! *Yata!* don't be mean to that poor boy, you know he good."

"I don't care, it's his momma's fault," Yata replied.

"No, it's Fritz's fault."

"How could it be Fritz's fault ?"

"—Fritz paid for that hoe's new teeth." Big momma Lucy shouted and leaned down to the floor.

Yata twisted her lip,

"You need to cut him off—get a real super—you should have been did that—but what will Ivory say?"

Big momma Lucy's face wrenched.

"I don't need Ivory's approval—this is my house—Fritz betrayed us and I'm going to tell her myself once I get some proof that he and that whore had those children together."

Yata crossed her arms underneath her blouse, she snapped her mouth, rolled her eyes and turned to the side of the house with the windows.

"I told you white people are evil, but you let Ivory marry that weird ass white man."

"Yata stop it!"

"Ummm, Fritz is going to Berlin right so what happens when he needs money for his ticket?"

"I'll pay for a one-way—I want him out of my sight." Big momma Lucy breathed heavily. A piece of spit drooled from her lip, and she sucked her nose so hard that her eyes went watery.

Yata slammed her hand on her hips,

"No Momma we ain't paying—He ain't going to Berlin—he doesn't deserve no trip to Europe after impregnating that hoe—I saw the little blue-eyed girl next to the water and she looks *just like him*, bringing all this hell into your house—I'm going to strangle him."

"Yata, enough !"

Yata stood in the center of the Livingroom. She had wide hips; getting around her was like getting around four door sedan with all that body she had. She was built just like Big momma Lucy but more muscular at the top. They say she was built like Serena Williams. Yata turned around and blocked half of the view with her full brown body. Some people used to say that she fell into a tub of chocolate when she was an infant so that's why it looks like heresy's. She used to lick her own skin to see if she was sweet, but she ain't taste like chocolate—just skin. Yata had a mushy booty cheek wedgie in her yellow cheetah shorts, walking while cupping her arm under her blouse and mumbling hateful words at Fritz as if she was preparing for an argument. She stopped at Fritz's royal blue hard case luggage near his room door. That's his favorite color. Everything in his room is royal blue because he thinks he is a European king. Yata walked over to the handle, spread her fingers, and pushed it down. The travel case flopped down with its zipper swinging. She twisted her lip and knocked down the one next to it. After that, she snatched his passport and vaccination card from the handle and the plastic string ripped.

"Fritzen Clayed. she uttered while staring at his dorky passport photo.

"*Damn you ugly.*" She laughed, she balled the vaccination card, shoved it into the dusty crevices of the couch, then she placed the passport into the cabinet with the pots. A place where none of the boys in the house would ever look because we never cooked or cleaned.

Big momma Lucy was leaning forward, black spots around her eyes, her nose blue, skin lifeless as a pot of old flowers. Her body slouched in between her legs. She tried to stare at her feet, but she saw four sets vibrating.

"Yata please! —*Take me to the Emergency room*—I can't breathe."

Big momma Lucy's second Heart attack was the worst one because she caught Covid twice, but somehow, she still survived without a ventilator. She said that the machine didn't keep her alive; God and her children did.

1

Dawn's dagger
March/9th/2022

I stood at Big momma Lucy's door frame. My grandmothers room always looked bigger than the rest because I used to crawl around her when I was baby, sitting near her doorframe playing with toys and listening to her talk on the phone. Here I am, sixteen years old and I am standing at Big momma Lucy's door frame with my fingers tugging to get my stepdad's attention. It was as if I were a child again and I was tugging him like those times I wanted to get snacks.

Fritz was hunched down, realigning at the cabinet on one knee like a proposal, but he wasn't taking anyone's hand—he was taking Big momma Lucy's paperwork and money. My Grandmother was recovering from her third heart attack—and he was stealing from her.

My face flushed pale,

"What are you doing?" I asked.

Fritz's blue eyes gleamed, his breath plummeted, and he kept digging with his jaw down.

"I'll explain later, Phillip," he replied his eyes bobbled at my brown skinned face, "this is grown-up stuff that I have to handle for your gram."

I let go of the cable wire and folded my arm. "Okay, but who told you to do it," I replied. "And why do you have your shoes on Big momma's carpet?"

I was ready to stand up to him for once. Suddenly, the doorbell electrified the tension-filled house — and I had a feeling that the bell saved us both.

Fritz froze, his right eye bounced toward the door, he swallowed hard as if he just swallowed peanut butter.

Fritz lifted himself with a paranoid muscle twitch.

"I'll get that," he muttered while straightening his wrinkled collar.

I raised my palm to block him from standing up,

"Nah, I got it," I responded.

I walked out of Big momma Lucy's room into the spacious living room, I buzzed the door, waited for the person to walk up, and to my surprise, it was a curvy brown woman. Her skin was moist like droplets of fresh flowers; she had thin drawn eyebrows, high cheekbones, and a wide head shape with a single strand tucked behind her diamond-studded ear lobe. The hallway smelled like coconut and honeysuckles. She wore black leather pants and red high heels that made her look as tall as a Macy's mannequin. She had red lipstick around her lips without a smudge. Long brown curly hair that tickled her shoulder. She stared at me without saying a word, her face clinched, she blinked three times in a row, and her lips parted.

"Phillip?" she said. She squeezed her purse handle, looked downward at her Jimmy Cho heels. She knew that I was Ivory's son because Me and Ivory looked like twins except, I had my father's head shape and muscular stature.

Dawn took a deep swallow,

"I'm Dawn," she said. "I'm here to tell y'all about me and your stepdad, Fritz."

"What about him?"

"Is Lucy home." Her eyes shook, she leaned closer towards the door and peeked into the house.

"No, She's at the Presbyterian for her third heart attack."

Dawn dug into her purse,

"I'm sorry about your grandmother," and at that moment I noticed that her wrist was red as if someone squeezed her by both arms. She extended her right arm, holding a piece of gold and unraveled her fingers. The gold wedding band was gleaming in the center of her palm. I picked it from her palm like a coin, lifted it and held it in the light. Ivory's name was engraved on it along with the year Fritz, and she got married which is two-thousand-seven.

Dawn's face squeezed as if she were nervous. She put her exotic red nails across her left arm and hunched over.

"I know all about your mother, Ivory," she said,

"he ain't no good. He has done a whole lot of sneaky things to your family—I mean we—I'm so sorry, Phillip."

"How did you get this ring?"

"I took it while we were in the motel—the Super Galaxy—that cracked out hell hole."

My skin buzzed, my face lowered, my eyes were still, and the color drained from my cheeks. I turned my cheek away from the door, my elbow aimed towards the back of the house, and at an angle, I saw Fritz forcing the off-white colored folders into a black Dunlop racquet bag with white words. He used that bag as a conversation starter to get to know white folks in Bed-Stuy, but at that very moment he was taking a backhanded swing at our whole family. He was as good as Venus and Serena—metaphorically of course backhanding all of us one like we were a green furry ball.

Each of Dawn's eyes looked like glass as she stood there. She squeezed her leather purse handle with both hands.

"He's a sociopath—somebody that would do anything to get what he wants—He always gets it," she uttered with a vengeful voice "He won't get what he wants this time." She stared towards her stomach. Her eyes bounced from her stomach to me, and she spread her fingers through her blouse. "It's my turn to get what I want—it's my choice and we are going to be safe this time." Her fingers spread and rubbed her stomach like it was a crystal ball.

My face went pale and there was no noise except

air creeping in from the roof door.

Her brown eyes darted, and she took a step forward with conviction.

"We met ten years ago. It was the fourth of July, and you were wearing a blue Berlin Bears jersey, blue jeans and Jordan's. You had rainbow stick of cotton candy and a soccer ball at your toe. You were so brown and cute back then with your little fat cheeks. I was by the beach with my day-one best friend Savannah. She is my family—she cared for me before I lost myself to him—I regret letting my friend see me become this unhappy person. —I'm leaving that Elf looking son of a bitch—If he shows his true colors on you or your grandmother best lawyer up, okay?"

I nodded. I understood what she meant by leaving, just didn't know what she meant by lawyer up because Fritz was our family. The fuck was I supposed to do? Sue him for stealing? who is going to help me tie my tie on my way to court!

Dawn sucked air into her nostril, she gave me a half hug and walked down the steps. Her red high heels clicked on the steps, and it sounded like she was walking on daggers.

2

Lucy's secret son
March/9th/2022

Fritz was kneeling in the center of Big momma Lucy's room, his backbones bulging out of his back and his right sneaker full of mud. He was reading the papers with a hunched body. Tiny words that looked like scribbled dots from the doorframe. I walked closer to him.

"You were cheating on my mother?" I shouted, I squeezed the ring in my palm, and I could feel it breaking in my grasp. I threw it in his direction, and it ricocheted off the wall, sounding like a penny and bouncing behind the mahogany headrest where Big momma Lucy keeps her back pillow. Fritz tried to catch it, but it slipped. It fell so low that even he couldn't reach it unless he moved the bed, but he was too occupied. His blue eyes bounced towards the Dunlop racquet bag he had near his foot, he pulled it closer to his thigh and muttered words under his breath.

"I'm shady?" He laughed, "You think I am the shady one? Check this out, you will see who is shady." He lifted his chin, reached into the File cabinet and pulled out an 8x11 photograph.

The photograph had a drip of cream paint, partially burned, and wrinkled down the middle. He stood up and as he walked closer to me, he tilted his body so that the picture was under the ceiling light. An old reddish-brown photograph of three black children standing near a Christmas tree. They were dressed down in spiffy little white and red outfits near a Christmas tree with lights. Ivory was nine years old. She had a red dress and white socks that came up to her knees. Aunt Yata, the youngest, had a white blouse and red pants. But then, an even younger little boy on the left was wearing red denim overalls with one side loosened. He had a snaggletooth smile, gleaming eyes, and a round lightbulb head shape.

My eyebrows dropped.

"Who's this ugly little boy?" I asked.

Fritz stood tall, his pudgy pink index finger pointed at the glossy photograph and bit down on his lip.

"That's your mother's brother," he said, "your Uncle Brian."

I angled my bed away from him, I held the photo near my rib and plopped down onto her mattress. When I sat, my body weight wrinkled the orange and brown bedspread.

"I have an uncle?" I asked, "wait, what?"

Fritz smiled with a underbite, he lifted his cellphone while walking, and put it to his ear.

"Yea, I'm coming, Reggio." He shouted with his back hunched. "We're selling today." He tunneled through the hallway and twisted the lock. The buckles on the Dunlop racquet bag dangled as he stepped out.

I glared into the reddish-brown glossy photograph, flipped it over and on its back were squiggly names written in faded ink.

"Lucy's children, Ivory, Yata, and Brian." The little snaggletooth boy looked like Aunt Yata the most. They had the same pinched nose and big Pufferfish cheeks. Ivory was on the left side, sitting next to Yata while holding a teddy bear. The photograph had a deep line between them and Brian, as if someone bent him out of the picture. Big momma Lucy was perfect in my eyes, but just like Fritz, she had some secrets too!

What if her angry son comes around and tries to take Big momma Lucy's money? Maybe that's why Fritz took the bag? I hate to speculate, but why did they lie about his existence, unless he is someone who doesn't deserve to be in the family.

New Landlord
March/9th/2022

On the opposite side of Brooklyn, something scandalous was going on with Fritz. Not scandalous like him fucking Dawn at a motel and claiming he's in Europe; that's light compared to what he was doing now. Scandalous, like having a relaxed grin, his legs wide open sitting in the back of an Uber. He held the Dunlop racquet bag over his shoulder, it was half-zipped opened with each of the folders semi-bent, he had his cellphone in his lap, typing the words "sell house" and "Real estate market for Brooklyn Brownstones."

He stared out of the window and smiled as if he were satisfied with the search results.

The Uber arrived at its location, Fritz stepped out, he slammed the door of the Honda accord, and the white car hummed away. Around his shoulder was the racquet bag and he held it while looking both ways, and squeezing the bag strap as if he were paranoid. He stepped towards Ricky's restaurant. It was a large warehouse with a pinstripe orange canopy decoration. The sidewalk was full of outside dining tables with overly large umbrellas. It reminded me of the ones on the beach that people used, but without the sand though. Fritz pushed the door hinges with his palms. There was supposed to be a security guard checking vaccine cards, but he was in the back with a pool stick near his rib.

The bar was dim, with electric chatter, laughter, voices muttering at once and Frank Sinatra stretching his voice over a Jazzy ballad in the background. There were memorabilia over the walls of famous athlete's jerseys and celebrity paintings. A dark space for dancing and an orange ambient under the bar table with a Latina bartender leaning over squeezing her boobs together with her inner arms.

Fritz walked towards the tail end of the bar table and his eyes caught Attorney Reggio sitting on a stool with his legs wide open. He had a big square head, gelled-down Guido hair, and a flabby fat face. He was watching soccer on the bar TV while slapping the table in a disruptive manner. His back straightened, and his cup was full of beer spilling over the counter.

"Hey, Fritzen," He screamed. "The man of the hour is finally here." his fat face widened. He had a half-loosened tie, hairy arms with yeasty beer leaking on his cuff links.

Fritz's bodyweight plopped into the seat. The nails

in the stool wobbled, and the table dipped an inch.

Regio smiled with an orange beam of light shining over his balding crown.

"Finally got rid of that crazy black whore," he shouted over the music, his double chin wobbled, "I hated seeing you with those niggers, been having dinner with them so long, I thought you were becoming one of them." He placed his large hands over the table and his wedding band shined.

"My wife sally has a sister who just graduated law school," he uttered, "what do you say you give her a pounding, she's a brunette with knockers down to here." Regio opened his cellphone to search for his Wife's sister's Instagram picture, but Fritz shrugged, he pulled the strap off his rib and loosened his racquet bag.

"I told you I'd get it," Fritz responded, his smile slowly built.

Attorney Reggio scooted side by side with Fritz and aggressively put his arm around his neck.

"We did it," he yelled in his ear, his eyes were low and swollen from the whiskey he drank. "The old hag is out of the picture, the money is ours, I thought you were going to be playing stepdad forever, but you did it, you sick son of a bitch." Reggio shouted. His breath stunk like he just drank a whole gallon of gas station gas.

Fritz unzipped the racquet bag and paused with a metal tip in his fingertips. The words stepdad forever kept replaying in his head and at the point he could see Merlo and Phillip in his mind. His temples moistened, chin rose, and his heart pumped in his earlobe.

"Bartender," Fritz yelled while snapping. His arm stretched while making a fast-snapping noise with his fingers. The lady's eyes opened wide; she was a pale-skinned Latina, with black hair and pink eyeliner. She wore a pink and brown blouse that stopped at her belly, and she had a tattoo of a dream catcher on her collarbone. She walked toward Fritz, put her forearms on the counter, broadened her cleavage, and partially opened her lips.

"What are you having?" she asked.

"Can I get a Jack on the rocks?"

"Yea, Papi," she responded, then her brown eyes winked as she reached for a glass.

Fritz's armpits were damp at both sides, his gelled-down, comb-over hairstyle poked up on the top of his hairline. He rolled his sleeve, reached into his racquet bag, and retrieved papers with small print. They were house deeds for the Williamsburg plot on Flushing Avenue, Prospect Lefferts Garden, and Big momma Lucy's house on Patchen Avenue.

Reggio smiled, he slapped the table again because his team was getting crushed on defense and then he went back towards Fritz.

"I got a thousand bucks on these chumps, you hear me Fritzen? Hey what are you looking at?"

"The will." Fritz blinked with an awkward twitch.

"There are always loopholes in this thing," he uttered while pointing to the racquet bag, "We don't even need a guardian to sign over the trust, just bring your stepson and have him sign over a few papers because his guardian is as good as dead."

Fritz dug into the bottom of the racquet bag, he picked up the old raggedy composition notebook and flicked through the first page. It was the most valuable thing in the bag, but you could not tell just by looking at it. When Reggio saw it, he dropped his drink and pointed with his index finger.

"You sly devil, that's the rest of Merlo's coach book" he yelled. "Merlo would come from the dead and haunt you for getting your palms on that.

"Too bad Merlo is dust in the wind." Fritz smirked, his blue eyes bounced over the bar counter, and he saw the bartender reading his lips.

The bartender was pouring the Jack on the side, her eyes bounced towards Fritz, but she maintained the same stiff position while pouring the glass. She knew that the two men were some bigshots because of how they dressed. Guys who wore suits often came in the bar and tipped big, but Fritz had a sneaky energy about him like he just came up on a lot of money. See when most people come up on millions, the first thing they do is go out for a drink and the seductive bartender, Halo, knew how to read every kind of customer.

Reggio laughed so hard that his double chin wobbled.

"Toast to sticking to our words and not getting caught up," he uttered, and they both gulped simultaneously.

At the backside of the dim-lit bar, the slacking security guard Osane was sitting in a steel seat with a pool stick in his hand. He was waiting for his turn, but he noticed an orange beam of light shining on man. A man he promised that he would kill if he ever saw him again. Fritz from Neptune Avenue. The hustler behind the biggest bust in Coney Island. Osane was merely a child back then, but he remembers the trauma that Fritz caused to the whole community. Osane had a wide cranium like Charles Barkley, a rough beard and tattoos all over the side of his face and gauges in each of his earlobes. He slammed his pool cue on the table, unbuttoned his security guard shirt, and threw it on the table like a bed sheet. It covered the whole green surface.

Lil Tony lifted his chin, then dropped his corona on the seat.

"Osane? what are you doing vato?" he uttered.

Osane pushed through a couple who was dancing then another and another. There was a chair at the edge of the bar, so he lifted it and dragged it to Fritz's side of table. He set the chair and stood with both hands around the top of it. The light shone around his eyes, and they were like darts, but frozen and lifeless.

Fritz noticed He was a light, brown-skinned Latino with a scruffy beard and a large body like a lineman on the football field. His talking delayed.

Osane lunged forward, snatched the book away from Fritz's fingertips and pages came flying out in a whiplash.

The Latino gang from the pool table slammed their pool cues down one by one, dropped their Corona's and They walked over slowly with a confused gaze. Confused at who would try them in their own bar.

Osane held the book with his right, he extended his forearm to Fritz's drink, and he pulled it in to his chin. He guzzled down the glass while staring at him dead in his eyes and the ice cubes tumbled with gravity.

"I needed that drink," he uttered, "it's been like sixteen years Fritz. you think I forgot what you did?"

Fritz blinked slowly and locked eyes with him,

"I've done a lot of things, to a lot of people, get in line with the rest of them." he responded.

Lil Tony was behind their table standing side by side with his brother Harry. They both look like motorcycle gang members who were just as dangerous with their knuckles as they were with guns. Harry cracked his knuckles so loud that it sounded like bone fractures and Reggio's fat face turned thin.

Fritz tried to stand up and Harry grabbed his arm and twisted it. Threw him down onto the seat and pulled his arm upwards from the back. He was so strong that Fritz's eyes teared up from the agony.

Harry's face crumpled,

"Don't make me send you to the light foo," he shouted.

Everyone in the bar froze in place, the ceiling fan spun, but nobody moved, the chatter turned into complete silence, and then the people in the bar instantaneously panicked. The floor was crowded, the music was loud, and people bumped and pushed to scramble to the exit.

Osane gave a chin nod to the bartender,

"Get going, babe," he said. She lifted her cellphone and ran to the knob- less kitchen door and almost knocked down the server with five plates of steak and potatoes.

Harry slammed Fritz's face to the table and Fritz's cheek was on the surface, pink and swollen as if he had eaten poisonous berries.

Fritz dropped his cellphone,

"Fuckin hell, let me go," He wined. "If you want to rob us, take my wallet, but that's my coaching book. you do not need that."

Osane slammed the table with his left hand.

"Coaching?" Osane shouted with his Spanish accent, "Merlo was the coach, you ain't no coach, you were a scumbag white nigga who sold Morphine in the hood, that's all you did back in the days."

Osane leaned to the side, he whispered to Harry, and it looked like he mouthed the word kill him.

Harry reached into his leather jacket and pulled out a black revolver with a groovy barrel.

Lil Tony snagged the racquet bag, and he placed it on his shoulder with wit halfway opened.

Harry twisted Fritz's arms as if he wanted them to detach like a prosthetic, then holding him up with the gun aimed at the back of his head.

Reggio was screaming with both hands cupping his ears. As the Frank Sinatra music played, Reggio tilted his head to his cuffs, and he started fidgeting with his wristwatch.

"Listen here, I've got a Richard Millie, brand new," Reggio shouted "I can get all of you a bussed down Richard Millie, let me go. I'm an attorney."

"Sit down," Osane spazzed, "ain't no bribery's happening."

The bartender pushed the kitchen open door, walking out with the owner, Ricky, an Italian man with a dark aura about him. He walked slowly and pulled a cigar from his blazer pocket. His eyes captured Fritz and then bounced at Reggio.

His posture perked up, he gazed at the TV with focus, put the cigar into a line of coc and sparked it until the tip was ashy orange. Ricky then puffed the cigar,

"Osane, I see caught the biggest rat in the city," he uttered, "do him out back, we don't want any more wet work in this bar

Cruiser Lights
March/9th/2022

As a teenage child, Osane was skinny and gawky. He bounced his half flat Spalding basketball in front of his building and shot with a fast release into his milk crate tied to a fire escape with cable wire. The first shot went clank, second was straight across and bounced into the square hole. A Dope boy came through with a wrist full of jingling ice, rainbow colors bouncing all in his canary diamonds, a purple bathing ape hoodie and fresh air forces.

"Yo Lemme get a shot, Lil homie," he asked while tucking his jewels in his collar, and Osane swung the rock. It was a Perfect chest pass just like Merlo taught him.

Since the park was closed due to a triple homicide shooting, he stayed on his block, learning how to shoot that perfect catapult-beak-finger shot where the ball didn't touch anything.

His mother just had one rule, she'd turn all sweaty and pigment pale,

"Don't go across the street, not for anything," she said, "if the ball rolled into the other side of the streets by accident, then just leave it, Papi." She rubbed his shoulders while staring down.

On the other side of the block, laid out on the floor, was a junkie named Horus. He used to have thick dreads, wore wooden beads with Egyptian gods on them, and sold oils on Fulton Avenue with black soap and shea butter. He also attended pro-black rallies and gave speeches in favor of black-owned businesses until he started popping pills. The white man's pills!

The drugs overwhelmed Horus so much that he'd sit down and scratch his own skin until it whitened like chalk lines. See, crack rocks and pills didn't discriminate; it went from white hands to black hands, black hands to brown hands, brown hands to young hands. Where Horus lived, there was a constant thudding sound, feet sliding across the ground and He was getting his high as often as three times a day.

Always hearing those feet thuds. In and out of the burgundy building came people of all walks of life. He was bent, slurring and shaking with his big veiny hands holding a bag of potato chips. He had wide eyes, a flat face, damaged skin that looked like monkeypox. He stood in front of Big Pea Suggs housing complex watching them cars drive by. The Shock houses were a stucco of buildings condemned from living in and used for pumping dope at night. One building was made of cruddy grey brick, another was stained yellow, two were brown, and the last one was burgundy. It had chunks of brick missing at the top. It looked like a war missile had hit and that's what opened the roof, but it was a ditched construction job. It still had a wooden green scaffold over the entrance and rusty bars across that peeled. The building was full of junkies, dealers, and sassy hookers who only stopped for niggas in half-decent cars. They had cottage-cheese asses and tits that looked like popped balloons hanging to their navels.

One of the grimmest drug dealers had the purest shit, a white boy named Fritz. He stood near the mailbox wearing a hoodie with his hands tucked into his pocket.

One October night, there was a rumbling off-white white and silver Benz coming through the block. It had icy bright headlights flashing the road, and the wheels were chrome.

Osane's youthful eyes widened from across the street. He held his ball to his chest and didn't blink because he knew it was his coach's car. He blindly began to step forward, but remembered his mothers' eyes drilling him.

Merlo's backdoor opened wide, and a light brown woman with long brown hair stepped out of his car. She was wearing a leather jacket and black pants. She slammed the door, alerting the crows on the balcony to fly away. The woman was walking shoeless against the pavement. She held her heels in her hand and she had a slow limping strut into the burgundy building as if she were coming for drugs.

Fritz was by the scaffold, he walked into the street pole with his arms tucked into his pocket. He stepped towards Merlo's luxury car and peeped into the windshield to see who he was. Merlo had the seats laid back; he was sitting inside typing into his blackberry phone. He had a gold watch, three gold rings and a bottle of water in his cup holder.

Fritz had a scruffy blond curly top, a beard that looked like he'd been in England wilderness with wolves and bears, and when he came to the car Merlo was ready to pull off.

Merlo's body slouched,

"Waddup, Fritz," He spoke loudly with his deep voice, he had a tilted blue fitted, bushy eyebrows and a charming half-smile.

"I didn't know that was you."

The driver's side door ejected, the car made a dinging noise and Merlo stepped out of his whip. He was a massively tall six-foot-six man, wearing a blue and white, long-sleeved shirt with the word berlin on it. He had gold jewelry dangling off his neck. He and Fritz stood at the headlights of the flashy car pointing and laughing.

"You are still good at fixing cars?" Merlo laughed. He pointed to the beaming bright lights. The car exterior was normal, but there was a scuff and a dent on the right side of the bumper.

Fritz dropped down on the beady pavement with his baggy pants sweeping the ground. He stuck his nostril under the car, reached his hand underneath the bumper and pushed it in from the inside. It made a snapping noise as he popped back into place.

After he helped him fix the dented bumper, there

was a hunch from Merlo. He examined it for several minutes, and a crackhead walked by staring at him as if he was the man. Big pea Suggs? Yea, Merlo had to be the man with a car like that.

Fritz then gave a slight temple thrust, swung his hand so the crackhead would move.

They stared at the car, while talking about high school, then Fritz pointed to the woman who walked from his car into the narrow path of the burgundy building.

Merlo's face scrunched,

"It was car accident," he uttered, "she didn't even press charges on me, she just asked for some cash and to drop her here to get something for the pain, so I was like cool."

Fritz nodded his head, sucked his teeth and gasped for a deep breath,

"Car accident! Damn Merlo you are going to total this sweet thing one day." He glared at the car with hateful eyes and shook his head.

After their brief conversation, Merlo walked towards his door, started his car and drove off into the road. Things seemed normal, as normal as it could get for *Neptune Avenue*, but hours later, there was an anthill of police officers surrounding the sidewalk. Sirens were ringing and blue flashes were bouncing off golden badges. Black guns, black boots, black booklets out gathering information and the yellow eyes of junkies telling lies.

Horus was laid across the burgundy building's steps with the sides of his eyes looking all bagged out and layered. The officer on the left side stretched down, bent his knees and he banged his flashlight on the handrail to wake him up.

Bang, Bang, Bang.

Horus's lips tightened, he yawned with a white tongue and his face looked like he gulped sour milk. He lifted from his cardboard box and walked away with an old unsteady limp. He was only forty years old but walked like he was eighty.

The EMT pulled up to the curb, the box truck lit yellow, red, and blue. The uniformed men toppled the sidewalk while rolling an orange cart into the building.

The burgundy building had friends laid out in the hallway. They were surrounded by clusters of trash, bags, and bottles. The E.M.T men rushed inside, and they had to make long strides to avoid the dust in the walls. They found the body of the woman they came for, then came back down with a long body bag latched tightly to the metal cart.

There were no dealers inside the burgundy building, but Fritz was still on the block near a mailbox with a paper bag and a root beer. He Boldly walked through the police officers, pretending that he was a local neighbor, but when he stopped, he spoke with authority.

"Excuse me." he said to the police. "Sir, the kingpin you're looking for, he was in a silver Benz. The car is rare man, they have only made three of them in Berlin so that drug selling motherfucker should be easy to find. Like I said its Silver FTH." He aimed his pink index finger in the direction that Merlo drove. His lip twisted to the side; he hunched while making darting eye contact. He provided the officers with the plate, description, and location.

The officers were so quiet, their pens were loud scribbling into their booklets.

Osane's mother stomped downstairs with her red and blue Puerto Rican flag pajamas. Her slippers slipped on the moist concrete step as she reached her son. She pulled him by his shirt to the point it stretched, and he dropped his basketball against the street to the road.

"Papi, have you gone loco," his mother snapped, "come upstairs ... Ahora! I mean it, Osane, come on."

She pulled him by his ear and dragged him inside the building and he couldn't take his eyes off Fritz. Fritz was him, he was the real kingpin, but the officers will realize the truth, Merlo was a good man. He died that night, which was a memory that he never forgot, even well into his thirties and he still could feel the hatred for Fritz.

Osane thrusted all the mugs off the edge of the bar table. Exploding glass sounds echoed one by one and left crystal shards on the flooring.

Harry walked from the bar wall with a long baseball bat. He handed it to Osane and the whole bar went silent.

Osane shook his head,

"I used to be shitty at baseball," Osane uttered. "they said I was too aggressive with the bat but here's what's going to happen, you lie? I'll get funky with this bat."

He squeezed the handle tightly, pointed it at Fritz's jugular and pictured knocking off that white boy's head with one swing.

Osane stepped closer,

"Who was that woman Merlo was driving in the

backseat?" Osane shouted loud, "I'm grown now, I'm old enough to know that niggas cheat on their ladies every once in a while."

Fritz's eyes grew feverish, his fingers started to twitch as he clutched himself.

"It's not what you think," Fritz uttered back, "it's a complicated situation."

"Put it in a nutshell." Osane snatched him by the collar and his coat wrinkled "White boy, I look like I'm playing. I'll send you to Merlo and let him deal with you for setting him up, taking his son and fucking his wife."

Fritz's eyes scattered,

"It was a car accident," Fritz replied, "Merlo drove her to buy drugs."

"Drugs? You're the one who sold that shit, not Merlo."

Fritz's eyes lit up, his mouth gaped wide and all ten of his fingers spread out, but before Fritz could tell another lie, a gust of wind whipped through the air. The impact of the bat was so loud that you could hear the iron thud through the bar music. Fritz's stool swung back, his body slammed, and his Burberry trench coat flapped against the floor. Both arms were spread, his shoulder slumped parallel to his head, and the ceiling fan spun dark vulture shadows around his shut eyelids.

"He dead?"

"If he aint, he gonna wish he was."

5

Homicide
March/9th/2022

The spring air was fresh, deafening with the sounds of birds, and wind and nature. There's a tree that stretches from the sidewalk over to the front of my stoop and a grey squirrel that climbs it with jolting speed. There were far-out train track noises, wheels screeching against the rail and the conductor shouting words over the loudspeaker. Sometimes there was violence in the hood, and other times it was like poetry.

Minutes after, T.T. jolted from across the street, walking like she had been told to step on fire. She was wearing a tight black and yellow blouse, some black jeans, and a pair of yellow Balenciaga's. She had a plastic grocery bag in her fingers that bounced across her thigh. She narrowed in, pulled the gate latch, stomped to the highest step, and slammed the grocery bag near my big toe. Ouch!

"Are you dumb," she blurted with her eyebrows pressed down. Her lips tightened, her nostrils flared, and her face trembled as she snapped her head. "Open the door," she screamed. Her chest bounced as she stood over me. Her eyes were wide and white.

I lifted myself halfway, "What's wrong," I replied. I awkwardly stood straight, and we nearly bumped into each other because she was rushing inside. Her hip knocked the wind out of my stomach as she rushed inside. The lobby lights clicked on, and I could see the lines in her face. Her face was scrunched as if someone did something wrong to her.

"Nigga, I need you to explain something to me, cuz this shit doesn't make no sense." She spoke with her back turned. She placed the groceries on top of the radiator, while breathing loudly and sat on a stack of mail and a screwdriver. She pressed her palms against her eyes and took a loud breath. It was so awkward, I mean, she wasn't my girl or anything so it was so weird for her to trip out on me.

T.T lifted her pink iPhone out of her pocket, the screen had H.D. on the left side, and the word live in blood red. She jumped off the sack of mail and each envelope flung to the ground. She pressed the volume button to its highest point, and the news anchor's voice sounded crisp. The white reporter, Shirley Ashton, had makeup so white that it made her look ghostly, she wore a bob cut and a brown blazer, she held a microphone to her chest and veiny hands that shook as she twirled the microphone. Her chin dipped downwards and came back up to the screen.

"Fifty-nine-year-old man, Edward Aberdeen was ambushed," she said. "Two shooters robbed a local massage parlor called the Pink Blossom near the Elmhurst section of Queens. The men fled into a black Supercharger Revolt GTSS, before witnesses say it disappeared into thin air. We believe that the car hasn't been on the road since the murder."

T.T. lowered the cellphone. She glimpsed at me as if I had an explanation for her, then slapped her thigh with her phone and waited for me to speak. She slapped it repeatedly and blinked with each slap.

"That's the car, right, on your roof?" She shouted, "Black Supercharger Revolt GTSS."

"I don't know, I mean, it could be."

"It is dummy." She pushed off me and leaned on the other side of the lobby wall.

"Explain!" she shouted, her eyes darting like scorpion stingers, "You and Lance murdered that Spanish man in a massage parlor? Why would you— did you do it for — Dutchess? —no you didn't! —please don't tell me you did it for her.

6

Vroom Deady's Landing
March/3rd/2022

Last Thursday, I was laying on my mattress, my face was sideways, smelling the bland scent of the cotton-filled pillow.

My eyes were shutting slow, then it happened, it crashed like a comet. I heard mechanical springs smash over the ceiling. My leg kicked, which sent my laptop flying off my mattress and crashing down to the floor. The battery ejected, which slid towards my door. The flat screen TV on my wall was trembling, I had a cup of water on my computer table, and the liquid was jiggling side to side with water, some above the cylinder. I jumped out of my sheets and walked to my room door.

There was no one home because Fritz was in Berlin

and Big momma Lucy was in the hospital. I walked through the hall, and the soles of my feet felt tremors. The mop and broom were knocked over. A can of Goya beans on the floor near the kitchen; they were knocked over and rolling to the center of the house. I thought there was an earthquake or something, but there have never been any quakes out in Brooklyn, so I went to the living room window. The barred- up view showed stragglers walking through the block like any old night. But directly behind my apartment door was where the real disturbance was; loud footsteps were bashing the staircase and echoing through the hallway, I twisted the knob to the front door. A gust of wind pushed sideswiped my face. First Deon, Slim Demon, and Kookah Bug frantically coming out of the roof door, sneakers slamming through the hallway, down the staircase as if cops were after them. Slim Demon swung around the banister to the second floor, he dropped a silver gun with a long cylinder silencer on it, it hit the ground hard and swung like a boomerang on tiles. Once he realized he dropped the heavy piece of metal, he scurried back, bent down and reached while fumbling it. His fingers tightened around it and then ran in an off-balance motion.

My face flushed, I blinked out of it and my hands

squeezed the banister.

"Yo, what's going on?" I screamed.

From the second floor, Sophia poked her head out of her door. She had an oily green face mask, her head tie was wrapped around her skull like a genie, and she had on a long white robe made of terry cloth.

"Who released Rikers island into my home?" she yelled, "what was that loud noise, and why is my bloody apartment shaking."

The roof door was halfway busted.

The roof door was magnetic, as if something gigantic were behind it and lights shining leaked through the frame.

I walked with my head leaning to the side, then peeking through the crack with my fingers spread against the door.

behind the door, I heard the wind swishing and vibrating, then a humming V8 engine coming from the other side. I twisted my head sideways and pushed with both hands to make the door shut. Then rested on it, but I could still hear the V8 engine noise. I opened the roof door again, and stuck my face through. A whole groovy sports car was sitting at the center of my roof, looking like a floor model for a lavish sports-car brand. I walked towards the driver's side, and the cold wind from the rooftop struck me. I grabbed the handle of car, stuck my head in, and the dashboard was still gleaming while flickering in code. I cautiously opened the car, sat inside the black seats; the wheel was to my chest and had red lacing.

The tip of my foot tapped the gas pedal.

"Vroom!" The engine roared with a ferocious lion spike, it wobbled, and I could feel electricity running through each of my bones.

After I told T.T. the story, she curled into a ball and used her right arm to shield herself from me.

"The real niggas who did it was the R.S.I?" she let out an aggravated scoff.

"So, they killed some nigga and dumped the getaway car on your house? Ughh, you're so fucking stupid."

T.T. didn't say anything else, but her expression was like a whole argument. She hated me for letting a murder case fall onto my crib because she was homeless and if she had this Brownstone, she'd treat it better than I could.

7

Rocket Science
March/9th/2022

T.T. opened her pink pocketbook, pulled the strap over the top, and wrapped her fingers around a rolled-up joint the size of a pinky.

"I'm ready to go," she said. Her eyes beamed, "I need to smoke ... like right now." Her brown arm stretched for the door, and each of her yellow nails wrapped around the gold knob. Suddenly, she froze with the metallic sun beaming over her face. Her eyes were squinted as if she saw something out of the ordinary coming from outside, so she formed a visor out of her flat hand. There were aggressive men wearing black shiesty masks, rushing up the stairs as if they were out of time. One man stocky, and the other was tall like hooper for a college division. He pushed at the center of the door and his hand knocked off the whole mailbox. The lobby door busted open wide enough to see the streets and cars. The taller man opened the door; he had a fade afro, a dented skull as if he had been shot in the forehead. He had tattoo of a black crucifix right above his eye, and a tattoo of the words R.S.I on his cheek. He had a chipped tooth, a large nose with an untidy mustache and purple-stained lips. It was that old greaseball, Slim Demon. He looked both ways and lifted a silver Smith and Wesson 9mm with a silencer. His forearm straightened and he stuck the long nose gun into T. T's ribcage while thrusting her into the lobby. She fell awkwardly and kicked out her foot which made the door slam backward. The radiator rocked and the grocery bag tumbled down and landed on the floor. The milk carton busted open, and milk was gushing out on the floor tiles.

Slim Demon's lip twisted, and his flailing nostrils looked like the inside of a sawed-off shotgun.

"Y'all bitches ready to eat sum lead," he shouted with a deep southern voice. I never heard Slim Demon talk before, but after hearing his southern voice, I knew that the car belonged to him because the plates read Georgia.

Kookah Bug shut the door and pulled down the

curtains. He pointed his .45 at me and his body was tilted. He had an oval-shaped face with a cone head, grizzly sideburns that grew in spotty and pulsating a double chin. A straight ugly motherfucker!

Slim Demon's attention reverted to me,

"You know what's about to happen." He turned around towards Kookah Bug and his voice amplified a notch. "This Ya bitch, pussy?" He screamed with his lips tightened, "I should buss her, but Ima pop you first for what you did with my whip, gangsta."

The light beams shined from the sky to the strands on my eyelids. At the center of the roof, The Vroom Deady car was still parked with the clouds running its reflection across the glossy body.

I couldn't tell Whether it was the wind giving us electric chills or the fact that I was about die. Slim Demon opened his door, started the car and he kept staring back. Tried to reverse the car in the direction I was standing in, and all he could see was the darkening grey smoke coming from the muffler.

Minutes later, Kookah stepped up to the roof with his chest bouncing, he had a long sharp scratch on his face that was tinted with a line of blood. My eyes ping-ponged back to the roof door and I had a weightless stance as I watched him.

"Where is T.T.," I shouted, "she aint have nothing to do with this, you know that?"

Kookah Bug bumped into me as he walked, he had an eye twitch and a shake in his forearm that looked involuntary. The back of his had the R.S.I tattoo written underneath the faded part of his hairline.

Slim Demon shut his car off. He had his knee on the driver's seat while digging into the glove department. He pulled out his insurance papers, shoved it into his pocket and pulled his afro out of the car. He looked down at the far-off concrete. The wind was heavy and people on the ground looked so tiny that you could become woozy if you tried to stare too hard.

I imagined myself running at full speed and pushing him off the roof to see him die; I can't lie, I wanted to kill him before he got to me, but I was trembling down to my feet. The air was tense, and each heart pump felt like a twisted hiccup.

Slim bit down his jaw and his temples had a muscle flex. He dropped his long gun to his skinny hip, lifted his pants higher then walked to the front of the car to take a seat on the slanted hood.

"We can't get down from this," he snapped while tapping his gun muzzle on the hood. "it's too high, we gotta trim Lul Bone and him, then leave for the country."

Kookah Bug's body flattened,

"Kill Lul Bone? hell nah, we caught that body for him and his sister. That our little man."

Kookah Bug slapped his forehead and everyone was quiet.

Kookah Bug walked towards me and stopped at the roof door, pushing me by the arm into the hallway. He lowered his gun down to his thigh.

"Listen, kid," He muttered, "I smoked that Shaq nigga on Patchen Ave. I still remember the look of his eyes when I hit him. He looked like he was having an exorcism or something. But that nigga I killed was a grown man though. I'm not bodying no little ass kids. Find Deon!" he stared intensely while pointing his finger into my sternum, "tell him he better get this fucking car down before they trace the shit, and we all go down for those murders we did for him."

Girlfriends
March/9th/2022

I walked down the steps in search of T.T. and once the lobby light flicked on, I saw that she was on her knees facing the lobby wall. Her wrist was tied behind her back; her hair and forehead was wrapped with brown duct tape. She had a muffled scream that sounded like a studio singer who got gagged in a recording both. Her whole body was full of red whelps like she had been beaten while moving backward. The wall had an ugly smudge right next to where she was standing, and the center of her head was swollen as if someone had banged it several times over.

T.T's brown body appeared a shade redder as if she were upset. Once she was cut lose, there was a large vein in her temple and she swung upwards into the air, and it landed in the center of my throat. She swung with her other hand, and I caught it in midair. She used her hand to lift herself off the ground and the top of her weave scalp hit my chin, she awkwardly turned around, got her balance, scratched, and clawed forward. Her face was full of energetic emotion, she took a long stride forward, and her long pink and yellow nails sliced into my forearm.

"This is your fault," she snapped, "you're so immature, all you had to do was call the police, you dumb ass." She leaned forward and pushed me in the shoulder, "9-1-1 hello? It's that easy! You don't use the resources to save ya fuckin ass?"

The echoes from her last sentence vibrated the hallway.

I stood up,

"Why would I call the cops, that's being a snitch." My arms reached forward preventing her arms from swinging.

T.T. held her arm above her head, squeezing a fist, then she unloosened it,

"You got me tied up in this stupid shit with them, Phillip, they kill niggas you fool, It's the R.S.I! they could have killed both of us."

Then she swung again.

The ground rocked as we slipped, she had a yellow flannel shirt around her hip, I pulled it by accident, and it flung to the floor. She pushed herself off me and wiped her face with her wrist pressed against her eyes.

"I'm going to Harlem," she snapped. "Rather be at my father's house, and he's a fucking woman beater, but I'd rather be there than here."

She shivered with emotion, she picked up her yellow flannel shirt and tied it around her wide hips. Her pocketbook was on the wood flooring, covered in milk, she lifted it and shoved her things back inside one by one. She pulled the knob and walked through the door frame into the dark streets. There was a gold earring on the floor along with a chipped yellow nail, she must have not noticed it before she left, or she did and didn't care.

Barbara was across the street, stone-faced, sitting next to a Puerto Rican lady with a light brown skin tone.

Barbara had on a long-sleeved plaid button-up shirt with a Black Panther T-shirt. She had some cream pants with green crocs, her legs wide open, and her elbows leaned on the step above. She waved at me like a stranded person on an island signaling a chopper.

"Come here," she hollered from across the street. At the same time, she was swinging her hand and smiling.

I looked both ways, then crossed the street and once I arrived close to those cruddy project steps, she tossed her small roach blunt into a Styrofoam cup full of Pepsi and it sizzled like frying oil.

By the trash can, there was an old radio playing "Rain on Me" by Ashanti.

Barbara looked like Lisa Leslie, she could even hoop like Lisa too, but she was too obsessed with females to go pro. She'd always say that she couldn't be in no locker room with that many females because she'd be all up on them, and slapping assess in the shower.

She smirked at me with a confused look, then tilted her head to the side with her eyebrows squished.

"Phillip," she uttered, "Who were the people in your grandma's house." She leaned forward while aiming her finger in the direction they walked. "I saw two men coming out, then an angry girl so tell me what's going on, you know your grandmother don't play when it comes to her Brownstone."

My eyes twitched, they dropped down, then I planted my foot next to the other. I looked at her with wide galaxy eyes.

"I don't know them," I replied, "They came in looking for Deon." I turned my face the other way and turned back to her again. "They were gonna hurt him because Deon was involved with some street stuff."

Every bone in Barbara's jaw went stiff, she lifted herself and then dropped again. Her eyes bobbled toward her cellphone, and she searched her own pocket to lift it

"Charlesha's son?" Barbara leaned up, her face frowned, and her fingers reached towards the Puerto Rican lady's leg.

She stared her down, while rubbing her girlfriend's inner thigh.

"Baby, let me and Phillip talk for a second." She uttered, her eyes were glossy, her voice sounded feminine and soft.

The girlfriend lady sucked her teeth, she walked towards the project door and pulled the wobbly handle. The door slammed so hard that the glass had a new crack in the center.

Barbara's eyes turned to me, and she didn't blink as she spoke.

"I've been in this neighborhood since nineteen eighty. I knew them fools weren't from over here," she uttered. But they aint coming for my Brown sugar! uh, uhm, he's a sweet kid, no, not my little man."

I dug into my pocket and put my head down to the concrete. Mind you that I'm the most dramatic teenager that ever lived in Brevoort.

I thought for sure that I'd die by Slim, and it was written all over my face. There was panic in my eyes, shakiness, fear and other strange body language that an adult could easily examine. Barbara was the perfect woman to talk to because she was overbearing when it came to protecting the children in the neighborhood.

My thoughts were so loud that she could hear them.

The edge of Big momma Lucy's photograph was still in my pocket, pricking my wrist so I held it at my hip. That long rigid line was large enough to separate the sea. Separate a family; my family and it did. The photograph sliced off Ivory and Yata from Brian. I stared at it, I took a deep swallow and stepped closer to Barbara.

"You can give this to Big momma Lucy if something happens to me." I uttered. My face shook as I spoke "You been here since nineteen eighty, this is Big momma Lucy's picture, of her children, it means something to her."

Barbara's neck snapped back

"What." She shouted.

Barbara stood up once more and her eyelids heightened as if she saw something gigantic. Gigantic like seeing the Titanic at the dock for the first time or a mountain like the Himalayas. She snatched the photo from my grasp and looked at it with budging eyes. She rubbed baby Brian's picture as if she had compassion for him. She held the photo with both hands and brought it closer to her nostrils.

"Of course, I knew Brian, shit! I grew up with him, he was my first crush... until he ..." her lips stopped. She took a deep breath while speaking mid-sentence, her left hand stretched towards the stony step and her fingers had polish that was clear and shiny. She lifted her bottle of Heineken and put her pink lips around it. The beer swirled down the green glass hole into her hesitating throat.

"Ya grandma aint tell you about him?" she uttered in a dejected tone. "Your own uncle?" She extended her chocolate brown hand towards me to return the glossy photograph. Her fingers looked sweaty at the tips. She scratched her jaw while leaning back.

"I don't want to get involved with that, Hunny,

I'm sorry," she uttered with a deep voice. Her left hand trembled as she retracted it. She reached for her old radio and twisted a knob so that that the music echoed into the open sky.

9

Find Deon
March/9th/2022

I walked towards the caged basketball court, and I could hear a loud voice shouting on a megaphone along with clapping hands. To my right, there were a bunch of cars parked on the sidewalk, girls eating food from a Halal truck and to my left was the rigid cage, with a line of men bouncing basketballs, wearing jerseys that were green, some orange and some blue. They were surrounding the scoring desk that read Summer Slammers. The tournament was organized for troubled kids in projects to prevent crime. But there were still shootings, and I don't mean at the three-point-line either.

A tall kid was in the center of the court, with his hands on his hips. He stood, then sped fast and had a catlike bounce to him. He was athletic and shifty like a brand-new sports car. He could switch hands with the basketball and get to the rim so fast that all I saw was a blur. I knew it was him at first glance because no one was as crafty as him. By him, I mean Him. Every neighborhood has a him. He was that kid, simply from his swagger, his style and his energy. The kid jumped high and landed smoothly, just like Deon. He was swift on his feet, just like Deon, he'd burst with speed and then dish the rock to his teammates, just like Deon. It was him and he wasn't in the streets gang banging anymore; he was playing basketball, his true love.

Deon glimpsed at Dustin and nodded while aggressively running down the court. Side by side they were like Mike and Pip. They both sat in their defensive stances and double-teamed little Lionel at the half court line. Deon swiped at the ball as if he were doing a karate chop and Dustin stumbled while dribbling. He lifted his head and tossed it to Deon, and he finished it with a rim- rattling dunk. Repeatedly, they crushed their opponents on defense and ran them into the ground on offense with fast passes, long range bombs and Alleyoops. My eyes couldn't shut, I walked closer to the crowd and everyone's body pushed and bumped into me like flesh bumper cars.

When I got closer, my eyeball leaked through a set

of bodies. I pushed through the backside of random strangers. Suddenly, Deon was running to rim with intense speed; however, there was a defender in front of him, but he didn't even stop and it seemed that it would lead to a sporadic collision. But then it happened and by it, I mean it. It happened. His arms and shoulders were covered in blue fogyish clouds. His chest was square, but his arms were glowing in-between the blue clouds. He pushed the basketball forward and it vanished into thin air.

The whole court went silent.

Deon was standing there, with a half-smirk like a street magician.

The blue clouds on his wrist were still, just like everyone's eyes and jaws. The ball vanished and re-appeared Dustin's two hands like a perfect delivery to the hoop. Dustin leaped up for a vicious rim-rattling slam dunk and the backboard vibrated so hard that I could feel the impact in my feet.

The announcer from the tournament had a bald head that shined from under the light. He held his microphone close to his bearded jaw like a comedian after a punchline.

"Oh my god," he snapped with a goofy tone. While holding one hand over his bald head, "we are not worthy, woah baby! what was that" he shouted, his eyes popped out of his sockets. He ran across the sideline rubbing his bald head, and scooting through the bench players. "Boy, what Michael-Jordan- Marvel-Comic moves are those! D-nice A.K.A Lul Bone! Collect the bones baby! we are not worthy!"

Even though Deon intimidated people on the court, he was so humble that he gave the opposing team handshakes after the game. His chin was forward, he slapped everyone's hand, and then he walked towards his sister Mary Ann.

10

The call

March/9th/2022

Deon stood inches away from me with his back turned. He was skinny but had football pad shoulders and when he spread his arms for defense. He looked like Jrue Holiday. Not in facial features, but the same slender athletic body type and a scruffy afro that looked like wool. He liked to slap his hands together aggressively and push opposing players around like a bully.

The R.S.I gang; his family it seemed, wasn't in the park backing him up and he didn't have his orange gang bandana wrapped around his head.

There were a lot of other gang members on their feet huddled up with plastic cups and spliffs burning like incense. They were rooting, rumbling, and rattling Deon's team, but after his magic passes, they cheered for him.

On the other side of the court, I saw Lance with his pants sagged low. He was slapping another kid with an orange foam finger shaped like a number one.

Usually, Deon would come close and give me a handshake, but he pretended as if he didn't see me in the crowd.

My arms flailed forward and I caught thin air,

"Yo Deon," I uttered, my voice cracked because I noticed everyone staring at me while puffing their spliffs.

"Please let me talk, remember the car on the roof, you gotta come to get it down, Slim Demon and Kookah ran up on me."

When I mentioned Slim Demon's name, everyone in the park turned to the side and talked louder to their homies.

Deon didn't show any immediate concern for Slim. He did leave the court, walk over to his sister and grab her backpack. He held the princess back pack with one hand and his little sister's hand with the other. He stood around some old gangstas with assorted color bandanas. I saw Homeboy Hustle from Marcy. Corner Pocket, from East New York, and a Spanish cat named Gunner P.

Everyone stared at me, as if I were a part of the

R.S.I and was about to bring negative energy into the park.

Suddenly, my hoodie pocket glowed like high beams.

My cellphone felt like a taser, and the screen was my mother's name.

I pressed the button and the heat from the speaking holes blasted me in the air.

"Where is your daddy, Fritz?" she screamed into my ear. "I've been calling him all day."

I walked out of the loud blacktop park, I took a seat on the flat head Johnny pump and stared through the gate. I sat there with my head down. There was a Corona bottle next to my foot and a moist pothole that shined like plastic. I could see the moon through the pothole water.

"I haven't seen Fritz since earlier," I yelled, "but he left me a photo of Brian."

The phone went quiet, my mother's voice gasped and began to space out and panic into half sentences. Her chopped words couldn't form properly enough to make sense, but I kept hearing her start off by saying let me explain. She breathed a deep, lively breath.

"I can't live with myself," she cried. She sucked her tears up, "I can't believe Fritz told you the truth about everything, Phillip let me explain what happened to us that night."

11

Ivory's Point of View
October/13th/2005

It was a chilly Friday, the thirteenth of October, months before you were born. I lived in Prospect Lefferts Gardens with your father Merlo, so I wasn't used to the tall trees and branches smacking my window. I was pregnant so I wore a robe around the house.

Merlo and I lived in a spacious two-family building. It was our first house, but it was nearly any space because we still had some of our things in bulky brown boxes. There were stacks of boxes lined up against the tall sliding windows; that's right, we had a relaxing view of the road, but I covered it up because I liked to walk around naked, and I aint want nobody to see my goodies. The boxes were full of Merlo's basketball stuff, clothes, and sneakers, but my stuff was on the left side near the bathroom.

I was seven months pregnant with you, my first and only son, Phillip. Merlo wanted your name to be Maasai, just like the warriors in Kenya, but your name became Phillip because that was the name of the prison doctor who was nice to me while delivering in Obbit Thorn. *A jail!* I had to deliver you in a *jail!*

Phillip McFlores was his name though. I was too emotional, crying about Merlo's death with a wrenching face. They told me I would die unless I calmed down because I had high blood pressure, and they were giving me an Epidural. I didn't care; I wanted to die that day and them redneck Doctors couldn't change my mind.

He held my hands, loosen the cuffs and even ordered the nurses to change my sheets so I won't get any infections.

How did it happen? How did Merlo die? I thought this day would never come. I hate explaining it. Merlo would go out and drink in Coney Island with his friends. Even though I told him don't drink and drive his fucking stupid ass car, he still did what he wanted. That October night, I bit my fingertips down to the whites; that's how anxious I was for him to walk through that door frame at ten o clock at least. I pulled at my dreadlocks, and I could feel the strands rip at the root. There were half-chewed nails that looked like crescent moons as I lined them up right underneath the keyboard and I kept drinking coffee. It was a bad habit, but I did it whenever I was having heart palpitations and I surely was whenever Merlo was out there with them niggas. He liked to hang in his old neighborhood, where it was known for selling dope, but if you ask me, Coney Island streets were more trouble than fun.

The theme park was just a cover-up for what really goes on.

I turned around, the computer desk was full of sticky notes and loose-leaf paper with my squiggly handwriting. Every calendar in the house had a sloppy circle drawn around my birthday weekend—a trip to the shady resorts of St. Croix Virgin Islands. We finally were going to do something together; I've always dreamed about seeing crabs at the shore, my footprints in the warm sand, and jumping into the sparkling blue water. It was my perfect getaway trip with him, but like everything else, it was canceled because of Merlo's Berlin calls that he wanted me to handle. That's right; I was his wife, agent, ride or die bitch, or whatever. I never liked to be called that, but I always stood there looking cute in my heels because niggas weren't gon see me stressing him about petty shit, hell, I never wanted him to be upset with me or us not speaking especially over his stripper baby mother.

Our Louie luggage was stacked in a corner near the door, if you opened the hinges too wide, those bulky cases would probably tumble into the kitchen. I'm not the messy one in the house, it was him, but I couldn't take the luggage down because I convinced myself that we could still make my birthday trip to St. Croix. It's my birthday, why wouldn't we go out? I mean, it would have been crazy talk for me to stay here for another two months of pregnancy and not do anything before our son came. It was our last chance! Maybe he was fooling around and wanted to surprise me.

I finally stood from the computer chair; I sat down slowly on the couch because my side was hurting. I opened my cell phone and called him, and you know what? I could tell he aint want to speak to me.

"I'll be there soon," Merlo spoke in a lifeless tone, he sounded as if I was sucking the life out of him as if our marriage wasn't enough for him to be happy. I walked to the kitchen, put the coffee glass under the machine, and let the water steam. Two mugs of coffee were perched near my table, red lipstick stains were on the rims, and saltwater tears kept coming down from my eyes. Every time I tasted the coffee, it tasted saltier. There was mirror directly across from the table, so I could see my reflection; people always told me I looked beautiful pregnant, but I felt like a disgusting cow. I didn't feel beautiful; I wouldn't have felt beautiful unless Merlo told me, and he'd never say shit.

This one white boy from Coney Island projects always liked my pictures on Myspace. He would always be on point with my birthdays, holidays, and everything. Fritz is what they called him, but he was a nobody, just there to entertain me whenever I was being a moody bitch. I opened my phone, and there he was, messaging me again.

"I hope I get to see you more," Fritz wrote. Something I wish Merlo would have said, but it was still nice to feel wanted by someone. I sat there staring at the phone screen, laughing at Fritz's goofy jokes. He had a dark sense of humor. Suddenly the lock on the door clacked, it nudged wide and Merlo stood in the door frame with a blue long sleeve shirt, he had his fitted on to the front, the blue one that I like so much. He had his gold chains on, rings, he was looking like a rapper or something. He opened up his lips and his mustache was lined up so perfectly.

"What's going on, Bumba" he said with his

earthquake voice. He tried to walk close to me, but I picked up the coffee mugs and brought them to the kitchen sink. Suds dripped down from my fingertips as I washed the dishes one by one. The last object to clean in the sink was the knife. I let the water splash over the blade, I lifted it up and watched his reflection through the steel. He walked past the tower of luggage, and he sat down at the computer table, hovering over the portfolio I made for his coaching profile in Berlin. That's all he fucking cared about was Berlin. I dumped the knife into the sink, my body rotated towards him, and walked toward him. He was so tall and lanky that we looked like father and daughter. My eyes rolled hard; I moved my hands through the air as I spoke.

"Merlo, what are you going to tell me this time," I shouted with trembling cheeks. "That you weren't fucking Cyn again. your old stripper bitch baby-mother while I was doing all your fucking paperwork like a dumb bitch."

"What the hell are you talking about?" he snapped back with his fingers open wide. I wasn't with Cyn! The last time I seen my daughter Shandy was when I was with you, I have a whole new baby boy to think about. I was in Coney Island with my folk drinking and blowing it down."

My anger didn't last long at all. First, I didn't have any evidence he was with Cyn, and second, I was the biggest dummy for him; whatever he said, I believed it to be the truth because he was just that type of nigga. He always seemed so genuine when he spoke about Cyn. He didn't respect her like he respected me so maybe he didn't creep out on me. He seemed sincere, and I trusted him, so we kissed while he pressed his chiseled body on mine. We undressed from the couch to the hallway and then to the king-sized mattress. I smelt him, and he smelt like he always did. No soap, or musky cologne, or anything to change the smell of his balls.

He threw me against the wall, then opened his mouth and kissed my neck. Then he lifted me off my feet and placed me on the mattress with ease.

I stood there and my cat was wet.

My legs couldn't go back behind my head like before, but they were open while he was ripping my guts. Lord I was so horny while pregnant, so I wanted all his chocolate self. His arms were all tight and sweaty as he killed this cat.

Merlo was partially drunk. He lifted himself from the dented bed and His eyes were puffy red.

"Babe, babe, babe," he spoke with his voice

smelling like liquor. When we get this money from Berlin, I'm going to buy both of our mothers a house, word to moms."

He loved his mother, so I knew when he said words to moms, that he was being truthful. He shut off the lights and pressed his chocolate body against mine. Then suddenly, my cell phone brightened the room, the light projected into the ceiling, and my mother's name was pulsating on the caller ID. She would normally never call me late, so I picked it up with urgency. My cheeks were colorless, and my arm created a soft dent in my pillow as I held the phone at the tip of my fingers. Lucy didn't sound like herself!

"Ivory," she muttered in choking desperation; it sounded like she was holding her breath underwater and finally got a chance to breathe. She spoke from her guts, sounding sad while hiccupping.

"Your brother Brian," her voice intensified with hiccups, "he was found dead on Neptune Avenue. Why Jesus? What could he have been doing out there? Please somebody tell me Ivory! Why!"

My right palm covered my mouth, my eyes busted out of the sockets, and the mattress shook like a waterbed as I hurried out of it. My heavy feet slapped through the hallways flooring and down towards the kitchen tiles.

The kitchen was silent.

Heavy needles darted my body which caused me to clench. I rested my back against the refrigerator with the phone pressed against my ears.

"Your brother is gone." Lucy screamed in trembling, cold agony.

My feet slipped, my body buckled, and my hand swiped every magnet to the point they all came crashing down off the refrigerator door. My tears dropped hard like AC drippage on a June evening. I was guilty of how I treated my brother over the years. He was different, but he didn't deserve to die, especially after I never got a chance to speak to him about what I did.

Merlo's long stilt legs stopped at the kitchen, his arms stretched over, and he hugged me tightly. I squeezed him until my knuckles turned white. He let me go; his jaw clenched as he handed me a tissue.

"I didn't even know you had a brother," he said in a low tone.

"What happened to him?"

"We never treated him like family," I responded. As soon as I was about to explain to Merlo why he was treated so poorly, a rock-solid set of knuckles throbbed against the hollow front door. The knocks intensified the second time around and it sounded as if someone had used a hard piece of metal.

Merlo's eyebrows wrinkled, he let go of me and he walked past the kitchen, around the couch, to look through the peephole.

It was two officers standing side-by-side.

Merlo looked at me and hunched.

"Officers Bumba." he uttered.

He took the chain off, twisted the knob, and opened it and the light beam shot into the apartment. There was a white police officer on the right name Scott Kramer, and Arab officer Jamaal Ahmad stood to the left. Kramer had a look of empathy on his face; his ears were red at the lining; he looked towards my pregnant stomach, and then his eyes bobbled to the messy bedroom and back towards Merlo. He took a deep breath, then spoke with his eyes. He was making laser eye contact, opening his police booklet and talking with a deep voice.

"Sir, you're the owner of that off-white and silver Benz parked in the front," he said, "It was seen on Neptune Avenue at approximately ten o'clock. We have a tip that an unidentified man was dropped off by your Benz to get drugs—he passed away from the Morphine, so we would like if you accompanied us down to the precinct to talk."

The apartment was loud with tension.

Kramer stepped forward, his holster for his Glock didn't have the strap around it and his left hand was holding his belt as if he were ready for someone to get out of line.

Ahmad's right hand touched the center of the door, his eyes dotted into the apartment.

Merlo's head snapped back, his eyebrows heightened, he kept his palm squeezed around the doorknob as if he was ready to close it in their faces.

"A man?" He smirked with confusion and the center of his face was as if he was ready to bust out laughing. "There must be a mistake, officer," he replied. "At no point in time did I drop off a man tonight."

I lifted from the tiles, with my gut full of fire. I stood by Merlo's side. I was dabbing my tissue against my eyes. All I could think about was my dead brother Brian. His mysterious life, his wigs, scarves, and skirts. His addiction to drugs, my mother said that he died on Neptune Avenue too. Maybe it was mass death thing going on or maybe it was *connected? No!* My eyes narrowed onto Merlo's solid shoulder blades. He shook his head with a sarcastic grin at the side of his cheek from the police across from us and then back to me.

Officer Kramer's grey eyes looked like silver dimes, his eyes bounced at me and to the bedroom, then back to Merlo. He stepped forward another few feet with his polished boot, and the light from the living room shined on his mottled nose. He took a deep swallow and then spoke hesitantly.

"The unidentified man didn't look much like a man," he muttered, his nose was full of sweat at the tip.

Merlo was briefly stunned, the cords in his neck curled, and he had a dumbfounded glow in the middle of his face. He shook his head while looking at me.

"I should have told you what happened Bumba," he said.

He placed his big hands on my shoulders. It's not what it sounds like, it was just an accident."

The tissue slipped out of my fingertips and down towards the floor. My jaw dropped into a horrific scream. My body hunched, my knees buckled and I was down to the floor. Kramer reached for me, so I raised my arm and altered my hand position towards his glock. Snatched it from his utility belt, lifted it and squeezed it towards Merlo. I squeezed that trigger so tightly, and an orange flash shook the whole house. Kramer backed away and reacted with a delay, but he pushed my arm, so the second bullet took a chunk of dust out of the ceiling. It rained sugar over our heads. And Kramer's lengthy arms managed to get tangled with my dreads, he locked his arm around neck and pushed my body. I lost balance with the gun, my torso was pointed down and my nose smelt like blood.

After the realization that Merlo had been shot, I was already being dragged to the cold floor. The officers wrestled me down in the center of my living room while grabbing my dreads and pulling my arm out of its socket. As I screamed, the officers yelled my rights. They said I had right's, they read them while they choked me down and pulled my loc's, but it felt like I didn't have anything, not even a baby in my stomach the way they were roughing me up.

I peeked over at the side of my eye and Merlo's wide legs were stretched across our travel luggage as if he were sitting on a floater. His legs wobbled with electricity from shock, his arm bent awkwardly with his knuckles dragging on the floor as if his forearm were twisted.

The police handcuffs hissed and tightened my

wrist. I remember the smell of the wood as my face was down and I remember the smell of blood as they lifted me up. And through the mirror I saw that my face had Merlo's blood splatter.

At the corner of my eyes was Merlo fighting with himself, his toes curved under his humongous foot, his body stretched across our travel luggage, and a splatter of blood oozing from the kitchen walls. The thing about bullets is that they shoot straight across, but blood splatters backward, forward sometimes telling a messy story.

Merlo's stomach was sucking in and out with his eyes to the ceiling. He squeezed his throat with one hand, and thick blood gushed through his fingers.

"Car accident," he screamed with a gargling noise. "A fuggin car accident."

Officer Ahmed bolted down on his knees, he grabbed a towel from the kitchen stove.

"Apply pressure to your neck." He screamed. Kramer lifted his radio from his shoulder and called for the ambulance.

As the officer kneeled to help, Merlo's face curved into a hideous twist, and he was nowhere near a hideous man. His mouth was covered in blood. The blood on his teeth looked like rows of red pomegranate seeds as he tried to breathe.

By the time the ambulance came, his legs were as stiff as firewood and his upper body was slumped awkwardly.

I went to jail that night looking for ways to kill myself. I wanted to hang with a sheet tied like noose because I had just killed the love of my life over a misunderstanding. *A car accident? Fuck! I'm so fucking stupid.*

As for my brother Brian, we damaged him in our house growing up. Long before Lucy purchased the Brownstone building, we were just a fatherless family that lived in the basement. That's the reason she doesn't rent it. It's our childhood house, and it's all guilt from Brian. We did not have a father growing up, so imagine having two sisters around a boy who seemed awkward at every given moment. Brian liked girls when he was younger, but he liked to dress up in women's clothes, so we clowned him. He liked to play with dolls, so we cracked jokes. Something odd was happening to his body during puberty, and his chest made a triangle shape just as ours did. So, we threw bras at him. Yata and I stood over his bed, we wound up our bras like slingshots, and they lashed across his head until he woke up kicking and screaming.

"Mommy," He screamed, he kicked and flung his arms like a little punk.

"Mommy, can you tell them to stop,"

Lucy never came for him. She stayed behind her room door with a bible to her breast crying tears of sadness.

Yata poked Brian in his soft jiggly arm.

"You're turning into a girl," she laughed. You'll never be a man! you're a sister boy, you're going to have your period like us."

Lucy wouldn't always pray. Matter fact she would avoid it altogether now that I can remember. She stayed in her room. Sometimes she would pray or watch movies, sometimes calling the pastor and asking for strength.

When Brian was fifteen years old, he stuffed his rolling backpack with clothes, zipped it, and threatened Lucy that he would move out. She didn't stop him like she would have stopped us; she closed her room door and prayed more. As Brian walked with his rolling backpack, he struggled with its weight and dropped at his knees.

The apartment was silent, then the door hinges squeaked and Yata stumbled out laughing and holding her stomach. She and I threw bras at him to remind him that he was like a girl rather than a boy. We sprayed our perfume nozzles onto his head until the back of neck was dripping in oil. I remember the hiccupping noise he made at the middle of the step because he kept crying. We didn't care; we just kept doing it until he was gone, and he never came back either.

I saw Brian before his drug overdose. *Yup!* He was in a motel—the Super Galaxy before it became all drugged out. He was a full-blown woman with tits, hips, and ass. That fool looked better than me and Yata combined. Yata told me after his transformation that he turned into a female so that he could disguise himself after robbery's he committed for drugs.

Fuck all the circus shit! I distanced myself from the family. I had my own family and I was with Merlo. We were waiting for our name to be called—to get a room and have a good night. I could have told my man who my brother was, but I kept my legs crossed, put my head on my man's shoulder, and didn't say a word. Which came back to haunt us all.

12

Lance's Get back
March/9th/2022

I didn't judge her.

By the time she was finished telling her story, the night sky had gotten slightly brighter.

I told her that I forgive her. Big momma Lucy always told me to forgive and as wild as Ivory was, she learned how to forgive herself first which helped her move on with Fritz.

I walked through the projects and stared at my house. I approached the sidewalk, my gate latch was wide open, there was a police car across the street, so the metal on the gate was reflecting red and blue colors. The stone steps led to the door, which had a slight crease in the strike plate. It was already cracked open, so I pushed it cautiously. The light from the lobby shined on a dark-skinned person who was on the inside.

My head tilted, and to my surprise it was Deon sitting there. He wore a stretched-out white T-shirt that revealed his chest plate and shoulder. His shorts had bloodstains, and his sneakers were scuffed to the rubber as if they were bent weirdly. He punched his fist into his palm while biting his lip.

"*you saw what happened?*" he uttered as he squeezed his fist. He took a step back and landed near the wall to retrieve his basketball.

The ball's surface looked normal, but it looked flat and wobbly when he touched it. There was a black piercing that tunneled straight through the rubber and out the other side.

"Look," he uttered, his lips thinned around his white teeth, "They shot at me while I was in front of my *little sister*, that shit coulda—." he scrunched his face and stared at me with eyes as if he were shocked. "That shit coulda hit her!"

My face had an involuntary twitch,

"What! Who shot—I mean who did this?"

Deon's eye was beaming at the floor, he didn't blink and he appeared as if he were shaking in cold nerves.

"Slim Demon did this shit," he uttered while squeezing the basketball. It whistled like Big momma

Lucy's Mac and cheese until all the rest of the air was gone.

Deon's face scrunched,

"I told the R.S.I what was happening to Dutchess. I told them about her sick ass godfather and Slim agreed to kill him. After he did it, his car landed on the roof, and he didn't trust me no more. He paranoid, he thought I was trying to set him up—Like I did that shit on *purpose*."

Deon face shivered, his eyes were puffy and red. He stared into his basketball and threw it into the floor tiles. He lifted himself from the carpeted staircase, his shadow shrunk and there was an imprint of his body where he was sitting.

There were police sirens ringing through the window over and over again. The blue and red lights shining through the curtains. Coming from the side of the street going in the direction of Chauncy Avenue Park.

I opened my finger and aimed it toward the window,

"Tell me every detail of what happened at the park!" I stepped closer and my eyes bounced around like a cat chasing a firefly. I shut the lobby door with my left foot and leaned closer.

Deon's face crumpled,

"I just finished hooping," he uttered, "I was giving Mary Ann the money we made for the tournament. Then I felt a shadow stretch over us. Slim Demon, he came from behind, he extended his arm, with a muzzle and started busting orange rounds. I held my little sisters down hunched in the middle of the court and I could feel people tripping, running and stepping over my spine. Lance pulled out his gun and busted back at Slim."

"Lance did what?"

"Lance yea," Deon's eyes dropped low, "One of the bullets flung through Slim and he collapsed at the three-point line with a disformed leg."

Deon face turned to the side, and I could see a scratch at the top of his hairline, ear bleeding with black blood and a throbbing vein in his temple.

The hallway was silent.

Ginger, the eldest sister after Mary-Ann, opened the door to the first-floor apartment and the hinges squeaked. It screeched loudly. She stuck her big afro out and walked over to Deon. She had a big brown afro and Harry Potter glasses, and her skin is the same color as manuka honey. She had one cornrow braid as if she was getting her hair done and then got up from the chair.

My face flushed,

"How did y'all get inside there," I uttered.

Ginger made a clicking noise with her teeth,

"Granny Lucy changed the lock," Ginger smiled, "But Deon has powers, so he invisibuled us in."

Then, feverish giggles erupted from the hallway walls. My eyebrows lowered, and I peeked over the doorknob. It was slightly cracked open, and a crispy light was beaming through the edges. The apartment was wide, glossy with lofty ceilings and sunny bright.

My eyelids widened, and I saw Dutchess's slender body shape. She was wearing a white top, cargo pants and a black pair of Air Force sneakers.

Deon stood up, he shut the door with his five fingers and his throat bobbled up and down.

"Don't focus on my sister's nigga." he uttered. "We have to get the car off the roof before the choppers catch it."

Deon knuckled up and used the side of his fist to crack the walls surface.

Doom! Doom! Doom! He knuckled the brown wall in a disruptive way. The vibration of the knocks throbbed into wavy ripples that flared with blue smoke.

Everything was in slow motion. Wavy blue ripples

were spinning from the center of the wall to the top of the decor. The air was visible, my hearing was distorted and the spot where his fist hit had a dark space with a spec of blue ambient light expanding brightly around our bodies.

13

R.S.I Murder
March/9th/2022

Deon didn't know exactly what he was doing, He had mystical powers— The wormhole was a special gift that he had, but he didn't know how to apply it.

For him, the wormholes were a curse because he barely went into the future, he'd instead be brought to the worst parts of the past. He saw his mother's drug addictions often, he had even seen his father, who was different from Dutchess's. He hated seeing his cursed family. He saw his sister. He saw the undeniable truth of Edward and what he did to Dutchess.

Deon's skin is as dark as an unused chalkboard, but the wormhole's light made his skin look ash bright. The kind of brightness that you would see in a tanning machine.

Suddenly, we were in queens. The sound of the flocking gun erupted through the air and Hispanic people on Roosevelt Avenue's sidewalk were pushing and falling in a frantic rush. Slim Demon and Kookah Bug popped out of the massage parlor and dashed back to the black Supercharger GTSS. it was across the street near the bus stop. The doors opened, and Slim and Kookah Bug, jolted inside while being chased down.

Slim had a sack of money in a fanny pack, dollars budging out and leaving a trail. He sat in the seat while breathing hard, clutching his gun handle.

"Start that bitch, *Lul Bone*," Slim Demon slapped the seat, and he screamed particles of spit at Deon. "*start that bitch dawg.*"

Deon grabbed the wheel, and thought of home, but that's when the Supercharger blew up with a bright blue ambience and landed on top of my house.

From that incident, we saw another situation and another. Then a flow of bright light spun around my body causing a sandstorm of blue waves. When I lifted my chin, a line of cars physically protruded, and the road was built beneath my feet. A green traffic sign for "Belt Parkway" was swaying above. I turned my head, I my eyes caught Deon at the street curb, his bicep covering Ginger and his knee up while the other was down. We weren't at my house anymore, instead we were in the street with cars honking, traffic poles and a long rigid road.

14

Coney Island Conundrum
October/13th/2005

New York City pavement felt like starfish skin. If you fell on the ground, and investigated the crevices of your palm, you'd see scrapes and tints of red blood. I know first-hand because There I was, in the middle of a crosswalk seeing cars and trucks lined up. Bright beam lights pushing me back.

One minute we were in Big momma Lucy's lobby and then poof, the roof was gone, and the night sky was burning black.

A grey Ford Explorer was blocking incoming traffic, waiting for the turning light to glow green. Its wheels were glossy and moist. The driver partially turned to enter the expressway. There was a yellow-orange autumn leaf caught in the tire that looked like a butterfly. The massive car hummed, and the driver appeared infuriated that we were blocking the road. Through the window glass I could see that he was a chunky white male with large glasses. He had a wide forehead with wrinkles that looked like knife slices. His face tilted to the side while squeezing the steering wheel with confused frustration.

"you kids! *Get out the streets.*" He yelled with his eyes popping out of his windshield. At the same time, he was slamming his hand into the honking sound. A silver Benz sped around the Ford; simultaneously a female pedestrian happened to be walking across the road from the side of the Ford, and she didn't see the Benz because of the explorer's body. The Benz driver stepped on the brakes, and a loud thunking noise echoed through the sky that sounded like a cracking football helmet.

The light turned green for a turn into the expressway, but Pedestrians surrounded the scene. Car doors clicked open sounding like briefcases. Random dull faces walked to the car accident to get a better look. A crowd of worried people huddled around the woman who had gotten hit. We heard the words

"Oh my god" and "Is she okay?"

The lady who got staggered by the car was brown,

with a small face and thin nose bone and flat cheeks. She had black curly hair that stopped at her thin, a bang, and thin shoulders. She wore black lipstick on her lips. Her lips made an ugly twist as she curled on the ground, balling a fist and cursing under her breath. She had on a black and blue striped shirt that exposed the chest plate on her upper body. She used her hand as a fan, each of her nails were gothic black and her hands full of veins. She had a small gold chain the size of a string, it stuck to her brown skin because of the sweat. She had a patent leather jacket halfway on, and a black scarf tightly wrapped around her shoulder. She kicked forward, trying to move her leg and as people stood around her, their bodies went stiff.

The lady sat on her ass with her palm pushed into against her nose. She had a strange carelessness while whispering the words Fuck my life. One leg was straight, and the other bent and she kept grinding her heel against the rigid road and it sounded like sandpaper. Her eyes shook with emotion and her mascara began to look like soy sauce leaking out.

Suddenly, the driver of the Benz pushed his door with urgency, his eyes raced and each of his fingers were spread while he sprinted toward the front of his wide-body car.

Scatterbrained-apologetic-indirectly expressing his faults. He was a tall, dark-skinned man with fine white teeth. He had a blue baseball cap on his head that was bent like a duck's beak. He was drenched in cold sweat and his pits were wet at both sides as he placed his palms over his temples.

"I'm sorry," he shouted. On his torso was a blue and white T-shirt with the words Berlin written across it and a Cuban link chain with a lion head. He walked over to the hood of his off-white car bumper. Standing inches away from his gold rims, he slapped his head and turned around to avoid the sight of the woman down on her rump.

"Fuck." He screamed. "I'm sorry."

"Somebody phone an ambulance," a random person blurted while staring into his gold rims.

The owner of the Ford Explorer driver stepped out, a hefty man with dark wrinkles in his forehead, his belt over his belly, and his arms swinging as he walked.

"*Are you nuts,*" he screamed while poking his finger at the Benz driver. "You need to have patience when you're driving that thing. You must be out of your meds."

There was a feverish wrenching feeling in my

stomach because I remembered seeing the man's face when Mother Megan came to my house with pictures of my father. I tried wiping my eye, but it didn't change the fact that he was *Merlo!* He was him, I mean, my dead father was right in front of me, and I couldn't miss him.

The white man from the Ford Explorer rushed towards the woman, he extended his arm like he wanted to lift her, but her leg weight was as heavy as a tree log. The hazard light from his car flashed onto them.

Yellow light-dark-yellow light, dark.

The white man hunched down, held her hand with his silver wrist watch shining,

"Jesus Christ are you okay," he muttered concretely. "I'm an off-duty firefighter, please don't move. I'll call an ambulance for you, Hun."

She grabbed his phone and shook her head left and right with a redness in her face.

My sneakers were scuffed with garbage truck juice from the sidewalk. I stood up with a dizzy wobble, I walked slow, then I picked up some speed. I arrived towards the car door, and my eyes caught sight of him *Merlo!*

He was everything that Mother Megan described him as, but he had a remorseful look in eyes. I mean he was me, just with darker skin and taller. I got three feet closer to him and stood by his driver's side gold rim.

I leaned down, then stared him directly into his eyes.

"Call Ivory" I blurted with a fast wrist flicking motion. Your wife will kill you if you don't let her know about this! Be a good husband for once."

Although Merlo's gold Cuban link danced in glimmering gold, the color in his face was lackluster and bland. His long fingers dropped into his hip, and he pulled the phone out of a phone case on his belt. He lifted it to his chin. It was an old brown Blackberry Bold that looked like a calculator. He froze with the phone at his ribcage, and he then angrily squared his chest.

"*Wait*, how the fuh, how do you know my wife?"

I snapped my fingers at his little blackberry cell phone. While I was trying to get his attention, I felt the air fading into black mesmerizing smoke.

15

See You Around
March/10th/2022

Big momma Lucy's building was back to normal. I could see the vibrant brown and cream paint.

The flooring was solid brown, the walls weren't shaking, and my stomach wasn't twisting into spirals. It was as if we didn't even move, but I was sure it wasn't some bugged-out hallucination. I saw Merlo and I saw Brian. I saw Slim Demon and Kookah Bug too.

I slapped over my eyes and rubbed it.

Deon held the door open, and Ginger walked inside with a look of excitement. Once the door slammed. He clapped his hands loudly and caught the attention of everyone in the house.

"I can't move David's car," Deon shouted, "I can't control shit, I can't control what I do or where I go."

"What you mean?" I walked in behind him.

Deon turned his face,

"I don't know what I'm doing." He whispered with his broad voice. "What if the car lands in the Atlantic Ocean! Nigga! You saw what happened with David's car the last time." His eyes bobbled to the ceiling while he talked.

We sat in apartment one for hours, huddled on the glossy tiles playing cards and talking. Just like during the pandemic, we didn't have food but after hours of talking, our minds weren't even on it.

As the time went by, Deon was in the corner, head down biting the rim of his cup and leaning into the window like a sad dog. His baby sister jumped on his lap, and he held her as if everything were okay.

Dutchess was next to me, she looked chubbier as if she had been eating more. I glimpsed toward her stomach, but she was wearing a shirt that covered the shape. She ran her hands through her hair, put a rubber band from her wrist into the back of her head and tied her copper-colored hair into a ponytail. Minutes later, she lifted me off the ground and pulled me into the hallway for privacy. She had a wide bowlegged hip shape, and a switch in her ass that snapped when she walked.

Dutchess shut the door, she slapped her spine against the wall, turned over and her eyes shook with a red moistness.

"Phillip umm. I have to be honest" She reached forward, retracted her hand and leaned back against the wall. Her copper curls pressed against the solid wall too.

Dutchess bit her lip, and stared downward then mumbled.

"It's my fault for the murders! Both murders! It's my brother! He saw my Godfather—and he saw Fat short Shaq black mailing me."

"Who's your *Godfather?*"

"Ed—Edward Aberdeen." Dutchess uttered. She then walked to the lobby door, stood there with a pale nose, she turned around, put her ass on the edge of the radiator and walked back to me. She reached to my face, ran her fingers underneath my peach fuzz chin and shook her head.

"Please don't judge me, Phillip." She lifted my chin higher, kissed me with her lips sticking to mine and dropped her hand but my jaw stayed high. She turned her neck, flicked her finger through her curly fry hair.

"Give me this—," she uttered while yanking my hoodie, "It smells like you sort of, but you need to stop smoking weed because it also smells like the Weed man's closet at the sleeves. *We are leaving!* Deon already told us that we have too and I' need something to remember you by."

16

Merlo Jenkins Estate
March/11th/2022

Bulky garbage cans toppled down from outside, I reached over to my curtain, and I saw Fritz being pushed out of a car, his T-shirt stretched into strings. He buckled down on one knee, shaking and blinking as if he couldn't believe what was happening to him. He lifted and then collapsed at the first stone step. It was strange to see him squeezing a step with his fingers. He lifted once more, grabbed onto a garbage can chain to keep himself up and wobbled into the gate. A big stout man walked over, grabbed his neck like an owner who wanted to discipline a mutt. He stood over Fritz and punched him repeatedly in the spine. The loud assault sounded like skin drums. Beating his ass. *Domp! Domp! Domp!* With each punch landing, his flabby back wobbled, his neck snapped back, and blood splattered in a drippy burgundy line.

"I'm not done yet," the man shouted while slamming his knuckles into Fritz's head.

He was a Latino gang member, a bunch of tattoos on his neck, skull, and fingers. He was about six feet, half balding wavy hair and a thick beard that looked like it had been braided and taken out. He wore a blood-stained wifebeater, baggy black slack pants with a leather belt in the loop. He looked like a crooked narc, but he ain't have any weapons on him and he wasn't law abiding.

I ran down the steps, skipping two and three at a time, to the lobby and then outside to the stoop. The man loosened his fingers, twisted his neck and froze in a punching position; his knuckles looked like a skin rash straight across.

"Ayo Pablo," he yelled something in Spanish, "*pop the trunk and come.*"

He looked dangerous, like on some mob shit, but they were all Hispanic. Slick, disciplined motherfuckers with nice clothes. One of his men, Lil Tony, handed him the racquet bag that Fritz had taken from Big momma Lucy's room.

He stepped forward with the bag's strap. He

unzipped and pulled the files, but that's when he noticed me watching him.

Osane's spine went slack,

"Young Merlo? That you," he froze while leaning, he dug through the duffle while keeping eye contact. "You look just like your dad, just your mom's complexion."

There were notebooks and mountains of cream folders with United States of America seals. One of them had Kings County written on it.

The man walked up to one step, and he blocked the view of Fritz; that's how massive of a mountain he was.

"My name is Osane," he uttered while rubbing his bloody hand across his shirt. "I'm sorry that we had to meet like this, but your dad was like a father figure growing up, and I couldn't let this puta slide. Merlo left all of this for you, but Fritz tried to steal this shit for himself."

Osane walked closer to me, he had a blood clot in his nail, I noticed it as he extended his arm. He walked to the highest step and handed me all the paperwork. Then he poked me in the arm with his index finger and stared at me with those wide brown eyes.

"Your father Merlo coached for nineteen

professional teams, his last gig was out in Berlin before he died, he was a genius at it, don't let this puta tell you lies."

Osane ran down the stone stoop, grabbed Fritz by the neck, and lifted him up from the ground. Fritz was as heavy as a cadaver, but Osane was strong enough to lift a whole casket on his own. He dragged Fritz to the first step and held him up by his hair strands, then slammed his teeth on the step.

He held the back of Fritz's head with his palm

"*Fritz the bitch!*" Osane shouted, "now tell me again, what did Merlo do?"

"Co—Coh—*Coach,*" Fritz shouted back with a gargling voice. Blood specs flew from his swollen gums.

The papers that Osane gave me were crispy white, with small print words that can give you a headache if you try to read it too fast. "Merlo Jenkins Estate," it read. There were house deeds for our Brownstone, Williamsburg plot and the Prospect Lefferts Gardens house. There were Life insurance papers, titles for cars and bank accounts. Bonds and certificates.

Fritz's fingers were scraped up, bloody and he reached forward. He hunched and spat out a string of blood that landed like maple syrup on pancakes. He crawled up the steps with his red chest being scraped by the stone.

"you are just a *boy*! you don't understand—you don't know who I used to be and what I had to go through. *What I sacrificed to raise you!*"

17

Fritz's Injuries
March/14th/2022

Aunt Yata's brown fingers grabbed the doorknob, she twisted the key and walked through the front door. The sun from the windows splashed into her face and she had a fulfilled smile. She and Big momma Lucy walked into the house, ready to surprise me, but the place was empty.

Big momma Lucy had on a black curly wig with a straight bang, a turquoise blouse with ruffles, and slack pants that could barely fit her wide thighs. She had hospital bands on her right wrist. Her brittle body wobbled as she leaned on a sturdy cane. She took a step and slowly walked inside the house. The floors were glossy clean, the couch pillows were straight, the rug was vacuumed, and the wooden tables looked polished. It's been a while since they weren't all dusty.

Big momma Lucy's eye squinted, she glimpsed to the back of the house and turned around with a crumpled face.

My room door was open, hers too, and the breeze from the wind made the curtain sway.

Big momma Lucy's brows dropped low,

"Where's my boy," she uttered with a confused look of sadness while wobbling. "He was supposed to be here for the surprise."

Aunt Yata walked over to the living room; glimpsed at the couch and back toward the kitchen. She lifted a pillow as if someone could fit under there and then threw the pillow back.

Big momma Lucy limped into Fritz's room; the doorframe was a dark cave, and he had a pile of trash sitting by the wall. She flicked the light. There were bottles of yellow piss, old boxes for fast food, and white paper bags for medicine.

"Oh my god," Big momma Lucy uttered with her mouth wide. She pinched her nose and her head cocked back. *"you are a wreck."*

Fritz's was sitting in his beach chair, while there was a Ford commercial playing across the TV. His face was straightforward, leaning back with his sloppy build. There were brown bandages around his head like a turban. He had a hard cast on his right leg, a sling with his arm hanging, and a stiff neck brace that hitched his head up an inch. His ear was red at the tip, he had stitches from the temple down the back of his head. Bulging stitches that were as big as lacing for a baseball. It was needed to keep his head from opening back up because he had a large gash in the center. Something that still looked like it was infected. Fritz's cheeks were swollen too. Swollen like he indulged in the sweetest batch of poison ivy and nearly died. His dark shadow was stretched against the wall like a fading ghost, he had his finger in the beach chairs cup holder flicking the remote control with his stiff finger. So much trauma was done to his back, that he could barely turn around to see who was watching him.

Big momma Lucy folded her arms, she stood there shaking her head as if she was disgusted.

"Look at what you did to yourself," she uttered with a stink face. "We gone pray for you, hope you have a full recovery because you aint staying in my house after that mess, you can go on with your baby's mother and *leave my damn daughter alone hear me!*

18

Brian's Last Batch
March/14th/2022

As much as I wanted to punch Fritz in the face, I didn't curl my fist and deck him with a Roy Jones haymaker. There are laws to protect people while dealing with injuries, so I didn't lash out on him for stealing like I wanted too. I smoked a lot more weed which helped me manage my anger.

I sat in the park with T.T. and we talked while sitting side by side. It was a new thing for us, but after Slim died, it was easier to have a connection, because we knew we could have been gone too.

I passed her the blunt and she hit it with squinted eyes,

"I'm high," she uttered with a smirk, "can we go upstairs now, I wanna eat."

We walked into the lobby and I held the door for T.T. she walked upstairs and her knees kept buckling. "I'm so high." She shouted with a smile.

"Shh, before Sophia hears us." I responded "you know she a rat."

As I opened the door to my apartment, Big momma Lucy was in the center of the living room with Aunt Yata. They had a bunch of bags as if they had just gotten off a Greyhound and was ready to check into a hotel. My heartbeat fluttered, I handed

T.T. the grocery bag and stretched my arms for a gentle hug. Big momma Lucy leaned away from the cane and spread her jiggly arms around me. Her eyes shut, she smiled, and her lips sat on her pink gums. When she opened her eyes, they shined like water with moonlight. She glared at T.T., her neck pulled out of the hug, and she rubbed my forearm while smiling.

"Phillip," she uttered in a confused voice, "who's that cute chocolate girl behind you?" She curved her neck around so she could see.

I smiled,

"This is my friend, —Tahiry."

"Tihara?"

"Tahiry, Momma."

"Oh, she is stunning." Big momma Lucy flapped

her wrist, she winked at me, pulled her finger up to my face and pinched my cheek. She redirected her focus to the home health aide, who was in the middle of the house talking with jawing words. Aunt Yata had her hand on her hip, speaking loudly back and snapping her head left and right.

The health aide was a petite Indonesian who was the size of a seven- year-old. She pointed to the picture to show them proof that she was a real home health aide.

Big momma Lucy's eyes bulged,

"Memory loss?" she shouted with a confused face. "There's no way, Fritz's just faking it."

The home health aide dashed away from Yata, she took the trash bags from Fritz's room and walked away waving us off.

Big momma Lucy's eyes were peppery, she extended her hands towards me, and I noticed something. Her hospital bracelets around her wrist. She had three different ones on like she had been bounced around from room to room.

She smiled at me and walked closer to my face.

"I miss you, my son," she uttered with a relaxed grin; she directed me to sit with her at the dining table. Peeling off her bracelet as she spoke.

"Ivory told me you found out about Brian," she uttered while blinking slowly, she sat down in slow motion onto her hemorrhoid pillow, and Aunt Yata straightened her seat.

"I messed up with him," Lucy uttered. "it's something that we have all been paying for and that's why everything happened the way it did."

"Everything like what?" I responded with my eyebrows scrunched.

"Having you as my boy is like my second chance."

Later that evening, my brown eyes barley blinked, I sat with a hunched body, while pressing my videogame controller.

T.T. sat behind me with her legs open. She twisted my hair with her small nails digging into my scalp.

I kept thinking about the passport that I had on my shelf, right next to the grease and yellow comb.

Fritz's passport which I found, and it looked fake as if he stamped his last few Berlin trips.

My eyes bobbled,

"My stepfather is lying, I bet I can get him to talk," I uttered.

T.T. smirked,

"Shit, I bet you won't, he's slicker than you think."

"Bet twenty dollars."

"Ouhh Bet it nigga."

I walked from my room to his dark door frame. The blue passport book hung off my thumb and index. I walked towards his enormous sized bed. A bed he kept with hopes of having Ivory in. I threw the passport on his mattress, then waited for him to say something. I crossed my arms like a club bouncer and cleared my throat.

Fritz had a hunched neck, twiggy blond hair with a long part in the middle of his head. Not a barber design, it was long gruesome stitches that looked like they tied his head with a baseball lacing. He reclined in his beach chair with one arm slacked. His legs wide open and his gold-bearded chin down to his neck. He twisted his lip while rambling.

"Yea, I lied about Berlin." He rolled his eyes and clicked the remote. "I was coaching there until they fired me, I wasn't Merlo, and I could never fill his shoes as a coach, but I filled his shoes as a man." He scrunched his face, then looked toward his large bed and glimpsed back at the TV.

"No, you didn't," I snapped back with my lips

thin around my teeth. "What kind of man are you?"

"An alive one," he scoffed. "I am the reason he's dead, you know."

"Ivory pulled the trigger, not you."

"I did whatever it took to get the cops off us; that's the difference between me and everyone else, I will do whatever it takes to get what I want. I tricked the cops; told them that Merlo was their guy and that's why they came to his door that night."

"What, you ratted?"

"I did whatever it took to get them pigs off me, I tipped them *false information* and the *cocksuckers* went with it! But that's not all." His neck straightened,

"—Your Grandmother, the Mother of Brevoort, right? She is not who you prop her up to be," He muttered with his lip pressed to his jaw. He had a raspy voice and a scrunched nose.

"She let me stay around because I told her the truth about Brian's lifestyle, that old fruit cup was a regular customer, and he popped my Percocet in handfuls. I knew that my work would take his measly life eventually."

"What? Why—?"

"See you're just a kid, you don't know shit about grown-ups."

The room turned cold. Fritz's face scrunched into a mean mug and the TV light dragged across his eyeballs. They were vein-filled eyeballs too that looked like he was in an electric chair.

"Those were my drugs, you twit," he shouted with sharp teeth and a snarling nose "and Lucy knew that shit too." he shouted louder. He smirked with an ugly puffy cheek smile.

"What?"

"Yea! Brian's last batch, they were my shipment. I was the biggest drug dealer in Brooklyn. I told your grandmother about Brian's addictive life, and since she is Christian she forgave me like a big dope. Since she didn't know shit about her own son, she kept me around to tell her more and more and more and I gave her all the details."

"She wouldn't!"

"She did! We were all stuck at a crossroads because I loved Ivory, so I came clean, I came to the house every week with flowers for her family and I helped her find an attorney for your estate. She needed me here, punk, and Ivory did too."

My neck curled downwards, my fingers were lifelessly limp, and the sweat at the tip of my nose dipped down to the sneer of my lips. Fritz was a few feet away from me sucking in oxygen as if he was smoking a square. His ear line was red, his disfigured face had muscle twitch and he kept blinking with alcohol eyes. He turned towards me with half of his face spooky dark,

"Brian's death isn't on me though, it's on Lucy," He muttered, "She shouldn't have abandoned her kid — she is a lousy Christian, and she has the nerve to judge Charlesha! At least everyone can say Charlesha is a real one."

My face tightened,

"Charlesha! The mother of your kids?

"Boy Don't."

"Don't what? it's true isn't it."

"Phillip just. . ."

"No! what about Deon, Dutchess and the rest of the girls, nobody cared that they were going through crazy shit—Y'all should have cared!"

"I don't have time to—you think I have fucking time to care, look at me motherfucker—I don't have it in me anymore."

He stared at me with a swollen, disformed head and his eyes bulging through the dark.

"Somebody should have cared though."

"wh—wheh. Phillip, where are the kids?"

"Y'all should have *cared*! because that car on top of our roof connects to a murder case—instead of Deon doing something productive with his powers, he killed a man, and him all his sisters including Livonia are gone."

"The fuck!"

"Y'all should have cared because they are on the run for a double murder."

"Fuckin Hell, Phillip!" He snapped back "fucking don't fuck with me."

19

Tiny scientist
March/14th/2022

Dr. Rancatipopo, the chief astrophysicist, looked like a body double of Albert Einstein. Wild grey hair and eyebrows. Tall in stature, lanky arms and legs and pale white veiny skin.

It was a chilly draft coming from his air conditioner, Rancatipopo took a sip of coffee and scratched his right wrist with his left hand. Another mosquito bite! He turned over towards his laptop projection shooting into thin air. There was a large glowing projection, he pressed the pin into his security system, it turned green and upon opening, there was a bunch of black people in a video recording. His eyeballs went from half-sleep to wide, and then peeled as he watched a viral video of Deon. Deon was summoning wormholes with blue smoke around his wrist, the same day he was on the basketball court.

Rancatipopo's sweat dropped from his temples as he scanned the video; there were thousands of brown faces in the bleachers cheering with their jaws wide and he hit pause to examine. From 3' o clock in the evening to 5' o clock in the morning he replayed the video, recorded the details and didn't budge.

The bright aura surrounded Deon as he vanished from one side of the court to the next in a millisecond. The speed looked like an edit!

Dr. Rancatipopo had many accomplishments, this new discovery made him feel small. He was no longer a lanky tall man with a PHD, he was a tiny man living on a tiny planet with a gigantic black child. Dr. Rancatipopo had Presidents, foreign Dictators, Doctors, Lawyers, and Scientist under his thumb, but the child's powers made their titles sound like a waste of college loans. Have a seat, this young boy shall be the new professor, that is if they can find him.

Dr. Rancatipopo's van engine roared through Tolls,

to Manhattan, to Brooklyn and stopped at the intersection of Patchen Ave. The reddish-brown brick house across the streets from the projects. He glimpsed and pulled the sliding van door open. He stepped out of his sprinter van parked directly under the tree with the red leaves and his coat whirled in the wind.

The block was silent, it smelled of garbage truck juice, weed and liquor.

Rancatipopo looked around while adjusting his tie clip,

"Bedford Stuyvesant, Brooklyn," he uttered with his nose-swooned Ukrainian accent. He rubbed his nose with a tissue and dropped it into his coat.

There was a storm of soldiers surrounding the stoop, the pavement and down the cemented grey sidewalk.

Soldiers with guns, standing in clusters of green.

They were waiting for a command by General Gotland. A man with multiple stars on his blazer. After a simple head nod, and a flicker of his wrist, slamming boots rushed into our lobby and the walls shook like earthquake.

The investigation was as if we were being indicted for something, as if we were criminals and they had busted us for major dope distribution. After a few seconds of door kicking and rumbling, a softer set of boots came back down to the lobby. *Doom! Doom! Doom! Doom!* and stood still on the square floor tiles. The soldier had his lips parted slightly, Jim Tibbers, the most overlooked squad member, had a choked face as if he'd just seen a phantom. The buckles on his helmet were still, the tip of his nose was pinkish-red, and his teeth jittered like he'd been freezing in the arctic.

"Doctor," he uttered and removed his helmet, "there is a suspicious vehicle on the rooftop; it's a Supercharger Revolt GTSS, no damage or clear details of how it was parked."

The center of Dr. Rancatipopo's face brightened, he had a vindicated grey bearded smile building, and he shivered while squeezing his suitcase.

"A car on the roof!" he yelled, his hand slapped the wall, his voice echoed to the ceiling, when he removed his hand from the wall there was a sticker on the paint that read property of the United States.

Dr. Rancatipopo opened his suitcase and jotted something down in his tablet.

"Get them out of the house, it's mine now."

Me and Big momma Lucy stood outside for hours watching the Soldiers parade around with rifles standard for war. It was supposed to be a typical church-going Sunday but instead our home was being ransacked from Sunday into Monday morning.

Big momma Lucy hobbled toward me with a face as if she were going to have another heart attack.

As the soldiers stomped on her daisies, she flinched with her eyes shut.

"Don't let these devils take our property," she shouted. Her voice was choppy, her face wrenched, the cords in her neck hunched as if she was ready to faint. She sucked air while squeezing the center of my buttoned-up shirt and exhaled in my face like a drunk friend who was ready to puke. Her curly hair bounced as she turned her neck towards the house; its reddish brownstone exterior looked like it was made of cruddy chimney bricks, and her eyes dotted back and forth. First, she looked at Ms. Moss's old apartment, then Sophia's and then ours. My Stepfathers royal blue curtains were shaking as if wind was blowing from the inside. There were soldiers on the porch, from the gate to the stoop and down to the parked cars on the other side of the street. They wore vomit-colored green. Arm pads, knee pads, and helmets squeezed around their uniforms. Their leather boots crushed the daisies in my grandmother's spring garden.

Big momma Lucy's chin lifted to the rooftop. The robotic soldiers were pacing back and forth, holding their rifles like Rockstar guitars.

Big momma Lucy sucked away the tears.

"Phillip," she shouted, "I don't know why you worked with those dang devils, but I don't trust them a mile away with water while being stranded in the damn desert." She threw her arm towards the roof; her apple juice skin color was pale as white smoke. Her gold Jesus chain stuck to her oily neck. She was sweating so hard that her pits were stained at the sides of her blouse. She lunged towards the soldiers with her index finger trembling.

"Get y'all filthy asses away from my damn flowers." She screamed with a chopped voice. She wobbled without her wooden cane, she was slightly off-balance, so I put my arms around her soft shoulder. I felt her tense as she was ready chicken wing me.

Her hair was messy, her face was wrenching in sickness and the back of her shoes were full of dirt because she was stepping in her own garden while pushing them away.

General Gotland saluted Jim Tibbers and gave him a stiff handshake, like how they tightened their thumb over your hand. Yea, a handshake like that and they locked eyes as if they were sharing a secret code.

The general leaned closer, his hairline pushed back and the edges of his smile were hard like dry clay.

"Great work, soldier," he said in a raspy voice, "something for the history books." His eyes gleamed as if he was sorry for doubting him for years. He shifted his attention to my grandmother's brown skin complexion; he stared with ice in his pupil.

"Escort Ms. Bynum away." The general uttered. His body language was so cold.

The sliding door opened then slammed, and birds flapped their wings from above the red tree.

We were in the Sprinter van, the seats smelt like chemicals, batteries and electronic wires.

The van started up, it turned out of the spot and a white soldier with an orange beard led us out of the block with hand gestures.

The van was rocking while we were being driven.

Big momma Lucy was across from me; She had her polyester church coat folded on her lap, both knees stuck together, her seat belt was tight across her chest, and her eyes were down toward the van floor.

20

The perks of the deal
March/24th/2022

Thirty-nine minutes after, we arrived at the location. A block away from my high school, there was the precinct and courts. We were in Downtown Brooklyn. The van stopped near the lavish Metaford Rose Hotel. There was a curving driveway that circled with parked limousines. There was a long glass waterfall around the entrance, and a red carpet leading to a revolving door in the middle. Grassy green potted plants were whirling around the outdoor patio and there was some bumblebees floating around it in a circular motion. There was a valet in the front with a red tailored suit; he wore white gloves on his hands and a flat hat that looked like he was conducting trains. He rushed towards the car, muttered words to Jim Tibbers in the passenger seat, stepped out, walked over to the back of the van, tampered with the door handle, and pulled the sliding door open until it slammed.

Our faces lifted at the same time.

Jim Tibbers stepped out of his seat, he stood there with his eyebrows scrunched. His hair was black at the scalp, short with a widow's peak. He had a youthful glow in the center of his face. He looked downward and spoke with a soft southern voice.

"I'm sorry about yawls house," he uttered. He reached out his hands for Big momma Lucy; when he touched her, he wasn't Rigor Mortis stiff like the Doctor or General Gotland; he held her fingers and assured her that she stepped out with both feet on the concrete.

Tibbers took a deep swallow and leaned toward Big momma Lucy. He put his palm in the middle of her back and leaned closer

"Check under the name Mar's." he whispered. "Dr. Rancatipopo is obsessed with space and what not— Mars is yawls new name."

My family walked from the van to the revolving door with our rolling luggage. It sounded like a skateboard crew because of the wheels moving with turbulence. Couple feet into the entrance, there was a porcelain floor that was slippery like sleet, but still hard and shiny. There were iced-out chandeliers hanging over our heads, a piano with red rope and black furniture with bookshelves.

To my right, there was a silky-clothed brunette with high cheekbones using the reflection of the glass to apply lipstick. She reminded me of Megan Fox. She had blue eyes that looked like ocean ice. She puckered up, turned around and grimaced. Soft swing music played in the background as she strutted and kissed this white man with a button-up shirt with orange palm trees. He grimaced a smile when he noticed me.

At the front desk was a man in a red suit. He had a jet- black mustache and a strong French accent. I rested my elbows on the marble counter and cleared my throat before speaking.

"We are checking in," I uttered. "Mar's is our name."

The French concierge glared, then he typed the name into the computer, and his eyeballs turned into solid white eggs.

"That's our finest suite," he said, "sure, mmm right this way."

He walked towards the lobby, there were soft

dinging elevators on each side, he placed a white square card over a metal sensor, held the elevator open with his hand, and smiled as he walked inside.

The suite had an oversized balcony, tall windows with water drips and drapes that wobbled. The room service workers rolled a stainless-steel serving dish on top of a cart to our door. She lifted the lid, steaming hot crab legs and shrimp were on the ceramic plate. Garlic bread and sauce made of wine. She brought another pan in and it had huge pieces of pink salmon with zig-zag flesh.

Yata was flicking through the widescreen TV. There was a large white banner across the bottom.

The reporter had protruding eyes. He didn't rattle while reading his cards, but he proceeded to clear his throat like he was sick. Not sick from Covid-19, but sick of the violence that he had to report in the black community. The reporter was in Brevoort, on the Fulton side right near where Barbara used to sit when she played chess. The red tree swayed from side to side and the reporter locked eyes into the screen.

"Live from Bedford-Stuyvesant," Cody McDonalds spoke "David Stennod, aka Slim Demon, opened fire in Chauncey Avenue Park. He is a confirmed suspect in the death of Edward Aberdeen, but he was shot and killed by an unnamed child suspect."

The child suspect was Lance. But if they caught him, they wouldn't charge him as a child; they'd charge him as an adult. I never understood why they would bring up his age if it didn't matter in a murder case.

21

Kookah Bug's charge
March/25th/2022

Downtown Brooklyn, over on Jay Street, not too far from where the Metaford Rose was, Kookah Bug was being interrogated for his crimes.

Detective Hendrix's throat shook, he bit into a strawberry donut with pink frosting and the sprinkles fell from his wrist to the glossy blue floor. He walked while holding an evidence box at his hip. His destination, was the small room near the detective's area for criminal lineups. The Detective walked while snapping his tongue against the roof of his mouth. He twisted the knob, then arrived at the interrogation room to see the inmate named Kookah Bug, dressed in his orange jumpsuit with his bearded chin down angled into his neck.

The Detective slammed the box on the table, he

pulled a plastic chair, and it screeched against the cold floor. He sat down with his donut in between his index and thumb.

The room was quiet, the detective looked forward and shook his head.

"Rick Springs" he uttered. "Darn it, another lifer, shame how you blacks throw your lives away."

Kookah Bug scrunched his face. His nose flared on both sides and his black lips were tight around his teeth. He had an afro that looked like black wool with a bald spot on each side.

Hendrix chomped the donut while digging to his left side.

"We traced the pistol that you were totting." Hendrix bit into the donut again and wiped his hands on his inner thigh. He reached over to his left and pulled out a plastic evidence bag with red words written on it. Rolling-Street-Infamy or other known as R.S.I. Inside the bag, was air sealed around Kookah Bug's .45 colt— along with a wrinkled orange bandana wrapped around the handle.

Hendrix glared into his eyes, waiting for him to react, he pushed the gun closer.

"R.S.I right." Hendrix uttered while chewing "I know you quite well, we are doing a R.I.C.O on your posse for the murder of Edward Aberdeen—Which means you're going down as a hitman"

Kookah Bug sucked his teeth,

"Fuckin goofy ass pigs" he mumbled under his breath.

"Earth to Ricky." Hendrix clapped his hand in his face, "Did the seventeen-year-old boy Deon Moss put you up to this murder? What about Shaqkris? It's a double murder. I think he payed you and David to do his dirty work."

The room went silent.

The murder of Fat short Shaq was an October evening and although Kookah Bug was in cuffs, he could still feel the kickback of the gun when he blasted live rounds on the busy sidewalk.

When Fat short Shaq stepped out of the Deli, he had a wide smile on his face like Zion Williamson. He stepped up talking to a girl on the phone, blinking slow, licking his lips as if he had swag. Slim Demon did a scurrying U-turn that sounded like a screaming tire; which is only rubber of course, but the tire sounded as if it were screaming across the road. The car rattled as it stopped at the edge of the pavement. The gunman Kookah Bug pushed the car door open and jumped out of the back seat, hunched low. He straightened his arm and bussed clouds of grey smoke along with five bullets! The first bullet ripped Fat short Shaq's spine, two in his head, the other bullets made his body bounce as if he were having seizures. Kookah Bug stood over Fat short Shaq's shit-smelled body and pulled through his true religion pockets. He squeezed the cash that he had and ran back into the car.

The adrenaline was rushing, the gun powder stunk and the car was speeding off.

Kookah Bug sat in the Supercharger GTSS, with an involuntary shake. As the car sped forward, he breathed hard and cleaned his hammer with an orange bandana. Kookah Bug slapped the seat in front of him and handed the wrinkled bills to Deon.

"Aye Lul Bone, give that to lil Dutchess for me." He uttered while breathing heavily.

That's how it went down.

While Hendrix grilled Kookah Bug, Dr. Rancatipopo walked through the precinct like a hurricane. The police officers' faces were stunned. They dropped pens, papers and lost focus as they watched him walk through the jail bars, to behind the desk and to the office. Dr. Rancatipopo kept his chin high while waltzing through the office down to the shiny blue police halls in the dark side.

There were doors full of police officers in uniforms. Some were laughing and talking loudly until they saw Dr. Rancatipopo and the only noise was the vents and the string tapping against it. The Chief of police had green eyes that gravitated towards him. His presence was like the sun and everyone else was just in his solar system. Next to him was the mayor, the Brooklyn Borough President, and members of the Feds.

One of the officers opened the interrogation room and waited for the Doctor to walk inside. His green eyes narrowed onto Kookah Bug, and his arms flailed below his hip in a relaxed way.

Dr. Rancatipopo scanned the room and adjusted his collar.

"We have to release Mr. Ricky Springs" he shouted, "He and Deon traveled through wormholes. We need extensive research with him, we need to know how that GTSS traveled from Queens to Brooklyn in less than a milli-second. We need to know exactly what Deon did and we need it at once.

Dr. Rancatipopo walked over, he shimmied the lock and everyone gasped for air as they saw Kookah

Bug stand without a chain on his wrist. He was a massive intimidating man, and his gun was on the table in plastic. He could have easily reached for it, but Dr. Rancatipopo was sure he wouldn't do anything foolish. Not with all them police there. So sure, he turned his back and walked out of the room.

Dr. Rancatipopo pushed the parking lot door and the sun rays shined across his balding head. To his surprise, he saw Fritz leaning on Bentley, side by side with Charlesha. They were side by smoking short Marlboro cigarettes and had an awkward look as if they just had sex and didn't want to talk much.

Dr. Rancatipopo's face widened with a smile.

"Mr. Fritzen Clayed, I see your head is in bandages, we will get you help." He reached toward the bandage.

"I don't need it." Fritz snapped back

"We will do whatever it takes to find your daughter Livonia. For you and your family! how about one million US Dollars for your cooperation?"

"I need my wife back!" Fritz yelled with his lips tight and his finger protruding. "where the fuck is Ivory! Bring her to me, that was the deal!"

22

Ivory's freedom
March/28th/2022

The sun shined through my tall window, and suddenly the whole room was full of light like those lofts in SoHo.

I received a screen shaking text from someone. My phone rattled with electricity and my eyes barely could see the name of who.

"She's coming up Dr. Bynum," someone wrote in all caps. The Phone number was Dr. Rancatipopo. He texted from untraceable robot-text numbers. I glared at the bright screen; holding my phone at my chest and sitting in my bed. I could barely smile, still somewhat in disbelief. *Ivory was set free from Obbit Thorn? and she was on her way to the hotel room!*

It didn't feel real. I sped across the marble floor, leaped over the area rug that looked like a polar bear's fur and left a trail of wind near Big momma Lucy. She was sitting near the balcony window in a white robe with her arms folded. Gold rings on both hands along with a bracelet that read Jesus on it.

Big momma Lucy scrunched her eyebrows,

"His girlfriend must be on her way up," she smiled while fixing her wig. "Phillip over there shining like a thousand- watt."

Aunt Yata jumped up, her body jiggled as she pushed me from the door and she was off balance.

"I ordered shrimp, that's probably my shrimp." she blurted while reaching for the knob. Once she twisted the knob, the hallway shined into our sunny suite. Standing at the front was Jim Tibbers, and on the left was Ivory trembling with one arm stretched across her stomach. She had a makeup-less face, her hair was wrapped in a bun that was darker than her hair color. She had a yellow shirt, black slacks that stopped right above her ankles. There was a long pause between her and Aunt Yata then their arms opened, and they squeezed each other while rocking.

"Oh my god," Yata screamed. She held her tightly while rocking side to side.

"How is—how did," Aunt Yata's chest caved in, and her body pulsated like back-to-back shotgun shots.

Ivory's eyes beamed from over Yata's shoulder. She stared at me with an emotion-chocked face and kept blinking. Ivory was somewhat tall, she had a flat face, a thin nose and a bright smile. She was even beautiful when she cried. She reached over her sister's back and pulled me into the hug.

"Thank you, Phillip," she said, "I don't know how you and your daddy did this but I'm thankful.

Yata pushed me in the rib,

"Now since you are so magical can you help your momma get her dreads back." She laughed.

Big momma Lucy got up from her chair.

"I cannot believe this," she said while walking with a limp "the joy that I feel is unimaginable, thank you Jesus."

23

Racism in the science world
April/20th/2022

I had to uphold my side of the deal with Dr. Rancatipopo. On the fifth day of April 2022. Dr. Rancatipopo escorted T.T. and I to Connecticut, into his self- funded college of Science and Math. He didn't do it out of the kindness of his heart, he and his company were producing a documentary about Deon Moss's gift and fascinating disappearance. To be a complete smart ass, they should of did a documentary on their disappearance instead. Where the fuck were these adults when Deon and Dutchess were going through it while living in that tiny apartment?

At noon, we walked into the college's library. There were rows of Mac computers, high-beam bright lights on the ceiling and glossy bookshelves by the thousands. There was crane cameras set-up, leather white couches and thousands of utility men standing around with jeans and baseball caps with the school's logo.

Rancatipopo college had a logo. The logo was everywhere and it was of a red planet dangling through the library.

I met a lot of smug white folk. Some were Doctors, Engineers, Astronauts and Politicians who had their fingers on big buttons. Everyone shook my hand the same way, all stiff and robotic. I looked in the corner and saw T.T waiting on the side with Big momma Lucy. They were both at the reference desk, far away from the camera lens. Big momma Lucy gave out coffee cups and T.T was near the donuts.

The host of the documentary was the news reporter Shirley Aston. She sat down on a white leather couch, with a deck of cards spread like a geisha girls paper fan. She had her legs crossed with pants that came up to her ankles.

The library was bright, quiet and the sound men kept walking by with their sneakers squeaking against the floor.

I could have answered each question and did things the right way, but Shirley kept talking about the environment we grew up in as if Deon was one in a million and that we were pieces of shit who were genetically pre-disposed to be fucked up.

Shirley's face went pale like vampire.

"I minored in urban studies at the University of Illinois," she asserted herself, "the ghetto has always been sort of like a wasteland—"

"Wasteland, what you mean?"

"Wasteland, a place where there's a lot of crime and less productivity—I suppose".

I stared at the college banner hung behind her.

"Mars is a wasteland too, but y'all want to fix it," I uttered back while staring at the school's logo.

I stood up, put my bag pack around my shoulder, "Y'all will die trying to water that dead planet but won't bring any life to the ghetto kids like me, T.T. and Deon. Gifted kids are probably rotting away somewhere just like Deon was—fix the wasteland instead of spending money on wars. Oh, that's right, wars are productive. No more questions about stupid shit."

I glimpsed over to see Dr. Rancatipopo and his jaw dropped from his chin and shook in a fast motion. He stood up from his seat with his high-water pants flapping up and down. He darted over to me while waving his hand to come back.

"Mr. Bynum," his voice echoed.

I pushed through the sound men, walked through the director, some foreign leader, a politician and few white men sitting side-by-side.

Walking away felt good.

T.T had a big smile on her face and shivered with happiness as I walked back to her. I stretched my arms around T.T, then Big momma Lucy, and they gave me a warm hug. We walked out through the library doors then the halls with classrooms, and then another door and another and while we walked, there was a stout security guard trailing us at every inch of the campus.

24

Deon Moss Physics Center
April/24th/2022

Multipolex, a private Space-exploration company, did many investigations into Deon's lifestyle. They jotted and typed until their fingers went numb. They were left with one glaring reality; if someone had the unique gift to discover something, it would be hard for them to make it out successfully because there's no bridge between us and them. Influences of Poverty interferes with the production of people. A fact, because while people like Rancatipopo get opportunities, People like Deon get bullets and rotten role models like Slim Demon.

Multipolex analyzed the environmental factors like gun violence, poverty, poor education programs, homelessness, Mental health and drug abuse. The odds of Deon making it out and becoming a successful pioneer at a university without a basketball scholarship were 0.001%. After the comprehensive trials, the hood was named an unlivable condition. Announced publicly and devoted to change.

Dr. Kuygbe Enyum, the CFO of Multipolex, gave my family a fifteen-million-dollar check for our house. Rather than letting the government get a hold of it, they revealed plans to build a museum out of it.

The Vroom Deady remained the main spectacle on the roof. The car served a purpose for everyone to take pictures of or at least dream something they may have never dreamed. The attraction was dubbed the Deon Moss Physics Center, an urban space station dedicated to ghetto children who might have never been interested in science. Instead of becoming Rancatipopo's house nigga, I signed on for research with Multipolex. They weren't as obsessed with finding Deon as they were with creating an easy pathway for the next. In our culture there were plenty of Deon's, but nobody cared enough.

One spring evening, a pigeon flew past my head and its flapping wings. I walked to the front gate and the latch was already opened. The stone steps had plates of grape tomatoes and Big momma Lucy was on her knees while digging in her garden, the tomatoes she planted were plump and pale green at the top. She glimpsed over her shoulder

"Phillip, you see this? Look delicious, doesn't it? it only came out like that because whatever you put in the soil is what you get back baby." Then she picked another and dropped it onto the ceramic bowl.

How did she not see that that simple idea works for children too? —How did they not see it?

Epilogue

In the backseats of the limousine, the shadow black tint shadow moved, the turbulent ride swept through the street causing Alejeh's body figure to be visible and then you could just see her body lining and then her beautiful face. The silence was awkward. Her body lining was inching closer. She sat next to Fritz, opened a napkin for him and pressed it against his bloody nose. The color of the napkin turned raspberry red. She crossed her elbow against his shoulder and stared into his blue eyes.

"I'm sorry your secret came out like that."

"I fucked up! I don't want to lie anymore. I don't want to be like this please. It's my fault! Everything is my fault."

"how did you and your wife meet?" Alejeh uttered while dropping the napkin and lifting a new one.

"you really want to know?" Fritz replied, he stared downward at his knees and his eyes bounced left and right.

March/11th/2005

Fritz walked with a limping hip, his knuckles inside his palm as if he were about to throw a punch.

"Claire Smithens," Fritz uttered, he wiped his nose, staring downward and spread his arms.

She was a six-foot, slim skimpy blonde who looked like Uma Thurman in the face. we all said she looked like Uma so she wore these yellow cat suits with her little tidy's bouncing. I still remember her laid out across the floor with a pink bong across her chest, eyes wide open screaming my name. she was known through the streets of Neptune.

One night, the skies were dark like barbeque smoke and the grey clouds were floating across the garlic moon. From a block away, you could see large groups of people standing in clusters, yapping, holding cups and pushing each other in goofy laughter. The door to the party was behind a zig-zag gate, a brown door with a screen, gold hinges with wobbly knob and cat scratches. The dope boys would come through and serve handoffs through the mailbox holes. My feet shuffled, I walked up the stone steps and grilled some punks selling their weed. Opened the door, there were people crowding the narrow hallway, out of shape strippers in the Livingroom, sliding up and down that silver pole with those asses jiggling like clam chowder. I sold sell a few beans near the coat rack on that particular night, grabbing the loot and crumbling it, sliding back to the coat rack and clutching my steel. I leaned on the wall, kicking my foot up and my hands tucked into my hoodie pouch. Black shirt, dusty Levi jeans with some Ed hardy converse.

My old friend Lincoln was a couple feet away smiling at shorty in a cheetah dress. Lincoln looked like a young Morris Chestnut, had a voice like Mos Def the rapper, so he had as way with the women.

My intent was to hustle some Oxies, but Lincoln, his intent was to do something different. What's the worst thing you could imagine a man doing? Linc did worst! he was a six-foot-tall animal. He stood there, clean cut with waves, freshly ironed brown Louie-V checkered board shirt, his muscles poking out and tattoo's on his forearm. He wore white pants and brown Louie loafers that were freshly polished. He danced, tugging some white bitches. Real arrogant prick he was.

Linc was a human trafficker. He liked all kinds of bitches, fat and short, white to black and even trafficked men, and Claire knew.

Alejeh's eyes bulged like it was getting pumped with helium. She scooted backwards, breathing in silence, wrapped her hand around the door handle.

"what?" she flinched back into her seat, her chest bouncing like she had been running inside her dream, her eyes bounced and her jaw shook. "a human what?"

"yea," Fritz responded, he grabbed a bud light beer from the cooler, snapped the cap off with his bare nail tip and took a sip "Linc was trafficking people back and forth through the states, men, girls anyone he could get his hands on."

Alejeh's stomach clenched, her eyebrows scrunched, and her hair bounded side to side.

"why-why were u hanging with a creep like that!"

"I was a fucking drug dealer, I wasn't exactly a boy scout myself, in the hood we all were animals, whose to say I was any better than he was."

"you are way better than him, I don't want to get to personal, but this shit really hits home." Alejeh unloosened the door handle, she hugged herself with her arms but still felt the coldness of Fritz's words. "that's so horrible." she muttered.

Fritz took a deep breath, he glimpsed at Alejeh and rolled over to the tinted window, speeding past buildings, roads, rocking back and forth as a limousine sped over potholes in the Manhattan. His eyes pupils appeared and large. Memories running across his wide eyes.

"I can stop telling the story if you want."

"no! go head, I'm sorry."

At Claire's house party, speakers were vibrating with Young Jeezy's soul survivor song. The walls were literally shaking, feet scuffing across the roof. I stepped up the stairs, bumping against people in the dark. My ears caught sounds of someone take a puff of something. There was black skinny couple near the rooftop, hiding their blunt. To my right, I saw the body shape of Ivory coming from the bathroom, she had a short skirt, her body jiggling and bouncing as she walked across the drug addicts. She had small feet, small petit hands and a pretty little face like Beyoncé the singer. My eyeballs were rolling as she walked out.

"hey." I uttered to her, grabbed her arm and she stared me down.

"who are you?"

I grabbed Ivory by the throat, pressed my pelvis against her and tried to spit in her mouth.

"what the fuck!" she shouted "you fucking creep."

She pushed me against the other side of the wall, walking fast, she glimpsed back and wiped her forearm.

I pushed my palm against my face.

Ivory stepped down from the staircase, then tapped her sister, Yata.

I stayed at the top of the stairs and watched her through the bannister.

"it's for Myspace." she shouted, "you ready, one, two, three." the camera flashed with a white polaroid flash. They smiled with bright teeth, then she took a snapshot as Ivory posed against the wall. She wasn't no type of bitch that I could go choke her, tongue her down and fuck her in the bathroom. She was a fly bitch. You had to be fly to get her.

The music blasted,

"if you looking for me I'll be on the block with my thang cocked."

Ivory had these long brown wavy dreads pinned into a bun. Chopsticks inside her bun. Her dreads were so wavy and curly, that it looked like she could take them out with a comb and her hair would be as straight as a white woman's. Two dread was hanging down across each side of her face. She had a choker on her neck, a white blouse with ruffles under a black fish net shirt. Her belly ring glittering like a constellation in Houston. She had a short pink school-girl skirt, poking her ass out like Ice spice and dancing in platform boots. She was singing the lyrics to Jeezy, she slowly thrusting her pelvis, every man turning their heads to see that freakishly gorgeous ass bitch.

Lincoln gave me a arm nudge,
"you see that dog." he uttered with a bright smile. "that right there is you."
"I'm here selling these beans, "I responded, and put the hoodie over my head and pushed through to the front door. "stuck up ass bitch."

Lincoln walked over to Ivory and greeted her in darkness, he gave her a kiss on the cheek and they started talking ear to ear. Smiling like Morris chestnut, brown skin player vibes. He was shouting through the music, ear to ear and every now and then smiling with his white teeth. Ivory yelled into his earlobe, a pretty stud diamond sparkling near her jaw; she wanted to kiss his ear at the moment.

Ivory's face exploded with a smile, she stared Lincoln dead in the eye and nodded.

"okay." she uttered with an uncontrollable smile.

"I'm trying to take you home with me." he shouted with his masculine. "you are the reason I came out tonight, you are the center of my world right now and i got to have you."

Ivory bit the rim of her cup,

"okay, Mr. handsome." she shouted through the music "I'm really down for whatever you know, it's the new year, new vibes." she bit the rim of her cup again, smiled and moved closer to him with slow blinking eyes. Lincoln gave her another hug, and they slowly walked through the crowd to the front.

See most guys still had beepers in 2005, but Lincoln was a fly nigga, he had a cellphone. He drove a 05 navigator, white body, silver wheels and he had his own apartment with a balcony. After Ivory walked into the passenger side of his truck, the door chopped and they drove off into the unknown.

Alejeh leaned forward,

"oh my god did Fritz!" Alejeh stretched her fingers

to his lap "you saved her? from the human trafficker?"

Fritz's face scrunched,

"no Alejeh." his face shook "who do you think I am? John Wick? I was never tough! I'm not that type of man! when I saw him drive away with her, I thought that I was never going to see her again."

"no, you were being petty because she rejected you!"

As the navigator wheels spun, Ivory and Lincoln sat in those swayed Louis Vuitton soft seats. They ping-ponged conversation while he glimpsed at her sexy long caramel legs. They spoke, giggled and almost made it back to the Reef house, but Merlo; her fiancé's name came up. That was the moment Lincoln panicked, driving backwards, and trembling.

Ivory stepped out near the stone steps of the Q train at Coney Island. There was leaky pipes and shrub bushes. you could hear the screeching train wheels from the sky into the open street. the Q had just screeched passed.

Ivory's eyes gazed at the moon, she walked the opposite way from the train to a path that led to the beach. The smell of sea life, foam water and sand crumbs were in her nose until she arrived at the boardwalk. She walked like a model, drägging a Louie sweater across her body. The sweater she took from Lincoln.

I was sitting on the brown benches, smoking a cigarette, and thinking about life. I never thought too deeply about my fucked-up actions, but that night I was feeling incomplete. I mean, I just had seen the most beautiful girl I've ever laid eyes on, and I froze up when she rejected me. I froze up so bad, to the point Lincoln had to talk to her. I actually never froze up with women. I spent a lot of time fucking crackhead bitches so I was the lowest of low, analyzing myself, and realizing that I had become a part of the underworld. anti-social, can't relate to normal bitches or have a conversation without dropping a red flag. Even Lincoln had a wife.

Alejeh's eyes brightened,
"his wife?"
yep, His wife was loyal too, even aiding him in his endeavors to traffick girls from Georgia to Florida and out of the country. But anyways, I was staring at the winking stars and suddenly the wood nails on my

bench rattled.

I turned my cheek and Ivory was sitting down with her palms over her eyes.

"hey you," I uttered "you're that shorty from Claire's party, are you okay?"

"yea." she rubbed her eye "I'm okay," while staring at the suddy black beach waters. The open beach waters made swish noises and gushed an open water sheet to the sand

"I noticed you, I noticed you when you came out the bathroom. that Jeezy song was playing."

"yea, that shit is hot, wait your that creep that grabbed me by my throat and tried to spit in my mouth,"

"why you tripping?"

"nigga, what. I should be asking you why the fuck you think it's okay to grab random women by their necks."

Ivory turned towards me, her eyes brows downward and her wrist curled upward in her lap.

"Do you have a lighter?" she muttered softly with her eyes bouncing, she shook her head.

"yea." I reached into my pocket, lifted a red lighter and extended my open hand. she uncurled her fingers and it was a brown joint in her hand, the size of a twig and it smelled like sour haze. she stared at me as if I were the cops, then turned her chin.

"you can't be grabbing women like that."

Ivory bit the blunt, created a barrier with her hand and sparked an orange flame.

"here," she uttered handing me back the lighter.

deep white smoke puffs floated out her mouth.

"you know what I hate?" she uttered while the sour scent dispersed, "I just hate when a man is intimidated by me, like these niggas act like they're street dudes, but so afraid, everybody is afraid of him"

"whose him?"

Ivory blew another cloud of white smoke from her mouth, "Merlo! like he gets to cheat on me with Cyn all the time, he thinks just because he have a baby with a bitch it gives him the right to still fuck her! ughh! we aint going to last as husband and wife if he does this shit! and it's not fair because if I try to get with somebody on the side, they always too scared to touch me."

Shocked by what she said, my eyebrows lifted, I took a sip of the cigarette, tossed it over the rusty pole into the crusty blue sand and looked over my shoulder,

"you talking about Lincoln?" I replied "you dodged

a bullet! Lincoln is a pimp."

Ivory paused, scrunched her eyebrows and laughed with the joint aimed my way.

"and what are you? a pimp too?" she dropped her chin giggling. "pimps don't spit in mouth's the first time they meet them."

I pinched the blunt from her fingers and held it to my lips.

"me, I'm just a corner boy, I aint nobody important." I twirled the blunt with my index and middle finger, then took an award pull that rocked my head back.

Ivory's face wrenched

"you aint never smoke no weed? it's better than them cancer sticks."

"well, uhh college dropout, got into selling drugs and pissing my parents off, cancer sticks was the best way."

Ivory's eyes squinted, for the first time she actually stared at me and noticed the color of my marble blue eyes, bearded blond jaw, dimple in the center of my chin. her jaw twisted angrily. she smiled and crossed her legs.

"you are a fucking gorgeous man." She uttered

while staring "and umm, you aint the only one who pissed off your parents! my mother is religious, self-righteous and completely nuts! sometimes you have to live for yourself!"

"fuck yea, live for yourself, even when you're in a relationship."

Ivory stared into my eyes and the moonlight bounced off us, her mind was running in circles and her eyes were telling a story like an audio book. There was a pitch-black silence, then a white man on his bike sped through causing a rumbling block noise on the boardwalk that made the wind spin.

"forget it." she turned the other cheek, hunched her body with the brown Louis Vuitton sweater.

I scooted closer to her,

"wait." I spoke softly, grabbed her by the hip and turned her chin back towards me. I squinted my eyes, and leaned in to her face. It was so romantic how we just stared each other down.

"you ever had a man spit in your asshole?" I puckered my lips.

Ivory's eyes swelled, she scrunched her face, shouted a laugh, blocking me with her palm.

"oh my god, you are out of pocket." she laughed.

"you are fucking funny." she grabbed the sweater sleeve, blocking me away with it.

Seconds later, she dropped the sweater, grabbed my chin. Bearded stubby hairs poking her finger.

"If you wanted to make-out, you do it like this,"

she smooched me, finger flicking the blunt away and plucked it on the bench. she wiggled her tongue in my mouth like a fish out of water. The kissing was wet, she grabbed my muscles, and then her fingers dropped onto my zipper. She used her nails to dig and caress my dick through my jean zipper. She pulled away from the kiss as if she was shocked by a bolt of electricity.

"is that a gun in her pants? I'm sorry." she uttered.

I pulled her face back into the kiss. I was kissing her while holding her neck, I pulled the gun from my hoodie and placed it on the bench. Blindly kissing her.

The kissed lasted a moment. All I felt was electricity between me and her. I opened my eyes and saw that her lips were still moving in silence. She was totally shit faced.

"I have a room in the trap." I groaned while squeezing her tidy's.

Ivory stared me with a cross-eyed smile. Her eyes blinked slow, she lifted her blunt and breathed in an exhilarated way.

"I'm coming though." her eyebrows lifted like she was surprised, blinking at my pants and shaking her head "are you sure you don't have another gun in your pants? you're a white boy, right? goddamn because I don't know any white boys who have a dick that damn big! that is just like a cucumber." she lifted her sweater, walking side by side with me.

Coney Island landscape shrunk as we walked the ominous streets. making a turn into Neptune Ave and 23rd street. Brick buildings, orange, brown and some just normal houses with canopies. to the right-hand side of the street, there was a rusty blue car with no wheels out front, with sharp rotors booted on cement blocks. a fat topless prostitute inside with a bald white man in a suit, unbuckling his silver belt buckle.

Ivory liked being a smartass, so she implied that I was the actual pimp and since I was good at being a dick, I told her if I was a pimp then she'd be my intern hoe. She giggled with a mean mug, slapping me in the shoulder and shaking her head. We walked through the block, the street poles were dim to the point you couldn't read the blurry parking signs. Past the trash bags and they became animated by wiggling rats, to the right side of the block you had a stucco of buildings with deteriorating brick. The first step to the burgundy building, it felt as if we were walking into a laced-out cave of death. An immediate itch feeling, the pathway was darkness, so I used my beeper for light. I kicked a bud light bottle and it rolled to the sticky trap near the couch. Before I shut the door, there was a man with patchy skin, doing cartwheels in the street, shirtless screaming. He ran in the middle of the pavement with a broken cassette player and chomped into a can of uncooked biscuits. He shivered frantically as cars skid through. I shut the door behind and his voice faded.

I turned my face towards Ivory, steering at her in the sheet of darkness.

"was that future husband?' I asked

"no," she nudged me while laughing. "but your future wife is in that jalopy doing something with papi."

I walked up the wobbly staircase, Side eyeing Ivory and thinking of what to say next to her. It wouldn't have been good unless I was being a jerk. I didn't have a mouth piece like Lincoln did. I had aggression. There was a large electrical wire hanging out of the ceiling, there was these gashes in the wall with slurring voices floating out. There was screeching steps, echoing door slams and fiends arguing about who owes who and dust at our feet. The building was so fragile that if you sneezed the walls, they would collapse like sand in Egypt. At the second flight of stairs, there was two dope fiends with skinny forearms drugged out with belts near their sides. We walked into the third floor and there was a large gash in the middle of the wood flooring.

"watch your step," I uttered "that is the gateway to hell."

"how did?"

"someone shot themselves in the foot."

"you're kidding?"

"no! it's not even a joke, Plasma is in kitchen whipping a chicken, just ask him yourself."

Ivory stepped over it, peaked in the room across. there was a long table, baggies and machines. clouds of powdery dust in the air and a constant sound of fan spoons moving. Plasma was in the dim light, he looked like a cracked-out grandmother hobbling around in the dust like a dark scientist. There were women in the darkness, they had face masks on and bonnets on their heads. Plasma had a cast on his foot, a hunch in his spine and he shivered in the darkness.

"Fritz, you can let boss know that we are closing

down at five?"

"iight Plaz" I replied.

I pulled the knob to my door and the air smelled like rotten food. I opened the window, flipped the switch to my generator and the bulb in the ceiling went bright white. The generator sounded like a chain saw, revving through the house. The walls were full of hip-hop posters like Biggie and Tupac. I Was the biggest hip-hop fan. In the corner wall was a Marbury Knicks jersey. There were a few car parts like a new head gasket, cam shaft, alternator, a throttle body and a suede blue vans car seat perched under the Tv. There was a tire next to my bed with a fluffy cat laying inside asleep. Vladimir was a quiet cat. My bed was in the middle with boxes on top. I dug through the box, lifted my radio and rested it on the floor. I plugged it in and ran Jeezy's soul survivor song. I lifted Ivory by the legs and her ass cheeks mushed through threw fingers like taffy. She had one of those super jiggly asses. I threw her on the mattress and the springs made a hydraulic noise. I pulled that pretty pink skirt down and her brown pussy was waxed. I went down on her and sucked her pussy while stroking my dick. She opened her blouse wildly and her tidies bounced out. Her nipples were dark brown like Reese's pieces buttercup and it made my dick so hard that it poked against the edge of the bed. She leaned forward, pulled me up and she stared at it. She had a cockeyed smile, grabbing at my dick with both hands and jacking it, sucking the tip and pulling me closer so I can stick it inside. First stroke, I could never forget because her pussy was hot like a furnace fire. No rubber, no nothing, just skin on skin.

"fuck me daddy," she uttered while squeezing my hips with her nails, biting her lips and staring at me with a docile head bobble. 'it's yours!" she moaned "I'm your filthy slut! it's yours!"

Alejeh fanned herself,

"wow," she uttered. "so, you been having sex with Ivory before she went to prison?"

"no," Fritz uttered "it was just a onetime thing."

"so how did you end up marrying her?"

Fritz's face scrunched,

"she went to prison for murder!"

"what about that human trafficker?"

"Lincoln Bijos is his name, everyone calls him Guidance and he is the leader of R.S.I."

Alejeh's eyeballs swelled twice its size, she stared angrily pushing her face closer.

"R.S.I? what the heck is that?'

"Rolling Street Infamy, right now Guidance is in prison at the Elides doing the nines!"

"doing the nines?"

"life sentence."

"is the Elides that same prison where the inmates."

"yea! that's the prison where the inmates took hostages and killed the correctional officers. the female correctional officers are still alive working as slaves for the prisoners. it's all fucking Guidance! I told you he was an animal!"

"oh my god," Alejeh uttered "that Trafficker deserves to die!"

"scumbags never die."

Fritz scrunched his face, he stared at his slacked arm and wrenched his lip. Shutting his eyes at the lifelessness of his fingers. Alejeh rested her left hand on top of his right hand. She then rubbed his fingers one by one, up his hairy forearm and his shoulder pulling him for a side hug.

"I thought you had something to do with the human trafficker," Alejeh uttered into his earlobe "that would have made things complicated between us" Alejeh's breast smushed against his slacked arm, her heart beating and her fingers inching up his jaw.

"complicated? what do you mean."

"we have something, I know you can feel it Fritz, we have something super special."

Alejeh rubbed his bearded jaw, getting close enough to feel his breath breathing on her upper lip. Her pretty soft pink lips. Then suddenly, the engine suspiciously cranked. The headrest for the backseat imploded forward with the speed yanking Fritz like a ragdoll. Alejeh's arms flailed over her torso. then a sudden impact sprung them to the seat across. there was a leaping vehicle bounce, then a water current smacking bubble crash that slowed the Limousine into slow motion as if they were sinking in quick sand. A swishing watery sound at their door, and coldness at their feet; water in those cake batter leather seats rising. The limousines car alarm echoed through the Manhattan sky.

ACT IIII

History Repeat's
September/15th/2023

Friday evening 5:45

Fritz opened his blue eyes to the sandy brown cinnamon ceiling, the gears in his head snapped. He propped his head up, his mind snapping, eyes bouncing under a vibrant chandelier bulb. His body twisted sideways only to feel the cushion of a red swayed pillow, neck cracks and spine tremors.

The red swayed pillow had diamond stitches, his fingers gripped it as he jerked his body, slamming his pale foot down onto the cashmere carpet. Fritz's ears lifted, he realized his kneecaps were exposed, white man had skin with freckles on some parts of his legs, long wild hair strands running down his grizzly legs. Wearing jiggly basketball shorts; his sons probably, he glimpsed around and smelled the aroma of a house that wasn't his. The first whiff was sweet scent of a chamomile ocean lake perfume. His eyes bounced, and his cheekbones lifted a notch higher. There was a pinging loudness in the circular structured Livingroom, an old man in a silver wheel chair at the corner of the wood cabin library holding his hands over the wood top piano with each finger spread like a puppeteer. **ping! ping! ping! ping!** The old man pushed the keys with blind rhythm.

Big momma Lucy was sitting down near the old man with her hazelnut mocha skin color. A pearly white smile with raspberry red lipstick. She had a curly hairstyle, a rose red blouse with black pants hugging her wide hips. She had hips that were shaped like a heart.

"Rigoberto, you are a musical genius" she clapped with a soft smile. "like Beethoven," while turning a cheek, glimpsing at the circular shaped fire place with white paint and roses engraved into the wall, her brown dandelion eyes darted, squinted and couldn't believe that Fritz was on his feet again.

"Fritz you finally awake?" she uttered with an animated face slouch, "I thought you was about to check out." she stood up, wobbling with a slight limp as she walked closer, you could see her yellow gold sparkling Jesus chain swaying on her chest plate. "since when did you have seizures, boy?" she uttered with a light pitched voice. "we know you had some brain bleeding a couple months ago, but can it be something else? you need to go to the hospital!" she uttered over his shoulder.

Big momma Lucy stood there, staring at Fritz with her eyes opened wide. She didn't say anything to him until he answered her.

"Lucy, will you get off my back? I will" Fritz grunted while locking his fingers, hunching and squeezing the cashmere carpet with his toes.

Suddenly, an unrecognizable man walked from the kitchen area with a Styrofoam plate at his belly. He had a plastic white fork in his fingers digging at a piece of mud brown cake. He had a balding crown, green hair inching out of his pale scalp. He had a blue dodgers baseball jersey, a white t-shirt with a small gold link chain. He had a full sleeve of squiggly tattoos on each wrist. He was a Latino man, no older than thirty. He took a bit of the mud brown cake while walking to the piano slowly.

"No! father that wasn't like before, remember you used to hit the high note at the end and then transition back," the man muttered comfortably, he bobbled his head with a mouth full of mud brown flakey cake. Aiming his fork toward Rigoberto.

Fritz's face scrunched, he squeezed the fibers of the area rug with his toes, bent his head to look for his gun.

"who the fuck are you" Fritz's eyes had a vicious twist, he partially stood and the living room spun. His head tilted, his cheek bones tightened and his eyes were pinging from lifting too fast.

The man walked over to Fritz, wiped his palm on his jeans and held his hand out for a handshake "I'm Cristiano; Alejeh's brother and that's my father Rigoberto." He muttered with a mouth full of brown cake.

Fritz cracked a knuckle, stared at his open hand, analyzing every wrinkle in his palm as if he were doing a crime investigation.

"I heard of Rigoberto, I just don't know you," Fritz snagged his moist Tank top from the floor tiles, it was slightly off the area rug, on the oily brown chestnut table across from the television.

Fritz spread his shirt wide, rubbed his nose, His blond strands were twiggy, the scar on his head was visible as he stared downward. He saw his gun tucked into a cotton blue towel. He reached for the chrome, grasping the handle, but Big momma Lucy grabbed Fritz's upper arm.

"come Fritz." She uttered in a fast whirlwind. She led him to the window, his gun remained on the ground twinkling like silverware.

520

"Fritz! look at this real quick" she muttered like a school girl about to gossip. Pulling him.

Outside the wide circular window, was a worldly balcony view of midtown Manhattan morning sky scrapers. Lanternflies smacking the glass as if they were drunken couples. Some walking across the invisible glass and flapping their lifeless wings.

The blue United nations buildings were in the view of the balcony, with hundreds of flags wiggling, whirling from sky high altitude. The FDR highway, the stone roadway and open landscape of Turtle bay fountain lake. The water looked like liquid metal from so high up. Far down the people looked like ants, surrounding the rippled lake water. The white Rose Royce Limousine, that belonged to Fritz was plunged in the rippled water and there was a sturdy red crane with a zip cable clamped to the ground, tinkering, lifting it with a zooming cord, a beeping noise and the water rippling, dripping and spilling into the concrete.

Fritz's face twisted, he looked at Big momma Lucy and his eyes were pinging.

"where's Ivory!" He shouted while squeezing the window glass." where the fuck is she."

Big momma Lucy's eyes twirled,

"she got herself arrested for a DUI," Big momma Lucy turned a cheek, shaking her curly fry hair. Her brown skin was close to the glass, it made her look a shade lighter. She shut her eyes, swayed her fingers across the glass to form a cross. Then she lifted one of her potted plants and carried it to the wood piano head for a bottle of water. Her body was jiggling as she went for a seat near the Rigoberto.

Rigoberto looked like a smooth Hispanic traveling musician. He turned a cheek and smiled with a single gold tooth on his left tooth.

Big momma Lucy poured a bottle of water into the plant.

"After your seizure, Ivory was acting all crazy so Jim went and got her from the precinct."

Fritz turned his face, biting his lip in anger and squeezing his pink fingertips into the tank top he balled up.

"the navy seal douche fuck!" Fritz's lips tightened around his teeth, he balled his shirt up and threw it against the furnace.

"fucking kill that motherfucker!" Fritz shouted, "he's a known coward, you know! Probably wouldn't even put up a fucking fight."

Big momma Lucy stood up tall from the seat, stomping towards Fritz and shaking her index like a windshield wiper.

"uhh uhhhh" she yelled loudly, "there will be none of that crazy stuff in my house Fritz, if you want to get like that, then take your behind back to your penthouse up the street." Her voice echoed through the hallow apartment. Rigoberto turned around, smiled with an elderly gold tooth grin,

"should we go."

"no, keep playing the piano." Big momma Lucy screamed. Cristiano took a seat and the house was silent. Yes, there was chandeliers and high ceilings, bouncing off the wall art, large plants and décor but you could hear the apartment breathe; that's how silent it was.

Gang Related
September/15th/2023

Friday evening 6:05

Fritz slammed his feet through the house, he stomped through the kitchen first, with his feet spackling against the Persian tiles, his cheeks trembling in rage as he walked passed the toaster at the counter top, on the quartz texture, there was a large iced orange cake. The cake looked like a basketball, with the word's congratulations, but it had been cut several times and eaten. The inside of the cake was mud chocolate and the crumbs looked fluffy.

Fritz turned the corner, dropping his jaw, opening the door to Phillips room. His son, who he had barley seen since he had been with Shandy for weeks.

The door knob wobbled, the light from beyond the door flashed in his face, there was three boys all sitting down holding game controllers near the wide movie-theater screen. Phillip lifted his cotton-like hair, it was scruffy and unleveled. He looked like he was growing a little peach fuzz mustache, lanky body and muscular jaw structure like a man.

Fritz stared back at his son, then blinked and noticed Lil Slida, and Jah Kraken; Two little juveniles from Bed-Stuy.

Fritz pulled the door back to his ribs until it went click, and his son was boarded by the wooden door. Boarded away from the family. Fritz turned the corner into T. T's room, there was feverish giggles and loud mumbles. "she is so crazy," T.T uttered, "she said she was going to kill you for sleeping with her man?"

The door was slightly cracked, with a scent of perfume mist in the air that smelled like coconut and berries. Alejeh was inside the room, sitting on a black and gold Egyptian silk bedsheets, there was a white chair, a thousand combs and brushes. T.T. twirling her hair while giggling.

As Fritz stood in the open-door frame, Alejeh lifted a white mirror, she saw T.T in the reflection braiding, then she turned her head partially in sheer happiness.

"Fritz your awake!" Alejeh uttered with a light voice, a soothing Latina ascent rolling off her pink tongue. "look papi, Tahiry is doing braids for me"

Papi? Fritz thought to himself. His brain pinging, his temples sweating and his bottom lip trembling.

T.T looked like a split image of a young Foxy brown, she was just standing there noticeably thicker. Fritz never looked at little girls, but T.T was nineteen years old, and he occasionally took a glimpse at her body since she was always in Big momma Lucy's house.

Alejeh was smiling, half of Alejeh's head had zig-zag braids through her skull dangling to her neck, and the ending of each braid was down to her ribs with color coded rubber bands.

T.T.'s room had a balcony view, a queen-sized bed with Egyptian brown silk sheets, a wall Tv and a jacuzzi that makes bubbles that sounds like a purring cat. Since she was in college, she spent a lot of time in her jacuzzi reading her books. Still surprised at the life she ended up having; from homeless to living the life of one of those white women who can do novelty things.

Fritz stared down at the ground,
"Tahiry?" he muttered "can you snag a pair of socks from Phillips room?"
T. T's lip stiffened, she rolled her eyes and her neck snapped in a ghetto way.
"he's your son, why don't you get them yourself."

The silence in the room was awkward, back in the living room you could Big momma Lucy and Rigoberto laughing as they played the piano.

Alejeh lifted from the seat, "I'll get it" she stared T.T. in the eye, smirked with half of her hair dangling down her back. She stood tall, her ass wobbled, her breast dangling through her white wife beater. She had one of those super jiggly bodies that moved even when she wore clothes.

Alejeh adjusted her stringy top as she walked, placing her palm on Fritz's ab's "are you okay papi?" she uttered.

Fritz took a deep swallow, responded with a slight head nod and an awkward eye twitch.

Alejeh stepped out of the room, walked down the slippery ceramic tiles barefoot and stood near the door frame cupping her elbow. She knocked on Phillips room with a candy cane shaped finger, then entered into the frame with a joyful smile.

"hey boys" she uttered "can I get some stuff really fast! it's for your dad"

suddenly the video game paused, you could hear a closet door grunt open and drawers rumbling and dumbling. Then a sneaker box thumping across carpeted floor. A loud thud that shook the hallway floor.

Alejeh walked from the frame with a fresh blue polo shirt, a fresh pair of black pants, boxers, socks and a royal blue and white Jordan ones.

"your size is a 12?" she uttered while holding the box at her breast.

"12.5" Fritz responded "but these will do, just take the insole out, how did you know my favorite color was-?"

"Blue?" Alejeh cleared her throat, staring at Fritz's eyes, and pointing her finger at them "dunno-maybe-ehh-from staring at your eyes so much." Alejeh uttered with a tight lip, smiling like a school girl. She hunched her shoulders, her cleavage bounced, she blinked softly, then used her left index finger to sway his bicep as she slithered into T. T's room. That moment, everything went in slow motion and Fritz could see him and her having the nastiest sex two motherfuckers could have.

Alejeh had a jiggle in her ass, a petit frame and every time she walked past, she had a sweet pomegranate-coconut-vanilla-honey scent. As she sat, it was a seductive smile.

Fritz took a deep breath, he walked into the bathroom with his head down. The bathroom lights brightened like caution lights. The gold and cream outline of the bathroom looked like some luxurious stuff you'd see in an Israeli diplomats' home. The tiles looked like plate designs, the pearly white toilet clean had a spray nozzle. There was a wall mirror that circled around the wall, tub and sink had gold and engraved into it and the faucet had a golden dove with wings in flight. When you twist the faucet, the dove splashes water from out its mouth into your fingers. Fritz ran the water from the shower, it rinsed over his head and he saw bits and pieces of last night. He felt the heaviness of his legs walking in four-foot-deep water. Pennies, nickels, Dimes and quarters all at his feet while hearing arguments vibrate his ear. Suds at his kneecap, he dragged his feet from the water to leap over the stone and onto the pavement. Holding his forehead upwards. Alejeh was holding on to his arm, "he had a seizure! excuse me" she shouted. "Fritz hold your head up," there were people jawing words, extending arms along with a crowd of unrecognizable pedestrians gasping at the disastrous fight. Ivory was kicking water at them, throwing her make-up at Fritz's back. The limousine drenched in cold water that stunk like seaweed. Blood coming from his nose, so he couldn't smell anything except the metallic smell of blood.

Fritz opened his eyes, he rubbed his face, stared at his fingers and realized that his ring was gone. The shower water splashed like slippery silver jewelry. He swiped the shower curtain and Big momma Lucy was near the bathroom door crack. Her hazelnut brown face made an awkward twist, her eyebrows scrunched. When she saw a piece of white milk skin, she flinched and she turned a side eye.

"Fritz! Cookie told me that you went in for a bath," Lucy spoke with her back turned while holding a white towel and terry cloth rag stacked up, she laid it on a stool, with a pink bar of soap and the wedding band glimmering on top of a towel.

"you dropped your band last night," Big momma Lucy uttered "Alejeh and Ivory was fighting in the street and she snatched it off before they arrested her!"

Fritz's eyes were in shock, he opened them wider and burning water ran down his eyelashes. down his nipples, genitals and toes, he stood there lifeless in warm water soaking in his own humiliation. The water beads smacking his forehead and running down his blond beard.

"fighting? What the fuck happened last night," Fritz rattled his head in the shower, lifted his hands and cupped his eyes to clear the water beads, he could see Rolling Street Infamy; someone from that street gang killing Dawn. His eyes widened and he trembled in place. "one more thing before you walk out," He shouted to Big momma Lucy.

Lucy lifted her head, and stared at the shower curtain. It was Himalayan pink salt colored.

"what?" she responded.

"can you tell Phillips friends to get the hell out."

"this is my house dammit."

"Lucy seriously will you just listen for once, those delinquents are murderers, they are in a fucking gang."

"no, this is my house."

"I don't give a rats ass, I need to talk to my son, he had a fucking busted lip and somebodies going to tell me why." Fritz's voice echoed through the thin water.

Phillip's Secret
September/15th/2023

Friday evening 6:05

Big momma Lucy stepped out, shut the bathroom door with a trembling earlobe. The house walls had slight tremors as if a house quake was happening.

Big momma Lucy wobbled in the hallways, shuffling her feet and stopping at her grandson's room. She wobbled into it, Pushed the door open and stood at the frame with a body lean.

All three boys stared at her.

"yawl my babies, so you know yawl can have as much cake and ice cream as yawl want. listen here, yawl gone take some and leave." she uttered with a serious eye twitch, "so go in the kitchen, take a piece then put yawl foot in yawl sneakers and get going, but oh yea wash them hands boys."

Jah Kraken dropped the controller for the game, lifted off the chair. he was a brown skin boy with a pumpkin pie skin tone, peach fuzz, long braids down to his neck, he wore a black Amiri hoodie, black nudie jeans with white sneakers. Lil Slida stood from the gamer chair. he is caramel brown, he had a scruffy little afro, a blue camouflage hoodie Amiri hood, ripped denim pants and ugly forest green uptown sneakers. He dropped his game controller too. They gave Phillip a handshake one after another, both walked to the door frame, spreading their arms and giving Big momma Lucy hugs while smelling like weed.

Big momma Lucy hunched her shoulders with a full side-eye. The boys walked out with saggy pants. they both had the tattoo of the number eight on necks. Her face scrunched in a confused way, wondering why she never noticed it before. Naïve. She scratched her brown curly hair, her ringy jiggled as she leaned closer and squinted.

"are your friends in a gang?" Big momma Lucy whispered while she scratched her back hairs, leaning closer to sit at the gamers chair.

Phillip shook his head, stared downward to the carpet and pulled his socks up to his calf.

"no Mama."

Big momma Lucy backpaddled, she lifted an old plate from Phillips headboard that had a stringy chicken bone, snagged a spoon and fork, a cereal bowl with a blue ring, and an empty glass bottle that smelled like sunny delight.

"your always leaving stuff in here, now I know where my dishes be ending up at, your dad is about to come talk to you."

"he isn't my dad!" Phillip blurted with an expression as if he tasted a lemon lime.

"now! I done told you a million times, don't discredit your daddy and his sacrifices he made to be here for you! he cares about you, fed you since you were a little docile baby boy."

There was a moment of genuine love between Lucy and Phillip, no words, just eye contact. They both knew that Fritz was no good, but somehow, Phillip couldn't snap back in the way he wanted to because Big momma Lucy backed him up.

Phillip turned over, he lifted the pillow and laid it over his head. Suddenly Big momma Lucy noticed that he had a dime bag of weed; weed to her looked like oregano because she always cooked with it so she jumped up. "Phillip what is that."

Phillip reached forward to snag it and shoved it into his right pocket.

"Uhh-uhh, that better be Oregano" Big momma Lucy shouted "not in my house boy! I already told you about that"

Phillip scrunched his face, scratched his sideburns in guilt. Then Fritz arrived at the door frame, he gave Lucy an arm tap and she moved out of the way.

Fritz pulled the open gamers chair, sat on it with his legs wide opened and his chest across the bar. He pushed the bar and the controller dropped to the carpet.
"Phillip I'm not fucking playing around with you!" Fritz pointed his index finger "you hanging around with all these motherfuckers and being secretive. What the fuck happened in crown heights with Shandy? I bet you were over doing some shit you weren't supposed to be doing!"

Phillip had a face of stone, his eyes bounced side to side and his ears low as if the words didn't rattle him.
"man leave me alone" he replied, He angled his body towards the Tv, pulled the game controller closer and his thumbs moved silently. The Tv flashed across his eyeballs.

Fritz's spine trembled, he lifted from the chair, slapped the controller down and stepped toward

Phillips frail little body. He yanked him by the collar, and aimed his index finger to his face like the muzzle of a pistol.

"you think this is a fucking game?" he yelled through his crooked teeth. "you're so tough now!" he pressed his fingernail into his jaw.

Phillips face tightened up, his eyes went from clear to cayenne pepper red and swollen. Tears rolled down his cheek like spring lake water.

"stop it!" Big momma Lucy yelled "don't do that to my baby boy"

She stepped in front of Fritz backing him away with her forearm, pushing with all her hips until Fritz was back against the book shelf. trembling books of physics and AP chemistry about to tilt onto the carpet.

"*Stop it.*" She shouted.

Phillip stood on his feet, his arms were at his legs and his fist were balled up and jittering. His head was boiling brown, he had snot bubbles popping at his nose, and redness creeping down his forehead. He kicked his own game controller which caused the Tv to collapse with a flash of thunder.

"you could never be my father" Phillip shouted with rumbling cheeks "what kind of father are you! you should go back to Neptune where you came from!"

Fritz smirked,

"if I go to the streets, I'll see you there you little maggot!" Fritz aimed his finger, stepping forward.

Phillip trembled,

"Nah! you let them nigga's beat you with a baseball bat! you a loser! what have you done with your life besides get beat up and live off my grandma!"

Fritz's eyes were opened wide due to verbal electric shock.

"you fucking punk! I raised you! you know what, I hope shanty's friends do more than give you a busted lip next time."

"what! you a fucking cornball nigga! you don't even know what I really be doing! Me and my niggas been running down on them R.S.I niggas! I put in pain for real and that's how I got my lip busted." Phillip tore off his shirt and tossed the stringy fabric toward Fritz's toe, "Kookah bug" Phillip shouted " he is in the dirt! and I did it for Short Shaq. Honcho is in the dirt too! And you know why I did it too!"

Fritz back peddled, suddenly he could hear his own heartbeat. He stared at the white walls, there was Picture frames of Phillip as a child, Phillips middle school diploma and honor awards. Fritz could hear his vison pulsate, he stared down at his arm and felt needle rashes running down the right side of his body and the room was spinning like just getting off a Coney Island ride. Everything was in slow motion. His heart beat was sounded as slow as a time lapse, every chamber in his soul sounded like clicks inside of clock. He stepped forward, balling a nasty fist, then suddenly he felt Alejeh pulling him out of the room. she had her arm around his waist, her forehead on his back, tugging him into the shadowy blue hallway. her arms had a loving lock, she had this desperate aura for life and structure. Her eyebrows upward, her skin filled with goosebumps.

Big momma Lucy backed up, shut the door with her hip and Phillip screamed through the wood door, the muffled words were clear.

"he should be thanking me and my niggas for getting get back on his dead bitch-he was cheating on Ivory with Dawn -and them Rolling street infamy niggas killed her! He aint do nothing." Phillip swung his wrist at the door. "he's a bitch-ass nigga."

Big momma Lucy's face loosened, her cheeks went lifelessly pale and her eyes wide and barely blinking at her grandson's stupidity. Her egg white eyes opened wide, she pushed her grandson back with trembling fingers. She could feel his blood in her open palms. the blood oozing down her fingers in slow drips. The reality of her Grandson getting shot as revenge. His organs out of his chest, leaking thick blood, going pale and shutting his eyes for good with a boneless neck.

"Phillip! you gotta go!" she whispered with a face tremble "I'm serious! there aint going to be no gang members in here! I'm sorry! get your stuff and go." She yelled with a chopped voice, her eyes ticking and her fingers trembling with the blood.

"no! why I gotta go," Phillip shouted, "Rolling street infamy killed Fat short Shaq!" Phillips voice went high pitched. "remember Fat short Shaq from the first floor.

"no, Phillip pack y'all things," she blurted.

T.T.'s room door barged open, she wobbled out holding a can of pepper spray like a piece of lit dynamite and stomping across the ceramic tiles.

She pushed through Rigoberto, Alejeh and Fritz, she banged the door and rattled the knob.

"Lucy no!" she shouted in calm fear "Lucy you can't! I'm." She stood there in loud silence, it was like a set stage for her to speak her truth. The arguments were like explosives, the dynamite rattling the rooms and T. T's voice was so light and weak. T.T. held her stomach and slapped the center of the door. "Phillip got me pregnant Lucy!" she screamed with emotion.

Fritz's eyes bulged, his jaw dropped and he grabbed Alejeh's wrist.

Big momma Lucy opened the door, light creped across her Oreo brown skin. "cookie." Big momma Lucy limped and spread her arms for a wide heavenly hug. She trembled with invisible blood all over her body.

"cookie! oh my goodness" Big momma Lucy uttered with a cold shake "is this true?"

Fritz walked to door frame and glimpsed at Phillip. He was shirtless, sitting on his bed while nodding his fever red face. He was crying with engine hiccups.

Alejeh put her arms around Fritz, hugging him tightly and rocking side to side.

Megan's Tea
September/15th/2023

Friday evening 9:45

Hours After the drama, Big momma Lucy stood in the center of the kitchen, swaying her fingers across her quartz countertop, lifting a plate of fried shrimp and fries, she shut the refrigerator door with a hip thrust, the light sealed away and the kitchen was dim like a cave fire. She hummed a Kelly price song, shimmying her shoulders and bopping her head. She wore a silk purple night gown; her love handles jiggling as she spun in a half circle. no matter what happened to Big momma Lucy, she was going to find a way to sing and dance no matter what.

Big momma Lucy opened the faucet and let her fingers rinse off in crystal waters, then suddenly her daughter walked into the kitchen. Yata was dark-skinned like black coffee, wearing a blue V-neck scrub with a glossy gold gain. She was holding a cellphone, with her neck slanted, staring into an iPhone.

"momma what should I say," she uttered with her fingers pinging across the screen. Her nails were yellow and white, clean from top to bottom.

"no start from the beginning" Big momma Lucy uttered with a wrenched lip, "what did Megan say?"

Yata smiled awkwardly, then with her wrist slacked, her hip to the side, flicking through to the message thread. She took a half seat on a dinning stool, she scratched her forehead, her box braids dangled down at the granite table.

"it's a teacup," Yata uttered confusedly "she just sent it a few minutes ago."

"why did she send a text of a tea cup?" Big momma Lucy scrunched her face, contorting her body and turning around and leaning her stomach over the kitchen sink. She lifted a sad brown rag and wiped the quartz countertop in circles.

"maybe she wants to have tea with you?" Yata replied "old people always drinking tea,"

Big momma Lucy squeezed her wiping rag, jerked her head back and made a stale face while her ringy brown hair bounced.

"I aint old! and I aint having no tea with that damn crazy woman" "maybe the teacup means tea, like drama or gossip?"

Big momma Lucy's eye twitched, she mumbled in silence and dragged her feet. She snatched the cellphone away with agility then busted with speed toward the coat rack,

"hello?" Big momma Lucy wrote, "hi Megan, what does that teacup mean?"

The message under shook, replied that Megan was typing, then the typing stopped and it just read that she seen the message. Something that rude people do when they don't want to talk perhaps? either way Big momma Lucy heard her loud and clear.

Big momma scratched her earlobe, walked closer to the polished wood hook, and snagged a bible black leather jacket. "you should probably get going" she uttered, she blindly walked to her bedroom door, thumbing her cellphone, dialed Fritz's phone number and it rung out for two extremely long seconds.

Fritz answered with an echo of a long road in his background. Tires swishing, smooth rumbling engine, chumming and crispy wind whirling at high speed. They had a decent relationship, but Lucy never called him late because she always called it devil hours. He was the devil in her eyes, sometimes.

"Fritz," Lucy hollered in gutted agony "Megan sent me a message of a teacup and tea for ladies usually means some sort of gossip-what's the darn gossip!"

"I don't know." Fritz muttered with a low jaw sputter.

"what if." Big momma Lucy's finger trembled, she fanned herself, then stood near her bedroom window, flamingo pink curtains whirled in her silence. The silence lasted ten long seconds. "what." Fritz uttered in desperation.

"Phillip could've. I feel like we are being haunted by that lie we all told Phillip! All of us, our whole family! God or karma!"

"Luce, it's all your fucking fault! linking Shandy and Phillip together in the first place! it's something you are responsible for!"

Fritz's breathing sputtering stopped mid-sentence, glaring into his rear-view mirror and seeing the pumpkin spice cream seats of his Denali. Rigoberto sitting with dimple shaped eyes, next to his son Cristiano.

Fritz hunched while driving, listening with a bucked eye over his shoulder.

"I'm almost at Alejeh's house" Fritz mumbled in a dismissive way.

"-she is in love with you-you know!" Big momma Lucy uttered back.

"what!" Fritz replied with scrunched eyebrows, glimpsing over at Alejeh's vanilla coconut fragrance. Her legs were crossed as she sat in the passenger.

"Alejeh." Big momma Lucy whispered softly while squeezing her body pillow and causing a crater

"after your seizure, you were all damp in your clothes, she took them off, laid your filthy gun down into a dry rag. She was rubbing your pale little nose with a towel, cleaning your blood. Mmmhmmm. I did the same for Ben, you know he went to war right?"

There was a chainsaw sounding engine, a wobbling speed burst and while the drive was smooth, Fritz's eyes were bouncing side to side in turbulence. He squeezed the leather laced steering wheel, staring forward at the long road. Alejeh, sitting beside him. She was a natural beauty, her high yellow skin, her long black hair was pulled out the braids so she had these natural ringy kinks. Mila Kunis. She looked like a young Mila Kunis with thinner eyes and a flat nose. She had pink eyeliner, pink lipstick and every time she smiled you could see her straight white teeth with pink gums.

Fritz gasped for breath. He stared down at Alejeh's thin little fingers, she had pretty nails, laffy taffy pink in the inside and her perfume smelled like shea butter and vanilla body scrub.

Big momma Lucy dug into her pillow, then tossing it to the mattress and laid down slowly, her legs trembled and her eyes shut.

"look Fritz I think this stuff was a blessing in disguise, "Ivory, my daughter might just be too much."

"no." Fritz shouted softly "look Lucy I'll call you in the morning."

"where are you going to sleep?"

"the penthouse"

"I pray for yawl! Fritz, you should stay with Alejeh."

Fritz couldn't. I mean he could technically, but he kept seeing the image of Ivory holding a knife at Alejeh's throat. He knew that there would be serious repercussions.

Eyeless Mother

September/15th/2023

Friday night 10:01

The escalade Trunk slowed down, the wheels made a rubbery noise as it parked between a black Subaru and a red Toyota with a slanted windshield. Headlights beaming to a license plate that read New Hampshire in white. The car hummed as it remained in place then clicked off with a screwy tank rattle.

Cristiano stood up with a hunch, pushed the passenger door outward, nearly hitting a cyclist and spread his arms. He laughed with his eyes bulged.

"you saw that papi! that was close" He uttered with wrinkles around his eye, giggling like a young child but he was just as tall and girthy as Fritz was. He had large hands, a large forearm and a big belly. He was a mountain of a man! Cristiano hunched forward, reaching his hand for a shake. "thanks Fritz," he opened the passenger door, and his heavy foot slammed against the ground. Cristiano walked to the back of the truck. His eyes beamed at the champagne brown exterior of the Escalade truck, not a scratch on the car. He glimpsed at the gaudy silver rims, it was well kept and as clear as a mirror reflection. Then he glimpsed at the license plate which read diplomat in sky blue and red. Cristiano's eyes widened, he opened the trunk and reached for his father's wheelchair while staring at the wide space. There was a large brown box full of party supplies and balloons, and bowls. It was a large space, could probably fit a whole washer and dryer. His eyes couldn't process that Fritz's family had some ties to the government though. It seemed like some deep ties to the government too; something that the average man couldn't buy, even if he was a drug lord in Tijuana Mexico. Cristiano worshipped them drug lords too; so, he was someone he knew better than anyone.

Fritz turned his cheek and Alejeh's eyes bounced magnetically toward the left side of the car. He smiled slightly, he blinked and tried to keep his eyes focused on outside of the window, the clunks of the wheelchair in the back rattling, and the loud air from the window. Zooming cars swished the road through Corona avenue, Bad bunny music bumping from someone's backyard and it all sounded so slow and distorted. "Why does good music play when your staring at someone whose beautiful?" Fritz thought to himself.

Cristiano softly slammed the foldable seat of his father's wheelchair, opened it up and rolled it to the left side door.

"ayo Fritz," he Cristiano yelled while squeezing the black handles and pushing the chair with his pelvis "you think your people can get rid of my felonies?"

Fritz glimpsed over his shoulder,

"Ivory still has hers," he uttered with an eye twitch. "if I could help, I would but you know how that goes with these government pricks,"

"why does Ivory have felonies though? How man Royce's has she crashed, bro?"

Fritz smirked, shook his head and his eyes landed on Alejeh.

Rigoberto leaned forward from the back seat, he had a bottle of orange prescription pills in his grasp. He opened the cap and plucked a white pill from it then he dropped it on his yellow tongue.

"forty-one, right? once again happy birthday Emperor Fritz." Rigoberto smiled "you should get some of these if you're feeling pain." The little label on the container said oxycodone. Rigoberto raised the cap, he muttered with an elderly smile, his dimple shaped eyes squinting and his lips twitching from an itchy tongue "I never wanted to be on these either, but it's the only way to slumber! I can't sleep! not after what happened to my Lisabelle! My Linda! I would tell you about her one day, but I might need more Percocet's to deal with that type of pain."

Fritz scrunched his face,

"Lisabelle?" he uttered with a half turn.

Alejeh jumped forward from her seat,

"papi" her eyeballs opened wide. Slapping his hands down.

"Ale, let me explain," Rigoberto waved off his daughter with a body tremble. His eyes turned glossy, pale and patchy. He shivered while unbuttoning his collar shirt, "Lisabelle is Alejeh's and Cristiano's mother," his voice went choppy and faded to a lower, more dreaded pitch "you know the motorcycle crash and the broken neck was easier to deal with then her being kidnapped."

"kidnapped." Fritz uttered with a look a concern.

"yes kidnapped!"

Alejeh extended her arm, cupped her father's kneecap and stared him down.

"papi enough is enough" she uttered. "you had too much bourbon!"

Rigoberto's eyes were dilated, the pupil broken brown, cloudy with patches.

"I'll find her one day" he shouted with a pale tongue, "Human Trafficking! Black men, they broke into my old house; first they gouged out Lisabelle's eyes like maniacs, which left her blind. She was traumatized, begging me to stay home with her. After she was weakened, they stalk our house, let us think things were normal, then boom! They took her from me; she was my sunshine and they took my days of joy!"

Rigoberto grabbed the driver seat, the leather was the same color as eggnog; he squeezed it, he had a compressed jaw, losing circulation in his chin and his neck thinning out to the point his veins looked like tree roots "I promise you my Linda, my sunlight, I will find you! Dead or alive; I will find you." His voice cracked.

Cristiano stood there, a tear inching down from his cheek. Alejeh had a tear running down hers too. It was awful every time papi got like that. His words were sound loud and heart wrenching that you could cry without even knowing Lisabelle.

Cristiano lifted his father by the hip, his arms flopped, his skinny legs dangled in his khaki slack pants, wobbling over the wheelchair. Cristiano pushed his father away and his dramatic voice muttered through the open streets,

"My Linda!" He sobbed emotionally with a stiff neck, the hairs on the back of his head sweating in cold chills.

Fritz turned his cheek, dug into his cup holder and pulled a cigarette that was all bent and twisted, he bit it his lips and sparked it with an orange flame. His wedding band gleamed as his fingers were curled on the steering wheel.

Alejeh rolled down her window, she blinked at Fritz and opened her hands with her palm upwards,

"can I." she uttered, staring at the cigarette, "when you're done?"

Fritz's eyes lit up, he handed her the cigarette and felt the softness of her gorgeous fingers. Her pretty vanilla scented palm, she was so beautiful that he salivated the taste of her on his tongue.

"I'm sorry about my father." Alejeh took a hit of the cigarette while leaning back into their eggnog leather seat. Her ringy black hair bounced as she turned her face to blow the ice-cold nicotine smoke.

Fritz took a deep breath, he gazed at her with the cigarette, her right elbow bulging from her inner thigh, her forearm straight, wrist slanted back with the ghostly smoke spiraling and dispersing upward.

"my mother wanted to be a singer, she had a beautiful voice, Rigoberto and her met in Spain and they performed show together from street corner to street corner."

"why did Rigoberto mention Human Trafficking?" Fritz replied with wide eyes. both of his blue pupils stuck to Alejeh.

"He's always talking about kidnappings because in Mexico, we don't know what happened to her; weeks after she had her eyes gouged, she could have just left on her own right?"

"damn," Fritz uttered with an eye twitch, staring forward through the windshield at the long road. He tugged the leathery laced wheel, moving it while in park. There was an awkward silence, then he began scanning information in his head and his eyes were like fireworks. **Guidance! Guidance! Fucking Guidance!** His eyes exploded from his own thoughts. Could it be Rolling Street Infamy? The organization that he started!

Alejeh handed back the cigarette, thrusted her ringy hair from her forehead and stretched closer with cocked eyes.

"look Fritz," she uttered while planting her hand on his inner thigh, "we both have knots on the top of our heads, I think we bumped heads last night during the

Limousine crash. "Alejeh moved closer, uttered with her breathe smelling like cold nicotine.

Fritz lifted his fingers, rubbing the lump above his eye trying to back his jaw away.

Alejeh smiled, leaned closer to his face, glaring at his knot and yanking his pale fingers away "your so awkward," she uttered with her pink lips near his. She leaned in and their lips magnetically bumped together for a sticky kiss. "your so fucking hot dude," she whispered into his mouth, running her fingers through his twiggy hair. She shut her eyes, her tongue poked out, and the kiss led to rubbing, heavy breathing and their fingers were digging into each other's clothes with blind passion. Fritz grabbed her stringy white blouse, yanking it down, and her cleavage jiggled down to the brown part of her succulent nipples. His heart raced, he kissed her neck while she moaned softly and the car felt like a toaster oven. Then suddenly, his phone vibrated in the cup holder. drilling the whole car, the rings went louder and louder. It was a drilling noise like construction workers in daytime fixing the road. He leaned back, he glimpsed at it and it rung with the words wifey. He slapped the dashboard and mumbled spit words that spewed through his shut lips.

Fritz twisted the key, he shook his head while squeezing the wheel and the engine cranked. He made a fist and punched the wheel causing it to honk.

Alejeh flinched,

"I'm sorry" she uttered, she fixed her blouse, opened the car door and stepped out but Fritz grabbed her dainty wrist.

"hold on" he uttered. "can we talk about this,"

"what is it to talk about? Alejeh replied

"she's my wife, I want this, it's just!"

"we only have known each other for six months, I can't tell you what to do, but if my partner drove me into a lake, id surely get a divorce."

"divorce" Fritz smirked "I'd have to leave the fucking country."

Then there was a pause that lasted a few seconds and a gear ran in Alejeh's head.

Alejeh sat back in the seat, shutting the door, she turned her body and glared into his galaxy blue eyes and smiled like a love-struck teenager.

"so, let's do that" Alejeh's eyes lit up "I've always wanted to go to Spain, there's so much wine, sunny views of the city, fresh buttery bread and we could make love until the sun comes up every morning."

"Spain?" Fritz grabbed her by the chin, took a deep breath and pulling her in for a passionate kiss. Their tongues flicking and moving. Alejeh reached for the car key, blindly cutting the engine off and pushing the car door open.

"stay with me?" she uttered grabbing his large fingers and holding it to her cleavage, lifting it and kissing his fingers. "please stay!"

Wormhole Alleyoop
September/16th/2023

Saturday night 2:03

T.T.'s chocolate body figure was stepping with soft feet. She had white socks, small dainty little feet that arched at the bottom. As she stepped into the doorframe, she held a satin black sheet draped around her shoulders like a vampire's cape. The mattress springs shook and her warm long-legged body laid next to her seventeen-year-old baby father, Phillip. Her jiggly brown breast on his chest, laying sideways. she stretched her arm, creating a tent of covers above their heads.

"hey husband," she muttered.

"he's gone?" Phillip whispered

"yea he's gone."

Phillip turned over on his side and the bed sunk to the left.

"why did you tell them about the baby?" Phillip whispered, then he pulled T.T closer and could feel her dark nose against his nose and the warmness of their breathe circulating in the fabric.

"we said we were going to tell grandma when I turn eighteen!"

"I had too or else she would've kicked you out"

They were silent, only hearing the sound of a chopper in the Manhattan sky. The choppers always would stay in place above the night sky; shinning with the billions of twinkling stars.

Phillip shut his eyes in the dark, rubbed his finger against T.T.'s belly, he caressed it, then stretched his open palm at her navel.

"you know that Lance is going to find out."

"fuck Lance," she shouted with a whisper, "Fuck Jah, Fuck Lil Slida, Dutchess and Shandy too"

"I slipped up babe," Phillip muttered with his head sideways. "I told Shandy that I'm not her real brother."

"why the fuck did you." T.T whispered while lifting her head off the dark pillow. Her frizzy hair matted against her neck.

Phillip squeezed his cellphone, turned on the flashlight and dropped it against the bed sheet. The beaming white light shined and he could see T. T's wrenching face. She looked like a beautiful vampire who was about to kill him or the start of a Horrific ghost story.

Phillip looked downward, tugging his phone charger, placing it inside the port and then staring back at her. He turned the phone over showing pictures of Shandy as a kid. She lived inside a humble two-bedroom apartment with her entire family. Her mother Cyn had to strip, Mother Megan was running a Caribbean restaurant called Island jenk's; until she went bankrupt and Remsen did construction until his back wore out.

Phillip flicked through the pictures, one by one showing the family, their tough life and living condition and arrived at Orlando. Orlando was a dope fiend, who had to go to rehab.

T.T. sucked her teeth,

"so, what!" she uttered.

"Big momma Lucy and Fritz are fucked up," he uttered "Shandy grew up in the hood with no father or no money."

"boo hoo," T.T replied "so why are you empathizing with her!" T.T. dropped the satin sheet tent, she leaned up with her thick legs straight, her pink sweat pants squeezing her thighs.

"didn't Shandy let her friends jump you in the heights, those boys were swinging on you like the golden gloves and she just watched."

"But when Merlo died all the money went to me, Grandma and Fritz!"

"so be thankful, Merlo left you the bag what the fuck!"

T.T. cupped Phillips mouth with every finger, stared at the bedroom door and contorted her body to the slanted pillow. Her eyes were like daggers tips.

"don't ever say that again" she whispered with her lips tight around her teeth, "I'm serious Phillip, you see how were living, if you skeptical of anything you better take it to your grave! T. T's eyes rattled with redness. "you see how fucking rich we are! I'm never going back over you feeling guilt for Shandy!' she shouted quietly.

Phillip knew for sure that Shandy is Merlo's daughter, but couldn't understand why his family, T.T. included, made it so hard for her to receive what she deserved. It was as if everyone was obsessed with money, and didn't care what was right or wrong.

Guidance
September/18th/2023

Monday morning 11:06

Shandy walked, the sun flashed her brown hair. She wore a hot pink golf cap on her head, a leather Balenciaga jacket and some tight jeans that hugged her hips. Niggas always used to say she aint have no ass, but she had a lot of cakes once she took them pants off. Her baby father used to call her ass a pie instead of a cake; because it was brown and round.

Shandy stretched her arm, pulling the glass door and walking up the groovy carpet, into the gate of Medgar Evers college. The door slammed and there was a thrust of wind that made her coily hair bounce. She had a thick ponytail hanging out of her golf cap. She smirked slightly, remembering when her best friend Abdul aimed his finger at her telling her that she looks like Naomi Osaka. She always thought Naomi Osaka was beautiful when her hair bounced around on the tennis court, so it wasn't a diss. She thought Naomi was fly.

Shandy had a strap with a lab top across her curvy little hip, a zipper half way open with the screen bulging out because she liked to type on the bus ride to school. She squeezed her nails around a coffee cup from a breakfast truck. Long hair don't care? sure because she didn't care! Unless she took a sip of her coffee and saw one of her long ass hair strands on the cap. Some people said that she looked like Zendaya the actress with all her brown hair, but Shandy preferred Naomi Osaka. lord, she loved how exotically beautiful she was.

Shandy walked through the long halls, her jeans had little stringy patches, she had the freshest air force ones on with the little piece of metal in the shoelaces. While walking through the long blue polished halls, she crossed into the cafeteria and it was mildly empty. She strutted slower and rested her MacBook bag on the granite table. The pink strap flopped, curling like a snake tail. she turned her cheek, examined the glossy blue cafeteria, long flat tables, vending machines and beanie seats for the students who liked to sleep. She noticed someone from her Philosophy class, but couldn't remember his name. Maybe his name was Fred or something, he had a monotone voice that irked her, but he sure did let her cheat on the mid-term quiz.

Shandy waved her dainty hand, remembering that her Grandmother always told her to be social around campus.

"Hey" she muttered with a slight smile. Fred's eyes bulged and he waved back while holding a lunch tray, then suddenly everyone in the lunchroom stared at her. Her anxiety kicked in, so she broke eye contact fast and lowered the brim on her cap. She pressed the button on her laptop to turn on the screen, then she scrolled through zoom and dialed a number. The wide computer screen flashed and then there was a notice that her call had been answered in blue words. The video background was a solid white concrete painted wall, chipped paint, hard blotches of ink in cursive letters that were written like graffiti. What was written? R.S.I. Then suddenly, there were slipper noises, long legs bending and a man stepped into the screen in navy blue sweatpants, he sat down on a metallic bed with an oatmeal creme pie in his hands. He had brown dusty cornrows in his head, was wearing a thin white tee and he had broad shoulders like a club bouncer. He had sunglasses on his face, a tattoo under his eye and a busy mustache. Her baby father looked like a young G Herbo, he had a voice like him too, but without the Chicago ascent. Virgil was living like them Chicago dudes too. That's how he ended up in Roderick Elderly maximum security prison. It was a prison known for ruining most men, but he looked rejuvenated ever since the inmates took the prison back.

"You hit me at the perfect time" Virgil uttered while peeling the plastic of his oatmeal creme pie, he stared at his cellmate, or someone out of the view of the screen and smirked with his chin up. He had a wide smile, dimples, a flat brown braid on both sides. "come here king" he shouted with a cheek full of brown gushed cookies. He chewed, he gave someone an arm thrust, suddenly, a tall brown skin man stepped into the focus of the camera. He was skinny' like malnourished kind of skinny. He had eyes like a praying mantis, all big and bulged. He had a balled head, a long shaggy beard, and big lips sticking out. He was in his early forties, but had some grey strands racing down in his beard. He sat down, big knuckles cracking, slouching with his legs open wide, his blue sweat suit looked freshly ironed and he had a cold stare.

Virgil put his arm around the strange man's neck,

"Shandy, I have somebody I want you to meet, this is my man Guidance. He's been like a father figure to me while I been at the Elides" he smiled with eyes like he had been staring at fireworks. While the two hugged, you could hear a basketball slapping the prison floor in the background. Voices muttering through the zoom call.

"father figure?" Shandy uttered.

Guidance smiled, made poise eye contact and slid a Glock from his waist. He placed the scratchy gun on his lap and hugged his arm around Virgil.

"this is my incarnation," Guidance uttered with his eyes squinted "he's a good dude shorty, we have been in here holding things down. you know, my life for his life and his life for mine."

"Guidance, I have class in a few, so what's the deal?"

Guidance glimpsed at Virgil, giving him a head nod and Virgil lifted from his seat. His slippers scrapped against the floor, when he walked away, you could see his sweatpants sagging slightly with a black Glock handle pressed against the cheeks of boxer briefs. Virgil stepped outside the cell, the prison bars grinded and shut with a loud vibrating cling. The basketball slaps became louder and you could hear niggas shouting about who fouled who.

Sometimes Shandy would listen to the background, anxious and praying that she didn't hear any gay shit going on, or the police storming the jail and killing the prisoners for what they did to the inmates. She often watched the news coverage of the police who surrounded the prison, watching with open ears and any updates on the hostage situation. It was going well, because the prisoners got what they wanted. They demanded food and toiletries on Wednesday and received it by Thursday.

Guidance's eyes bulged, his facial skin was as tight as brown leather, muscles in his cheekbones and fat black lips that looked like he burned them while sucking fire.

"it's been 150 days since we took these cells back," Guidance rubbed the hard-white prison walls "we lucky to still be alive, your man is good dude and if he could, he'd be there for his Junior, but do me a favor, Talk to me about someone. someone I've taken mutual interest in; Phillip?" Guidance stared with a psychopathic eye dart.

Shandy placed her face closer to the screen, her nose was so close that it looked like she was cockeyed. she smiled awkwardly.

"you said you knew my dad right, Merlo" Shandy placed her fingers around her coffee cup and took a sip, then her eyes bounced side to side.

"shawty, Merlo was my ace boom!" Guidance replied.

"Phillip said that Merlo aint his real father, I think that little boy has a crush on me and is lying about our dad; he's a weirdo."

"mm," Guidance smirked with a slick grin, and planted the back of his skull against the solid white wall," he took a deep breath, folded his arms and turned his jaw to the jail bars glaring at the basketball game in the mess hall

"that isn't news to me though." he ripped down a piece of paper from the solid white wall, he aimed it at the screen and it became gigantic and blurry. The newspaper was old needle bled ink, dark grey paper and nearly chipped at every angle. the headline read "Human Trafficker Lincoln Bijos sentenced to life on August 26th of 2005."

"what do you mean," Shandy uttered "what does your life sentence have to do with anything?"

"you ever heard of Claire smithens Coney Island parties? It was *a lot of freaking going on*, let me explain what happened one night."

Claire's Party
March/11th/2005

Flock of people flooding the front yard playing dice and drinking 40 ounces. The crisp cold air shaking out of their mouths as they shouted and laughed. I walked up the steps, bumping through; the step had a dip that lead to a brown dented door, gold hinges with wobbly knob that shook outward. Inside the apartment was human furniture because everyone standing in the center of the living room or blocking the walkway. Fella's wore Leather 8 eight ball jackets, or Pelle Pelle; they weren't wearing the Gucci and Louie V like me. Ladies stared in silence. Above our heads was a dim bulb that flickered in and out like some haunted shit, but everybody was fucking wasted and having fun. There were smoke rings on the ceiling, smoke rattling out of the speakers and out of shape strippers sliding up and down with that funky smell. I loved that funky smell, funky pussy and ass all in my nostrils. Bitches with blackness in between their legs, bumps, stretch marks. I'm a psychopath for pussy.

I kissed Claire on the cheek. Walking behind me was Fritz, he gave Claire a head nod and then then leaned on the sweaty wall.

Shandy's face went pale, her head cocked back and she put her fingers around her mouth.

"Fritz" she uttered with bulging eyes, she lifted her coffee cup, there was brown stain on the cover that looked like brown lipstick "why would you hang with Fritz?" Shandy uttered.

"To me, Fritz was no threat" Guidance replied while cracking his knuckles "Fritz? he was like a partner to me! we had! we had a murderer on our asses, telling us what to do."

"a murderer?"

"yea, you ever heard of P-89 Suggs?"

"no"

"P-89 Suggs, a kingpin who ran all the operations in Coney Island! He supposedly yelled at Fritz; telling him that Pill sales weren't enough, how he wanted Fritz to help him gather people."

"gather people" Shandy's eyes bulged, she turned her head left and right. She was slightly afraid, reminding herself that this Guidance person was too far away to be a threat.

Guidance smiled like a maniac, he had slow blinking eyes and a delay that look like he was counting fireflies.

"yup, snatch a girl from the party, bring her home and then. I don't want to say the rest. god forgive us. Fritz was in the corner watching like a creep, scoping all night and clutching his ratchet."

"what about you." Shandy uttered, "what! what was your job?"

"for the dirty work," Guidance, shook his head, rubbed his long beard, pulling it to be straightened. There was a tattoo of R.S.I on her hand, under his wrist and thousands of scriptures written on her forearm that looked like a bible psalm.

"yea, I pulled a lot of people into my truck. I aint gone lie." Guidance uttered in a delusional voice.

My intent was to have a good time at the party, before I had to do what I had to do, so I was dancing, and smoking with some white bitches from Canarsie. Christie and Paulene, two blonde, Russian Jews who had smiles like Camren Diaz and the other; Stacey keibler. Fritz was fifteen feet away, standing by the crowded door, getting bumped by people stepping in. He was flinching at the bright flashes of people's camera phone, jumping out pictures and hiding his face like a vampire in daylight. Camera phones were just getting popular around that time, and Fritz was a caveman.

At around 12' o clock, I was slurring, eyes blinking slow and feeling off balanced, so I went for a Styrofoam cup and asked the lil bitch in the kitchen for water instead of whiskey. There was a small board of wood that kept the liquor bridged away from the party, so we had to as the bartender. I slammed a wrinkled five-dollar bill on the counter and she handed me the cup. stumbling to the door, I barely could remember her face. I kept seeing P-89 in my head like a mushroom trip. He was watching me somewhere, waiting to kill me and Fritz. At any given time. P-89 had resources to gun us down from the roofs, get us stabbed in the subways or even while we were at home, in our vulnerable moments.

P-89 Suggs forced us to take all kinds of bitches, fat and short, white to black and even trafficked men, and Claire knew too.

Shandy shook her head in confusion, snapping out of the conversation and running circles in her own mind.

"oh my god, like what would P-89 do with the men?" Shandy uttered "is P-89 gay?"

"you ever heard of the black market? let's say you're fifty-eight years old and you have your hands on a hundred grand in savings, you are on a waiting list for a new eyeball, or kidney and it's taking forever. Me and Fritz basically did the dirty work for P-89 Suggs so you'd be able to get it. a new Kidney faster than any Organ company could get for you, you want honesty; that was our job."

Shandy's face wrenched, flashing images were in her head of her baby father being involved with him. Shandy jerked away from the screen.

"oh my god, Guidance you're the fucking devil" she held her face away from the screen. she trembled in her seat. The cafeteria went blizzard cold, she covered her fingers with her mouth, her eyes bounced as she jerked her neck back. "are you serious? this is horrible" she held her stomach. She stood up, walking away from her laptop. School officer, with a flat top, brown skin and a mustache walked past her and squinted his eyes.

"you okay?" he uttered.

"I know" Guidance leaned away from the camera, Then, Guidance lifted a water bottle and sipped it with his shaggy beard. His Adams apple bounced up and down as he drank. His psychotic eyes waiting for her in silence.

"come on lil girl, I have to tell you about Phillip before you cancel on me."

At Claire's house, I was smoking a roach while a white girl danced on my dick. Speakers were vibrating with Cassidy's I'm a hustler song. I glimpsed over and saw the baddest bitch at the party. Ivory! She had these long dreads, the side of her head shaved completely, gold hoop earrings. she was against the wall shaking her fat soft ass, her ribs moving like a gypsy.

I pushed off the white girl. Ivory wore this little white blouse under a black fish net shirt, Her belly ring glittering like a dime at the bottom of a wishing well. She had a short pink skirt, with her honey brown legs jiggling. she was poking her ass out and dancing in platform boots. Puffing a blunt in darkness while bopping her head.

Fritz walked over, her bottom lip pulsating. He gave me an arm nudge,

"you see her" He uttered, "that's the bitch we need."

My eyes blinked like a sandstorm,

"I got this white girl over in Gulags room!"

"no!" Fritz shouted with thin lips " Her!"

"alight," I responded, gazing at Ivory with a fast beating heart, short breath and nostril sweat. Gulag was my best friend. He was a Russian kid who held things down after I went to prison.

I put the hoodie over my head and turned my cheek. One by one, I was bumping and knocking against people. Human furniture! they were always in my way, and I was a strong nigga even back then, I had the presence of a mule. I walked over to Ivory and greeted her in darkness, I gave her a kiss on the cheek and whispered into ear.

"you looking good baby" I pulled off my hoodie, diamond stud on my earlobe blinging, looking like a young Morris Chestnut. That's who people said I looked like. Holding out my flip phone, I was smiling with thug charm.

Ivory's face was tightened, she snapped her head back and stared me up and down "oh, okay, thanks" she uttered with a face wrench, turning her cheek and I could see her side of her head that fully shaved. What a dime piece. She danced, brushing the wall with that Jell-O soft ass.

"you ever had extasy?" I uttered through the chopping music, I opened my left hand and there was a lil lady bug of white dust on my fingers. Ivory snatched that thing and giggled toward her sister, holding her fingers open like it was gold.

"so, you have a flip phone and Ex?" she shouted, tippy-toeing with her lips at my ear. "you must be hustling? Her eyes widened, she smiled with a Beyoncé facial structure.

"I don't even got a phone yet and I have a job with the board of education, you must got it like that." She uttered.

"yea, shorty, I hustle, you could say that."

While the music blasted, she just stared at me.

Yata, the dark skin sister grabbed my lower arm, and yanked me closer with desperation. She placed her palm on my shoulders and tippy-toed to my ear.

"Hey daddy," she shouted through the loud music "that's my sister, I was wondering, can I get one too? we are trying to party!"

"hold on" I replied, while glaring at her with an awkward eye twitch, I back peddled, bumped a couple people on the pathway as I stepped to Fritz, nudging him in the arm and smiling.

"yo, Fritz, you have another Ex Pill for her sister!"

Suddenly, Fritz's face tightened, he flicked his wrist, aiming his desert eagle at my stomach, he grabbed me by the neck with his massive hands and threw me against the wall with ease.

"Linc, do you think this is a fucking game, get the girl so we can roll!" he pressed the gun at my stomach and I could feel the ring of death pressed against my skin.

Fritz bit his bottom lip,

"quick fucking horsing around, you get the bitch, we get outta here! You understand?"

That was the first time I noticed the anger of Fritz, he had a coldness in his eyes too, a constant eye twitch and underbite breathing heavily. The rage he had was nasty, as if he didn't care about anyone's life. He breathed spit particles while tucking his gun.

I always thought to myself that if Fritz was this bad ass motherfucker, then how was he was just worker like me? P-89 Suggs must have been Satan himself.

Minutes later, there were some young boys by the brown gate rapping in a cypher, some dealers across the street, and hoes wearing thin clothes walking with pocketbooks stuck to their hips. Waving at cars, they were prostitutes and everything went silent for me. I rubbed my face with a wet napkin, put some dark shades on and I walked over to Ivory. By then, she had already taken the extasy, she rubbed her Jell-O soft ass on my pelvis, shaking and moving sensually. I glimpsed in the corner, staring at Fritz who was watching me, then I broke eye contact with him and held Ivory's petit hips.

Sean Paul's song "I'm still in love" was playing. I loved that slow Caribbean drum, that soft voice chanting I'm *still in love*, over and over

Ivory shut her eyes,

"you dance like a Jamaican man," she slurred while thrusting her dreads on me, she squatted down, holding my kneecaps as she corkscrewed her ass cheeks into my pelvis. We called the wining.

"you like that shorty?" I grabbed her hips, running my finger up her backside and squeezing her neck like she was my bitch. How high she was, she was my bitch so I squeezed her neck. "I'm trying to take you home with me," I whispered in her earlobe. "how that sound?"

Ivory nodded her head,

"what's your name again," she shouted through the slow drumming music "you know what, it don't matter, I'm really down for whatever." she turned around, placed her arms over my shoulders and we were eye to eye. Then pushed the hoodie off my cranium and her smile went even wider.

"you are such a handsome man," she uttered, "I've never had a man make me feel like this" she locked eyes with me, then locked my hands with hers. We slowly walked through toward the brown door, I saw the vibrating walls, could feel the vibrating floors and on the way out, everything went in slow motion.

Ivory stepped out of the doorframe with a wobbly body frame, half-way stumbling and yawning. I dug into my pocket for keys. A '05 navigator, white body, silver wheels. After she walked into the passenger side of my truck, the door chopped and we drove off into Neptune Ave.

The road through Neptune Ave was dark, I slowed down and stopped through a side block on 30th street. The engine creaked, we were under a tilted hanging tree near an alleyway narrow white house garage that smelt like moon shine and Ginkgo nuts. Me and Ivory crawled from the front seats, louis Vuitton peanut butter leather seats scuffing and denting. We went toward the backseat undressing. she got on fours like a cat, crawling, bending her back with the perfect arch. I yanked down her skirt until it was at her kneecaps while she was on fours and my heart was throbbing. She lifted a leg, I pulled her skirt off like a piece of Kentucky fried chicken skin. Her ass was in my face so I spread her cheeks open and I licked her crack down to her juicy pussy, then my tongue went back up to her asshole and I was fucking her with my taste buds. Her fat brown ass tasted like a fresh batch of banana bread. The windows turned Smokey like a steam room.

As I was eating her ass. she turned over, lifting my shirt and scooting closer. Six-pack of condoms in my hand, ripping it open with my broad shoulders, I unbuttoned my pants, pulled for a condom, but she peeled it right off with her backhand and slapped it on the car floor.

"no," she shouted, "I want to feel it," and she threw her brown pussy onto my dick. "please daddy, let me feel it," There was no tightness, I was balls deep inside her wet pussy, and it was warm and full of spit suds. She threw her ass back and the smacks sounded like water splashes. After about two minutes, she had her eyes shut and moaning like a mindless bitch.

"yea fuck me with that long dick, fuck me Merlo, uhm I missed you! yea!"

my body stiffened, my dick softened and my eyes were pinging. First of all, I knew she wasn't talking about me; because I had a small four inched dick and second, she mentioned Merlo.

"wait?" I lifted my body weight from her spine, my shirt jiggling. My fingers were twitching as I reached for my belt. "Merlo?" "Merlo, you mean Merlo Jenkins?"

Ivory cupped her mouth, jumped up with electricity and stretched her arms towards her fishnet skirt.

"you know my fiancé'?"

"your fiancé? bitch what! you aint tell me that Merlo was your fiancé!"

I opened the back seat, walked back to the driver's side and started the car.

"fuck" I uttered frantically, the view of world spinning around. I could see Merlo in my head, shooting me and burying me with his own two hands for kidnapping his woman.

"you don't understand bitch! this is not what you think this is." I clicked the car in drive. "we gotta go! I'm dropping you at the train stop! For safety."

Shandy's eyes were twice its normal size, she blinked slowly and breathed with a chocked neck,

"so, you are Phillips real!"

"yes, he's my son!" Guidance leaned closer to the computer screen "I counted! That night was in march and Phillip was born in December, right?"

"December 27th."

Guidance smiled with a validated eye twitch,

"yea he's my son, yup no doubt about it-after that night I quit! I quit the Human Trafficking shit and Five months later I was arrested in Georgia and extradited back for Kidnapping, sex assault, attempt murder and Human Trafficking of ten or more people."

"wow" Shandy uttered with a pale face.

"yea, and that's not even the full story! you see Fritz wasn't just a corner boy selling ecstasy, he was the kingpin! that P-89 Suggs nigga wasn't our boss! Fritz was! He manipulated me into doing his dirty work for an imaginary person. Then snitched on me to get me life."

Shandy's eyes bounced around with horrified anxiety!

"I never trusted him" Shandy replied, she shook her head and her lip twitched with coffee drips "he always seemed off to me!"

Guidance swayed his hand across the metallic prison bed.

"I'm, here for life because of Fritz! you know, when my nephew found out Fritz was living in Brooklyn after sixteen years, I was going to give him mercy, I just wanted to find my son! but Fritz fucking killed my nephew Dadrian in at the auto shop!!"

"why?"

"he was fucking paranoid, he knew I was the real father of Phillip! but fuck all that, can you tell me where my men can find my son?"

Shandy got silent, she blinked away from the computer screen staring the security guard in the eye as a call for help. He didn't get the hint, he turned toward the vending machine and ordered a Pepsi.

"100 Beekman towers," Shandy uttered "that's where Phillip lives, their family came up on some money. He lives in Manhattan. it's a green scaffold with a doorman and gold-plated frames for the windows he's on the 46th floor. what are you going to do?"

"my son is safe, but I can't promise tomorrow for anybody else.

Fighting Wife
September/18th/2023

Monday morning 11:45

The sunlight crept into the curtains, stretching onto the banana yellow pinstriped bed spread of a queen-sized mattress with ruffle pillows. Two sets of feet parallel together, slightly touching, Fritz laid in bed with his arm stretched to the side of the pillow, while leaning his naked body on Alejeh. Her thick ringy black hair in his face, he blinked twice and clinched like he had just woke from a coma. He opened his eyes, and saw her kinky black hair strands coming from her golden scalp then released his smile he held back. Her watermelon kiwi scented hair on his nose, her pineapple tasting pussy on his upper lip and her soft naked body leaning on him. He lifted from the springy mattress, he placed both hands on his temples and dragged them down his horrified face.

"fuck," he screamed with his throat expanding. Breathing hard, eyes racing as if he had the anxiety bugs crawling in his brain.

Alejeh lifted her chin, staring at Fritz with squinted eyes, yawning sideways, her pink tongue and tonsils were visible.

"Fritz, are you."

"no," he lifted the bedsheets, his armpits smelled like sweat and onions "what the fuck happened?" he shouted.

There were clothes peeled off, slung around the small bedroom, a scratchy wood desk with his jewelry stretched out and his Desert Eagle glistening in the morning sun. No sight of condoms.

Fritz lifted the yellow pinstriped bed sheets higher, scanning the bedroom for his underwear and snatching his briefs from the ending of the mattress.

"Did we?" Fritz glared around, noticing that his penis head was full of dried juices. "I gotta go." he stood, bent down and shoved his foot into his black jeans and hobbled around until his leg was in.

Alejeh lifted from slumber while on her knees, planted her palm on the yellow pinstriped bedspread, she hooked her forearm around him and pulled him back to the bouncing mattress. "hold on," she uttered "do you want Turron before you go?"

"No," he shouted "do you know what my wife. My wife Ivory will do if she finds out?"

Suddenly, the phone vibrated with a zap that sounded like an electric drill. The sunny bedroom turned dark and ominous. Their heads turned at the same time glaring at the phone of cellphone of death. Fritz walked to on the head board, lifted it and held it to his reddened earlobe.

"Ivory? he muttered.

There were loud screams coming from the phone, a scream that sounded as if her madness came from her gut more so than her throat. His twiggy blond hair began to sweat, his pale skin went rash red and his body slouched while standing. Ivory's words were a hurricane of torn; tearing into Fritz's mind and ripping their last piece of foundation of love.

Alejeh's breast dangled as she walked across the mattress on her knees. She stood from the yellow pinstriped bedspread, planting her foot on the carpet and walking around until she stopped in front of him. She had the perfect hourglass shape, a gap in between her legs that looked like an upside-down pyramid, perfectly perky boobs and a bubble butt. Absolute bombshell. She grabbed his finger, stared into his eyes with an emotional pause.

Fritz lifted his face, it was fiery red, he spread his lips around his teeth and breathed particles of spit.

"Ivory!" he shouted "you fucking drove me into a lake you crazy bitch! what do you expect!" He screamed. He pushed Alejeh away slightly with a stiff wrist and turned around toward the curtains.

Alejeh pulled him closer "please don't." she smiled awkwardly while reaching for the phone. She grabbed it and the cellphone screen went dark. Once it was away from his ear, she pressed the button to end the call and there was a loud silence in the house.

Fritz slammed his hands against his temple, wiping his fingers to his cheek.

"we made a fucking mistake." He whispered with sleepless eyes, "I have to go."

"no, we didn't." she replied in desperation, reliving their sex.

"Ivory's outside right now." he muttered, walking to the blinds and lifting it with a finger.

Suddenly Alejeh walked toward the icy bright window, pulled the yellow blind aside and pushed her nose into the glassy view. Ivory was in a wide stance, as if she was about to pitch a baseball; she threw something while screaming from her guts. She was wearing a long-sleeved, with a silk silver head tie wrapped around her skull. She had stripped white and black shorts for jogging and some Nike tennis shoes. In her hands she held a Long lanky pair of blue jeans. She slashed the pair of pants into his windshield, then turned around and grabbed a handful of linen shirts from a popped trunk and lashed them one by one onto Fritz parked Escalade truck. The same truck that she and Fritz were gifted by the government.

Alejeh turned from the window, planted her body on the mattress, sticking her legs into her gym shorts. She put on her Cinco de mayo air max sneakers while pouting her lip. Her chest bounced, eyes raced as she stuck her foot inside. She flicked her long lock black hair into a bun, dipped her fingers into Vaseline and rubbed it on her face.

Fritz grabbed his gun, he tucked it into his waistband and then he lifted his shirt, pulled it over his torso and his hair blond hair instantly went thin and thorny. He turned around, pulled the knob, the door opened and he slithered out of the crack.

"if you're smart, you'll stay away from me, ok?" he shouted "just pretend we never met."

Alejeh sucked her teeth, shook her head and opened the yellow wood door to the opposite side of the house.

Fritz walked through the living room, which was the backside entry, a slower way out of the complicated house. Rigoberto, was inches away from his bedroom door frame. Rigoberto rolled his wheelchair closer, holding the gloves in his lap. he wrenched his face in confusion.

"Fritz my buddy, is everything okay?"

"fine" Fritz squeezed the doorknob."

"My friend, you could take the back door it's faster, in Alejeh's room" Rigoberto pointed with a veiny finger aiming at the windy room.

Fritz turned his cheek, standing his shock, he dragged his feet back to the bedroom, opened the front door and there was windy balcony of sunlight pouring in from Alejeh's room, a gapping doorway into the street of Corona.

"that yellow door? I thought that was the bathroom" Fritz uttered, He ran back, pacing down the steps. There was swaying clothes, buckets with suds and old bottles for detergent.

Ivory was in the middle of the street, her lanky body was pivoted, she swung, grabbing Alejeh into her breast, her head locked, her face down at the pavement, throwing uppercut punches with her right hand.

"you young little bitch" Ivory shouted pulling her down and yanking her around until the world spun.

"I should've never let you around my fucking husband you little man stealing bitch!"

As Ivory kneecapped kicked her, cars from the road stopped in traffic and people stuck their heads out to see. Jaws dropped as the girls thumped it on a busy road. An avocado vender scrambled away from her box of fruit, running toward them while brandishing a large broom stick.

"mita!" he shouted "detener! detener! permiso!"

After the shock of them fighting, Fritz grabbed Ivory by the hip, pulled her off and there was a psychotic stare. Ivory rolled over, swung at Fritz, hitting him in the head with the back of her fist.

"this is what you do!" she screamed "this is what you been doing for the past seventeen years?" Ivory threw a roundhouse punch, landing right on his chin and knocking him back a few inches. Everyone in the streets screamed while holding their mouths. Screamed at the violent nature of a black woman who was completely fed up with a cheating husband. while holding his mouth, Fritz opened his crooked jaw, yawing with pain. He tried to stand, but he was wobbled so grabbed a shackled bike tire and pulled himself into balance.

Ivory shimmied her ring finger, tossing the diamond ring at his chest and planted her toe in the concrete.

"I never loved you!" she shouted. "no, don't, let go of me," she screamed at a random person trying to hold her back. Ivory walked to her car; a silver Audi r8 with a diamond gloss paint style. She lifted bulky black trash bags from the trunk and dropped them at the curb.

"fucking designer jackets" she shouted," designer shirts and jeans," she tossed them over her shoulder and the expanded like open parachutes.

Fritz glared in agony, trying to stand and suddenly he felt his arm numbing. a fever of rash needles creeping down his brain, to his shoulder and wrist.

Cristiano stood on the corner, he had a blunt in his fingers smoking while clutching his knife. He didn't want to step over to his brother Caté, who already separated Alejeh from the nasty cat fight. He resented Fritz; not just for all the money he had, but for bringing problems he was slowly bringing to his family.

Killer's Karma
November/3rd/2023

Sunday morning 12:06

Fritz bobbled his head down, walking across the glittery road of Manhattan. A sunny spec of light shining off his leather jacket which was coffee brown, but had a laminated shine. His inner shirt was white and his pants off white. He crossed the street and arrived at the building where he and Ivory shared a penthouse. The taxi's rolling through the street, honks from the road and the smell of cigarettes. Fritz pushed the front door, through the outside glass he could see inside the lobby. He could also see the mirror of himself; some greys in his eyebrows and a protruding jaw.

Fritz wheezed slightly, pushed his palms into the revolving door handle and it swept open. The spin was fast, oxygen less and when he arrived inside the lobby it smelled like lavender and pomegranate. A big red couch in the middle with a book shelf behind it. Fritz glimpsed at the old white doorman who had a bald head, scruffy face hairs down his jaw. He wore a collared shirt that was ironed with a slick tight blue blazer.

James Eastwood was the doorman's name. His clammy pale his palms up, tussling a food delivery person and shaking his head side to side.

"hey, you have to take the freight elevator, it's at that back entrance." James uttered while back hand thrusting.

"que?" the delivery person uttered with a blank expression

In that same moment, Fritz walked toward the food delivery person, and his feet clicked again the marble floor. He placed a palm on the Hispanic man's shoulder and it was a second of awkwardness.

"el edificio tiene otra puerta" Fritz shouted, and then smiled. He aimed his finger and pushed the delivery man to the revolving door "sal y ve al otro ascensor." Fritz spoke with a slow delay in his words.

"Gracias Hermano," the delivery person smiled with a gap tooth.

After a month of being with Alejeh, Fritz could speak Spanish.

James had wide eyes, a bushy grey broom hair mustache and his pink lips bobbling.

"good morning sir." James uttered in reply,

Suddenly, the windy lobby went quiet. James lifted his eyebrows, turned his shoulder and reached toward the white telephone with the squiggly cord at the front desk.

"I'll give to Ivory a call to let her know you're coming up"

Fritz strutted into the elevators. He pressed the button and it glowed yellow. Standing next to a pot of shrubby green plants that shook if you walk past it.

"Mr. Fritzen Clayed?" James uttered with his words bouncing off the high ceiling. His finger up and his neck.

"hold on let me give Ivory a call before you go up."

"fuck you mean? This is my house! I still pay the bills!" Fritz stepped into the elevator and pressed PH-01. The elevator mechanics cranked, ratcheted and the doors clunk shut.

The turbulence made his ears pop, there was a vibration under his feet and then a fast upward light headedness. The elevator doors clicked and racketed and rattled open. Fritz walked through the bright grey carpeted hallway, there was illuminated doorways for the other three penthouse apartments, a faint noise coming from the four doors. a voice of a mother perhaps, or the voice of a daughter mumbling something you could barely hear in a joking way. Charlie and the chocolate factory running on their Televisions.

Fritz always thought that his neighbors were shady. All they did was talk about people and smile in his face. Fritz walked passed every door imagining what he might say to his wife. Imagining what he'd say before he strangled her to death. He had only murdered one man in his life, and wasn't sure what he could do with his wife.

Fritz's feet stopped, PH-01 was at the left side, near a plant pot that looked like a palm tree from Barbados. He stepped toward the scruffy welcome mat. Black and blue knitted with squiggly words. It was out of place and the spare key was gone. The door slightly cracked open with sun light bouncing from the window. Fritz's eyebrows dropped and he backed away. He heard a tweet, a small blue jay tweeting behind the door. He took a deep breath, pressed his ear into the hallow door; there was a loud TV running in the background.

Fritz shut his eyes, he slowly pulled his Desert eagle from his waist and it sparkled like chrome. He pushed the door open with the Barrell of the gun and it made a creaky noise. He could see a small square view of the kitchen countertop. Sunlight stretching across the home decor like a summer morning in Cali. He squeezed the rubber grip of his Desert eagle.

Fritz shut his eyes, breathing loudly, running the smooth elongated Barrell down the center of the door. Pushing it open enough to see what else was going on. He stuck his head inside the apartment and there was flashing images of Jim with his wife. He couldn't bare it.

There was a bottle of white wine on the countertop with two glasses. Skinny glasses that were as thin as flower stem but the cylinder was empty. Fritz's heart was beating fast like a drum after mushrooms. He saw flashes of all of the nights he spent with his wife, her brown body, her hair her purple skirt being lifted in Vegas. His muscles shook, his bones trembled and there was a repugnant feeling in his gut. Fritz pushed his foot against the door, bit his bottom lip and walked inside the penthouse with his nose down.

"Jim" he shouted to the high ceiling and glaring at the walls which were naked of his portraits. His medals and awards for coaching in Berlin. There were no portraits of Phillip; their son, none of Ivory either. The hallow apartment was nearly lifeless; as a someone about to move out. Fritz stumbled as he walked, dragging his feet across the carpet that looked like the scales of a clown fish. His heavy gun toward his kneecap. Long path to the bedroom, Fritz noticed there was a musty stench. He remembered how Ivory hated bad scents and how she'd always light one of her scented candles if there was a smell of sex, liquor, dirty socks and cigarettes. Fritz twisted his face in a wrenching mean mug; sticking his ear in the direction that he could hear noise. He scrunched his face, pushing the door open with his fingers stuck to the polished handle. The door creaked and the light from the hallway crept into the room. Fritz glared at the mattress which had a long foot hanging at the edge of the bed.

Fritz eyes turned twice his size.

"what the fuck is this" Fritz shouted with his guts, he pulled the bedsheets back and the wind made a rippling noise.

The sheets, revealed a burgundy wound on a man in the bed with a contorted neck, slacked shoulders. There loud funkiness, an electric feeling in the room and a big furry fly that landed on Jim's open eyeball. Fritz dropped his jaw and smelled the dead space between him and the man. A piece of his skull was blown backwards. Chunks of brain meat pinned to the wall.

Fritz back away and slammed against the wall; he placed his forearm over his nose. "Ivory." He shouted, backing out with a chocked feeling in his throat.

He stumbled back to the bathroom knob. He pushed the door inward and his feet turned into cinder blocks. His eyes froze, his face snapped back. Ivory's head was inside the clogged toilet with her hair floating in the bowl. Purple tint across her body, slouched with her back bones poking out of her lifeless spine.

Fritz backed out, landing his bodyweight against the wall and tumbling down, he crawled backwards, lifted the phone to his jaw.

"Eastwood! call the police" he shouted *"somebody fucking strangled my wife!"*

New Love

October/30th/2023

The morning sun spilled through the shaded window. Alejeh's room was full of Aztec carpet, a small couch that looked like a poncho and white wolf fur. She had wooden desks, wooden bedframe and white walls with a homemade dream catcher above her mattress. Fritz stood up from bed; his chest wheezing, his index finger curled with a stinking cigarette, and a shoulder slouch. He yawned like a grizzly bear waking from hibernation. He looked to the side of the mattress which was empty as a shower noise rained in his ear. He walked, spreading his left palm against the window, shoulders slacked, winking at the sun sparkling buildings protruding through the shade. He pulled aside the shade and saw a white jalopy van across the street with a rusty interior hogging the parking spot. Old thin tires, black hubcaps and on the body of the van, there was graffiti words written all over like subway carts in the 90's. The van rattled and a short man with tan brown skin stepped out; white sandals, slapped the concrete and his shorts jiggled. Alejeh's eldest brother Caté. He had black scruffy hair coiling out of a trucker hat, wrinkles in his forehead, an America stripped T shirt with a black beard that made him look homeless. He dropped his forehead against the tall tree near the yard, unzipping his shorts and pee'd a gold arching splatter against the rigid tree bark causing the squirrels to climb and the birds to float. The man turned around, put a kneecap into his van and grabbed a box of pink dragon fruit.

Alejeh crept from Fritz's backside, she placed a palm over his spine and reached for his cigarette.

"Good morning, Azul," she said with a wide smile, after jumping into the shower, her hair was straight and ringy at the same time. Moist eyebrows, white teeth and a fresh vanilla smell coming off her skin. She rubbed honey lotion on her forearms and spread it in a circular motion. Fritz glimpsed over his shoulder, pushing his pale face toward hers for a peck kiss. She held his hand afterwards, pausing and getting stuck in his time lapse. He was the hottest man she had ever laid eyes one. She could stare at him all day, but her pussy cat would start to purr and they had already fucked at 4am.

Fritz's blond hair was looking all shaggy, his cheekbones were pink and his eyes had small rings as if he were tired. Fritz usually tapered the sides of his head, giving him that handsome billion-dollar businessman appearance, but he was looking more like her brother Caté.

Fritz squeezed Alejeh's ass and it jiggled while being grabbed.

"your brother? why does he live in a van?" Fritz uttered, his nose all in Alejeh's face.

Alejeh blinked slowly, pressing her nude body against Fritz's pelvis.

"My brother Caté has too much Orgullo," she responded while lifting her honey lotion, rubbing her thigh with that milky texture and bending over.

Fritz stepped back, sitting in the couch and tilting his head.

"Orgullo? what's that?"

"Pride," Alejeh lifted her leg, her fat pussy looked like a brown diamond. She leaned closer to Fritz's ear, she rubbed his earlobe and dropped her leg across his lap like a motorcycle rider. She kissed Fritz on the lips.

" Caté would rather be known as the Avocado man, who lives in a van, then to be under this roof living with papi."

Fritz squeezed her tidies, pulled the lotion, he rubbed it on his hand and slapped her shoulders, spreading it out across her neck.

"gracias Papi," she uttered. She shut her eyes, moaning in silence as he rubbed her. His touch was so smooth and sensual. She was smiling as his bed hands massaged her soft skin. Her head snapped back and then she could feel her pussy purring. She pulled Fritz's arm and they both stood up. back peddled towards the yellow pinstriped sheets on the. The shade flickered and sunlight in the room turned dim like a brownout. He kissed her, grabbing her by the chin in darkness, his big hands squeezed her neck, his beard stubs stabbing her face, his blue eyes glowing like an exotic animal in the artic. He was gorgeous.

"are you ready for this?" Fritz uttered.

Alejeh blinked slow, snapping out of her trance that he had her in.

"yes," Alejeh uttered, with her eyelids lowered, hazy as if she were high off life. High off what the relationship was turning into

"I can't wait to know everything about my man."

"don't have any expectations." Fritz pulled out of the kiss, still squeezing her big fat brown ass with both hands "and if tell you to go inside the car, then make sure you do it, something bad can happen." He uttered with straight face.

"okay Daddy," Alejeh uttered with an angry smile, her nipples got hard and a coolness ran down her spin to her pussy. Fritz's eyes made her so wet, and when he kissed her neck and screamed for Jesus Christ. Lord have mercy! Take it! He squeezed her neck, pressing her down against the mattress and pulled his dick out of his boxers. Alejeh's eyes rolled to the back of her head and her fingers spread against his back; scratching him with her cat-like claws as she moaned in his ear.

Marcy project's
November/2nd/2023

Fritz stepped out of the bedroom, he had a black long sleeve Gucci shirt, red and green stripes on his sleeves, a black pair of leather jeans and Givenchy sneakers.

Woah!

Alejeh's father, Rigoberto staring at him. Smelling the billion-dollar man walk through the narrow hallway of the shuttering window blinds. Rigoberto had a frog faced smile. After saying good Moring to a man two times already, what is it really else to say to him? Rigoberto was hawking Fritz every hour of the day but not hawking as a protective father would do, he hawked him like a celebrity. Collecting Fritz's articles from online as a basketball coach in Berlin, his son discovering wormholes and his life as millionaire.

Fritz looked handsome as he walked through that narrow hallway. There's a table of clay statues that

Rigoberto has for the bad spirits and every time Fritz walked passed, the incent would shut off. The house went silent.

Fritz had so much that he could easily pay for Rigoberto's spin surgery so there were no problems between he and him.

Alejeh and Fritz could afford the finest hotels on the east side of Manhattan and fuck with her tidies slapping against her stomach. Spill liquor all over its thousand-dollar carpets and make a baby with blue eyes. Rigoberto treated Fritz like he was the second coming of Christ.

Rigoberto wiped off a wooden seat.

"Azul," Rigoberto uttered toward Fritz waving with an elderly fragile posture "would you like some coffee? the Cuban way?" As Fritz glared in the mirror adjusting his gold chain, he turned a cheek, "wassup Rigoberto, I'll pass on the coffee today," Fritz stepped out of the Livingroom, nearing him, seeing his wrinkled skin, his spotted brown head, grey hair sprouting of his ears and his dimple shaped eyes looking like it was almost time to shut. Walking through the small house, the Livingroom had walls that were red like tomato paste, a thousand candles surrounding a picture of Lisabelle. She was praised as a goddess in their house. There's a big kitchen with an old box stove and a laundry machine that rumbled with a red generator on top. Fritz stopped and crossed his arms. He saw four white Mexican ceramic mugs with colorful Mayan skulls, steamy black coffee with smoke rings hovering like hookah. Rigoberto limped toward his Frying pan, slapping the spatula on some fresh purple onions, "Azul, come on its the Cuban way, can you at least try some." Rigoberto uttered while scraping the pan, a bowl of brown porridge in a bowl.

Fritz grabbed the handle of the mug, it felt like a fiery hot crucible. He blew the smoke and took a sip. The Coffee tasted like chocolate and cigarettes.

Alejeh had her hands in her hair, using a thin blue comb to draw a curving part down her brown scalp. A mirror reflection of her and her ringy long hair hanging down to her yellow cleavage. There was a black blow dryer, red tubes, tops, brushes, make-up, lipstick, baby lotion all lined up on the bathroom sink. She stared at herself. A perfect dime! Still insecure about how everyone would react to the news. The news that she is Fritz's girlfriend and his wife Ivory is no more. She smiled in the reflection and turned her cheek to snap her earring in her earlobe. She could imagine her mother who was gone. Her mother telling her to go to Spain with Fritz and enjoy the music of Barcelona, the humble food in Madrid or the historic castles of

Granada that looked like fantasy views in Kings Landing. Thinking too far ahead, as most women. She smiled in secrecy.

Rigoberto was standing, hunching over the stove while talking to Fritz about Manny Pacquiao's fight with Miguel Cotto, eyes wide open, forehead full of wrinkles. Manny's autographed glove on the Livingroom wall, he shivered in happiness. pointed with a frail body frame, wobbling over to the glove and yapping words that made Fritz slouch. Blinked his eyes slowly as if he were about to go to sleep.

"old man, shut the fuck up already." Fritz uttered, he stood up, walked away with a brush of whirly wind the made the house cold.

Fritz was a nasty motherfucker.

Walking down the black steel staircase, the morning sun ran across their bodies giving them that golden glow. The wind was chiming, Fritz's spikey hair shaking with animation. The vehicles on the road were bouncing with Latin music, swerving, skurring with farting engines down the intersection of Corona Ave.

Caté, the avocado man had a long line of people at his desk. Flies whirling around, giant leaves of aloe Vera in his hand. He wrapped it for a customer.

Another Hispanic family was holding oranges like a grenade in battle, lifting it and bagging the best ones in foggy plastic fruit bags.

Fritz pressed the car key, triggering the champagne Escalade to start. The car rumbled like a wildcat. Fritz didn't have a car since 2019. He refused to get one, but ever since the government has been in his family's life, he was given the truck as a gift.

Fritz grabbed the door handle and sat inside the soft cake batter seats.

Alejeh was wearing a nude brown body suit, she had a mink vest and some white Balenciaga sneakers. She kissed Fritz, then walked over to Caté pulling her pocketbook off her shoulder. She lifted a few singles and dropped it on his desk full of Aloe Vera, she turned to her left, swiped a pink dragon fruit with green leaf thorns.

"Gracias Hermano." she uttered with her pink lips, a soft smile that only a loving sister could give to a brother.

Caté nodded with his brown skin shinning in the morning sun, he smiled with a handsome grin and his missing tooth was exposed. He reached for his reflective machete, which was about the size of Alejeh's whole arm. Caté slashed a separate Dragon fruit causing it to split and then shaving the edges off until the oily texture of the fruit looked like white dice was oozing with black seeds. Everyone on the sidewalk line started to clap as if his cutting was some kind of street performance. He smacked the dragon fruit in a plastic container, twisted a rubber band around it, pulled a fork with napkin in super speed, handing it and smiling with that missing tooth on his top teeth.

The claps grew louder, "Caté! Caté! Caté!" Spanish folks fist pumped.

"que tengas hermanita." he uttered in a deep Latino voice. He had a strong Latin accent, as if he didn't speak any English since he came over the border as a migrant.

"Te amo hermano." Alejeh smiled at him, then turned towards Fritz while walking toward the tall escalade. She sat down inside the leather soft seats. she had the mink over her body, covering her nude brown body suit, but her nude brown body suit still exposed her thickness. she had thick thighs, a fat camel toe, a diamond shaped space in-between her legs so if she stood up, you could see right through to the other side. mm! she looked delicious and Fritz couldn't resist. He glimpsed toward his woman, kissing her with a smile, he turned his cheek to the house, staring at narrowness of the entry and then to the top step. Cristiano who was standing at the top, wearing a white shirt with blue Laker shorts. A twisted lip, wrenched face as if he had some kind of hatred for the Caté. Cristiano tucked his hands in his pocket, kicked a rock while shaking his head.

"what's Cristiano's deal?" Fritz uttered with a stone face, scratching the back of his head.

"don't scratch it." Alejeh shouted, "you have to get your head checked, because what if it didn't heal. She swallowed a dicey piece of fruit, holding another on the end of her fork.

"well, Cristiano. we made a deal that we wouldn't have any secrets so I'll tell you. Ehh, Cristiano and Caté are 15 years apart. Cristiano is twenty-five and Caté is forty, Caté has always been a man to us. They have a bad relationship because when Cristiano went to Prison, Caté helped the cops identify him and he made statements."

Fritz's eyes bulged,

"a rat? he ratted out his own brother? what did Cristiano go to jail for?"

"credit card scams."

Fritz shook his head, giggling while he turned the wheel and the view of the houses running across his slanted window. His pale fingers on the leathery part of the wheel gliding through the orchestra of noise on the street road, he couldn't help but to think about them screaming in detective rooms in Spanish. Fritz had been in plenty detective rooms himself because he is a known snitch. His eyes were low, glimpsing at Alejeh while he drove. He glared with wide blue eyes thinking about his son Dayton and Phillip. They are 15 years apart too, and they don't even know each other. What if they get old and shoot each other in the streets or they rat each other out over some dumb shit like Caté and Cristiano. Fritz's eyes twitched with allergies, or simple emotions that he couldn't express because he held back so much to his wife Ivory. But he could be honest with Alejeh. His daughter who is gone Livonia, is something he still hasn't vented to anyone about. Couldn't tear up or show his depression because of what Ivory might have done if she knew he cheated on her with Charlesha. The woman who everyone called a crackhead. He felt a pain in his chest, slightly stabbing feeling as he navigated though the traffic.

Fritz stared at the rearview mirror and then turned a cheek to Alejeh.

"My sons, Phillip and Dayton are fifteen years apart, I can't imagine them. you know what, let me just say this, your brothers need to come together." Fritz uttered while staring with darting eyes, A Chevy Malibu was in front of their escalade and the brake lights were ruby red. An orchestra of traffic and horns were blasting like instruments. The wide landscape of the road had some funky exhaust gas whirling, green liquid dripping on the road. "your brothers need to come together, seriously." Fritz shouted louder.

"no," Alejeh uttered "Cristiano actually scammed Caté, which is why Caté lives in that van." Alejeh took another bit of the dicey fruit and chewed away the memory.

"what the fuck!" Fritz turned his cheek, he blindly reached for his cup holder, blindly pulling his cigarette from his Marlboro pack. He stuck his head out of the window, punching his horn along with the others.

"come on! let's get going mother fuckers!" Fritz shouted loudly with the cigarette bouncing at his lip. He glimpsed at Alejeh eating the dicey fruit, curled his finger around his cigarette and sparked it with his neck down. At the same second, A white Porsche crept, inching slowly from the passenger door side, an Asian American woman with brown hair gazed into the car. She had flat cheekbones with an angry smile. She inched closer, searching inside the car seats. She broke focus, her eyes bounced side to side and she dropped her cellphone in her lap, inching forward with her eyes straight.

Fritz sped off of the highway, he circled the block, pulling into an old half caged parking spot with dumpsters near a silver gate. A rusty hydrant, a fat bag of autumn leaves at the curb. He smelled sewer leaves and rust. Alejeh glared at the tall red buildings across the street, moved her neck and dumped the plastic out of the car window.

"is this the projects?" she uttered, her white nails gleaming as she sucked the rest of the cigarette.

"yea, its Marcy projects" Fritz replied "my son doesn't live in the projects though."

Lexington avenue, a block and a half away from there was a parked Lexus car, along the pavement were a bunch of antsy people at the bus stop. They were scattered, leaning on the glass, shouting while on their cellphones, kids dribbling a basketball and some people making loud huffs to show that they were irate from waiting. Opposite to the bus, Fritz and Alejeh walked, they looked like a power couple even though there was a vast difference in age. Fritz walked by the people smelling like Tom Ford cologne. There was a long line of apartment buildings with silver windows, flat brown brick houses with yellowish bricks in the upper part. tenements with fire escapes zig-zagging down the building stoop. Bright yellow deli was on the corner, glittering with yellow and orange bulbs. Savannah; all the way up on the third floor stuck her face out of the fire escape window. She examined the whole block and her eyes landed on him! She pulled her head back inside the Livingroom and slammed the window down with a vibration.

For about ten minutes, Fritz and Alejeh waited near the bus stop glass, over hearing others complain about the Bk100. It was always running late, and that's why they never bothered to pay for public transportation. Suddenly, the metallic brown apartment door opened and you could see a quick flash of the silver mailboxes before the door closed. Savannah walked out holding a tiny sand brown boy, he wore a blue puffer coat, some baggy white jeans and Jordan 3's.

"mommy, that's daddy?" he uttered with wide doe eyes, tinkering with a toy car that looked like hot wheels.

Alejeh gripped her own lips, turned her cheek toward Fritz, "oh my god," she uttered "he is so cute."

Fritz's eyes twitched, he bit his bottom lip, he walked toward Savannah, digging into his pocket and pulling out a flat wad of cash.

There was immediate silence.

He stared at Savannah; She was absolutely beautiful, looking like Rubi rose the rapper, but Fritz never talked about her beauty. He only handed her cash.

"how's your mother doing after therapy?" Fritz uttered with sweat coming from his eyes and nose. He tried to give her a handshake, handing her the flat wad of cash as if it were a drug deal.

"fine.' Savannah replied awkwardly, taking the handshake. She shook her orange hair so that it flicked over her face. She was shaking her leg while standing. *Shaking! Shaking! Shaking!* in place. There was a million words screaming through her twinkling brown eyes and phrases that made her jitter and shake. Her own thoughts forcing her to tremble cold. Her vocal cords swollen, holding back while shaking her foot. Just say it! Savannah just say it! just say it!

"How come you never come see me and Dayton unless you giving me money." Savannah blurted loudly, "Fritz, you always giving me money, I don't care about this shit." she squeezed the cash, holding it above her head as if she was about to throw it. "money is not enough! Dayton is always talking about where's daddy, you told me after Dawn was dead, that we were going to Have a fucking relationship."

"easy." Fritz flared his face, clutching his buckle and stepping in front of Savannah.

"bitch, calm the fuck down," Fritz replied, aiming his finger in her face. He knocked her head back with his finger and pushed closer to her. "I loved Dawn! It eats me up every fucking day!"

"who is that Mexican bitch you with?" Savannah shouted "you be eating alright, I bet you eating all of her little taco. You don't see your son because of her?

who the fuck is she?" Savannah snapped her neck in a ghetto way, her eyes shaking from left and right.

Fritz grabbed his son by the pits, lifted him up off the ground into the sky like a basketball player about to dunk and hugged him with one arm. He took a wide stride toward Alejeh, four footsteps and he stood in front of her

"Alejeh, this is my son Dayton, remember what I told you at home? no secrets between us you hear me? this is my son! my boy and Savannah is my baby mother, he turned around to Savannah "Savannah this is my girlfriend, Alejeh." while pointing back. Dayton smiled, reaching for Alejeh's large watermelon shaped breast.

Alejeh waved at Savannah, she broke eye contact, reached forward, locked her fingers with Dayton's little fingers and smiled with a tearful joy. He peanut butter brown skin and sandy blond French braids that zig-zagged to the back of his chunky little neck. When Alejeh touched him, he growled with a girthy nasal voice box, a loud tooth spitting smile. He looked like an 80-year-old drunk with missing teeth.

Livonia
November/2nd/2023

Fritz laid back, his twiggy hair down over his ears and laid against the leather head rest. As his nostrils were upward, he could smell the car freshener. A green tree flicking back and forth, latched below the rearview mirror.

Alejeh had her legs crossed, resting her head on his shoulder, and blinking slow while puffing the cigarette. a slight tick in her muscles, she clutched his cellphone, rolling through the google maps.

"I love Dayton so much." Alejeh uttered, then pulling the cigarette away, turning and blowing the smoke rings at the window, "he is so perfect."

Something about the word perfect caused Fritz to flinch. He started breathing hard and rubbing his pant legs.

Fritz's body shook, and it wasn't the seizures, neuropathy or nerve damage he obtained, he shook because of the simple fact that he couldn't see his daughter. For him, things couldn't be perfect because he knew his daughter was gone forever.

The plan was to see Dayton and Livonia, but he had to come clean about his little princess. He grimaced, turning toward Alejeh with his eyes bouncing left and right, staring through her as he melted within.

"we were supposed to see my daughter Livonia," Fritz uttered with his nose twisted, he used his sleeve to wipe his face. "but we can't, because she is probably in another dimension."

Alejeh froze with the cigarette at her tips,

"ughh, what? did she go missing?"

"Phillip told me that her and her siblings went into a wormhole. Have you ever heard of Wormhole Alleyoop?"

"What?"

Fritz shook his head, he took a deep breath and cupped his nose with his left hand.

"me and her mother! We weren't watching over like we should have. Her brother and her sisters all left this world and fucking Phillip watched them go! I fucking hate that little son-of-a-bitch sometimes."

Alejeh hunched, leaning closer to Fritz's bicep and rubbed his arm with her long pink and yellow nails.

"Azul it's going to be okay!" Alejeh reached her arm over and lunged her arm around his neck to hug him.

Suddenly, a draft of wind shook the driver's side window, that same white Porsche from the highway sped by the gated side of the parking lot, then stopping, wheels bouncing as it drove up the flat sidewalk part. The Asian American lady with the brown hair stopped the Porsha Truck, blocking them from leaving. She stuck her arm out. Screamed loudly and punched the steering wheel with something that looked like a gun. Rocking back and forth in her seat and her hair shaking wildly like she was a at a rave dancing. She began to scream through the glass,

"ughhh." she shouted with a thin space of insanity between her eyes.

Fritz turned a cheek, he flared his nose and stared the woman as if she was insane. He rolled his glass down, stuck his head out the window with a nasty grimace.

"lady, I know that Porsches are padded but you might need to go check yourself into a real padded room. Get the fuck out of the driveway." he uttered into the wind. He rolled his eyes with his eyebrows scrunched, his hand reaching toward his desert eagle inside the car door.

The lady's desperate eyes turned into scorpion stingers, gushing sweat and glossing with sadness. She had a vein in the middle of her forehead pulsating. Her brown hair looked like wet seaweed. She was at the end of insanity, ready to down a whole crowd of people with live rounds.

"have some control over your bitch." she screamed, her head lights shined like electricity in a power outage. She turned the wheel speeding backwards. The tires screamed against the road. Then doing a U-turn and speeding away up a one-way. Her car was flopping around, leaving a trail of grey smoke. Her license plate was white framed with the digits of an army sergeant. Fritz recognized the army plates because he had been in many situations with them ever since Dr. Rancatipopo and general Gotland took interest into their family. As a matter of fact, the woman looked like Lily Tibbers; Jim Tibbers wife. Fog in his memory, he turned over and shook his head.

Alejeh turned her neck, placed her fingers over her heart beat as if she was stunned. Her head cocked back, her lip twitching and breathing with a whistle in the back of her throat.

"who's that bitch?" Alejeh muttered, "is she."

Fritz shook his head,

"not one of mine that's for sure." he replied, placing the pale cigarette to his lip. He then slapped his pant leg, he had a flashing phone, vibrating with the word son on the screen, he bit the cigarette and swiped right on the call.

"hello," the voice of Phillip protruded through the phone. "dad, Tripple plat's car is parked out front."

The name Tripple plat pinged in Fritz's eyes. It was like a long falling pit into the center of hell. Only lasted a split second, but he felt the agony of being burned in his gut. He could hear the vibrant echo of the name over and over. The man who killed Dawn. Blasted her like she was an animal and killed her boyfriend over nothing.

Suddenly, life flashed before Fritz's eyes. He hadn't thought about death since the doctor let him know he had a brain hemorrhage! Fritz always thought he would die from his diabetes, sudden heart failure from neuropathy trauma or something health related. He could feel the bullet that Tripple plat was going to shot him with [piercing his chest plate while he was fucking Alejeh and flattening him to leave her screaming].

Fritz reached for his gun,

"Tripple plat?" Fritz shouted, his eyes bounced side to side opening wider and wider.

Alejeh crossed her arm, turning her neck and biting her lip.

Fritz shook his head.

"where's Lucy?" He shouted into the phone, breathing heavily, he could feel his arm going numb and the static of needles rushing down his temple.

Phillip had a nose full of snot as he spoke on the phone.

"Lucy? umm, she babysitting the white baby from downstairs, Ernie. She has been doing marathons remember, so she has been walking while pushing the stroller," Phillip uttered in fear. "I don't know what to do dad, I'm scared."

"fuck!" Fritz screamed "how the fuck did he find out where y'all live." Fritz's eyes bulged, the cigarette dropped from his lips into his pants zipper.

Phillip started coughing, his words fragmented and slurred.

"I don't know." Phillip uttered, "but Shandy's baby father, Virgil is in the gang!"

"call the cops, call Dr. Rancatipopo, call the navy seals, General Gotland and everyone! stay on the phone, I'm on my way."

Urgency
November/2nd/2023

The rolling wheels were rippling in the wind, speeding into sparkling lights of Manhattan sky scrapers.

Alejeh sitting right beside him; had glimpsed into her cellphone, scrolling through the plane tickets she had purchased behind his back. She squinted her eyes, almost pressing for a cancellation. Barcelona was the city; she wanted to surprise him, but the day was going downhill quickly.

Fritz's eyes had electricity in his eyes as drove through traffic nearly inching an accident every minute.

Alejeh anxiously shoved her cellphone into her pocketbook, crossed her fingers and watched her man drive. He had his big pale hands turning the wheel, wind bouncing off the windows. He vroomed toward the green exit with white words; 47th street midtown. Then making a dragging let turn, speeding whip lashes passed one police cruiser. Alejeh's kinky black hair shook left and right, she glared at him waiting for him to say something to her or give her a commanding glare, but he didn't. He just melted away while listening to his son's confessions. Over and over Phillip explained things that should have been kept to himself.

Phillip explained how he got close to Shandy; parties, family events and loitering in the street as her protective brother and then it led to feelings he shouldn't have felt. After feeling those strange feelings, he realized that Merlo wasn't his real dad.

After Phillip came to that reality, he realized that his sister; who didn't get anything out of her father's death, needed to know. And after that information was given, the whole street turned against him.

Alejeh grimaced,

Whatever Phillip was talking about, it seemed like he wasn't cut out to be a thug. Alejeh knew a thing or two about gangsters because when Cristiano went to prison, he had stories about real thugs. Real racist thugs that will run in ya cell and scrap on concrete floors until your tired; and then a razor is running down her face.

Alejeh reached forward, rubbed Fritz's leg and blinked in an innocent way. Begging for his attention, but she couldn't get him to break focus on his son.

Through the windshield, there were thousands of scathing tall Manhattan buildings, sky scrapers with black tile windows and statues of the four fathers along the grassy flat gardens. Alejeh flicked her hair with her right wrist, and twisted a ringy stand into her index.

"Azul, I am sorry about everything that's been happening," she whispered with her mouth closed. she talked just loud enough for him to hear, but didn't interrupt Phillip from spilling his emotions.

Fritz nodded his head, he glared at the heavy police presence flooding the traffic stop. South of First avenue, cop cars were lined up as if a president were coming. An area where the president did come through for United Nations matters. A white cop had his hand on his utility belt glaring into every car windshield. he stared and gave a wrist flick forward letting them know their SUV was good. Fritz turned the wheel, pulled into the parking near the vegan burger hut, and it smelled like French fries and crispy onions. He stepped out of the car, stomping toward 50th street.

Alejeh felt the adrenaline as she stepped out along with him, she clutched her pocketbook tightly holding it at her ribs while running in a nude brown body suit. They sped walked, nearing the lanky tall building towering above the city clouds. Turtle bay towers was the most luxurious apartment buildings on the eastside.

Phillips voice was still deep, but shaky and he kept stopping to breathe.

"Dad, Jah Kraken died while on his way to the emergency room," Phillip uttered, "it's all because of me, if I didn't introduce Shandy to my friends, then this would have never happened."

Fritz froze, took a deep breath, he shut his eyes and shook his head.

Fritz knew that the violence would only get worse between Rolling street Infamy and them. Guidance was out for revenge after being sent to prison for life, the death on Bone, and then Honcho and Kookah bug. The beef had reached a point of war between them and he could almost feel the bullets zipping through the wind in a brazen Manhattan shoot out. Fritz wasn't the only one, Big momma Lucy had visions of Phillips death since she found out he was a gangbanger.

"we have to go." Fritz uttered lifelessly "listen here Phillip, we will go to a different country, somewhere in London? you could go to college out there or something, we can bring your mother, T.T. Lucy too. we have to leave the states." Fritz's eyes twitched.

As Fritz yelled through the phone, Alejeh froze in the street. She dug into her pocketbook, holding her cellphone tightly. Wanting to show Fritz the plane tickets to Madrid, Barcelona and Granada. Maybe they all could go as a family. She flashed her cellphone.

"Azul." She screamed "we can go to Spain together as a family."

Fritz glimpsed over and his eyelids went thin around his eyeballs. He stretched his neck forward and kissed Alejeh with a blind kiss.

"Spain?" Fritz yelled into the phone. "listen kid, we are going to Spain."

Alejeh felt vibration in her stomach. her eyes shut and fanned herself.

"thank god" she uttered, "thank god he said yes."

Medicine

A stony road toward the entrance of Turtle bay towers. Autumn leaves spinning across the skinny branches, dog owners walking across the sidewalks and grey smoke disbursing from a manhole at the center of the street. Fritz walked toward the large green scaffold with a fast face flinch. He met a fat balding white officer who had a PD bullet proof vest and big boots that were laced tight. He had a canine on a short leach, it had a shaggy brown fluffy fur coat with a fox face, black muzzle, breathing with a long tongue that rolled towards his nose and hypnotic brown galaxy eyes. The officer bobbled his head, turned sideways to his partner who was brown skinned with a hairless face he looked like a teenager, but had height as if he were a pro basketball player. Eyes shaking, mumbling and a fast wrist flick toward Big momma Lucy. She was coming from around the corner with a stroller. He bobbled his head toward to Big momma Lucy as if he wanted her to hurry up.

As the doorman walked through the glass door, he whistled at the officers, then stretching a long green hose on the eastside pavement.

"no killers around here, trust me, if it was, I'd know about it." The Doorman, Andrew Blaow sprayed his green hoes, pushing the pressure to the curb as suds dripped toward the sidewalk.

"orange car was out here all night." he uttered "my relief wrote it down inside the log book, but why would a killer be doing his work in an orange Camaro?"

Big momma Lucy pulled her leather gloves off her fingers, her sleeves jiggled with black fur that looked like panther. She opened her cellphone and walked over to the doorman "Hey, Mr. Blaow, mm, can you send the policemen the surveillance from last night?" then her eyes dropped toward the baby in the stroller. Her eyes always twinkled when she stared at Ernie and the universe slowed down to the point she could see his happy future. He had green eyes, laying down with his foot in his mouth. She was the nanny for the children in the neighborhood, but Ernie might have seen her as a mom. He stuck his foot in his mouth and smiled with puffy cheeks.

"boy, you sure can't talk ya way out of this, stop putting your foot in your mouth," she pulled his toe off his gums and fold her arms.

Big momma Lucy clapped her hands at the police man and her coat jiggled. She shook her head and her hair bounced, her eyebrows scrunched as she rolled the stroller to the cops.

"I know yawl think my grandson is some kind of fibber, but why would he prank call yawl? the boy smokes all that reefer, he wouldn't want yawl around here if it wasn't am emergency."

Fritz stood across from Big momma Lucy. His head dropped down with the phone at his ear. Fritz believed every word his son was saying. Every fragment of Phillip's vocal chamber made his eardrum shake down to his clammy purple heart.

Alejeh stood behind Fritz. The German shepherd with a long rolling tongue was smelling something on Fritz so the dog barked a shotgun.

Fritz pulled the handle to the tall glass doors, the bottom of his feet still moist from the doorman's hoes. Walked into the building lobby and the door did a sweeping smack shut.

"Lucy, listen, we have to move-to a different country."

"are you on drugs, Fritz" she shouted with an echo.

"Phillip told me about these people, they are after our family; they are coming." Fritz grabbed Lucy's arms.

Big momma Lucy pulled her pocketbook from the stroller and swung it across her forearm, slapping quarters out of Fritz's chest.

Fritz grimaced,

"what the fuck," he shouted.

"you are like a nasty water bug that need to be crushed." she yelled with a deep southern accent, tightening her neck. "you bring these people to my family, you a gaddamn *Devil!* That's what you are."

The bouncing echo of words made Alejeh flinch. She took a step back, fold her arms and bit her lips.

"Azul?" she shouted in her head.

Fritz pushed Big momma Lucy, aiming his index finger in her face, "you let Shandy into your house, Shandy is responsible for all of this!"

Big momma Lucy walked toward the large lobby mirror, adjusted her collar and fanned herself.

"I will get rid of you." She shouted.

Suddenly, as Fritz was talking, there were four policemen on the inside of the building. They had a suspicious vibe.

Fritz smiled, leaning over and then awkwardly waving. Eyes twitching as he glared at Big momma Lucy.

Alejeh covered her mouth. She shut her eyes and took a deep breath.

Fritz yanked Alejeh by the arm and her body jerked. He walked through the lobby then arriving at the elevator. He pressed the button and suddenly he felt anxiety fire in his stomach, a tweaking headache in his brain, spasms in his muscles and thousands of pins and needles running a rash of nerves vibrating down his forehead to the right side of his face. It was like an instant dose of pain. His face twisted like a faucet. He could hear his own thoughts running across his eyes. His skin twitch, his eyes shed a tear that trembled in a zig-zag. He slapped his palm against the center of face and slid down to the slippery marble floor. His view became blurry, his nose bled a thick trail to his lips and everything went pitch black.

The police flooded the lobby, running towards him, stretching their arms to help him up. Alejeh dropped on her knees. Her ringy hair bouncing over her backside.

"hold on," she screamed. Her hands stretched to his jaw, holding his face to her cleavage "give him space, give him space." She threw her arm above the huddle. she dug into her purse, lifted a bottle of prescription pills and twisted the cap. "he is dealing with a lot, give him his space." she pulled a bottle of Poland spring water out of her pocketbook. "give him space."

Big momma Lucy pushed the stroller into the hallow elevator, she let go of the handle and ran towards Fritz.

"give him his space, yawl. You heard the woman." he shouted with reluctantly. "he just needs to breathe, it's this brain hemorrhage situation, he will be okay."

Seconds later Phillip pushed the staircase door open and it slammed with a metallic vibration.

'dad?" he shouted while standing over him "dad? you okay?"

Big momma Lucy rubbed the top of his head. Knowing that she wanted to kill him a few seconds ago for pushing her. She had this weird love for him. He was her son in law; but the secrets that she kept for him made her develop a strong tethering love for him.

Big momma Lucy grabbed his ear and stretched it.

"this is what you get for pushing me, boy! You have to be a better person, Fritz! That's why this is happening to you." Big momma Lucy glared at Alejeh, and his lip pulsated. She removed her arms from Fritz as he laid across the floor.

"where's his other medication?" Big momma Lucy uttered.

"it's at home." Alejeh responded, "I'll get it." She stood up, went into his pockets and pulled his key ring out, "and I'll come back." She uttered.

Jim, the coward
November/3rd/2023

When Fritz woke up the next day, he pushed the bedroom door open and saw Phillip inside the long circular house. The red couch was against the wall with raggedy clothes and socks all over the pillow cushions. Phillip' now standing Six feet, he had a long torso, flat chest and long chicken bone legs. He held a lighter near his throat. His flat fingers laid across Lucy's kitchen counter.

Phillip flinched, tucking the joint in between his palm and thigh.

"you okay, dad?'

Fritz flared his face,

"this is your grandmother's house!" Fritz twisted his mouth sideways. He walked closer to Phillip while and scratching his twiggy hair and could feel the painful scar in his scalp. His skin was purplish pale like a Deadman who drowned.

"your homeboy, Jah what was it like to lose him?" Fritz uttered.

There as a long silence between them. They just stared at each other and blinked.

Fritz's eyes bounced around in a sad way, knowing that he doesn't have a connection with his own son.

"where is your mother?"

"mom is with Jim."

There was a pinging loud silence in the house. Fritz turned around, smacked his hands over his blue eyes and you could see that back of his neck turn rash red. He walked over to the piano and swiped all the music books off with his left hand. "that fucking whore ass bitch." Fritz shouted, then he kicked a wall with his bare foot, shattering the glass vase that was holding potted plants. "you saw them? you fucking saw them together?" Fritz shouted while walking closer to Phillip.

"yes." Phillip uttered while protecting his jar of weed that was on the couch. Fritz turned his back. He walked across the porcelain tiles, his ears red and his back bones bouncing like a hockey player who had just went blow for blow with an entire team. He shoved his foot into his sneakers, walked toward the coat rack and shoved in arm through. His face was as if he were calm, but that's when Fritz was most dangerous. He grabbed the doorknob to Phillips bedroom.

"you know, they used to call Jim a coward when he was in the Navy right?" Fritz smirked with a wrathful eye ping, he dug into Phillips closet and thrashing all of his sneaker boxes. "Jim was known as the coward. I overheard that his comrades stole his food, hazed him and they even tried to sleep with his wife, now that motherfucker is sleeping with my wife." Fritz shook his head. He zipped his jacket, walked towards the dresser and lifted his desert eagle. He noticed that his car keys were gone.

Dead
November/3rd/2023

Fritz walked the long luxurious halls with a slouching spine. Mindlessly rocking side to side as if he were drunk and depressed. He held his chin up, glimpsing at every door and catching a reflection of himself on the Luxury hallway mirrors. A strung-out dope fiend looked healthier than he did. On another note, why does all these luxury residential buildings have mirrors installed in the hallway? Maybe it's because those rich pricks like to bask in their own greatness.

Light beams flashed him, his sneakers stomped across the carpet that ran through the halls like a mohawk. He rubbed his large pale fingers down his face, hearing the muffled voices of the neighbors in his brain. "Shut the fuck up" he shouted loud. He slouched lower and almost dropped to the carpet but his palms held him up. His eyesight was blurry, his body itching with heat, he unzipped his coat and could see a drenched T-shirt with his chest hairs smelling like onions. He Stretched his arms and straightened his back with a crack that sounded like a pool ball clicking against another. He laid across the wall.

"she's fucking gone." Fritz screamed to himself. He stood, scratched his nose and his bare fingers made him think of his wedding band he once wore. His wife who he was happily married to. It was a flawed marriage, but it couldn't be questioned in the presence of a divorce lawyer. He caught a glimpse of himself in the lobby mirror again, his face looked slightly skinnier from hot sweat. Whenever he'd skip out on carbs or steak, you could see his chin dimple.

The detectives believe that it was a suicide murder. The last Eight hours, Fritz spent with his ass nailed to a hard metal chair, and a bowling ball of light in his face. Questions about his marriage. A blobby neck detective that looked like Rod Stewart. absolutely frustrated, that he had to grief his dead wife in front of men in tailored suits while he smelled like onions. And on top of that, the NYPD used weird tactics to get your DNA. They'd offer you some fatty mayonnaise glazed chicken sandwiches and a bottle of coke, then swab the trash for your saliva so they can record it in their database.

Fritz's nose flared. He shook his head and dropped his chin. His brain flashing gunshots and through every shot he could see Ivory's lifeless body slumped over a toilet seat.

Escape
November/5th/2023

Fritz arrived at Big momma Lucy's front door and felt a ghost over his shoulder.

He stood still. The cold breeze ran through his hair. His eyes bounced. He stood there flicking his ring of keys and dropping his eyebrows.

"Phillip?" he uttered to himself. Then pulling the brass bladed key like a pocket knife and stabbing it into the lock, He squeezed the silver knob and pushed the heavy door outward. He let out a devastated deep breath. The misty cold draft of Big momma Lucy's house felt like menthol to the chest, chimes to the ribs and tornados of goosebumps all over his pale skin.

A long circular space that leads to the white wall Livingroom, a view of the gated fireplace a long with pieces of Art on the floor waiting to be hung. A retro pair of Jordan fours with its laces dangled along the floor. Phillip and T.T. were further inside the swanky

Livingroom. Phillip was on the red suede couch near the window while holding a green bottle of Sam Pellegrino. His neck was broken with emotion, his wooly afro down as T.T. was right beside him rubbing his backside. She had white teeth that you could easily see even in the dim room; her chocolate hand on his back as her hair dangled at her jaw.

"it's okay Bookie." she uttered to him. Although T.T and Phillip were two years apart, she sorts of played as a mother figure to him. Her skin was dark chocolate, but the inside of her palm was peanut butter brown. she grabbed his arm, hugging him to form a shield.

Fritz darted towards Phillip, stomping across the carpeted floor and kicking one of Phillips sneakers out of his path. Biting his bottom lip, he grabbed him by the arm and lifted him up to his feet.

"stop dad," Phillip shouted with hazy eyes. His eyelids dropped down and Fritz lifted his chin with his open palm. They stood eye to eye.

"fucking Phillip," he shouted, aiming his dirty fingernails into his stepson's eyes, getting closer to him and you could smell the onion sweat.

Fritz squeezed Phillips jaw.

"your fucking so stupid," particles of spit came out of his wolf-like teeth, he had warmness in his breath that smelt like cigarettes and an ugly face twist,

"Ivory would have never let Shandy come over to the penthouse! did you tell Shandy where your mother lived? Is that how they tracked her! I'll kill you son of a bitch."

Phillip backed away, smacking his backside against a large oak brown table stand. Then stretching his hoodie over his afro. He then smacked his hands together and lifted a leg. Cursing loud and pulled the string on his hoodie so that his face was closed into the hoodie hole. He backed off from his father, smiling with sadness and landed near the fish tank hiding in the corner. Phillip touched the glass and turned around to sit next to his bottle of Sam Pellegrino.

Fritz stomped over, pushed his chest into Phillip, knocking his bottle down to the couch. Then yelling so hard that the floor and the walls had tremors. The bottle rolled down to the carpeted floor, spilling and dragging juice guts on the fabric. Fritz hunched down, stabbing Phillip with his index finger and shouting with a cracked voice.

"you wanted this gang life, right? Bitch! You hear me? You wanted to be a criminal so bad now you got it!" Fritz grabbed the bottle of Sam Pellegrino from the floor, and tossed it towards the kitchen cabinet. A line of sparkling juice stretched across the room it shattered into a thousand green shards. The juice splashed like ice rain and soda suds.

Phillip lifted the couch pillow, holding it against his face and crying. He could see his mother in his head; feeling guilty about her death as he hunched down to his knees.

Fritz placed his heavy fingers on Phillips shoulder, pulling him closer, ripping his hoodie off his head exposing his little flat afro. At that moment everything was in slow motion.

"I hate the pigs!" Fritz shouted with a crack voice, screaming over Phillips head. "I had to tell the police a lot of shit about our life and they are coming here to get take you for questioning next, we have to get out of here."

Fritz had an ugly face twist, staring at his disgrace of a son and shaking his head. He stomped towards the bedroom, shaking the whole house with each step. He was a heavy man. You could hear the piano keys making little soft pings under the shut piano hood. the chandelier had a soft spin and the clown fish were hiding in their rocks.

Fritz took a stride into the dayroom, there was an additional flatbed black couch, a lipstick red pillow on top. He stomped through the narrow walk-in closet, and it smelled snake skin leather. The light bulb shined bright and it was just about as spacious as a bedroom. The wideness of the closet was partitioned to form two gaping spaces, the upper part had multicolored handbags, the middle row had blazers and blouses. He walked through the blazers, dresses and skirts dangling smelling like sugary perfume. Color coded stiletto shoes lined up like glass bottles at the open bar, there were blue pairs, red pairs, white pairs, snake skin, any style you could think of. As he stepped further into the closet, it smelled like crocodile leather and he looked down to see a rare collection of snakeskin boots. The collection that Ivory owned. She valued them so much, that she bought an extra set and kept them at Big momma Lucy's house as back-up in case she lost hers at the airport.

Fritz hunched down at the shoe and his breathing was chocked up. He squeezed them while walking out of the narrow space. He slammed the unzipped luggage at the center of the Livingroom floor. Dust swirling around the Livingroom smelled like a gator in Mississippi.

644

T.T. put her arm around Phillip, she shook her head and fanned the little gnat dust from the blue luggage, then turning back around and fixing Phillip's hoodie so he could put it back on his un-evened afro.

"I'm sorry, Bookie" she uttered. Hugging him with her breast near his ear.

The silence was so loud that you could hear the fire detective beep, Clown fish swirling and outdoor birds chirp. There was a constant stomp. Fritz's body casted a long shadow as he stood in the center of the Livingroom. Navy blue suitcase in the center of the floor, with a shaking zipper, opened wide. it was the one Fritz used for Berlin trips. A white suitcase, the one Big momma Lucy used to go to Georgia and a pink one that was set aside for T.T just in case they ever went traveling as a family.

One by one you could hear slams, metal hangers raking against the closet bar. Fritz slapping shirts, pants, sneakers into the luggage. He angrily turned a cheek, glimpsing at Phillip with those frozen blue eyes. His nostrils flared and his face had wrinkles in his nose bone.

"you think I'm horsing around you little motherfucker! get up and pack. you think I want the police digging into our lives for the next five years? I warned Ivory about this shit! nobody wanted to fucking listen, nobody ever listens to me!" he shouted from his guts and his eyes were pinging with madness.

Phillip stood up with his chest shaking, gasping and laughing in heart wrenching pain. He walked into his bedroom closet and stood at the thousands of shirts and pants that he never wore. Being rich never solved any real problems for their family. He stretched his arms across his stomach, his head dropped down and he stayed there.

T.T. stood up, she walked over to Fritz at the center of the swanky apartment. Her arms crossed in a ghetto way, she began snapping her neck, her long weave shaking at her jaw.

"why do we have to go, you seem like you aint giving us a choice." she shouted with her white teeth showing.

Fritz's eyes landed on T.T.

"you fucking naive little broad!" he screamed, "you think life is about choice? huh! life is about survival." he aimed his finger at T.T. pulled her by the arm and yanking her towards the bedroom. "you don't have a fucking choice! you woke up this morning, right? did you have a choice? now let's get fucking packing!"

T.T.'s eyes bulged. Her jaw dropped as she stared at her bedroom door. At that moment, she wanted to kill Fritz because he was so disrespectful and aggressive. He dragged T.T. to her bedroom then stomped off as if he had the right to do whatever he wanted. T.T. rubbed her nose in sadness.

Fritz stomped back to the Livingroom; he felt himself being more militant than he had ever been so he took a deep breath. When things slowed down, he had relived the memory of seeing a dead navy seal laying in his bed, his Wife murdered in the bathroom and that the Detective at the precinct; Edgecomb was implicitly accusing him of being the man behind both bodies. Detective Edgecomb even took his desert eagle to run the ballistics.

Big momma Lucy opened the apartment door, her frizzy hair dangling over her distant eyes. Her make-up melting across her cheeks. She looked like she was stunned by a stun gun standing in her own misery, the door propped wide open behind her and the draft from outside coming inside, she lifted her chin and her skin was ghost pale like she was thawed out in cold snow. Her armpits were oily, her kneecaps were weak, she stepped towards Fritz, each footstep was a dragging step. She walked into Fritz's arms with her nostrils smothered by his large chest.

"they got my daughter." she shouted with muffled words, her back bounced like she was being shot with a shotgun, "they got my daughter." she shouted, yawning for breath and evening ignoring the onion smell of Fritz's clothes. Her legs trembled, holding on to Fritz's biceps. She glared upward at the thousand-dollar chandelier, and her tears were rolling down.

Fritz held his arms over Lucy, hugging her while crying. Standing in that one spot of the house that seemed to be the highest. Phillip stood in the corner, feeling as if he couldn't experience grief along with his family. He hugged himself, walking to the edge of his mattress and trapping his grief inside his hoodie. He pulled the strings, crying cold tears for his late mother.

Fritz stepped away, walking toward the bathroom. He had brown make-up smudges all over his grey shirt. His eyes dropped downward, he took his shirt off and dropped it against the bathroom tiles. He walked with a limp, digging for his cellphone and held it to his ear. The pink bathroom carpet was silent, absorbing all of his footsteps as he stepped, sweeping the door for a soft slam. He slapped the toilet seat lid, making a thud. He blindly sat, sitting with his cellphone pressed against his right ear and his left hand running down his eyebrows.

"hello," he uttered, "Alejeh." he spoke, while looking away, he slapped his forehead and took a deep huff "Ivory is dead. "he muttered with an empty voice, his throat slightly cracked and he yawned for a new breath.

"dead?" Alejeh's voice interrupted in a careless way, almost as if she thought it was funny.

Fritz held the phone away from his jaw, he stared at the device with his eye's ringing. He felt a shiver run down his spine. A shakiness in the wind, the shower curtain flicked in a ghostly way. There was a whistling of air, and then the image of Alejeh doing the unthinkable.

Fritz shook his head, he blinked with a brain whistle behind his cold eyes. He placed the phone back to his ear, "Alejeh? where the fuck was you this whole time?"

"I went to pick up your medicine." she replied in a fast tongue snap, "and then something else came up."

"take three days to get medicine?"

"I can't talk about this unless your here. Come to me when you can because it's important."

Fritz grimaced his face, stretched his index and thumb across his forehead while slouching.

"okay." He uttered.

Taxi

November/ 5th/2023

The sounds of humming of cars vrooming by, murmurs from children yapping to their parents about what they want from a local eastside ice cream shop. Fritz walked with his head down, blindly stomping and nearly collided into a pedestrian woman. *Doof!* their shoulders brushed. She was a five-foot-six blonde with eyes like Megan Fox. She wore a long Burberry scarf around her neck and glared at Fritz's Burberry coat.

"excuse me sir." she muttered, slightly astonished, angrily eying him with a twinkle in her pupils.

"sorry." He uttered back, "hey you know any good places around here for a drink?"

And suddenly a shooting static of nerve twitches ran down his skull. He turned away and walked with a body jolt and slammed his fingers against a public trash can. There was a spit blob on the rim, plastic cup of skinny chicken bones and rice. If his condition wasn't going to make him throw up then it would have been the stench of that disgusting garbage can food.

Fritz dropped his eyes at his reflection on a pothole pond a few inches from the stony curb. He was completely disoriented. He saw doubles of himself. On the other side of the street pavement was the E train entrance at Lexington and 53rd. The smacking metal sounds of the tracks clicking were fracking under the pavement and you could hear the wheels rumble an earth quake and loud machinery imploding, winding whirling into the gaping tunnel smelled like wires and sparks. Fritz stood near the subway steps, scratching his forehead, waiting for his ride to Queens.

In between his index and middle finger was a cigarette burning with a tint of grey and orange. Thoughts of Killing Alejeh? Fritz scratched his forehead. Scratching the thought out of his mind of her doing the murder. He knew that Ivory's death wasn't a Murder-suicide situation. His stomach felt as if it were being turned with a wrench. He placed his left hand over his belly and went to the curb to vomit.

The Uber driver had a white grand Cherokee, oily black wheels and a glossy body. The window rolled down and a man in his mid-40's who looked like Eddie griffin. He wore a brown leather jacket that looked like Grandma's leather couch. He was holding the steering wheel, he had a lump of skin on the back of his neck and grey hairs coiling out of his shirt. He had a Jamaican accent, staring at Fritz with one eyebrow low, "you Fritzen Clayed?" he shouted.

Fritz, grabbed the handle, still clutching his cigarette bending for a seat.

"can I huff this cig, I'll dump the ashes out the window," he muttered while digging into his deep pocket.

"no" the man replied with aggression.

Fritz shoved his hand deeper into his Burberry pocket, pulled out a stack of hundreds and dumped it in his cup holder. He slammed the door before the man could respond.

"okay corona queens bro?" The Jamaican cab driver uttered, while he lifted the cash and swiped each hundred across his big dirty fingers. His eyes bulging through his car mirrors. The driver pressed the button on the dashboard, the car fan started to swirl, fresh cold wind blew inside while sounding like a vacuum.

Hurling through traffic, the car sped and the wheels wobbled at the rigid road of Koch bridge. The drive sounded soothing because of the wheels swishing against the flat beady ramp. Fritz lifted his blue eyes, leaned forward and cleared his throat.

"mm ummm, you know where I could get guns?" Fritz uttered.

The man went silent. His eyes exploded through his mirrors. He clutched the money that Fritz gave him and stuffed it in his side door.

"ayo whutless man, you must be out of your blasted mind!" he turned the steering wheel, twisted his neck sideways to see if the police were behind his car.

"I'm driving to your destination, man dats all".

those new cabs aren't like old taxi's from back in the days, back in the days, the drivers used to know all the spots, warehouses, gun trades, drugs and Trafficking spots. Motherfuckers knew it all. These new drivers don't take risks.

The driver arrived at 110th street, a Cuban restaurant with a blue scaffold, a watery hydrant spilling Icey drip. A Latina woman with a shopping cart full of sliced pineapples and watermelons. Churros and candy. A wobbly ATM machine in the corner of laundromat. a little boy selling candy yanking a fat Latina woman by her long white bubble jacket to get her attention.

Fritz pulled the handle to the Uber car and stepped out. Caté's old white van was across the street, there was a bunch of old Mexican men with thick mustaches playing dominos in the cold. Alejeh's house is in between two large houses as if it were being squeezed.

In the night time, you could hear cat's meow as they squeezed through the tight buildings. The 2-family house seemed to look larger than it was in the day. The trees in Corona Queens were massive, scratchy branches twisting around the roof and spilling leave thorns into their yard.

Fritz stepped toward the charred gate, grabbed the latch and pulled it open, the latch made a popping noise. Fritz walked into the back entrance. "Alejeh" he shouted. At the garage entrance, there was a large row of snowmobiles with stickers, fishing equipment and a box shaped couch with an orange cat sitting on top. The left side of the garage was open and there was a long wood table with thousands of Christmas ornaments.

Fritz had barely gone through the back of the house, only for a quick smoke, but as he stepped inside the busted concrete, he noticed Alejeh's body figure at the glassy door. The backside entrance illuminated, her eyes darted and the glass cube door pushed open. She stood with her arms in her pink shirt sleeves. She wore a yellow cardigan sweater, black leg-ins hugging her hips. She lifted her head and her eye size became bigger.

"Azul?" she uttered with dotted eyes "remember we." She whispered and suddenly Fritz lunged at her.

"you fucking killed her." Fritz aggressively tugged her, her eyes bulged, squeezing her elbows, lifting her and pinning her against the ash white wall.

"killed who?" Alejeh responded with her voice echoing and one slipper off her foot.

"fucking Ivory, you willed her?" Fritz screamed particles of spit and his eyes grew larger as he breathed.

"no," Alejeh replied with a soft tone, "I told Rigoberto about Rolling street infamy, I shouldn't have told him your business like that, I'm sorry. I didn't call you hear for Ivory!"

Suddenly, in the blink of the wind, Fritz's face loosened, his eyes dotted as he let go. Then allowing her to put her foot back in the slipper.

Fritz bit his bottom lip, bent down close to her face.

"so, you told your father, what is it to talk about?" he grabbed her neck and slammed his jaw into her lips for a forceful kiss. Sucking her bottom lip, her pink bottom lip jiggled.

Alejeh, opened the glassy door, it was a brown door, made of glass that looked like ice cubes. probably really unsafe for the neighborhood, but nobody would know how easy it is to break in because they would have to trespass. As the door opened, there was a pathway of Smokey darkness. There were water damaged tiles, water damaged walls and pipes above their foreheads, chipped paint, yellow foam to keep the walls in place. As she walked through, she stopped near a wood storage cabinet, she pulled the drawer open.

"Azul, do you have your magnum?" Alejeh whispered while holding the drawer, "please don't bring it upstairs today, leave it down here because."

"I don't have it." He interrupted.

She turned to him, half of her face was light and the other half was in darkness.

"are you sure?"

"no, the detectives took it, why are you asking?"

"no guns at dinner. That's all."

Suddenly, Fritz could feel a ghostly presence around him. There was a long dusty set of staircases that led into the basement.

Dinner

As Fritz walked upstairs, the light flickered and the walls were full of dusty spiderwebs. *Zap!* A fat fly buzzed past his earlobe and landed at the brown bulb, ping-ponged around a vent. He swatted it away, walking into the brown staircase. They arrived at the second floor.

Alejeh turned the knob to the house door and Fritz was by her side. She shut her eyes and shook her cheek, knowing that she was about to betray him. She pulled the knob and the apartment opened like a different dimension. The wide space of the Livingroom felt dense. The furniture appeared closer and the space to walk through was jammed with Rigoberto's wheelchair. Straight ahead, Jesus Christ crucifix was over the box television, stick figurines, clay vases and a cluster of pans that looked like battle shields. There was a wood Jesus crucifix that Fritz had seen many times and a red bandana covering the eyes as if someone wanted Jesus to be blind. Plastic wrap spread everywhere as if one of the boys were painting the Livingroom. There was foggy plastic stretched over the couch set, the doors shut with plastic from the top to bottom. Plastic on the flooring and plastic over the potted plants, Rigoberto's acoustic guitar and piano.

Alejeh turned her face, she bit her lip and stared toward the floor.

Cristiano was to the left, shutting his bedroom door. He had a bald head, wearing a white tank top with his prison tattoo showing. To the right of the house, Caté was in the kitchen and you could hear a piece of steel grinding against another piece of steel. It sounded like he was playing a steel violin. *Shring! Shring! Shring! Shring!* the sound was very loud. And at the center of the house, Rigoberto seated in his wheelchair, he rolled from the walkway toward the dining table. He lifted rifle with a wood handle and cracked it in half. He didn't look at Fritz either, his eyes were down as if he were reading the carpet. He kept his chin down as he loaded the cracked the rifle.

A loud thud of footsteps ran up the backside of the staircase and the whole door went dark as if Andre the giant was behind the door. There was a big Spanish Mexican man with a massive face tattoo above his eyebrows. He had a black leather biker vest with a skull chain. There were green tattoos on his fist, big buff silver belt on his waist, ripped blue jeans and leather brown loafers.

Fritz stepped in, staring at the large man. A man who the family called Big burrito. He was their cousin. Sort of like a family enforcer. The light swung as he shut the door behind him.

"what the fuck is going on." Fritz shouted.

Rigoberto raised his long rifle, pointing it and trembling in clammy sweat.

"what the fuck is this?" Fritz uttered, turning his neck and gasping. His eyes pinging and his head ringing with anxiety fire. Fritz pulled Alejeh's dainty arm and pinned her closer, but she pushed off.

"Fritz, there's somethings being said about you." She uttered while rubbing her elbow, shaking her head and sadness.

At the dining table, there was a small cellphone on beady Aztec table cover. A voice of an old Latin woman speaking through the phone in a whimpering tone. Her voice was like a person who had been screaming and breathing dust particles for so long that they lost their voice and tried to speak again in darkness but was so weak that their words weren't connected to their spirit anymore.

Alejeh fingers dropped to her legs. She stepped away from Fritz and the room became heavy. She walked the narrow path towards Rigoberto who was at head of the table. The wooden seat that she sat in had beads on the backside. When she sat, they sounded like marbles. Alejeh locked her fingers around her blue rosary and shook her head while pulling the chair closer to the table.

"mami, ya llego." she uttered into the phone. Her eyebrows were low, her arms folded to her breast and her chest bouncing.

Suddenly Lisabelle choked.

"Fritz, you disgusting animal!" she screamed

"what you done, you deserve to die! My eyes gouged out with car tools? I lived in the dark for so long, screaming and serving you in this cellar." she shouted with her voice wheezing. Her words cracking, the whole house went silent and everyone could feel the chills of vertigo. "you monster! there was a little girl I met. Her name was Livonia! She was only twelve years old before they took her. They separated the girl from her sisters and these men tore his skin open like a piece of plastic. I could hear her gasping, sneezing at night because she had allergies and the walls were so dusty. Sicker than an eighty-year-old after they ripped out her liver. Her liver! Her fucking Liver. A twelve-year-old girl! You sick fuck! The nightmares we lived! you are a monster!"

Fritz's jaw dropped. A tear ran down his cheeks and his face was pale as snow. His jaw dropped an inch lower and the tear shook down faster. His head spun as he trotted back to the door.

Rigoberto aimed his rifle a notch higher, he had a shivering bottom lip, red sleepless clotty eyes and off beat head nod. Tears rolling down his face, he pulled the trigger and **Bow!** a whole chunk of wood exploded from the side of the house and you could see the upstairs apartment.

"La Plaga!" Rigoberto shouted while crying, he popped his rifle open and reloaded. Two bullets on his lap that were the size of Double-D batteries.

Fritz let go of the knob, landing on his leg and covering his head of dust shards.

Alejeh raised her arm, slapping the weapon away and squeezing the muzzle, "No Papi please, wait!"

Alejeh glared at Fritz with her mouth yawning.

"wait."

Fritz trotted backwards, everything moving in slow motion in his head. All he could think of was his daughter in darkness. Wood chips all over his hair. He backed for the door knob, stretching his fingers around it and pulling it open.

Cristiano slammed his feet while walking over to Fritz, his hand smacked against the wall of the door. He snatched Fritz by the neck, putting him in a full nelson headlock and dragging him back inside the house. Fritz's heels dragged against the flooring till he reached a seat.

"my daughter." Fritz shouted, my fucking kid." there was dust particles everywhere which caused him to slide.

"Puto, you going to die today," Cristiano shouted, slamming Fritz into one of the polished wood chairs with rolling red beads.

Alejeh stared at Fritz, then mouthing the words "Livonia! Livonia! His daughter? *Wait*, he didn't know papi!, please stop."

Cristiano grabbed a chunk of Fritz's blond hair, he squeezed it while pulling his face upward and his eyes were at the ceiling.

"you know I was locked up right? yea I was at Eldies right before the inmates took the prison foo."

The apartment went silent. Cristiano had these red cheeks, biting his bottom lip while talking. "I fought with the essays, dealt some cigarettes with the skin heads, but one of the biggest weirdos I met in prison was Guidance! Turns out he wasn't so weird after all. He helped me find my mother foo."

Fritz's face scrunched,

"please I have to get to my fucking kid?" Fritz shouted in cold tears. He hadn't cried in his adult life, but at that moment he could feel the feverish sickness trickling from of being gutted. His jaw was aimed at the ceiling, one eye shut and his tongue pushed back into his tonsils.

"please!"

Cristiano grabbed Fritz throat, locking him in a sitting headlock that slowed his breathing like asthma.

"I called Guidance" Cristiano uttered, "and Guidance called someone named Felony Fred. We found my mother with their help. We found her Foo!"

"no please! You have this shit mixed up." Fritz shouted.

"Felony Fred told us that you were the creator!"

Cristiano squeezed his right fist, punching Fritz in the temple over and over and he could hear the pounding on his brain.

"you traffick people ehh," Cristiano shouted, "fucking weirdo."

"stop" Alejeh shouted.

"no, this one is personal." Cristiano yelled wrapped his swole bicep around Fritz's throat. It was a ruthless headlock which narrowed Fritz's breathing until he saw fuzzy flower white walls. The tip of his nose turned cold blue and his lip had a pulsating vein in it.

Lisabelle's voice cracked,

"Mi Nina pequena," she sucked her snot while talking over speaker phone, "it's been so long since I was able to braid your long black hair while we talked about Ricky Martin, I miss you so much! I will be getting on the ship to Florida then a plane to New York! I'll be back home. Guidance says that in order for me to come home back to you, one thing must be done! Mi Nina, this has to be done."

The whole house went silent. You could choking, hear the wood cracks in the seat while Fritz squirmed in that headlock. His leather belt zipping against the beaded seat.

The flooring had tremors that caused vertigo. out of the yellow lit kitchen, Caté walked inside the living room, big brown sandals slapping against the floor, *Domp! Domp! Domp! Domp!* He stopped in front of Fritz, casting a tall dark shadow. His long dark hair strands ringing over his ears and sideburns. His almond butter brown skin slightly red from unhinged anger. He had a thick straight mustache, the scent of liquor coming from his heavy breathing. Tears on his stoic eyeballs looked glossy, a twisted bone in his cheekbone and an awkward nose twitch. He lifted the wood handle of his machete and the blade looked like chrome.

"La Plaga!" he mumbled, "La Plaga!" his machete went to the left side of his torso and the light bounced right, then when he swung right Fritz's knees straightened like he was being electrocuted. His chest gargled, his throat flinched and there was a red zig-zag blood string that flung forward. The last gasp of wind fell back into his windpipe, his fingers stiffened and his body deflated with shock and back weight.

Things were in slow motion.

Alejeh had her eyes shut, she held the cellphone while contorting her body away from the plastic wrapped flooring. Something gooey dripping from her forehead. She could hear the floor plastic throb. It was as if someone were bouncing a slab of ham over and over. It rolled to her foot and when she opened her eyes. She saw his blue eyes staring upward. In-between her feet, was his square-shaped head rolling like a bowling ball in vomit-like blood strings. She screamed so loud that the walls shook.

Cristiano grabbed his sister from the backside, held her mouth so she couldn't scream. His mustache all in her earlobe, blood all over his skin and heat from his breathing.

"shhhh." He shouted with his teeth closed. "stop screaming. this was for mother."

Epilogue
November/12th/2023

The funeral flowers were propped up in white vases. The windows had steel crosses and tinted glass. The wooden pews were polished with paper portraits.

The casket was white. Long pink sheets handing off had gold embodied dandelions. Ivory was inside the casket with her grey coated flesh aimed at the ceiling.

To my left, there was a few people from the neighborhood who walked to the casket and stood over her in sadness. People from the church were lined up and holding paper fans. Eyes full of sadness and lip shaking.

At ten o clock, the preacher stepped toward the microphone. He spoke with his eyes inside a piece of paper that looked like origami.

I saw my mother's dead body the hour before service so I didn't go up to see her. She looked beautiful as always, high cheekbone and pretty slanted eyes. She wore a pink dress, her long brown curly hair to her shoulders. Black eye liner, white eye shadow and some brown make up that made her jaw bone appear as if she were a model. Holding an entanglement of dandelions that had yellow pedals. My mother loved to plant them with Big momma Lucy.

Big momma Lucy wobbled to the front, holding a paper fan. She swung it up and down and grimaced in pain. Ivory's casket was still but when Big momma Lucy grabbed it, it shook with life.

"my daughter." Big momma Lucy cried.

To the left side, was my pregnant girlfriend T.T. who had no words for me, but sealed it in her respect for my mother. Her nostrils gusted, she made sucked her teeth with a shut mouth and stared me down. On the way here, she had two bottles of water inside her purse. She didn't offer me one. When I told her about Rolling street Infamy and what Tripple plat did, she blamed for me it. She told me that the police will come for me and my stepfather Fritz.

To my right side was Aunt Yata. She couldn't stop crying. She held hands with my Aunt Joi and their hysterics felt like it was aimed at me because they got louder and louder until my ears rung. They wanted me to crack. They wanted me to admit that it was my fault for bringing the Gang violence to my religious family.

After an hour and a half, in the middle of the preacher reading the introduction to the obituary, the doors swung outward. It was a squeaky noise. My head spun toward the back of the seating area with the flowers. It was Mother Megan. Mother Megan walked in with her arms crossed, holding a long black rose at her elbow.

Mother Megan was wearing a black hat, net over her eyes. black blouse with ruffles at the neck. She had black slacks and flats. she stepped toward Big momma Lucy twirling a black rose in her grasp. the whole church was silent. she stopped at the casket and placed the black rose on top.

"mm" Mother Megan uttered. "she lifted her fingers and formed a crucifix in thin air, then her eyes examined Ivory's dead body. "mmm," Mother Megan muttered, "when you steal riches from another family, you become arrogant and forget that it aint yours. whether or not you conscious of it, you still receive the worst karma. I'm not sorry about your dead daughter, because you weren't sorry enough for my son when yawl! She turned to all of us "yawl murdered him." Mother Megan took a step back, pointed her finger in Big momma Lucy's face "You took his hard-earned money! you know that little red boy wasn't his biological son! A blind man could see it."

Mother Megan pointed her finger at me, smirked while shaking her head.

Big momma Lucy's eyes flinched as if she was caught in a snow storm. shielded me.

"I want justice." Megan shouted, "and I'm ready to fight until we both wither away. I'm taking it back for Shandy! that's her daddy's money! the white man can steal, yup, he sure can, but god is going to strike him down and all of his negro hoes that defend him. Yawl keep hiding him. See, I know what yawl doing."

A lot of bad had to happen in order for us to get this quality of life. Only weeks away from turning eighteen, I kind of see why Big momma Lucy and Fritz did what they did, but it came with a cost. when you steal to create generation wealth, your inheriting bad karma. this is why Fritz is always paranoid. This is why Big momma Lucy has heart problems. This is why my mother is dead. We are cursed.

Care about the children!

Before its too late.

The end

Simple son novel